The
Blood of
Whisperers

Silence rang long and tense in this hall that was both so large and suddenly too small. He was an emperor. I had interrupted him and spoken roughly. He could reprimand me if he wished, but when he let out a tired sigh, I knew he would not. "Ahmet is nosing around this too, Darius," he said. "It will do no good for either of us if it comes out."

"What does he say?"

"He warns me that you aren't who you say you are. That you really serve the Otakos and want me dead. That you have a secret."

"And what do you tell him, Majesty?"

Kin looked at me then, a smile pressed flat between his lips. "That all men have secrets."

THE
BLOOD OF
WHISPERERS

THE VENGEANCE TRILOGY:
BOOK ONE

DEVIN MADSON

www.orbitbooks.net

ORBIT

First published in 2013
First published in Great Britain in 2020 by Orbit

1 3 5 7 9 10 8 6 4 2

A CIP catalogue record for this book is available from the British Library.

ISBN 978-0-356-51530-4

Orbit
An imprint of
Little, Brown Book Group
Carmelite House
50 Victoria Embankment
London EC4Y 0DZ

An Hachette UK Company
www.hachette.co.uk

www.orbitbooks.net

For my parents.
You have always supported me. You have always believed in me.
I could never have come so far without you.

And with the fall of the axe comes change
With its sharpened edge, gods perish
Long live Emperor Kin
Man
Soldier
Usurper

1. ENDYMION

We are judged. That is what the Sixth Law says. The gods are always watching. They can hear the whisper of our souls.

"Are they watching me now?" I asked when Jian stopped the wagon for me to piss. He had been talking of the gods and the laws ever since crossing the border that morning as though being home made him a different man.

"They'll be watching me bang your head into a tree if you ask silly questions like that."

I glanced over my shoulder as I finished up. "Is it wrong to be curious?"

"It is to be a nuisance," Jian said, twisting and untwisting the reins in his hand. "Be quick, Endymion, or we won't make it to the next town before nightfall."

"You know I wouldn't mind that."

"Yes, but this time you might. We're getting low on supplies."

The folds of my Kisian half robe fell back into place as I returned to the cart. It wasn't as comfortable as the tunic I usually wore and I kept fiddling with the knot in the white sash, but at least Jian hadn't expected me to wear one of their big fancy robes. It was already hot enough without adding all that extra weight.

As I settled myself back on the seat beside him, Brother Jian set the ox walking. "You'd do well to listen to the laws and stories rather than mock them," he said, gruff words spoken to the ox's back.

"I have listened to them for at least sixteen years. I still don't want to be a priest."

Jian shifted his weight on the hard seat. He looked at me. Looked away. Opened his mouth only to close it again, and I knew there was no escaping the coming argument.

"You have to aspire to something, Endymion," he blurted at last. "I know you say you'll figure it out, but you can't just wander around—"

"You do."

"I travel to bring the word of the gods to those who need to hear it. I bless those in need and I give guidance and hope, and with your abilities, you could be so good at it, you could—"

"But I don't want to use it."

"Why not?"

Because it stretches me thin. Because it hurts. Because it makes me feel like I'm not here. Because it's getting worse.

Words I could never say. Especially when Jian turned that concerned look on me. He wanted to help, but all these years together had proved he couldn't.

I withdrew an arrow from the quiver at my feet and, rather than look at him, checked the fletchings carefully. "I guess I'm just not a good person like you," I said, knowing it was the quickest way to end the conversation.

"I know that's not true. A man is made the way he is for a purpose. The gods judge harshly those who reject that purpose and—"

"Let the gods live a day in my skin before they judge me."

His hurt flared, or maybe it was mine; I couldn't tell. Only that for an instant, it was hot enough to rival the sun. Then Jian sniffed and settled in for a few miles, glaring at the ox's rump. Blessed silence reigned.

It was a stifling day, and as the afternoon wore on, heat rose shimmering from the road and everything seemed to droop. It had been six years since we had last been in Kisia, and I had forgotten how hot and humid Kisian summers could get. The air was thick with the buzz of insects, and my linen robe had long since stuck to my skin. No matter how Jian tilted his woven hat, sweat covered the back of his neck and pasted his dark hair to his head in curls.

The ox plodded on, the desultory rattle of the wagon our constant companion. Few other travellers were braving the heat, only the occasional carter long inured to the weather. And soldiers. We had passed three bands of them so far that day and come across another in the middle of the afternoon. A dozen in total, colonising a patch of shade where the road branched. Their tense irritability spread from them as they ordered every traveller to stop and have their cargo inspected.

"This is new," Jian mumbled, slowing the ox as we approached. A mule driver with half a dozen animals looked up as we halted behind him to await our turn. "We might not make it to Hoturi before dark if this takes too long."

"Might not be a bad thing, it's bleak there," the mule driver said, standing amid his animals, the languid swish of their tails sending their bells tinkling. "A patrol from the local garrison got slaughtered a week or so back. Left in pieces, I heard," he added, glancing at the soldiers and lowering his voice. "Tiny pieces."

"Pieces?"

"Like a burst plum, I heard."

The man seemed to be enjoying himself, but before he could elaborate, a soldier called him forward, and he moved up with a swish of his tasselled guiding whip.

"Names." An imperial soldier stood beside the cart with his arms folded. His face was flushed and he looked ready to murder someone, but the fear scratching at his skin was far more awful. I looked away.

"My name is Father Jian Eko and this is my novice, Endymion."

"Eko? Like the court priest?"

"Yes, but once we take the Oath of Word, we give up all family ties."

"Father Kokoro Eko is your ... ?"

Jian sighed. "We have the same mother and the same father."

"So he's your brother?"

"No, because when we take the Oath of Word—"

The soldier waved him into silence with an irritable shake of his hand. "And what's in your wagon, not-the-brother-of-our-illustrious-court-priest?"

"Nothing more than our belongings and many copies of the Word of Qi if you are in need—"

Another irritable wave of the hand. "I'll have a look."

Not a request. He was already walking toward the back of the wagon when Jian thrust the reins into my hand and hopped down. I gripped the worn leather tight and stared at the road, breathing as slowly as I could, though the pressure of fear and nervousness pressed in more oppressively than the heat. Behind me, the wagon shook. Footsteps tramped around inside. Muffled conversation continued, and I just stared at the road and recited the death prayer in my head over and over until Jian returned. He must have taken the reins back too, for we were soon moving again. The ox plodded on, and bit by bit the fear ebbed away.

I let go a long breath. "What was all that about? Even the soldiers at the border gave us less trouble than that."

"I don't know, but I don't like it," Jian said. "There's still time to turn around. We could pass the winter in the north and skip all the snow and ice. And the rain."

No longer having the guards' fear clogging my veins, I shook my head. "Someone attacking patrols of soldiers has nothing to do with us. I can't make a decision about my future until I understand my past." He took a deep breath, ready to argue, so I added quickly, "Speaking of the past, since when do you use your last name when asked to give it? And I'm not a novice."

"Since I got the feeling Kisia isn't safe right now," he said, ignoring the second part. "Being related to His Majesty's own priest might at least smooth the way."

"You mean being *not* related to him."

Jian smacked my knee and barked out a laugh. "You watch it, boy."

The afternoon shadows lengthened as we neared Hoturi, and climbing onto the roof of the wagon, I watched the sun begin to set, gilding the sharp, craggy slopes of the Kuro Mountains. They framed Kisia, their distant outline a work of art upon the misted sky. I had spent most of my life outside Kisia, but even in Chiltae, the image of the western mountains could be found on pots and frescoes, and seeing them with my own eyes gave me the feeling of coming home.

Home. Wherever that was.

Hoturi was one of northern Kisia's largest trading posts. About a day's travel south of the border, it was where most travellers stopped for the night, leaving it a bustle of constant noise. Usually, cities crept up on me, first one heart, then ten, then hundreds, but Hoturi hit me like a thrown stone. I gasped, gripping the edge of the roof. We weren't even in sight of the city and already it was screaming. Bleak, the mule driver had called it. Grim and wrathful would have been more accurate.

Step after heavy step, the ox drew us on.

The mountain groves thinned, and a gatehouse rose from the cleared undergrowth, tiles missing from its roof like a toothless grin. Its painted gates were still open, and against the darkening sky, crimson flags snapped. Just like the soldiers on the road, the gate guards were inspecting a merchant's cargo. As we approached, there was much gesticulation, papers changed hands, and eventually the man was waved in.

"You had better get down here," Jian said. "They might take exception to me bringing a monkey in with me."

With an effort, I prised my fingers from the edge of the roof and climbed down beside Jian. "Try to relax," he whispered. "And have your papers ready."

I took a deep breath and let it out as Jian slowed the cart, bringing the ox to a halt in front of the gate.

"Papers."

The guard held out his hand, and I dropped my papers into it, taking care not to touch his skin. Not that the precaution helped when he stood so close. Trying not to breathe him in, I stared at the row of gold fasteners along his shoulder, each moulded into the long dragon of Emperor Kin Ts'ai.

"Endymion?" the man said.

"It's a Chiltaen name," Jian returned, leaning a little across me to address the guard. "It means lost sheep."

"Then he'll have to register with the—"

"Chiltaen by name but not by birth, Captain, as the papers say."

The captain grunted. On the other side of the wagon, Jian's papers were handed back to him. "Have you been here before, Brother?" the other guard asked. "I can provide you with directions to the Sanctuary Square."

"Yes, I have," Jian said. "Thank you. On the north road not far from the bridge?"

The man nodded and stepped back. "We'll search your wagon now."

Beside me, the captain was still frowning at my crumpled papers. He let out a discontented huff, his breath sour. "You're not a novice."

"No, Captain, he is not."

"Let the boy answer for himself," the captain snapped. "You are not a novice, boy?"

"No." I forced the word out through dry lips, wishing he would step back, that he would take his weight away from me. Jian had said that with the peace, it wouldn't matter that I looked Chiltaen, that it wouldn't matter I wasn't a novice, but these men were tense and angry and I dug my fingernails into my palms.

"Yet you travel with a priest?"

The wagon rocked, footsteps sounding inside. A step, a pause, then the murmur of voices.

"I am an orphan," I said.

Again, Jian leant across. "We are travelling to Shimai so he might take the oath and become my novice."

The captain glared at Jian. "I don't like the boy's papers."

"They are as the governor made them."

He looked back at the document, running his fingers over the seal and feeling the paper.

The others returned from their inspection. They exchanged nods and the captain pursed his lips, his troubles seeping off him like a stench. He looked at me. He looked at Jian. He looked down at the papers and, licking his fingers, pinched the corner. Long seconds went by.

A gong sounded, its deep tone reverberating over us. Upon the walls, a guard rehung the striker, the last light forming a halo about his head, while down on the road, his fellows hurried about, preparing to close the gate for the night.

"Very well, go through," the captain said. "But if you make trouble, you won't easily be forgotten. The streets around the garrison are closed and a curfew will be enforced at midnight. Enjoy your stay in Hoturi."

He handed back my papers and stepped away, leaving the road open. Jian took up the reins and, giving thanks, drove us in beneath the stone arch. I could feel his relief as we passed into Hoturi, could taste it on my tongue. But it only lasted a few seconds before souring into horror. "What—?"

Death met us inside the gates. A pair of gibbets stood on either side of a great tree, its branches and the hasty structures filled with dozens of corpses swinging gently. I felt nothing from the dead, but the fear and disgust of people around me buzzed like flies, and Jian's fingers tightened about my hand. "Read the sign," he whispered.

It had been hammered to the tree trunk, its neatly painted words reading: *For the crime of witchcraft.* Two men hanging from the main branch had large eyes painted on their bare chests, or what was left of their chests. The summer heat and the crows had left the bodies foul and oozing.

"Witch—?" The word stuck in my throat and I had to clear it and try again. "Witchcraft?"

Jian didn't answer, but the flicker of his gaze toward my wrist was enough. Behind us, the gates slammed closed.

"We should...find the Sanctuary Square," Jian said, glancing back at the gates. "Get some rest."

I didn't answer, couldn't, just sat stiff and tense as the ox pulled us on through the town. Despite the dead hung as a warning and the oppressive anger, the people of Hoturi acted like it was a normal day. Shopkeepers were closing their shutters and bolting their doors, while street merchants filled the dusk, stalking citizens with their produce, their food trailing mouthwatering odours and their hands held out for coins. A boy was lighting a string of lanterns as we passed beneath. Perched like a sparrow upon the eave, he held the tinder between his teeth, a bag of candles hanging from his waist. The town bustled in time to the beat of its own fear. And from every corner, guards and soldiers glared.

Jian glanced at me. "How are you holding up?"

"I'm fine," I lied. "Just hungry."

"We can eat as soon as we stop. There's some leftover smoked fish and yellow beans."

"Ginger?"

"If we're lucky."

He might have said more but was forced to mind the road. It was no easy task to avoid the slew of carts and palanquins clogging the streets, most citizens having no time to spare for a shabby prayer wagon.

"Well," Jian said as he navigated a sharp turn into the walled square. "I think the walls have grown taller. You'd think they were ashamed of us."

The walls encircling the Sanctuary Square hid us completely from the rest of the town. There was a well and the usual bags of grain but nothing else to make priests feel welcome. At the other end of the square sat another wagon, the ornate designs upon its panels weathered beyond recognition.

"It looks like times are hard everywhere," Jian said. "Or the people aren't valuing their souls as they should."

While we tended the ox and gathered a meal, the priest from the other wagon ambled over, fatigue marring his gait and staining the air around him.

"Well met, good brother," he said as he neared. "You wouldn't be Brother Jian by any chance?"

"I am," Jian said, his hand stopping halfway to the outer lantern, tinder burning in his fingers. "Why do you ask?"

"Ah! A letter came for you a week or two back. I wasn't here, but the priest who was gave it to the next wagon to arrive, and then last night it was handed to me with instructions to pass it on. Seems whoever wanted to get in touch with you knew you'd be coming through here."

The tinder had gone on burning all the way to Jian's fingers, and as the man finished his explanation, Jian yelped and dropped the smoking stub. He brushed his hand upon his robe, then held it out for the letter. The priest handed it over, his brows lifted in expectant curiosity. But if he had hoped for an explanation, he was to be disappointed. Jian looked at it long enough to ascertain the seal had not been broken before tucking it into his sash. "My thanks," he said. "From where have you travelled, Brother?"

"I was in Risian a few nights back, but I have been keeping clear of the big towns as much as I can. The reward is not worth the trouble."

"Ah, Risian. We are headed that way ourselves. Any news we ought to know?"

The priest grimaced, his whole face contorting as though he had just bitten into a lemon. "You want my advice, you won't go south. Go east. Go west. Keep to the small roads and the villages and hope this all blows over soon."

He made the sign of Qi as he spoke, honouring the dead.

"Is it as bad as that? We've heard there have been clashes over land redistribution since the peace treaty, but not that it was more than a nuisance."

The man tilted his head to the side. "You've come from Chiltae?"

Jian nodded.

"I'm sure His Majesty will be glad to know the worst of it hasn't leaked out yet, though it's only a matter of time. The fights over the land are getting worse, and the return of the Vices is a whole other thing."

Despite his visceral fatigue, the man agreed to walk with Jian to the nearest shrine so he could impart the whole story. Curious though I was, I was glad to be left alone, but there was no peace to be had when my thoughts kept veering back toward the hanging bodies and Jian's unwilling glance at my wrist. I plucked at my sleeve as over and over one question plucked at my mind. Was my Empathy witchcraft?

When Jian returned, we ate in silence as long as I could bear it, which wasn't long. "Who are the Vices?" I asked before he had taken more than a dozen mouthfuls.

Jian heaved an enormous sigh, puffing out his cheeks. "Monsters."

"Monsters?" Disbelief coloured my words and Jian frowned.

"As close as man can get, and you know I am not one for exaggeration. A group of men with…abilities that make yours look laughable. They came from nowhere about eight or nine years ago and, within a season, were the terror of the empire."

"I don't remember them."

"You think I would tell a ten-year-old about the hundreds of whores who were killed and turned inside out or the two dozen people at a teahouse who were all found strangled? I don't even want to tell you about it now."

A patrol from the local garrison got slaughtered a week or so back. Left in pieces, I heard. Tiny pieces. Like a burst plum.

"Why do such things?"

Jian shrugged. "I don't know. Because you can? For power? To make people afraid? If they ever caught them or found out who they were or why they did it, then it's more than I ever heard."

"They weren't caught?"

"No, and you can be sure they had the empire in such a fearful frenzy that His Majesty would have paraded them through the streets if they had. They just…faded away. You see, they used to leave a mark at the scene of every death. An eye."

"Like the one painted on the dead men at the gate."

He nodded. "It made me feel sick to see it again after so many years. Brother Catuxi said he heard rumours of their return a few weeks ago. As if the attacks on northern strongholds weren't enough of a problem. We shouldn't have come. We can leave first thing in the morning."

Whenever Jian lied, a twinge of guilt and shame always followed, but though I waited for it, it didn't come.

"You're not just saying this so I'll agree to go back to Chiltae." Not a question, a statement, but still Jian shook his head. "You really believe in this stuff."

"And of all people, you don't?"

The squirm of horror in my stomach was made all the worse for the hope it was only mine. Jian had never seemed to fear me before, and yet... "You think I'm in danger here," I said. "Me, specifically, because of this." I touched my inner wrist. "Because I'm like them."

"You would never do any of the things they—"

"Then you think I'm like them but with better morals. Is that why you want me to be a priest, to make sure I never turn into one of them?"

He rose onto his knees, pushing back from the table. "Where is this coming from? If I have ever said anything to make you believe—"

"You don't have to say it. I feel it. What does the letter say?"

The sudden change of topic made him blink. "The letter?"

"The letter someone sent to you here. What does it say? Is it about this? Is it about me?"

Jian gave me his chastening look, a look beneath which I had always bent, always quailed, but anger kept me buoyed, and it was he who looked away. A few long seconds passed, then with a grunt, he tugged the letter from his sash and threw it on the table. The seal had been broken and the scroll unrolled just enough to reveal Jian's name at the top in the neatest calligraphy I had ever seen.

I snatched it up. Jian flinched as though he would have liked to take it from me, but he sank back down on his cushion and said nothing.

Dear Jian,
If you have received this letter, it is because despite my strongly worded advice, you have chosen to go ahead with your plan to bring the boy into Kisia.

I bristled at *boy* and at the stiff tone but read on.

Given the current tensions, this course of action is even more unwise than when you first projected it, though if wisdom was capable of turning you from your path, you would have abandoned this long since. Therefore, I have made the necessary arrangements to ensure a safe meeting. I dare not write the place for fear of this falling into the wrong hands, but you know it. It is the same location where you came into possession of the boy in the first place. I will be there alone at the day and time of your birth, but a wise man would not come. A wise man would give the boy a different future.
May Qi guide your steps.

I set the letter down.

"We can be across the border by tomorrow night if we travel swift," Jian said. "We could—"

"Where is this place?"

He hesitated, staring at a few grains of rice spilt upon the table. "It's...a little inn off the main road, a few miles north of Shimai.

I used to stop there a lot. It won't be easy to get there in seven days though. If the trouble in Risian is as bad as Brother Catuxi said..." Jian trailed off and a sad smile turned his lips. "You want to go anyway."

"I have to know, Jian. I dream about her every night. Could you just walk away from that?"

"No, I suppose not."

"You don't have to come. Tell me where to find it and I can go on my own."

"Persuading me to let you go on your own will be about as fruitful as my attempts to persuade you to give this up and take the Oath of Word." He laughed but there was a flash of bitterness only I could feel.

Although half our meal remained, it had long since gone cold, and neither of us showed any interest in picking at the leftovers. Darkness pressed close to the windows and I felt tired, constricted into a body smaller than I had woken with, but sleep was far from my thoughts.

"I think I might go for a walk," I said.

Jian smiled, a sad thing brimming with the disappointment he always tried to hide. "Are you sure that's wise given how many soldiers are around?"

"I will keep to myself and give them no trouble."

He did not argue. "You do whatever you need to do. I'll be right here."

Right there with his sad smile and his barely concealed repugnance, but though I hoped one day these would be powerful enough to turn me from my course, today was not that day. Taking my cloak, I stepped out into the Sanctuary Square. The night was still young. Still warm. In his wagon, Brother Catuxi was singing. It made me smile.

The smile soon vanished as the onslaught of the town hit me from all sides, the emotions like waves buffeting me in a stormy sea.

Do whatever you need to do.

I carried Jian's words with me like a mantra all the way to the pleasure district. I held them close as I sat in the alley outside one of the rich brothels and let the waves of euphoria wash over me, drowning out everything but the kernel of shame deep inside that was the only sign I still existed at all. And once curfew had been called, I carried the words back with me, an excuse to cling to like a life raft in the face of Jian's silent but inevitable disgust.

———————

It took six long days to reach Risian, leaving us all exhausted, especially the ox. One more full day on the road would get us to the inn near Shimai on time, but for now, the spreading town of Risian promised rest. Until the gate guard looked at my papers.

"I don't like these," he said as though they had looked at him askance. "Take yourselves elsewhere."

"Elsewhere?" Jian leant over, his face red from the summer heat. "We have been on the road since dawn. We need rest. Our ox needs rest. Where else are we to go?"

"There is a village a few miles east. A hostelry there might take you in."

"So might we rest in Risian's Sanctuary Square. Endymion's papers may be travel worn, but they were written up and signed by the governor the same as yours and mine. Please let us in. We must be in Shimai tomorrow, and it will add considerably to our journey to have to go around Risian on cart tracks."

The guard rubbed the paper between his fingers and peered again at the signature scribbled on the bottom. "What is your purpose in Shimai?"

"I am to meet one who was once my blood—Father Kokoro Eko of the Imperial Court."

"Is that so?" The guard went on rubbing the paper between thumb and forefinger, though it seemed mindless now, his thoughts elsewhere. Everyone else who had been stopped at the gates had already passed on into the town, leaving newcomers to stare at us. Their curiosity nagged at me. "Well I'm afraid you'll be late, because I don't like these papers. They're good, so good they might even be real, but it's not a risk I'm allowed to take. I was born in Giana. My papers have Governor Ortono's signature, and it doesn't look like this."

"What governor doesn't rely on his secretaries to—?"

The papers were thrust back into my hand. "The answer is no. Now move out of the way, you're blocking the road."

Considering the anger and frustration that bubbled inside him, it was impressive how calmly Jian thanked the man and blessed him and turned the wagon around. People grumbled as we got in their way and threw Jian unwanted advice on how to better handle the reins, but the guard who had refused us entry remained impassive.

While the wagon turned, I had a good view down the main avenue into Risian, and there were the same trees and gibbets hanging with bodies that had graced every town along the way. There had even been collections of them swinging by the roadside, some burned to charcoal, others left to be pecked apart, always with the same warning sign. *For the crime of witchcraft.*

As they disappeared from sight behind the wagon, I fiddled with the band of cloth wrapped around my wrist and wondered how many of them had been like me.

———————

By the time we left the Willow Road just short of Shimai, we had already missed the rendezvous. Jian tried to be hopeful despite his fatigue, but under the weight of his frustration and my own doubts, my head drooped like the red and yellow wildflowers that ran in patches beside the road. To keep myself afloat, I took to loosing arrows into every passing tree and dashing back to collect them. Jian warned me I would tire myself out, but as archery always kept me calm, he didn't try too hard to dissuade me.

Not wishing to proclaim the arrival of a travelling priest, Jian parked the wagon in a distant field and walked to the village wrapped in a travelling cloak. I remained behind and fretted, and by the time he returned, I had not only loosed the ox from the wagon's shafts but also washed some of our clothes in the sluggish stream, put on the rice, boiled water for tea, and climbed into a cluster of fruit trees to pick sour plums. These I peeled and sliced with the quiet focus I only ever found when completely alone.

"He was there last night," Jian said, returning while I was loosing arrows into yet another innocent tree, taking solace in the rhythm of nocking, drawing, and loosing. "But he left a message with the innkeeper. He won't be seen two nights in the same place, but there's a small estate a half mile south of here, and he'll be there tonight and only tonight. Then he goes back to Mei'lian."

"An estate?" I lowered my bow. "You mean the home of a lord?"

"More likely a merchant or a councillor if it's small, but yes. It would have been better to have met him at the inn. The innkeeper is an old friend of mine."

Worry itched at me, but with answers so close, I could not abandon the search now. I had been given to Jian as a child, too young to remember more than a few closely held memories and images of my former life. Jian had taken me in, had treated me as his own; he had fed me and educated me and helped me develop ways to cope with my unusual burden, and yet for all his kindness, I had never been satisfied. He could tell me nothing about my past.

This time, Jian didn't say we could turn around and go back to

Chiltae because he had already said so a dozen times. Nor did he show surprise when I said we would go to the meeting. More than ever, I needed to know who I was. And what I was.

We tended the ox, cleaned the wagon, said prayers, and ate our meal in silence, and when darkness fell, we gathered our cloaks and started for the estate.

The heat had not abated, but wind whipped at the skirt of my short robe as I slid my feet into my reed sandals. To reach the estate of the unknown maybe-lord, we had to walk a short distance back toward the Willow Road, following the innkeeper's instructions beneath the faint guiding light of a half moon. We walked in silence, there being no point in voicing the anxiety that hummed between us like the whirring song of cicadas filling the night. We made it part of the way without needing the lantern, but unable to find the right turn, Jian soon gave in and knelt to light it.

While he worked, hoofbeats sounded on the road ahead. They started as a rumble beneath my feet, only to grow until galloping thunder split the sultry air. Jian stood up and, gripping my arm, tugged me to the edge of the narrow road. But they must have seen the lantern, for the line of riders squeezed to single file at the edge of the track, hooves kicking up dry clumps of grass as they galloped past. Crimson sashes flew out behind them, as the group of black stallions re-formed their lines and charged on into the night.

The last rider slowed as he passed, turning his skittering mount back to glare at us. A young face beneath the helmet, but there was no time for more than an impression of hauteur before he dragged the reins around, dug in his heels, and urged the horse after his companions.

"What was that for?" I coughed, dry dust tickling my throat.

"A warning, I think. We should have moved out of their way faster."

"They didn't ring us off. Surely we would have heard the bell." Soldiers had clogged every road and town in the empire since we'd arrived, but there had been something different about this group. Each horse had perfectly matched its fellows—sleek and black, their tails whipping out behind them like the long ponytails of their riders.

Jian shrugged. "You know how bad my hearing is. Let's just say it's encouraging they are hurrying in an away-from-us direction."

We met no one else on the road, and following the instructions left for us, we reached the side gate of a walled compound just as the moon was reaching its zenith.

"Last chance to walk away," Jian said.

I peered at him over the top of the lantern, its light deepening the lines on his face. "Why? I understand being worried about the soldiers and the people being killed for..." I left the word *witch-craft* hanging, unable to say it. "But...we are just here to find out who I am and where I belong. Why should we be worried?"

Jian's face grew all the more lined as he grimaced.

"Do you...do you know something you haven't been telling me?"

"No! I don't know who your parents were."

"But you know something else?"

When he looked away and did not answer, I drew a deep breath and knocked on the door.

A soft footfall scuffed beyond. Someone had been waiting, and the door opened just a crack. The smell of salted fish breathed into our faces. "Who's there?"

"My name is Brother Jian. I am here for..."

The man grunted and the door swung wide, admitting us into a courtyard garden, its path stretching all the way to a well-lit manor house. "The other is here." He jerked his head toward a well-lit pagoda. "In there."

He went away on the words, taking his lantern with him. Jian hesitated. Caught between these walls, every breath was saturated with the sweetness of summer flowers, while the sounds of laughter and conversation from the manor were like ghostly voices on the air.

"Come on," Jian said, striding the short distance toward the pagoda. It owned only a single inhabitant, a man kneeling at a narrow table, his eyes fixed on empty air. Jian's brother. I could not have mistaken him. From the flat forehead to the square jaw, the trappings of the priest only made the likeness more obvious.

"Good evening, Jian," Kokoro said, making the effort to rise. "You have grown old."

"I could say the same of you. More so."

Jian was right. The difference in age was marked, although it was possible Father Kokoro looked older than he was—his face lined by troubles, not years. His eyes had a sharp, glittering look as he turned them to me. "And this is Endymion, I presume."

I bowed, showing the respect his position demanded. "Father Kokoro."

"I expected you last night."

"We were detained," Jian said. "We have been having more and more trouble with Endymion's papers."

"That," Kokoro said, resuming his place at the table with a groan, "is because they are forged."

I stared at him. "Forged?"

Taking the offered place at the table, Jian shot me a warning look. "That has never been a problem before, Kokoro."

"That's because checking papers is no longer merely a task to keep the gate guards busy. They have a reason to fear imposters. Surely you have noticed the tone of the empire has changed. You should have stayed in Chiltae." Kokoro looked up at me with a smile and indicated a place at the table. "Do join us, Endymion.

You may as well, since I believe it is to talk about you that I have been summoned."

"I want to know who my mother was."

Father Kokoro's greying brows shot up. "Your mother?"

"I dream about her."

"And what is it you dream?"

I closed my eyes, and there inside my lids the images of her played, taunting me with their heartache. "She has golden hair and is wearing furs. She talks to me, smiles at me, a rare smile because I don't think she smiles often. She's more like a doll—fragile and beautiful and cold. There's a man there too sometimes, and she hates him, and I hate him because she hates him so much it hurts her, and . . ."

There was hunger in Father Kokoro's gaze when I opened my eyes. "You hated him enough to kill him, perhaps. And then her?"

"Kokoro! He was just a child!"

The older priest shrugged. "We'll never know what really happened."

The possibility that I might somehow have killed my mother left me breathless, her sad, anxious look taking on new meaning. But surely I would remember that, would remember something more than the feelings and the brush of new furs against my cheek. "Who was she?"

Again, Father Kokoro gestured to a place at the table, and I knelt beside Jian, the throb of his mortification like an external heartbeat. Kokoro exuded no such emotion, just sat calmly, his expression one of faint interest. Beyond our lit pagoda, night birds sang through the ongoing chatter and music from the manor. "Yes, I know who she was," Kokoro said at last. "And I know who your father was. But why do you need to know? They are both long dead."

I had known that, or at least told myself I had, even if a small part of me had continued to hope. The barb cut as deep as he'd meant it to, but I clasped my fingers tightly on top of the table and said, "Perhaps if I know, the dreams will hurt less. Perhaps I will feel less alone and adrift." There were more words in my heart, but under Father Kokoro's stare, I could utter none of them. My soul withered beneath his gaze.

"You would feel less adrift if you took the oath," he said at last.

"I don't want to be a priest."

"That is a pity."

"Why? Because in taking the oath I would give up my name?"

"Endymion," Jian warned.

"No, Jian. I want to hear everything he has to say. You think your name is so special you must be parted from it, child? Such dreams of grandeur! Is that why you do not wish to be a priest?"

How could I put my reason into words this man might understand? "I don't think I was made to help people."

"Then what were you made to do?"

"I don't know yet," I said.

Kokoro leant forward, an ugly sneer turning his lips. "Well I do. You were made to steal and to hurt. You were made to break and destroy and kill. I know better than you what you are, Endymion. Your father was an Empath, too."

Every word had been like a punch, but at the last, my breath caught in my throat. "He was?"

Kokoro looked at Jian. "Why did you bring him to me?"

"He wants to know, and if he will not take the oath, then he deserves to know who he is. I could have taken him straight to Lord Laroth for an answer, but this was easier."

The older man reached across the table and gripped Jian's clasped hands. "Do you have a death wish? What did Nyraek tell you?"

Jian leant back as though from a furnace. "Only that he was not like a normal child," he said. "But he is harmless. He suffers under a great burden, but that is far from his fault."

"You're a fool. It may not be his fault he was born an Empath, but he is far from harmless."

"I'm right here!" I snapped. "Would you prefer I left so you can talk about me in peace?"

"Infinitely," Kokoro said.

Jian shook his head. "No, stay. We came all this way, and you are old enough to know whatever Kokoro can tell you."

"You mean he is of an age to be more dangerous than ever." Scowling, Father Kokoro looked even older, his face criss-crossed like crumpled parchment.

Someone cleared their throat. A servant stood waiting in the archway, a tray in his hands. Receiving a nod from Kokoro, he entered and began to serve a meal. Jian and I never ate what the nobles called their midnight meal, and I stared hard at the bowl of sugared beans placed in front of me, not sure what to make of such hospitality. Did the owner of the manor know who the court priest was entertaining in his garden?

My bewilderment increased when the liquid that flowed from the teapot's earthen spout was reddish brown, its aroma sweet. Roasted tea. It was a delicacy I had never tasted, our meals more about sustenance than elegance.

While the man finished serving, Kokoro picked up a bean and crunched it between his teeth. I pushed the bowl away, wanting nothing but an answer and to escape. "Who is Nyraek?" I asked.

Kokoro ate another bean and nodded at Jian. "You could have asked Jian that."

Not meeting my gaze, Jian looked away and sighed. "Nyraek Laroth is the man who brought you to me. He was the fifth count of Esvar."

"Was?"

"I heard he died not long after, though his son, Lord Darius

Laroth, is minister of the left in the court of Emperor Kin. He is the only other person I thought might know who you are."

"But why did his father give me to you?"

"Because Kokoro told him where to find a priest he could trust to look after an orphaned child." Jian still did not look at me, but something in his words twinged a dormant memory.

"It was raining," I said. A careworn man dressed in a dark travelling cloak, raindrops shimmering in his hair. He had protected me from the storm as best he could, holding me close on the steaming horse, his scent a mixture of sweat and blood and fine jasmine oil. And—I put my hand to my throat. "He gave me a pendant."

"Oh he did, did he?" Kokoro said, still chewing on those damned beans and looking from me to Jian as though we were a practiced entertainment. "The eye? Understandable that you took that from him, Jian. I honour your wisdom."

"You took it?"

Jian dug his hand into his sash pouch and withdrew a fine silver chain, its pendant shaped like an eye. The very same eye that had been painted on the dead men back in Hoturi and on many more along the way.

"I take it back," Kokoro said, humour vanishing. "It is foolish to have kept it at all, let alone carried it on your person."

"Nonsense, I am a priest. Who would question that I found it on the road if I spoke such a lie?"

Hardly meaning to, I snatched the glimmering pendant from Jian's hand and turned it over, awed by the sight of something both new and old to my gaze. I had worn it before, I was sure I had. An elegant spider was engraved on the back.

"You should never wear that here," Kokoro said, eyes locked to the pendant. "Nor even carry it. It is called the Eye of Vice, and it will get you executed as a Vice whether you are one or not."

"Then why did Nyraek Laroth carry it? Was he a Vice?"

"No," Jian said. "They did not appear until years after his death. I know, I checked the records. Nor was he the only one to wear this. I understand it was a popular symbol for love and protection in the court at one time, is that so, Kokoro?"

The court priest nodded. "On that piece of information, if nothing else, I cannot fault you."

I looked from one man to the other, an idea sending my heart racing. "Was...was Nyraek Laroth my...my father?" I had to force the words out, so foolish they sounded, so hopeful and arrogant to even consider I might be the son of a lord. Yet the mother in my dreams had never been shabbily dressed. She wore silks I could never have imagined.

Kokoro sipped his tea. "Go back to Chiltae, Endymion, take the oath and become a man of the gods. For your own good."

"Why? Because when a man takes the oath he not only gives up all blood ties but also all rights to family property?"

The old priest crunched another bean between his teeth, his jaw shifting as he ground each grain of sugar. I watched him closely, hoping the lines on his face spoke some message his emotions failed to convey.

Kokoro lifted his brows. "Trying to read me, Endymion? I know you can lift my emotions out of the air, but I am not one to wear my heart on my sleeve."

"I want to meet Lord Laroth's son."

"I do not think you can hear what you are saying, boy. You are a vagabond demanding to meet not only a lord but one of the highest-ranked ministers in the empire."

"Who might be my brother."

Kokoro's laugh rang out through the garden, silencing the birds and cutting across the babble of a fountain. "You naive, foolish child," he said, anger coursing through cracks in his composure. "No matter who your parents were, you are a bastard as well as a freak. You get nothing, deserve nothing, are nothing. Take him away, Jian. Do not take him to Mei'lian. Do not seek out Lord Laroth. Make him take the oath and I will forget you were fool enough to bring him to me."

Jian's hands trembled around his teacup. "Drink up your tea, Endymion, and we will be on our way." His tone was jovial, but it hid nothing.

I threaded the necklace around my neck, its pendant heavy. "No." I glared defiantly across the table. "I want to know who I am."

Kokoro reached for another bean. I wanted to slap it out of his hand, but I controlled the urge and said, "Tell me, and I will take the oath and go back to Chiltae."

"If only I could believe that."

"It is not important, Endymion," Jian said. "When you take the oath, you will have no family. Let us give thanks for the hospitality and we can go."

No family. But it would be a lie. Nothing could change the blood that ran through my veins, as nothing could change the blood that ran through theirs.

Kokoro's hand was on the table, the distance between us nothing. There was no guarantee I would find what I wanted, but I would never have another chance. I gripped his wrist. Kokoro flinched as I forced my Empathy through his dry skin, forging a connection. Fear poured into my heart. It turned my stomach sick, every vein seeming to run with its poison, and there in his mind's eye, I could see myself.

Father Kokoro snatched his hand away. "You have no idea what you're doing," he said, his breath coming fast.

"You're afraid of me."

"By the gods I am, and I have good reason." He looked toward his brother, half risen from the table. "I'm sorry, Jian, but you've left me no choice."

"Sorry for what? Don't do anything stupid, Kokoro."

"I'm afraid it was you who did that. You should never have brought him here. Guards!"

Heavy footsteps sounded in the garden, my heartbeat rising to their tempo. A dozen armed guards spilled into the pagoda.

"Take the boy," Kokoro said. "Endymion, you are under arrest. You are a traitor to the great Emperor Kin, first of his name, and to the Imperial Expanse of Kisia for the practice of witchcraft. You will be executed for your crimes and your body returned to the soil from which it came, the mercy of the gods willing."

I heard the words but could not move, could not speak. A man grabbed my arm, pulling me roughly to my feet.

"Kokoro, don't do this!"

"I must," Kokoro said. "I'm sorry, Brother. Bind his hands and do not touch his skin."

Sudden fear loosened their grips, and I backed away, hands lifted before me. The guards followed warily. "Just let us go, Kokoro," Jian pleaded. "We will leave. You will never see us again."

I bumped up against the stone wall. One of the guards unclipped his scabbard from his belt but kept his sword sheathed. "Come on, boy," he said. "Fighting us isn't going to end well." He lunged on the words, the butt of his scabbard jabbing into my gut. Breath burst out of me and I could not draw it back in. Someone grabbed my arm, and I flailed, trying to find skin, to share my fear and my pain, but chains clicked tight.

For the crime of witchcraft.

Rope tightened at my elbows.

When the crows were done with me, there would be nothing left but bones.

"May the gods judge me as they judge us all," Kokoro said as I was pulled toward the garden stairs, still dazed, every shallow breath agony. "Sometimes we do things because they are right. But sometimes we do things because we must."

2. HANA

Firelight and grumbling met us at the small camp, but though the waiting men might complain, only one dared call to us as we reined in.

"You're late!" The complaint came in advance of its owner, though I caught sight of him soon enough, wending his way through my Vices as they dismounted. They looked strange in the uniforms of imperial soldiers, but I had to admit it had made travelling much easier.

"And you lack patience," I said, jumping from the saddle to land before Shin. With a lantern held at his side, his face was lit from beneath, leaving his long scar carved in gold from eyebrow to chin.

"It was your boss who said we had to be in by sunrise."

The alliance between the rebel Pikes and the Vices was months old, but it had taken me a single day to realise that despite holding no official position in the group, Shin was their leader's closest advisor. He seemed to exist only to serve his captain. "You have the goods?" he said.

"Of course we have. Avarice. Ire. Bring the sacks for the captain—I mean, for the captain's arse."

Shin's brow furrowed. "Arse?"

"You're always following Monarch so closely. Seems appropriate to me."

The man grunted but said nothing as Avarice and Ire brushed past, their arms straining beneath the weight of two bulging sacks. These they dumped beside the nearby fire, and ill ease temporarily forgotten, Monarch's rebels gathered around. A few tugs on the knots, and imperial uniforms spilled out. More sacks followed with more uniforms, and while the Pikes piled in, snatching up tunics and sashes and mail, I turned to address the Vices. They weren't my men, technically, but my guardian had ordered them to obey me and so they did.

"It's going to take the Pikes some time to get ready," I said, yanking up breeches that kept threatening to fall down. You'd have thought womanly hips would make keeping them up easier, but either I was too skinny or soldiers' uniforms really hadn't been made with women in mind. Probably both. "While we're waiting, you can see to your horses," I went on. "Then you can rest. And see if the Pikes have any food. It's going to be a long night, but Malice will be waiting for us at the other end."

No agreement, no salutes, no exuberance. At home, they smiled and laughed and joked like any other group of men, but every time we worked a job, they became cold statues of themselves. Aloof. Guarded. Even with me.

Conceit remained while the other dozen dispersed, and good to his name, he folded his arms and smiled his pretty smile. "Were there any... special orders, Captain?" he said, tapping his sash pouch to indicate where I kept the ink canister Malice's message had been in. The blood was probably dry by now, but I could have made a show of checking it and might have for anyone other than Conceit. His tone and expression—his very existence—mocked.

"If there were," I said, making no move toward the blood-filled canister, "I would have given them to you. Avarice remains with the horses, the rest of us travel with the Pikes to get them through the tunnel. Those were our orders."

He bowed, and I couldn't put my finger on what he did that made it appear contemptuous. "As you command, *Captain*."

Conceit walked away, skirting the Pikes still fighting over the best uniforms. I had no idea how many rebels Monarch commanded. Malice thought it as many as a thousand, maybe two or three thousand, given who he was, but only forty had been chosen for this mission. No doubt only his longest-serving, most loyal men for such a task.

"Captain Regent?"

Shin was at my side again, and I rolled my eyes. He always hovered close when we were around. People made a lot of fuss about the Vices' reputation. "Yes, Shin? There is nothing amiss with the uniforms, I trust?"

The long scar that bisected his eye left it lidless and unblinking, and he turned it on me now. "No. Monarch wants you."

I ought to have expected the summons, yet it sent my heart thumping. I'd needed to piss for the last few miles, but Shin started walking with the unspoken assumption that I would follow, and I did. I had not been playing this game long enough to keep Monarch of all people waiting.

In silence, Shin led me away from the fire and out into the dark trees. Shin's lantern swung gently in his hands and he made barely a sound, nothing like my clomping feet, incapable of taking a step without cracking sticks and dry leaves and sending animals scurrying.

Monarch wasn't far, just far enough that the noise of the camp faded to little more than a background hum cut by the occasional shout of laughter. Here in the trees there was just the buzz of insects. And the creak and twang of Monarch's bow. An arrow thudded into an unseen target.

"Regent is here," Shin said, halting far enough back that even with the lantern, Monarch was little more than a collection of shadows against the night.

"Yes, I heard him coming." Twang, thud.

I reddened like a berated child but folded my arms and refused to be drawn into a retort.

"Leave the lantern and go back, Shin," he added as an arrow clacked against the sides of a quiver. "I want everyone ready to leave within the hour."

"Yes, Captain."

I gripped the handle as the lantern was thrust into my hand, but Shin didn't immediately let go. Standing close, his eyes scoured my face for a long moment before he let out his usual grunt and the full weight of the lantern dropped into my hand. Without a word, he brushed past in the direction of the camp, leaving me alone with the rebel leader and the hammering of my heart.

Twang, thud.

I tightened my sweaty grip on the lantern and ventured a few steps closer. Monarch had no light of his own and had to be loosing arrows blind. Which was, I had to admit, fucking impressive.

"You had something you wanted to say to me?" I said, swallowing the desire to praise his skill.

"Yes."

Up close, the light from my lantern fell upon his face, upon his strong jaw and his heavy brow, upon long dark hair pulled back into a messy topknot and the stubble of a beard he must have grown since the last time I'd seen him. Papa Orde would never have let himself be seen with a beard, but the kindly couple who had looked after me in my youth had been farmers, not exiled scions of imperial blood.

"Well? What is it?" I said when he lifted his bow again rather than answer. "If you want us ready to go within the hour, you had better—"

"I want your word none of my men will get hurt."

Whatever I had expected, it hadn't been that. "What?"

"Your big boss man's Vices," he said, lowering the bow. "They can do some fucked up things, and I want your word they won't turn their freakish shit on my men."

Stung by the injustice, I said, "Surely if that was a concern, you should have made it a condition when you first struck this deal with Malice."

He turned, fixing me with his bright blue eyes. The Otako eyes, some called them, and I had been glad a hundred times over that my own were dusky rather than luminous. "I did," he said. "But I don't trust your Malice any more than I trust his Vices."

"But you trust me?"

"Ish." His scowl fled before one of his sudden smiles—ever an unexpected peek of sunlight through storm clouds. "Did you know my men think you must have some amazing, hitherto unseen power, because why else would the Vices answer to a little boy who looks like he's run away from his tutors to come play soldier in the woods? Whereas I think you're just a little boy who's run away from his tutors to play soldier in the woods."

The smile was gone with the words, and he stepped closer, tall and imposing and still holding his bow. "But they listen to you, so I want your word none of my men will get hurt. The tunnels are narrow and dark. Easy places for accidents to happen."

I swallowed the mortification of his words, and for a moment, I felt exactly like what he had said of me, only he would laugh to know I was really a woman dressed as a boy who had run away from his tutors to play soldier. Before I could reply, I had to remind myself of who I was and why I was there, of everything I wanted to achieve.

"I cannot control accidents," I said, drawing myself up. "But you have my word that my Vices will do all in their power to ensure every Pike gets into the city unharmed. That is, after all, our mission."

It wasn't entirely true, but I could no more tell him Malice was on the hunt for new blood than I could tell him who I was. That I was an Otako too.

Monarch's brows lowered, forming one long dark band in the shadows. "That is not very reassuring, Captain Regent."

"I am afraid it's all the answer I can give, Captain Monarch. You would perhaps like to dig your way through to the capital instead?"

"As His Majesty will be leaving for Koi within a few days, that isn't an option."

"You could ambush him on the road."

"No." The scowl darkened. "I don't want to give him the chance to die in combat. I want him to die like—"

He broke off, though I could guess the words he left unsaid. *Like my father died.* Tianto Otako had been emperor for only ten days before he had been caught and executed for treason. For ordering the assassination of his own brother, Emperor Lan Otako.

My father.

Standing silent, I clenched my teeth as surely as he clenched his, neither of us willing to let out words that might condemn us. I wanted to hate him for the harm his father had done mine. I had tried to hate him, but just when I thought maybe I could, he would let down his guard just enough that I could see his hurt—deep, bruised to the soul—and the urge to tell him the truth would surge to the surface.

"No." He shook his head before I could speak. "No. I will tear him down slowly for what he did. Just as I will tear you and your Malice apart if anything happens to my men."

"They will be fine as long as your guide knows the way."

And just like that, he had swallowed the hurt down where no one could see it, and his smile was back. He even laughed. "You give as good as you get. I like that. In fact, fool though I might be, I like you, just not your friend or his Vices." He paused, and I could find no words to fill the silence he left me. "If they weren't so damned useful, I'd have let them all go hang by now."

"A warning to watch our backs?"

"A man should always watch his back. And so should a woman."

There was no particular emphasis upon the word *woman*, but I froze like hunted prey as he stepped back to his mark and lifted his bow. Woman. Surely if he knew, he would call me on it, and yet... Monarch turned to look at me even as he loosed an arrow at the unseen target. "Will you be coming with us all the way to Koi, Captain?" he said.

"Yes." I hoped the word didn't sound as breathless to him as it did to me.

"Good." He took another arrow from his quiver and, looking into the darkness now, added, "I look forward to being able to spend more time with you than the snatches we have been afforded so far. I get the feeling there's more to you than a boy playing dress up."

He did not look my way again or seem to expect an answer, but if he had, I could not have given one, could do nothing more than mumble something unintelligible and turn away, all too conscious of how hot the night was and how close the air, like I was trapped in a travelling chest and there was no space to breathe. How could one man be so disastrously alluring without seeming to even try?

Fiercely reminding myself that he thought I was a boy, I tramped away with the lantern in hand, blindly at first, then in search of somewhere to relieve myself. Somewhere far enough from Monarch and far enough from the camp that I could be alone.

I found a spot a little way out, and having made certain no one else was around, I set the lantern down in some scrubby grass. A few steps away, I untied the strings of my breeches as fast as I could, yanked out the roll of fabric Malice had assured me I couldn't be a man without, and squatted in the undergrowth. I breathed out a sigh as I pissed onto the leaves, taking care as always not to get any on my breeches or, gods be feared, my feet. It wasn't an easy task, but I had grown up with the farm boys back home and had plenty of practice. Mama Orde would have been horrified had she ever found out.

A twinge of yearning for her homemade seared apple and ginger cakes hit me at about the same time as the sound of Shin's voice sent my pulse into a panicked frenzy. I stood hurriedly, drips dribbling down my legs as I yanked my breeches back up.

"Those uniforms are good," he said, stopping nearby and beginning to untie his own breeches. "I'm impressed."

"Damn it, Shin, I didn't hear you and you scared me half to death," I said, glad the darkness hid my red cheeks. "Am I not allowed an instant of peace around here?"

He grunted rather than answer, and though I could only make out his outline, I looked away as he relieved himself a few steps from where I had been crouched. I half turned to depart, only to wonder if that would be a strange thing for a man to do. Ought I talk? Or did men stand in companionable silence like priests at prayer? Mama Orde had always prattled in an attempt to block out the sound of a woman doing anything so unsavoury as passing water.

"I hope our horses will be properly cared for while we are in Mei'lian," I said, deciding at last that having stood there so long, I had to say something. "Malice will be disappointed if they aren't."

Shin adjusted himself and began retying his breeches. Head on the side, he regarded me curiously a moment before saying, "His ponies will be just fine." And he walked away out of the lantern light as though nothing had happened.

Preparations were well along when, after cleaning myself up as best I could and readjusting my breeches, I returned to the camp. The Vices had finished seeing to their horses and were sitting around one of the smaller fires, keeping their distance from the Pikes, who were still changing into the uniforms we had brought for them. They were joking and laughing as they did so, preferring constant chatter to the fear that was no doubt beginning to eat at their stomachs.

I made to join the Vices at their meagre meals, only to halt. I had lived around them for the last few seasons and they called me captain, but I was no more one of them than I was a Pike, and feeling out of place despite it all, I hovered at the edge of the camp.

Preparations continued. Soon all the Pikes were dressed in the imperial uniforms we had supplied and were checking over their weapons and helmets and bags. Shin moved about, giving orders, but it wasn't until it was almost time to go that Monarch emerged from the trees, his bow, Hacho, in the holster upon his back. His men quieted at sight of him, their last words dying away as he stood before them, a grand figure with squared shoulders.

"It's time to go," he said. "This isn't going to be fun. There will be some places in the tunnels where we can walk, others where we have to crawl on our bellies like worms, and some where we have to stand back and let our Vice friends clear the way. No talking, no laughing, no complaining. Once inside the city, we make for the safe house. If you have any questions, now's the time to ask."

"Do we have to wear these tight breeches?" a man called out. "My balls are going to drop off."

Amid the laughter, someone else said, "No great loss there, then."

"Yeah, you're the expert on balls, Kai."

I recognised the complainant as Wen, one of the few Pikes I had seen recruited. He was tugging at the inside leg of the uniform, happily drawing attention to his bulge. "Perhaps I need a larger size."

"Enough." Monarch did not have to shout to cut through the laughter. The men fell silent. "Once we're safe, you can check to see if you still have your pair. Let's go. I want a lantern bearer every third man in the passage."

The group broke up, moving forward, a few wary glances thrown back to check if the Vices were following. Ire led them over. He nodded to me as they joined the Pikes to get their lanterns, a half smile the only sign of his usually buoyant humour.

"Joining us, Captain?" Monarch said, striding along the line to hand me a lantern.

"Of course." I tried to ignore the thrill as his hand briefly touched mine. "Will your bow hold up all right in the passage?"

He reached over his shoulder to touch it. "Oh, she'll hold up. She's never let me down. There aren't many people who can say that about anyone."

Almost I pointed out that his bow wasn't a person, but he trained so much that perhaps it had taken on a life of its own.

To my surprise, it was Shin who led the way out of the camp. At every mention of a guide, I had assumed it would be someone paid well and brought in for the purpose, not that it would be Monarch's taciturn arse. No one else seemed to find it amiss, or at least no one said anything, and leaving the dying fires behind, we pushed our way through patches of brambles toward a forest pool. In single file, our oddly assorted group made its way around its edge and down a slope where water followed in trickles. At the bottom, Shin stopped before a short rock face and ran his hands over it in search of the narrow fissure Monarch had spoken of. And it was narrow, narrow enough that I began to wish I had left the Vices to do this mission alone.

Monarch turned his back to the stone face. "All right, this is where everyone shuts up," he said. "Not a word from here unless it's absolutely necessary. We don't want red belts waiting for us at the other end, so anyone who makes a noise will be answering to Hacho."

As though in proof, he removed his bow from its holster. The men shifted their weight, but Monarch seemed disinclined to kill anyone just yet. Instead, he nodded to Shin, and the big man turned his shoulder and squeezed through the fissure, the light from his lantern making the stone slit glow.

Monarch followed and I followed him, leading the Vices through first, because when shit went wrong, they were the ones we needed up front.

The narrow opening in the stone led down, the passage slick with mud and every breath carrying the stink of sodden soil. Ahead of me, Monarch had to duck his head to keep from hitting the low ceiling, while a hiss from behind me was the sound of Ire doing just that.

Down and farther down the tunnel led, until we came out in a broad passage, its stones faintly green in the shifting light. Fearful emperors long dead had built quite the network of escape tunnels in and out of Mei'lian, but over the years, earth tremors had collapsed whole sections, leaving them impassable. In some places that would mean just having to climb screes of cracked stone and slither on our stomachs through spaces so narrow they were like the guts of the earth, while in others we would have to rely on the skills the Vices carried with them in their skins.

Once we were all present, Shin set off along the tunnel. For a while, we were able to walk upright, nothing to complain of but the silence and the oppressive heat. With every step, the air seemed to grow hotter and sweat prickled my skin. Ahead of me, Shin shifted his lantern from hand to hand. When we came to the first narrow squeeze, he pushed the lantern ahead of himself, a grunt of effort the only sound he made as he scraped along over sharp stones. The rest of us followed, the smell of sweat filling the space like raw wool.

It was a relief to come out the other side, but there was no reprieve from the heat, and all too soon we reached our first complete cave-in. Ire and I examined it while the Pikes took the time to rest and Monarch hovered, his anxious scowl all the more marked in the lantern light.

"If this chunk here is solid then Apostasy could do it," Ire whispered, resting his hand on the large piece of ceiling that blocked our way. "Otherwise I'll try. What do you say, Captain?"

"It's sweet of you to ask as though I have any idea," I said, the heat and the fatigue leaving honesty the simplest answer. "You do whatever you think is best. Just take care no one gets hurt."

He pressed out a wan smile. "Yes, Captain."

Under the watchful gazes of the gathered Pikes, Apostasy took up a position beside the block of stone and set his hand to it. While some of the Vices enjoyed the showmanship and the attention, Apostasy was not one of them. He stared at his hand rather than at the shocked faces around him as the rock vanished from view.

A scowl from Monarch quieted the outbreak of whispers, and with a frown my way, he walked through the space first to prove it was safe. One by one, his men followed, and once we were all through, Shin walked on. Behind me, Apostasy whispered to someone about "contiguous matter," but even in the cramped space beneath the ground, the Pikes kept all the more distance between us and them. It only got worse when Ire's touch turned a series of boulders to dust, and Parsimony and Conceit together lifted a boulder that should have required at least ten men.

Eventually, after hours of dragging ourselves through narrow, dust-clogged passages and breathing in each other's stink, the air began to change. Breathing became easier. The gentlest of breezes ghosted through the passage. Shin stopped, and without looking around, he handed me his lantern, its handle damp from his grip.

A cart rumbled overhead.

Monarch followed him to the wall, the pair running their hands over the stones until they found one that stood proud of the others. Everyone gathered as first Shin and then Monarch began to climb, catching hold of thick roots and pulling themselves up to disappear into the darkness.

Handing my lantern to Ire, I too began to climb. I was not as tall as Monarch, but I had grown up climbing trees on Papa Orde's farm and knew how to shift my weight. Grasping hold of the root,

I swung my arm up, gripped the ledge, and pulled myself through the hole in the stone ceiling. Monarch helped me to my feet, and one by one, the others joined us in the old hay room above, grumbling in whispers. Cut, grazed, and filthy we might be, but we had all made it into the city alive. And as soon as we reached the safe house, we could rest.

A moonlit stable-yard stood outside the hay room. At the end of the yard, a gate led to a narrow lane and on to another courtyard shadowed by the broad canopy of an old magnolia. The Kissing Tree, where couples hung offerings to the god of love. Dozens of lanterns hung in its branches, flowers too, and strings of red beads and crumpled shreds of parchment.

The men rested beneath the tree's emerald blanket, an odd collection of Pikes and Vices licking their wounds.

I crept on to the end of the courtyard to be sure we were alone. A city street stretched away beyond, lined with closed shops, their signs turned down and their windows shuttered with latticework. In the distance, an open plaza was hazy with lantern light, the city a mess of shapes and smells and shadowy figures going about their business in the early hours.

Wen and Kai were waiting at the gate when I returned, the shadows of shifting leaves upon their faces.

"No guards," I said. "But there are people around. Go carefully."

They nodded, and striding off along the street, they looked enough like a patrol making their way back to the guardhouse that I let them go.

Beneath the tree, the others clustered together like a pack of lost goats. I caught Monarch's eye, but he seemed content to let me choose the next pair to leave. It had been a long night for everyone, all of us tired and sore and dirty, but both Ire and Apostasy looked ready to drop from all the extra effort they had expended. They went next, then two Pikes whose names I didn't know, and in pairs the group dwindled, our caution squandering what was left of the night until, with dawn approaching, only Monarch and I remained.

"The sun will be up soon," I said, turning to leave. "We had better go."

"Not yet." He grabbed my arm and pulled me back, hard enough that I almost bumped into him. "I want to know what a girl is doing running with the Vices."

I choked on my heart as it made a fearful bid for freedom up my throat. "I—"

"Don't deny it, we don't have time for lies." He hadn't let go of my arm. "Are you one of them?"

"Yes! No...I mean, I don't have...can't do...Please let me go. We have to get to the safe house."

"To stop Malice wondering what happened to his little girl? Is he your father? Is that it?"

"No!" The idea of Malice having children made me laugh. "No, he just took me in. The only grand secret is the one you already know."

"Why then? Why dress up like this?"

Genuine confusion creased his features, and I thought of just how much easier life would have been had I really been born with something stuffed between my legs. "Because people listen to men," I said. "Because no one tells a man he can't do something."

"But no one will take an interest in you either," he said, his smile artlessly lopsided. "Or want you to share their bed."

An attempt to say that this was part of the point died unspoken as he leant in close. "Do you know why it's called the Kissing Tree?" His voice was little more than a murmur now, his breath warm.

"Not exactly, but I could take an educated guess," I said.

"It's where couples kiss goodbye."

It was like a dream, blurred around the edges. His dry lips brushed my cheek. His breath ghosted across my face. Despite every reason I had chosen to dress the way I did, I yearned toward him, only to find nothing but the cool night air.

Monarch stepped away. From across the courtyard, Shin was watching.

"Another time, sweet Regent," Monarch said in a husky whisper, stepping aside to let me pass. But I couldn't move. I wanted him to kiss me, even just quickly, anything but parting like this when I could imagine the touch of his lips and his fingers in my hair, the strength of him and the fire of his skin.

He smiled, a single dimple appearing beside his lopsided grin. Then with a tap on Hacho, he strode away along the road.

"Looks like you're with me, Captain," Shin said when at last I joined him. Whatever he had seen or heard he said nothing, just turned away, leaving me to scamper after him like a dog.

Monarch had vanished before we reached the street, no sign of his prominent figure or Hacho's reaching tip. In the predawn light, the city was no longer quiet but full of shutters slamming open and barking dogs. Carts rumbled past and the air was rent by hawkers greeting the morning with their cries.

As soon as we could, Shin veered off the main road, cutting down a side alley into a tangle of narrow passages, the houses so close they blocked the pale dawn sky from view. Courtyards connected the passages like the rooms of a palace, curtains left to draw the line between inside and out. Laundry and drying herbs hung from lantern strings like a makeshift ceiling shifting in the breeze.

Sound returned as we came out the other side. The streets opened up, allowing us glimpses of the bright sky, and we soon found ourselves in a quiet, well-kept district. Here, the alleys led to the back doors of larger establishments, and it was down one of these that Shin turned. We were nearly to the safe house, but at the corner I stopped. In the distant morning haze, the grand spire of the inner palace peeped just above the crowding buildings. Up there somewhere, Emperor Kin might even now be sitting upon the Crimson Throne, though it had never been his birthright.

It was mine.

3. DARIUS

I knelt at the table, tapping one manicured finger upon the polished wood. The emperor was keeping me waiting. It was his prerogative, of course, but that didn't lessen my frustration at such wanton wasting of my time. It had been light when I arrived, but now shadows grew in every corner, claiming the room with their reaching fingers.

One by one the lamps were lit, spreading their golden glow across the reed matting. The imperial lantern lighters went about their job in trained silence, unacknowledged ghosts who allowed the court to function. I watched them glide around the room, giving me a wide berth. Minister Laroth was not a man one wished to inconvenience.

An uneven step approached, one leg dragging, the other spry. Cups clinked. A tray was lowered, a little unsteadily, but the boy was getting better.

I turned to find him bowing, nose pressed to the floor.

"Pour," I said. "You don't need to prostrate yourself. Remember that liars and sycophants walk these floors. I would not wish you to catch their sickness."

"The court has a sickness, Excellency?"

"Most of the time the court is a sickness."

"And you, Excellency? Are you sick?"

A surprising question from anyone's lips, even more so from

those of a servant. Safer to keep his mouth shut and his eyes on the floor. He would have to work on that.

He had already reddened and looked away, and sure he had realised his mistake, I merely said, "You are fortunate that your ability to count above ten makes you invaluable. One day you will be a secretary and look down your nose at everyone. As for sickness, let us say I have some symptoms. I am a brilliant liar, but I have not been at court long enough to develop such an important skill as sycophancy."

"A great inadequacy, Excellency," the boy said, trying not to grin and failing. He would have to work on that too.

"Indeed," I said gravely. "Serve the tea."

Bowing again, he did so, his hands still a little unsteady. The first time, he had shaken so fiercely that tea splashed across the table, which made the mere tinkle of ceramic a decided improvement.

He handed me a cup, and while I sipped, he watched me with an expression rather like that of a puppy, unsure whether it would receive a pat or a kick.

"It's good, you little wretch," I said. "Now be off with you."

At the head of the room, a pair of doors swung open.

"Ah, good evening, Laroth," spoke a hated voice in its sickly-sweet tones. "Are you here to see His Majesty? How sorry I am that we kept you waiting. We got to talking, you know how it is."

I set aside my cup and looked up, wincing theatrically at the sight of Councillor Ahmet's robe. The busy turquoise silk did his ruddy complexion no favours. "Ah, Councillor, I wonder at him being able to stomach the sight of you for so long. Prolonged exposure to that robe would make anyone feel bilious."

The boy snorted. He had the sense to look at the ground, but the sound drew Ahmet's attention. "Ah, is this the crippled serving boy I have been hearing about? What strange taste you have, Minister. He is not even pretty."

"I am quite pretty enough for the both of us," I said, signalling for the boy to leave. He did so, bowing only perfunctorily before hobbling out.

Ahmet watched him go, but his sneer was for me. "There is nothing more disgraceful than a vain man."

"Better a diamond with a flaw than a pebble without." I rose from the table and, leaving Ahmet to struggle for a retort, made my way to the open doors.

The imperial chancellor stood in the aperture. "His Majesty is waiting for you, Your Excellency," he said.

"Then I will go in. Good evening, Councillor."

Ahmet's face had reddened, making the contrast with his robe all the more hideous, and after a lingering glare, he marched out. No doubt he would go bluster at his secretaries. I had been the focus of his ire ever since Kin had given me command over Kisia's military districts instead of him, and in the years since, his anger had only festered.

"His Excellency Lord Darius Laroth," the chancellor intoned as I walked into the throne room. "The sixth count of Esvar and minister of the left."

The throne room was a semicircular marvel. On the highest floor of the grand spire, its roof soared away to a distant peak, while red glass windows stained all light that entered—or would have done if the sun had not already set. At night, no amount of lanterns could have made it bright, so dark was the floor, but a pair shone on either side of the emperor's dais all the same. He sat on the Crimson Throne, its curls of lacquered wood reaching far above his head as he stared into the distance, a line cut between his brows.

I knelt at the Humble Stone, touching my forehead to the floor. He did not immediately order me to rise, and when he did, it sounded as though he had only just remembered I was there.

"Number forty-eight worrying you, Majesty?" I asked, shaking out the skirt of my robe as I got to my feet.

He laughed, the lightening of his expression improving his appearance. He was not handsome in the common way, his brow too heavy, his features too thin, but he did not require beauty the way other men did. Emperor Kin had been the youngest general in Kisian history, a brilliant tactician at twenty-two years of age. Perhaps he had been handsome then, but sixteen years of battling for stability had left their mark. Where most leaders grew fat in their power, Kin had wasted away in his, leaving lean strength where once there had been brute force.

"Perceptive as ever, Darius," he said, indicating that I should come closer. "It certainly feels about time for it. Assassins have always liked the days before I travel north, perhaps in the hope my guards will be distracted by packing their bags. Come, sit."

"Thank you, Majesty."

I approached, and stepping up onto the dais, sat down upon what had historically been the empress's divan. Except that disregarding the advice of his council, Kin had not yet married, choosing instead to name an heir from amongst his family.

"You would think that after so many attempts on my life, I would be inured to them," he went on as I sat. "But I find there is nothing so bad as feeling sure one is coming. When death comes for me, I would rather it took me by surprise."

"Like a warrior in battle?"

For a full minute he was silent, considering. I was used to his ways and waited, listening to the guards shift their weight behind us.

"I used to think so," he said at last. "But what is honourable about dying in battle? Every war we fight is a failure of my duty. Is stability not what an emperor should strive for? Prosperity. Health." He sighed. "At least I fought every war for the right reasons."

"And Kisia is grateful."

Again he considered. "Is it? I wonder. Your father fought for me, too. I remember."

It was hard to forget. He had fought for General Kin until he had been sent home in disgrace, released from service for turning on his own men. The unspoken question often followed me through court, tangible and prickly—had I inherited the madness as well as the title? Not here though, never here, and Kin's acceptance of me allowed me to let out a breath I would otherwise have held. "Yes, Majesty, I imagine he is as difficult for you to forget as he is for me."

Despite the honesty of the words, I did not allow myself a wry smile, for too much hurt would have shone through its cracks, hurt I could not let free. Rigid control. My father had been proof that without it, I would lose everything.

"For everyone, it seems. Councillor Ahmet mentioned him only an hour since with that arch look he has whenever he thinks he is uttering tasty court gossip. I tell you so you know to be careful there. You may have made an enemy."

"Ahmet and I are old enemies, but he is not the only one," I said. "I'm afraid I still do not fit in at court, Your Majesty. I do not simper and flatter enough. I do not enter into their games and their power plays and their trysts. What does it matter to me if a certain councillor we've just been talking about has been taking Lord Oro's third daughter to his bed?"

"Except when you can use that knowledge to make sure a certain councillor doesn't argue against your district redistribution scheme."

I pressed a hand to my chest. "I?" I said in a tone of mock disbelief. "What a thing to accuse a man of, Your Majesty, I am quite shocked."

He grinned, and for a moment, his anxieties about assassins vanished. "You are every bit the monster they assure me you are, Darius, just not—" Kin broke off, seeming to realise too late the infelicitous nature of his statement, and for a moment, I might have been kneeling on the cold stones of that snow-dusted courtyard again, head bowed, tears streaming as freely as my pitiful, begging words.

I ran a hand down the skirt of my robe, smoothing the silk against my leg. "Was there a reason you sent for me, Majesty?"

"Merely for the company. I trust you have time for a game or two, Laroth."

Errant was always his escape in sleepless times, capable of clearing the head as little else could.

"Of course, Majesty. There is always time for Errant."

The chancellor had been lying in wait, and with a nod from Kin, he slid the intricately carved and painted board onto the wide arm of the throne between us.

A small box came next. The chancellor had to use a silver coin to prise its lid free, sending the scent of old spices wafting out. Kin tipped the box and a rain of wooden discs scattered across the board, white on one side, black the other.

I drew back my right sleeve, folding the silk to keep it clear of my hand. Kin had carelessly rolled his despite the expensive fabric, drawing attention to his lingering inelegance. He looked well, had moulded over time into the image of an emperor, but his hands still gave him away. They were the hands of a soldier.

Kin watched me set my pieces as I watched him set his. Observation was one of the most important parts of Errant and the part most people forgot, along with remembering you were being observed in turn. I had begun our very first game sure that, whatever his tactical skill upon the battlefield, he would be as easy to read as any other soldier. But I had been wrong. Kin had a restful, focussed state where there was nothing except the problem at hand, and it was a skill worthy of respect.

Wasting no time, he made the first move and I mirrored it, all attention on the game. For a time we did not talk, no sound in the long room bar the click-click of pieces shifting across the wooden board. I watched his hands. I watched his face. There would be a strategy in his game, no matter how random his choices appeared. He never did anything without reason. Watching a man play Errant once could tell more about him than watching him live for a year. Games with Kin always reminded me that beneath the silk, beneath the smile and the calm and the gravitas, beat the heart of a ruthless man. He would not spare me if I got in his way.

"Any more news on our expected assassins?" he asked, moving another piece seemingly at random.

"Nothing new, Majesty." He already knew the answer. That meant it was worrying him even more than he was willing to admit. "The information may yet prove false. However, the guard has been doubled and the square as well as the surrounding streets were to be cleared from sundown."

"No curfew? You know I hate curfews. All they do is force our enemies deeper into hiding. I prefer them where I can see them."

"No curfew, Your Majesty. In this case, General Ryoji has deemed it unnecessary. If we were not in Mei'lian, it would be a different matter of course."

"The fact that most wait until I am outside the capital before making an attempt on my life does help me sleep at night."

"Well, you may sleep soundly, Majesty," I said. "No one will reach you here."

"Will you be sleeping soundly, Darius?"

Another member of the court might have taken the opportunity to fawn over their emperor, but that was not the reason he kept me.

"Yes, Majesty," I said. "I intend to be sleeping as well tonight as I do every night."

Kin scowled. "It is not you they are attempting to assassinate."

"Very true. Although I don't think I would feel otherwise if it were. A man must sleep."

He moved another piece, but it was me he looked at. "You're always such a serene devil, Darius. No, composed. In calligraphy, the word is more spiky and you're nothing if not spiky. You know I heard Lady Meche say she is quite sure you are not alive at all, but have been reawakened from the dead." He laughed. "Did you refuse to be excited by her numerous charms?"

Happy to keep his thoughts in less anxious channels, I said, "Sadly, yes. Though every servant who brings my washing water stares at my scars, so it was only a matter of time." Once again, honesty edged me too close to old hurts, always a danger with him. "However, do let me assure you, Your Majesty," I went on, "that the moment I start to smell like a corpse, I shall have myself buried immediately."

"Are you ever serious?"

"Occasionally."

He snorted and moved a piece dangerously close to my king. I looked back across his field, seeing and discarding leaping strings and patterns until I could see his complete passage, cunningly hidden by two measly leaders branching off to one side. I took in the placement of my own pieces and knew I had lost.

"You know I've got you," Kin said, his eyes flashing triumphantly. "In this court of liars, you're in a league of your own, but even you aren't made entirely of ice."

He could have crowed, could have made me play it out, but though it was a rare win, he just swept the pieces off the board as he spoke, impatient to start the next round.

"Was it your father who taught you to play?" Kin said as he slid my pieces back to me across the board.

"No. He was always at court in those days."

"Oh? Before my time, I think. Tell me about your early Errant education then. You must have had a good teacher."

I had, just not the sort expected of the eldest son of one of the empire's wealthiest lords. And not someone I wanted to tell the emperor of Kisia about.

"You don't like my request," Kin said. He pointed at my left hand, where I had been turning a piece over and over.

I stopped and tugged on my sleeve. "I was merely thinking, Majesty, of what I could say that would be worthy of your time."

He set his last piece in place with a snap. "Well done, Darius. You remind me that as I am the emperor, there is no such thing as a friend. Play."

Having no answer I dared speak, I focussed on the game, moving my first piece as a strategy formed in my head. Kin glared at the board and moved his front man. In someone else, I would have put this down to stupidity, but in him it was moody resentment. He no longer desired to play. It galled me, but I hid the anger behind the cool mask of Minister Laroth and refused to let him draw me out.

Half the round had gone before he spoke again. "It has been a week since the last report about Monarch's whereabouts," he said as though disliking the silence. "I hope the great rebel is not ill."

"It would be a sad end to his reign of terror, I admit."

"Have you heard the rumours?"

"Which ones, Majesty?" I said, turning one of his pieces, black for white.

"That Monarch is Katashi Otako back from exile."

Kin pushed a piece across the board with the tip of his finger, and I stared at it rather than immediately answer. The whites of his nails started farther down his fingers than was normal. A childhood of nail biting? An interesting detail, given I had never seen him present anything but a confident exterior, restraint almost as important to him as it was to me.

He cleared his throat. "Surely my minister of the left has thoughts on this point."

"I have heard the same rumours and hearsay you have, Majesty,"

I said. "But yet no evidence to connect these rebels to more than a few northern families upset by the treaty. The Meis and the Rotas especially. And you got my report that General Tikita refused to engage them at—"

"It's him."

"Pardon, Majesty?"

"Monarch. Who but Katashi Otako would call himself that? He is too much like his uncle and his father." He didn't even look at the board as he made his next move. "It worries me, Darius. I thought I was doing the right thing when I chose to be merciful and spare the boy's life. The north might have revolted then if I had killed him, but they are doing so now anyway. All I did was put it off long enough for Katashi to grow into a leader they all want to follow."

He pushed a piece forward as he spoke, and so poorly was it placed that it was clear he wasn't focussing on the game at all. It was so unlike him it troubled me.

"It is done and cannot be undone," I said, turning his piece. "But if you are so sure, we can alter our current plans to account for his involvement."

Ready to be finished with the game, I took a piece and leapt it along a string of his, turning them as I went. The third one bore a crown on its underside. Kin was neither surprised nor annoyed, conceding the round with a shrug.

"Something else is troubling you, Majesty?" I said, leaving the pieces where they sat, not sure either of us wanted to play the third round.

"Yes." Kin did not look at me, staring instead at the pale Humble Stone set into the shiny black floor. "Yes, there is, Darius."

I waited, more sure with every passing second what he was going to ask. When he did speak again, he still did not look at me. "I know I promised we would not speak about it again, but...the Vices—"

"I'm afraid I have no answers on that subject. I have heard all the reports. If they are back, then I don't know why. If they are working with Monarch, I don't know why. I gave my word when I took this position and I have never betrayed it. Now you need not break your promise either, Your Majesty, unless you have reason to disbelieve me."

Silence rang long and tense in this hall that was both so large and suddenly too small. He was an emperor. I had interrupted him and spoken roughly. He could reprimand me if he wished, but when he let out a tired sigh, I knew he would not. "Ahmet is nosing around this too, Darius," he said. "It will do no good for either of us if it comes out."

"What does he say?"

"He warns me that you aren't who you say you are. That you really serve the Otakos and want me dead. That you have a secret."

"And what do you tell him, Majesty?"

Kin looked at me then, a smile pressed flat between his lips. "That all men have secrets."

I returned the smile. "Shall we finish the game, Majesty?"

With only the distant sound of footfalls for warning, the double doors swung open and a man dressed in full imperial armour strode in.

"General Hade Ryoji," the chancellor called, rushing to greet the newcomer. "Commander of the Imperial Guard."

A dozen soldiers entered behind him, dressed in layers of leather and mail over dark linen. A wide crimson sash proclaimed each an elite member of the Imperial Guard, loyal to the throne, and when the general knelt, each of his men knelt behind him.

"What is it, Ryoji?" Kin said as the man rose, pushing a lock of hair back from his eyes. The guards stood in turn, their hands falling to their weapons.

All trace of General Ryoji's usual sparkle was absent this evening.

Many had thought him too young for his position, but he was a favourite at court, handsome and charming. Unfortunately, his first year in the job had brought with it not only a dozen attempts on the emperor's life but also the rise of the rebel Monarch and his Pikes in the north. It was leaving traces upon his face. Bit by bit, his countenance was growing stern, as Kin's must have done years before.

"My apologies for the interruption, Your Majesty," General Ryoji said. "There is an intruder in the palace."

"An intruder? What sort of intruder?"

"It is hard to say, Majesty. We don't know how they got in, so I've brought you my best men and must request you remain here until we know more."

"A prisoner in my own palace?"

General Ryoji bowed. "For your own safety, Majesty." He turned to me. "Your Excellency, your presence is required, if you would come with me."

"How sad that you don't find my safety to be of such importance that you would have me venture forth into danger."

"As you will be doing so in my company, I hope you don't feel you have anything to fear, Excellency."

"But I don't see that at all," I said. "Here are twelve of your best men to guard His Majesty. If you are equal to even half of them on your own, I would be amazed. Surely, I am worth half an emperor. I mean, just look at this robe I have on; this purple thread is far more expensive than His Majesty's crimson."

The general opened his mouth, closed it again, scowling as he sought a retort.

"But not more than my gold," Emperor Kin said and, with a quelling look at me, addressed the commander of his guard. "I will not be kept blind of what is going on. Speak, Ryoji. What has happened?"

General Ryoji shifted his weight from one leg to the other. "As you wish, Your Majesty. In the course of her usual rounds, one of the serving girls came across a dead body in the council chamber. A very recently dead body, branded with the Traitor's Mark." He let out a long breath. "And the Eye of Vice."

I forced myself to breathe evenly despite the tightening of my chest.

All men have secrets.

"And what has this to do with Darius?"

"The body in question has been..." The general paused, eyes flicking my way. "...Has been propped up, positioned, you could say, kneeling in Minister Laroth's customary place at the council table."

In the silence that followed, I thought I could hear the lanterns burning. Their orange light reflected off the gold fasteners that ran the length of Ryoji's leather-clad arm.

Getting no response, the general cleared his throat. "We are still attempting to identify the body. Minister Laroth's assistance may prove useful."

I got to my feet, shaking my sleeve back into place. "I am all yours, General," I said. "With your permission, Majesty."

Emperor Kin unrolled his own sleeve. "I will see this travesty," he said, rising and holding up a hand before General Ryoji could speak. "No, General, I will not be dictated to in my own palace, not by assassins and not by you. Bring your men if you will."

"Yes, Your Majesty, but—"

I met the general's gaze and shook my head. Kin was determined. Not to see a dead body, but to show none of the fear he had freely admitted during our Errant game. One could not but admire his courage, though on this occasion, I felt more like damning it. The Eye of Vice was the last thing I wanted him to be reminded of tonight.

It had grown late while we played and the inner palace was quiet.

In the anteroom, my tea set had been cleared away, the room bare but for the flicker of lantern light upon the wall. Kin did not speak as General Ryoji led us the short distance to the council chamber, and all I could do was follow, our wooden sandals clacking out of time with each other's step.

A long gallery led to the council chamber, one of its walls home to an enormous scroll depicting a famous battle. Most councillors and officials liked to stop and point out figures they claimed as their ancestors, but I always walked past it as fast as I could. Tonight was no different, the dark-clad man with the long ponytail near the front seeming to watch me as I passed.

I touched my chest, fingers gliding over silk in search of my raised scar. I had hoped the rumours of the Vices' return were exaggerated, but for the mark to show up here inside the palace...

Two of General Ryoji's men were waiting inside the council chamber, the only other live occupant being Master Kenji, the emperor's physician. He had his chin propped on his hand, head tilted to survey the slumped figure at the end of the table. "Your Majesty," he said, rising quickly to bow before Kin. "This is no pleasant sight."

"I am used to unpleasant sights," Kin said, the hem of his crimson robe sweeping across the matting. The room looked as it always did. The windows were closed, the paper screens whole and untouched, even the flat cushions upon which we knelt sat neatly squared to the table. Only the body was out of place. Was I looking for signs? There wouldn't be any. He was always neat.

"Who's the boy?"

"I don't know, Your Majesty." Master Kenji gripped dark hair and pulled up the slumped head. Despite the branding on both cheeks, the face was all too familiar. My eyes slipped to the tea tray on the table. Each cup was painted with the Laroth crest. No wonder his skill had improved. The boy had been practising.

"His name is Kun."

Every eye in the room fell upon me.

"One of yours, Excellency?"

"Yes, General. My new serving boy. He could count."

I fought the urge to curl my fingers to fists, fought to keep the mask in place. No one would have begrudged me a show of emotion, but this had been done to elicit just such a reaction, and I would not give him the satisfaction of knowing how much it hurt. In truth it was my own fault. I had shown the boy kindness. Who was it who had said the hand of every Laroth was poisoned?

Brandings aside, the boy looked peaceful, as though he had merely fallen asleep at a dull task. The only sign of foul play was the blood splattered across his pale woollen robe.

"These are fresh brandings," Master Kenji said, touching his forefinger to the boy's cheek. There, seared flesh stared back, three horizontal lines crossed by one diagonal—a traitor's brand. Every guardhouse in Kisia owned a Traitor's Iron. It was the mark on his other cheek that was more unusual.

"The Eye of Vice," Master Kenji said, turning the boy's head. "I never thought to see it again."

An intricately patterned eye had been burned into his left cheek. It was all too familiar, and I went on staring at it long after Master Kenji moved on, searching for the wound that had stolen a lifetime of beats from the boy's youthful heart.

"The blood doesn't seem to have come from anywhere, Your Majesty," Master Kenji said at last, placing the boy's arm back upon the table. "Apart from the brands, his skin is intact. There are no wounds. He was a healthy boy, Excellency?"

"As far as I am aware," I said. "He came from a good family. A weak leg, but that should hardly have killed him."

General Ryoji crossed his arms. "Poison? Does that mean his murderer bled on him, Master Kenji?"

"The blood is certainly odd, General," Kenji said, pursing his lips. "But we make no wild summations in my line of work."

The general turned to Kin. "We are searching the palace from ceiling to cellar, Your Majesty. If the intruder is still here, we will find him."

Master Kenji straightened from his examination of the boy's scalp. "And I will get one of my apprentices. We must move the boy and examine him properly if we are to find out what happened. With Your Majesty's permission."

Emperor Kin grunted, looking at neither man. Taking this as assent, Master Kenji bowed and left about his business. Ryoji moved to speak to the guards on the door while Kin leant against the windowsill, one sandalled foot peeking from beneath his great crimson robe. My gaze slid back to the dead boy kneeling in my place. Master Kenji would find nothing. The only message here was now drying upon Kun's clothes.

My heart beat loud in my chest. There was a drop of blood on the boy's hand. Still wet. I pressed my finger to it, every muscle tense.

Darius.

I snatched my hand away, leaving a fingerprint on the sticky blot and a flush of hurt and anger coursing through my skin. It had been years. Why now?

I touched the blood again, like a man already cut wanting to be sure, doubly sure, the blade was sharp.

I hope you haven't forgotten me, yes?

"Darius."

My heart leapt into my throat. Kin was standing beside me.

"Yes, Your Majesty?" I said, habit alone producing a dispassionate tone.

"Is there anything about this you ought to tell me?" He kept the words low enough, private enough that even the guards would not hear. I could tell him much and yet nothing he did not already know.

"No, Majesty. I think we both know I am the target of this, not you."

He nodded. There was another blot upon the boy's neck.

"Interesting, this pattern of blood drops," Kin said.

"Certainly strange," I agreed, and I could not keep from touching it again, though the hurt was a stab to my heart.

I haven't forgotten you, it said. *Sunset tomorrow. You know where I'll be.*

Kin reached to touch the blood on the boy's hand, but I gripped his wrist. "Don't. Your Majesty." I let go as fast as I had taken hold of him, the affront to his position enough that he could dismiss me. He narrowed his eyes but lowered his hand.

"Are you sure there's nothing you ought to tell me?" he said as I used a corner of Kun's robe to wipe the wet blood from his hand. Dried into the fabric, it would be useless.

"Vice blood can be a dangerous thing, Majesty." I used the boy's collar to clean his neck. The rest of the blood had already soaked into the robe. "Safest not to touch it."

He wanted to meet. He had gotten into the palace with ease, proving anyone might die next if I did not go.

"Then perhaps," Kin said, lowering his voice to little more than a murmur at my shoulder. "You have upset more than just Councillor Ahmet."

"They will have to try harder than this." I threw my shoulders into a shrug, forcing coldness to my lips. "Servants are numerous. Even if they can count."

He touched my arm as I made to move away, and almost I shook off the kindness in such a gesture. "I trust you, Darius," he said, his low voice for my ears alone. "I will make sure no breath of this reaches the court, but I hope you will never make me think better of my decision. You are the best minister of the left I've ever had and I like you, but you will suffer for disloyalty the same as any other, do you understand?"

"Perfectly, Majesty. An emperor is only as powerful as the men he can behead."

He stiffened. The flash of a snarl crossed his features, and he might have struck me had he really doubted my loyalty. Instead he stepped away. "You of all people know I am not cruel, Darius. Go. You ought not be here longer and I have had enough of you for tonight."

I bowed. "Then I will wish you a good night, Majesty." And with one last glance at the boy, I left, swallowing the bitter tang of guilt.

4. ENDYMION

A single candle lit the passage beyond my cell; a fat, wax-streaked stub in a sconce. It threw little light, allowing me to retreat to the darkest corner, though all hope I might be forgotten soon died.

Slow steps came along the passage, the sound echoing back from the stones of my prison. A soldier stopped at the very edge of my cell. He was carrying a wooden bowl and a tense expression.

"Hey," he said, reaching in quickly and dropping the bowl. Watery slop splashed over the side. "Are you really a demon?"

I had spent the last few hours returning to the conversation with Kokoro, trying to divine some meaning from all he had said, to find something in the tangled memories, anything, that might prove my lineage and save me from this hell. I touched the pendant tucked beneath my robe.

"No," I said, unsticking my tongue for the first time in hours. "I am no demon, no witch, and no traitor."

"What's your name?"

I pulled my knees up to my chest and said nothing. It would make no difference if he had already chosen to believe me guilty.

"The old man we brought in with you says your name is Endymion."

"Then why ask me?"

He took a step, no longer hiding in the shadow of the wall. "What about your family? Do you have a family name?"

"They're dead."

"Killed them, did you?"

Father Kokoro had said so. I turned my head away, staring at the candlelight on my prison wall. The air was stale, chilly despite the summer beyond these stones. My watcher did not move.

A scream sounded. Distant, muted by the walls, yet I could feel its anguish. It came again, rising in pitch. Begging. Pleading. My skin chilled, my insides hollowing with dread.

"What's that?"

The man stepped closer again. "Your old man," he said, taking hold of the bars.

Anger pulled me to my feet. "He told you my name, what more do you want? It says Endymion on my papers, doesn't it?"

"It sure does, but those papers didn't come from any governor. Father Kokoro says you're a traitor and a demon."

"If you want to know who my family is, then ask Father Kokoro," I said, advancing on the man.

He backed away from the bars, baring his teeth. "Stay back, freak."

"You're scared of me? Is that why you're torturing an innocent man? A priest?" Each question spat from my lips, but Jian's cries for mercy did not cease. "You want to know if I'm a demon? Come closer and I'll show you."

The guard spat on the stones, barely missing the fraying edges of his reed sandals. "I'll see you hang first."

I gripped the bars, the cold metal doing nothing to cool the fury bouncing back and forth between us. "If I am already condemned to die, then why torture him? Why does it matter who I am?"

"Because the captain is in trouble in Mei'lian." Leaning against the far wall, the guard grinned. "He's out of favour with the district commander, and some boy who the court priest has locked up for witchcraft could be of interest to those who care about such things. Maybe you're a demon. Maybe you're a Vice. Maybe you're the by-blow of some lord who's paying handsomely to have you gotten out of the way. Such things are worth the captain's skin to know about, if you catch me?"

"And if I told you I was the son of a lord, what would you do?"

"I guess that depends which lord and where the money is. If it's in seeing you dead, it won't matter. And if you're a Vice, I'd light a pyre for you with my own damn hands."

"I know only one name, and it's the one you have. If you think I have another, ask Father Kokoro for it."

Jian's screams broke off, the cessation of sound making breath catch in my throat. "If he dies, you'll be sorry," I said. "He's Father Kokoro's brother."

"I thought priests didn't have brothers, but you're the novice; you should know."

"I'm not a novice."

"No, then what are you? You could tell me, or he will eventually. He'll talk before his precious gods grant the mercy he begs for. Everyone does."

"How can he answer what he does not know?" Talking to the man was like talking to the wall, only more repetitive. Perhaps I would have better luck with the captain. "Listen," I said, pressing my forehead to the cold bars. "If your captain wants to know something he can use at court, then you bring him here."

"So you can practise your witchcraft on him? I'm not that stupid."

"Aren't you? You've been standing there awhile."

He looked down, pressing his fingers to his chest as though

expecting some part of himself to be missing. "What have you—"
He broke off, scowling. "Oh, you freak me out, you do. I think you
are one of them Vices." He backed away.

"I'm not! I don't know who I am, but"—I raised my voice as
he kept backing farther down the passage—"it was Lord Nyraek
Laroth who gave me to Brother Jian, tell your captain that! Tell
him—"

But the man had gone, leaving me to breathe the stodgy fumes
of his fear. The bowl he had left behind sat on the stones just inside
the bars. Runny porridge, the golden millet grains already cold to
the touch. Trying to imagine it was something else, I dug the spoon
in, shovelling the cold sludge into my mouth and swallowing as
fast as I could. When I had finished, I reached through the bars to
place the bowl in the passage, but it fell from my grip as another
scream ripped through the building. The bowl rolled away, hitting
the opposite wall. Between each agonised cry came a string of shrill
words, every one familiar. Qi's invocation of death.

"Leave him alone!" I shouted, shaking the bars. "How dare you
torture a man who serves the gods? Let him go!"

New footsteps came along the passage and another man
approached. He wore the uniform of a soldier, but where most had
only a narrow sash to display their allegiance, this one had a band
of crimson silk elaborately knotted over his scabbard. One hand sat
upon his sword hilt.

"There is no need to shout, prisoner," he said. "My name is Captain Ash. You have been imprisoned for attacking Father Kokoro
with witchcraft, and yet—"

"Attacking him with—?"

I suppose I had when I gripped his hand, but it had harmed
no one, not even him. Empathy didn't hurt—couldn't hurt anyone
but me.

"And yet," he went on as though I had not interrupted. "You knew Lord Nyraek Laroth." The captain tightened his grip on his sword. "Tell me how that is."

"I didn't know him, I . . ."

He waited after I trailed off, only to heave a sigh. "No? That's a shame. Your papers are forged. You have been arrested for witchcraft and treason. You'll be executed in the morning."

"No! Wait!"

The captain scratched his nose and stared at me through the bars. Having removed his hand from his sword hilt, he seemed unsure what to do with it, and it hovered in front of him, a hesitant dragonfly above the smooth surface of a pond.

"Lord Nyraek Laroth," I began, feeling for a reaction more than watching for one. "Gave me to Brother Jian as a child."

Annoyance sparked. "That's an easy lie. Lord Nyraek Laroth is dead."

"Then ask his son!"

The captain's brows shot up. "Lord Darius Laroth? The imperial minister of the left?"

"Yes."

My words shocked that hovering hand back to its place on the sword hilt. The captain laughed, and the spice of true amusement jolted through my Empathy. "The Monstrous Laroth? You want me to call the Monstrous Laroth here to identify you? Is he a friend of yours?"

"No."

"Then if I were you, I would go quietly to the noose rather than seek him out."

His words didn't bode well. "Why?"

"Why?" the captain repeated. "Because he's a fucking cold bastard. I've heard he doesn't eat or sleep, and that he has this long, ragged scar across his chest from where someone stuck him"—he lunged forward, imitating a killing blow—"right through his heart, and he didn't shed a single drop of blood."

"Everyone bleeds."

The captain shook his head. "Not Minister Laroth. He has no heart. I hear he even killed his own father."

I thought of Nyraek Laroth. His breath had stirred my hair, drops of rain falling upon his hands as they held tight to the reins. "Why would he do that?"

The captain shrugged his large shoulders. "Why not? The Laroth fortune is immense. Men have killed for less."

"None of that frightens me," I said, though it was a lie. Courage is easy to find when the other option is death. "Send for him."

"Send for Minister Laroth? He isn't a stable boy. I won't put my head on the block for you. If you have nothing else to say, then—"

I gripped the chain around my neck and yanked. Its clasp snapped, and the pendant almost slid free, but I caught it in shaking hands and thrust it at the captain. "Nyraek Laroth gave me this. Do you think he would have done that if I was not worth his son's time?"

The captain didn't seem to hear me, so focussed was he on the eye in his hand. "This . . . is the Eye of Vice."

"I know. But he gave it to me years—"

He turned it over. "And the Laroth family crest." Captain Ash whistled low, then having turned it over and back again, he started to laugh. "Yes, this'll do. This'll do nicely." Closing his hand over it, he said, "Thank you. Thank you very much indeed." And without awaiting an answer, he turned and strode away, my only possession tucked in his fist.

"Wait! Captain? Are you going to send for him? Are you going to let me go? Captain!"

All that returned was the echo of my voice.

Afraid I had made a very bad bargain, I retreated, shivering, to the corner. Sleep would have been good, might have eased the pains all over and the thumping of my head, but it would not come easily. I tried to curl myself up like a cat, but the stones dug into my shoulder and chilled my cheek. I tried to lie on my back, but my head seemed to be the wrong shape. There was nothing soft, nothing to lure me toward slumber except fatigue, which slowly dragged me toward oblivion.

A succession of loud clangs jolted me awake. A guard strode past my cell, letting a wooden baton strike each bar as he passed. When he reached the end of the passage, he stopped. "Sorry about that, freak. Did I wake you? My friend Cati was asleep when one of your Vice pals burst him into a thousand pieces."

Calm, I told myself. *Don't say anything.*

I laid my head back on my arm, but as soon as I found a comfortable position, the clanging started again. The man was walking back the other way.

Exhaustion leaked from my every pore, but it was some minutes before I once more slipped toward sleep. Perhaps I managed it for a moment, or was once more on its cusp, before the sound came again.

"Hey, freak," another voice said, banging on the bars. "I hear you're the whoreson of a priest. Do you know what we do to bastards of Oath Men?"

Laughter rang loud, then another voice said, "Nah, he's one of them Vices. Just a shitty one."

"Well maybe that's how the demons are made. In the wombs of women who lure men from their oaths. Is that right, freak?"

Calm.

Jian had always made me chant it like a mantra whenever the cruelty of the world became too much.

"Not talking? We'll make you. We'll start by pulling off your fingernails, one at a time, bit by bit."

I closed my eyes. Last time we'd crossed the border there had been a man in one of the border towns, vociferous in his support of Emperor Kin's claim to the throne.

"Then we'll stick hot needles through the tips of your fingers."

It was high time for change, the man had said. *"Gods? Is that their excuse for rutting each other like rabbits? Empress Li must have been the most used whore in Kisia. So many royal whelps, all with a different face to show the world."*

The crowd had been enraged, and infused with their anger, it had taken Jian's grip on my collar to keep me from rushing at him.

Calm, I had chanted. *Calm.*

The guards banged on the bars again. "Hey, freak, are you listening? We've burned some of our demons. Would you like that? We could make sure you burn real slow, that you feel your skin blister and pull away from the soles of your feet."

"Do you know what burning flesh smells like, freak?"

Clang.

"It's a smell you won't forget until the day you die." They laughed. "At least for you that won't be very long."

Clang. Clang.

"Are you still trying to sleep, freak?"

"You'll have plenty of time to rest when your body is turned to ash. Was it you who turned the whole garrison in Ji to ash? Huh? Was it?"

Their aggression weighed upon my shoulders and clogged my nose with its stink. There was fear and anger too, but it was being sucked into a great cauldron of cruelty. Their blood was hot, their hearts pounding. They were so excited their cocks hardened against the fabric of their breeches. *If I move*, I thought. *If I make a single sign of weakness, they will tear me apart.*

Grateful for the bars, I kept trying to rest, to let their words become a lullaby that rocked me to a terrible sleep, but they would never let me manage more than a few minutes at a time. For what felt like an age in this timeless hell, they took turns strolling past my cell, banging their batons on the bars and throwing out choice taunts to the acclaim of all. They even began to laugh at one another, turning on comrades who showed less enthusiasm for the sport, until every dozing moment was filled with noise.

"Hey, demon, your mother must have been a godless whore."

Calm.

The mantra meant nothing when her sad smile filled my memories, the touch of her soft hand upon my cheek so real my skin tingled.

"I've heard that demons are the children of dead men. I guess that means your mother was such a whore she mounted a corpse. Anything hard would do for her, it didn't even have to be warm."

I was up, chest slamming into the bars before I could even think. "You disgusting little maggots," I snarled, grabbing at one through the bars. "Come in here and say that. Just come a little closer and I'll make sure you never speak again."

The dozen guards outside my cell leapt away from my reaching hands. "Are you threatening us, freak?"

"Just come closer, I dare you. If you are the best of the emperor's men, I weep for Kisia."

I had never wanted my bow so much, never wanted so much to fill anyone's flesh with arrows. My hands opened and closed as I eyed every soft target on their bodies. Eyes. Throat. Crotch.

Every head turned as a shout echoed along the passage. "The minister! The minister is here."

The guards' unspoken leader blanched. "So soon?" He pushed through his knot of men. "Let's go. I don't want to be dessert."

Each man dashed off at a fast trot, leaving me to the music of running steps passing back and forth above me until the whole building stilled. Slow steps emerged from the silence, each the loud, staccato clack of a wooden sandal on stone. A shuffling companion followed, the air stiff with nervous tension.

The captain came into view, his lips caught in a grim, satisfied line. "Prisoner," he said, once again resting his hand upon his sword hilt. "Bow before His Excellency, Lord Darius Laroth, the sixth count of Esvar and minister of the left."

The man of my imagination died. Here was no burly warrior or harsh-featured monster. Lord Laroth was fine and slight with skin as smooth as cream. He wore his silk robe with neat precision, every line so straight he was more statue than man. Never had I seen a more beautiful face, but there was no smile, no life in his cold violet eyes.

"You do not bow," he said, speaking in a voice that might have been ripped from my memory. "Do you know who I am?"

Dozens of guards stood crammed into the neck of the passage, watching.

"Yes," I said. "You are Lord Darius Laroth."

"And yet you do not bow."

The minister came a step closer. His face was immobile. I could read nothing in it and resorted to my Empathy, reaching it out toward him like a formless hand prepared to drink in all it found. Anxious glee hung about the captain, and hunger pervaded his guards, but the minister had nothing.

Lord Laroth regarded me steadily. He did not move. He did not tap or twitch or scratch, his body guilty of nothing but the occasional blink, and even that seemed deliberate.

"Pull up your left sleeve," he commanded.

Breath caught in my throat. He knew. My saviour had confided in his son. Yet there was still no softening of his features, no recognition.

Pinching the fabric of my sleeve, I drew it back, exposing the twist of silk around my wrist. The minister's eyes darted to it. "Who was your father?"

In the passage, one of the guards sniggered.

I let my sleeve fall. "I am not sure. That's what I want you to tell me. Your father gave me to Brother Jian. Please, they are torturing him for an answer he cannot give but you can."

"Ah, I see. Perhaps you think you might be my father's son? Allow me to disabuse you of the idea. My father spent a number of years as the commander of the Imperial Guard and was therefore privy to every bastard the ladies of the court needed to get rid of. There were many. You are not special." Minister Laroth turned to the captain. "Captain Ash," he said, his slow blink strangely sinister. "This boy is no one important. Your devotion to our emperor is certainly to be commended, but I think we can dispense with this charade. By order of Emperor Kin Ts'ai, first of his name, this man is to be branded a traitor and exiled, and he is barely worth that much of our time."

"Branded?" I gripped the bars, pressing my face to the cold metal. "I have committed no treason. Please." I reached out my left arm, wrist turned up. "Just tell me who I am and let me go."

A slow step brought him closer. "Are you sure you want that answer in front of so many witnesses?"

"Yes."

"Very well. Your name is Endymion and you are the bastard son of a dead man who has no honour left in this world. His name will not save you. Captain, carry out the sentence."

The captain bowed. "Yes, Your Excellency, but what of the charges of witchcraft? Father Kokoro—"

"Father Kokoro?" A frown flickered across that serene face, but I could feel no confusion, could feel nothing. "Father Kokoro is a pious man prone to see evil where there is only stupidity. This young man may be a traitor, but he is no more a witch than I am."

"He threatened us!"

Murmurs of agreement came from the crowd of guards.

Minister Laroth's eyebrows rose in slow disbelief. "You question my word?" With a final step, he closed the gap between us, gripping my hand and squeezing it to the bar. His fingers were warm. He was alive—a living, breathing man beneath the smooth facade—yet when my Empathy touched him, it found nothing. There was no emotion, no soul, just a frightening blank where his heart ought to be.

"What are you?" I whispered.

"I could ask you the same question."

He let me go and stepped back. Every eye was on him, every breath held close. Glancing around, he spread his hands in a theatrical gesture. "I am, as you see, unscathed. Brand him and put him on the next cart to the border. I don't want to hear any more about this, Captain, and gods help you if His Majesty comes to hear of it."

"Yes, Your Excellency."

Grey silk twisted about the minister's feet as he turned, and sending guards scattering before his imperious step, he was gone, the truth with him.

One by one, the guards returned like stalking wolves, their grins wide and slavering. "That's disappointing," said the man I thought of as their leader. "We wanted to see you burn, freak."

I let go of the bars and stepped back. "You heard him, I'm not a witch. Nor a Vice."

The man's lip curled. "Just a traitor. Open the cell, Bale."

"We should wait for the captain to get—"

"Just do it or I'll brand you too."

Bale took a ring from his belt, keys clinking. Their threats were all too fresh in my mind and I backed away another step. "Stay away," I said. "Or I'll hurt you all."

Their leader stepped up to the door. "Hurry up with the branding iron," he said, his lips drawn back from his teeth in a cruel smile. The key turned in the lock. My fingers trembled, heart hammering loud in my ears. I wanted to run, but there was nowhere to go.

The door swung in and I took another step back.

"Afraid of me, freak?" the man sneered, entering my cell ahead of his pack.

"No."

His teeth seemed to lengthen in the shadows. "We'll see, shall we? We'll see if you squeal."

Movement flickered in the corner of my eye, but I was too late. Someone grasped me around the chest, stitched leather arms ending in stained hands, crushing the air from my lungs. My assailant breathed in my ear, hot and damp.

"Get him on the floor."

Faces were everywhere in the thickening nightmare. Hands grasped my feet. I tried to kick them off, but the unyielding arms tightened about my chest. I could barely breathe. Light flashed in my vision. Men gripped my hair, my robe, tearing at the fabric like vultures at a carcass.

"Hold him down!"

Hands pressed me to the stones. They swarmed over me like a suffocating blanket, my every gasp a taste of hatred. I tried to find skin, to tear at hands and faces, to share my fear, but every touch was so fleeting that nothing passed, leaving it to pool in my body like poison.

"Out of the way!"

The mass of bodies thinned. I tried to squirm free, but the men had me pinned to the cold ground, their grips like steel. Coals hissed. An orange trail blazed before my eyes and I lost all sense. Panicking, I tried to buck them off, to bite, to claw, to rip, to spit, anything that might gain me freedom.

"Hold his head down or I'll get it through his eye."

A weighty hand pressed upon my temple. Unable to move, I stared at the worn sandal before my face: broken reeds and broken toenails. The smell of dirt. The smell of blood. Anticipation. Every moment, I imagined the branding iron hovering above my cheek, and every moment it didn't come was worse than the last, the latent heat like a candle held too close.

The sound came first. The hiss of searing flesh. Then the pain drove from me all power of thought; behind my eyes a world of white-hot agony. There was no end to it; even when the weight of the metal was drawn away, the pain went on. And the smell. It was like acrid charcoal. That was my skin I could smell, my blackened flesh.

Their grips slackened and I rolled over to retch, only for the heat to press into the back of my head. The hiss was louder, the stink of burning hair clogging my every attempt at breath. Bile leaked out of my mouth, and like the roar of a single beast, the men jeered.

The iron twisted. It ripped at hair and skin, tearing flesh. I could no longer even scream. "Give me the other iron. This one's going cold."

The ambient heat returned, and in my heart came a dreadful urging, a voice I'd never heard before. *Do it*, it said. *Do it and you'll suffer.*

The iron touched my flesh, and my hatred chanted back. *There will be justice. You will be judged. You will suffer.*

A scream was wrenched from my lips, owning all the torment I could not contain, all the hatred, while the great heaving injustice of it all wept from my skin.

Their voices died. Grips faltered, but it was too late. My pain burst forth, turning one cry into a harmony of many, each delicious in its anguish. Darkness gathered at the edges of my vision, but I swatted it back, wanting to remain, to revel in the justice. But I could not fight it. The night called and I surrendered, letting it drown me in tortured screams.

5. HANA

I woke to the pressure of a hand on my shoulder and had jolted half upright before I registered Conceit's amused face. Or rather two of his amused face. He was playing his trick just to mess with my tired mind.

"What?" I hissed, aware of the stertorous sound of others around us still sleeping.

"The master—" one Conceit began.

"—is here," the other finished, and my gaze flicked between the two copies of him. "He wants—"

"—to see you."

"Upstairs. Captain."

There were Vices with stranger and more impressive abilities, but his had always been the most disconcerting. One of the Conceits wasn't real, wasn't solid, but it was impossible to tell which without poking him.

"I'll go up," I said, checking my clothing before slipping out from beneath the blankets. Everyone else appeared to still be asleep, the Pikes spread out across the floor in what had once been a grand kitchen. Monarch lay against the wall, rolled up in some furs, a lock of dark hair straying across a brow that frowned even in sleep.

I picked my way over slumbering men toward the door. A few glanced up before rolling over in search of sleep, but Shin's gaze followed me all the way out into the passage. There the dusty floor was thick with strange scents and memories of people long gone. It must have been a fine house in its day, owning more fretwork than I had seen anywhere and even plush carpets in the upper rooms.

I found Malice in one such room, reclining upon a divan with a book, his long ponytail snaking across worn silk. Despite my quiet steps, he looked up at my approach, the tip of a finger marking his place on the page.

"This is an interesting choice for a safe house," I said in greeting. "Given the area we came through this morning and its faded finery, I'm going to guess and say it was a whorehouse."

"Quite correct, my dear. Sadly disused now."

"There are a lot of rooms. I hope they had a big laundry."

One thin eyebrow rose. "The laundry is no larger than in any other establishment. Long-dead men need no clothes washed, yes?"

"Perhaps not, but the live whores surely needed their bedding changed."

The other eyebrow went up. "You think men need clean sheets to copulate? What a strange idea. Men are animals. What dog complains of its quarters while it has a bitch to rut?"

"But the women—"

"The women?" Mock incredulity stretched his features. "What say did they have?"

I immediately felt foolish, but his expression softened into a smile. "You have such fierce idealism, my dear. Do not let anyone tell you it is a fault, yes? You are the moral light by which we must all seek to be guided."

"You're laughing at me."

"Only a little." Malice set his book aside and patted the divan for me to sit. "Tell me about your journey through the tunnels. Clearly it was a success, yes?"

"Oh, like Conceit hasn't already told you about it."

He clicked his tongue. "Now, now, don't be petty, my dear. It was Ire and Apostasy who reported how it went. But they are very dull, yes? They cannot tell me why my girl looks so put out. Monarch not behaving himself?"

He patted the divan again, and giving up on being a statue of pride, I slumped down next to him. "He knows I'm—"

"You smell like him," Malice said, tracing a finger the length of his nose. It was an oddly distracted mannerism for a man who always appeared so calm. "Be careful there."

"He knows I'm not a man, but I didn't tell him who I was."

"Good. His father had yours assassinated so he could take the throne, yes? He won't spare you if you get in his way. Don't forget that."

I sighed. "I know, I know, but do you really think he would harm me?"

"He wouldn't help you to the throne, that is for sure. What happened to the ferocious girl who swore to sit on her father's throne, no matter what?"

There was no answer I could make without betraying the hopes I had begun to cherish: maybe Katashi already knew who I was, maybe he was playing along with my game, maybe it was me he had tried to kiss beneath the tree last night, not Captain Regent.

"Hana," Malice said, his striking features unaltered by the ten years I had known him. "I've always looked after you, yes?"

"Better than Darius."

"We'll leave him out of this, I think. He has chosen a different path. Although I am sure he would agree that Emperor Kin's sole claim to the throne is that he has it. He took it, and if you want it, you have to take it back. With your own hands. Monarch's plans are all very well, but they don't help you. You're an Otako, a daughter of the main line, yes?"

"But I'm a woman," I said. "No man would bow to me. No man would fight to put me on the throne."

He let out an irritated snort. "You have been spending too much time with your cousin. His opinions, like his smell, are an insidious stench, yes?" Malice trailed a long fingernail down my cheek. "You are Emperor Lan's daughter. Katashi is a traitor's son. Remember that."

"There was no proof."

"As there is no proof to whether the world is round or flat. What matters is what people believe. Emperor Kin rules Kisia, and in his version of history, your uncle was a traitor, yes?"

"Yes."

"And his son was exiled as a traitor, yes?"

"Yes."

"Almost you make me regret we searched for him at all."

"No." I thought of the kiss that had come so close to my lips. "It's . . . comforting to know I am not the only Otako left."

Malice let out a long sigh, once again running fingers through his silken hair. "That is sweet of you, but you forget that while his father and yours were brothers, they were not friends. You must take what belongs to you now or not take it at all."

"How? If I claim I am the daughter of Emperor Lan, people will just laugh at me. At least Katashi looks like an Otako. I don't. I don't even have birth papers."

"No, but they exist."

"Where?"

"Where do you think?"

I searched his face for an answer but found none. Neither of my guardians had ever been expressive. "I don't know," I said. "In the palace, I guess."

"And where are Katashi and his Pikes going today?"

"Into the palace." He was going for the crown, or rather Shin was while Katashi created a diversion in the square. Though what he meant to do once he had it, I wasn't sure. Even the possession of the Hian Crown could not change that his father had been executed for treason, that he had been exiled, that by the laws of the very empire he sought to rule, he had no true claim upon the throne. Not like I did. If only I could prove my name.

"Where would my papers be?"

"There's a small archive near the throne room where all the imperial documents are kept—it shouldn't be hard to find, yes?"

"The throne room? That's... not easy."

"Why not?" Malice said. "You'll be wearing the uniform of an imperial soldier, and with Katashi's diversion and the theft of the crown, no one will be looking inside for traitors."

Could it be that easy? Could I really just... walk into the inner palace unnoticed? "But what if someone sees me?"

"What is there to see? You are a soldier. Tell them you are look- ing for Minister Laroth's office with a message from your com- manding officer, yes? Unless you don't trust him."

I crossed my arms over my chest as though to defend against memories of my other guardian. "He chose to work for the Usurper instead of me."

"That is very true." Malice reached into his sash and withdrew two vials of clear liquid. "Here, take these, my dear. You never know when you might need a little extra help." He placed both in my hand. They were icy to the touch and I recoiled, nearly drop- ping them.

"What are they?" I asked.

"Tishwa."

"Poison?"

"A scholar of you farmers did make, yes?"

"Are you mocking me again?"

Malice laughed. "Not in the least, lamb. A dose of this will kill a man in less than a minute. The weapon no one expects."

"Perhaps I could just kill Emperor Kin and be done with this."

It was almost entirely a joke, for not only would he be surrounded by guards; even if I succeeded his ministers were unlikely to give the throne to his assassin. Malice did not laugh, however; he just shrugged. "It makes no difference to me, yes? If you want the throne, you take the throne, but at least a dead man won't fight you for it."

"But—"

He held up his hand. "No, no; no more words. It is late and I am fatigued beyond measure. If you do not want your father's throne, then by all means leave your papers where they are and walk away. Just remember that a leader does whatever evils are necessary. Both Kin and Katashi know that even if you do not."

I knew a dismissal when I heard it and had grown used to his oddities. Already, Malice had opened his book and was hunting for his page, his mind elsewhere.

"Thank you," I said, standing to leave.

Malice looked up as though he had forgotten I was there. "Anytime, my little lamb. If you choose to go, I will see you back at Nivi Fen, yes?"

"You won't wait here for me?"

"Like an anxious parent? No, lamb, I do not think so. I have my own plans."

"Anything exciting?"

He smiled. "An old friend."

Knowing I would get no more from him, I bent to kiss his cheek in farewell. "No one ever had a better guardian."

"That is undoubtedly true. I wish you good fortune, little lamb. Don't let the great Katashi take what is yours, yes?"

All I could manage was a smile, and having tucked the vials safely into my wristband, I returned to the kitchen. Dawn light had begun to spill in through the high, narrow windows, and the smell of millet porridge made the old space more comforting. A few Pikes were still asleep, but most were sitting up or stretching, poor sleep and worry lining long faces. Monarch sat on one corner of the bench with Shin tending a gash on his captain's forearm.

He won't spare you if you get in his way.

The words repeated in my head, and perhaps sensing me, Monarch looked up. I turned away, busying myself with a tie on my tunic that had come undone while I slept. He said nothing and the tension grew, the urge to ask unspeakable questions fading from my tongue.

You are Emperor Lan's daughter. Katashi is a traitor's son. Remember that.

Slowly, all the Pikes rose from their mats and shovelled down bowls of porridge. One by one they disappeared to relieve themselves, but otherwise none wandered. They all knew who owned the safe house, and though they might travel through the tunnels with Vices because they had to, no Pike would risk coming face to face with Malice, the Vice Master. I had often heard them whisper about him when they thought I wasn't listening.

Unlike the boisterous excitement from the night before, the Pikes prepared for the next part of their mission in a quiet trance. Half were to go with Shin into the waterway, half were to take up their positions ready for the diversion. Both groups would have to wait until dark to act, but with the streets around the palace blocked off from sunset, they had to move out in daylight. Hence the uniforms.

While the men were dressing and checking their weapons, Katashi strode around the room, stopping to speak to each of them in turn. He was easily the tallest, and his skill with his long bow had broadened his shoulders and thickened his arms until every other man was a mere shadow next to him. He ought to have been intimidating, but when he stopped to smile and utter encouragement, bolstering the morale of his rebels, I could not believe he would ever do me harm.

I could tell him. At the very least, he wouldn't harm me while Malice was still upstairs.

What happened to the ferocious girl who swore to sit on her father's throne, no matter what?

She had fallen in love with a handsome face. How pathetic.

I looked away, determined not to be seen watching him, but he soon walked over. His scent came before him, intoxicating despite the overabundance of sweat.

"Have your Vices abandoned you, Captain?" he said, his deep voice like a purr.

He leant against the wall beside me, and I turned my head just enough to breathe in his smell. "No, they haven't left me. I just prefer the sounds of common talk rather than silence."

"And your big boss?"

"I'm not sure. He was here this morning, but he wasn't staying. He's very . . . transitory."

"That's a fancy word for a manly cutthroat."

Laughter brightened his eyes, and even though I knew he was mocking me, for a moment I just didn't care. "Then I'm a fancy cutthroat," I said.

"But not a manly one?"

"I . . ." My cheeks reddened beneath his laughter, and I looked away.

"Angry with me for seeing through your ruse?" he said. "Don't worry, your secret is safe with me. So long as you don't stare hungrily at anyone else, you might yet go undetected."

If I had thought myself mortified before, now I wished I could melt into a puddle of shame. He had caught me looking. For how long had he known and how often had I stared?

"Don't be embarrassed, sweet Regent," he said. "I like that you look at me. And you can have that kiss when I come back."

"Who says I want it?"

He laughed and pushed himself off from the wall. "I wasn't suggesting it would be a sacrifice on my part. Quite the opposite. And besides, getting to know each other better will make the journey to Koi far less boring."

His careless words sent a wave of heat through my body, but by the time he had walked away, it was equal parts desire and anger. Malice had dressed me as a man and given me command of the most feared group of warriors, but it meant nothing to Monarch. As a woman, I was someone to while away a boring journey with, someone to tease and mock, but not someone worthy of respect. Would he respect me any more if he knew the truth? Probably, but I wanted to be more than a wife, more than a woman, whatever my name. I wanted to be his equal. His superior. I wanted the throne more than I wanted him.

You must take what belongs to you now or not take it at all.

He didn't look back as he sauntered away, just touched the tip of his bow as though to be sure she was still with him. His men had almost finished their preparations, and keeping an eye on them, I began to make mine. Malice's plan was risky, but no one was going to fight for me if I would not even fight for myself.

Alone in my corner of the kitchen, I checked my weapons. A sword and two knives sheathed upon my belt—an imperial soldier's weapons, along with the two vials of Tishwa and the needle Mama Orde had given me threaded into the sleeve of my under tunic.

My fingers fondled the needle. Shin was talking to his small group while Monarch's team of decoys checked eath other's uniforms. I could stay. I could wait. I could go back to Nivi Fen with the Vices. But nothing would change. I would be no closer to my goal. And there would never be a better opportunity.

With one last look at Katashi, I stepped into the passage that led to the street door and let myself out into the sunshine.

After so long in the dim old house, the brightness left me blinking a few seconds on the doorstep. Fortunately, this end of the Pleasure Quarter was all but empty, its run-down houses nothing to the bright new ones near the entry gate where strains of music called despite the early hour. Down that end, people bustled as though at a market, and although I knew my imperial uniform was all correct, I turned down an alley rather than push my way through the crowd.

The plan was for the Pikes to exit the safe house in pairs, several minutes apart, to avoid someone noting a large crowd of imperial soldiers. The infiltrators would leave first and meet at a well in the Silk Quarter, before Katashi's decoys each made their way to their designated positions close to the palace gates.

Though I had thought I knew where I was going, the twisting alleyways eventually spat me out too far west, and as I stood on the corner trying to plot the easiest way to the Silk Quarter, a trio of city guards strode past. Whether because they didn't see me or because I looked the part, they continued on their rounds despite the panicked thud of my heart. Once they had disappeared into the bustling crowds, I crossed the street, ducking between two carriers. Another alleyway greeted me and I turned down it, slipping on foul-smelling slop splattered on the stones. No one laughed, though several people watched me steady myself on the wall, and I soon realised that in the uniform of a soldier, I was little better than a ghost. No one had eyes for me because no one wanted to draw attention to themselves, allowing me to stride through the city as though spirits cleared the way.

Knowing no secret back routes, I had to keep my eye on the sun and the grand spire of the palace to find my way. I had thought I'd been making good time, but all too soon, gongs began to announce the midday hour. A man darted from a robe maker's shop to strike the one hanging from his balcony, before nodding to me and stepping back inside while its resonant boom rang on.

I had a head start, but if Shin knew a more direct route, he might yet beat me to the meeting point, so I sped up, veering around two men arguing on the corner. More shouts spilled from an open warehouse door, the scent of spices mixing with the sodden smell of oxen and mule shit.

By keeping the palace ahead of me, I soon found myself on the Silk Road, where rows of shops showed colourful faces to the street. Two guards raced past and, in my haste, I almost ran into them. Acting on instinct, I fell back, heart hammering, but they did nothing except adjure me to watch where I was going as they sped toward the Divine Square. It was unlikely Katashi had already reached it, let alone been discovered, yet I could not but worry. Getting caught would be the end of him. His true name would not save him any more than mine would save me. Once, the soldiers had been Otako men, employed to protect us, but that time was long gone.

There were many entrances to the Zavhi Waterway, avoided by all but the poor bastards whose job it was to ensure the city's cisterns went on functioning. Every well and drain would lead there eventually, but just climbing in and wandering around was a fast way to get yourself lost, or drowned, or both. Shin had given his men detailed instructions to find the right well, but though I had listened, the closer I got the more afraid I became. Twice I almost turned around and went back, but Katashi's mocking smile kept me going. I would make him respect me.

I came at the meeting place from the south and at first saw nothing but a well, its chain and bucket worn and blackened. Had I beaten them all here, or lost my chance entirely?

From the shadowed eaves of a nearby house, someone waved. Narrowing my eyes against the sun's glare, I made out two figures and had started toward them before recognising them as Shin and Wen. I tried to be calm, to walk with ease though my lungs sucked in fast breaths and my pulse pounded.

"Captain," Shin said when I drew close. "Trouble?"

I took a deep breath. "No, only a slight change of plan," I said. "Malice has offered me as an extra pair of hands. Just in case."

I knew the Pikes had wondered from the start what special ability I owned, and now I was glad I had made no effort to correct them. Let them wonder if it got me what I wanted.

Wen looked to his leader, and as had become his habit, Shin peered at me as though trying to see something beneath my skin. "And Captain Monarch agreed to this?"

"Of course," I said, scowling back and trying not to think of him watching us beneath the Kissing Tree. "The success of this mission is pretty fucking important to him."

Still he peered at me and didn't answer. Wen shuffled his feet as though he'd rather be somewhere else.

"All right," Shin said at last. "You can come, but I'm watching you."

"Keep your eyes for what needs it," I said.

He didn't shift his gaze. "I will."

Wen cleared his throat, but fortunately, another pair of Pikes soon arrived and the tension waned. Eventually, seven of us were gathered beneath the awning, nothing between us and the well but a stretch of sun-baked road.

"All right," Shin said in his low growl. "The idea is not to look suspicious. We stride out there as though we have orders to search this part of the waterway. If anyone asks, give them attitude. If anyone stares, glare at them. We are disgruntled soldiers who really would rather we hadn't been given this job. Understand?"

One by one, they murmured agreement, and with a nod to his men and a scowl at me, Shin led the way out onto the street. A buzz of excitement ran through me. I had done it. I was going with them into the palace.

Shin had already attached a rope to the top bar, and while the rest of us stood around looking annoyed, Wen climbed onto the edge of the well. With a nod from Shin, the wiry little Pike began his descent into the darkness. One by one the others followed, until it was just Shin and me at the top. At my turn, I climbed onto the stone wall, but rather than hold the rope out to me, Shin folded his arms.

"I know who you are," he said. "And you shouldn't be here."

His words almost sent me reeling back off the stones. I gripped the edge for support. "What do you mean you know who I am?" I said, mimicking Malice's sneer. "I'm a Vice."

"You're a princess. You should go back."

I parted my lips to deny it, but something in the way he went on staring with his scarred eye stopped me. He knew. He didn't just suspect, he *knew*. "And if I don't?" I said instead.

"I can't guarantee you'll be safe in there."

"I didn't ask you to. I can look after myself. Now if you're done wasting time looking like idiots up here, I'll climb down."

For a moment it looked as though he would refuse to hand me

the rope, but before I could snatch it from him, he thrust it out. "On your head be it," he said, the words rough as gravel. Once I took it, he turned away, arms folded, and did not look at me again. And with shaking hands, I climbed down into the darkness to await nightfall.

6. DARIUS

I had thought my visit to Shimai could not get any worse, but before I could even conclude my negotiations with Captain Ash, a message arrived from the teahouse across the street. Father Kokoro wanted to talk. That the old bastard had been involved in all this, I knew, but that he would force my hand surprised me. He had been at court longer than I, but we did not often cross paths. I'd never had an interest in seeking pardons from the gods.

He sat waiting in a private room, already sipping tea while a spray of afternoon light filtering in through the windows turned his grey hair to gold.

"Ah, Your Excellency," he said as though he couldn't have been more pleased to see anyone. "Do come and join me."

"Father Kokoro." I slid the door closed behind me. "You save me the trouble of sending for you."

"Yes. I heard you were called to the guardhouse and, even more interestingly, that you chose to come."

I watched him closely as I crossed to the table, choosing not to answer until I could make some sense of what he knew and what he wanted. Captain Ash had been easy. He had wanted money, lots of it, and a promotion to a different military district. Both small prices to ensure the existence of an Eye of Vice bearing my family crest did not become common knowledge.

Settling on the cushion opposite, I said, "You have something you wish to say to me, Father Kokoro?"

"I rather think it is you who have something to say to me, Excellency."

Faintly smiling, he looked like an absent old man, a part he played admirably. I would not give him the chance. I removed the necklace from my sash and dropped it on the table in front of him. The weight of the pendant made a satisfying thud, leaving the silver eye staring at the ceiling. "Can you explain why a boy, imprisoned at your command, was in possession of this particular trinket?"

"A step too far, Excellency. You admit you know why it was brought to you, when you should have feigned ignorance."

"If it is a game you want, we can call for an Errant board."

His smile broadened. "I would not presume. Beside your skill, mine is meagre."

He sipped his tea, his restful demeanour grating. It was one I often used to great effect, but he had been perfecting it much longer.

"We play at cross purposes," I said. "But I have no desire to prolong my stay, so I will begin. This pendant belonged to my father."

"Perhaps the boy stole it."

"That boy is no thief. Did you really think I would not know him? Tell me, Kokoro, how is it that Prince Takehiko Otako just happened to come your way?"

"Very clever, Your Excellency. Did you tell him?"

"No. You would not have risked me seeing him if you thought I was such a fool."

There were words neither of us needed to speak. The boy was dangerous. Despite the current unrest with the Pikes, Kisia had grown used to its soldier emperor. Kin had been competently holding the empire together for sixteen years, and they had been prosperous ones despite the many incursions into our territory by Chiltaens and the ever-restless mountain tribes. But the glory of the

Otakos had never dimmed. The people had never chosen to have their rule ended—this family to whom the gods themselves were said to have given Kisia. Katashi Otako was enough of a threat, and he had never been heir to the Crimson Throne. Takehiko had.

Father Kokoro went on sipping his tea, a picture of innocence with his greying, frazzled hair. It was hard to tell just how much he knew. Did he know the boy was an Empath? Did he know how dangerous that could be in a position of power?

"The last surviving son of Emperor Lan," Kokoro mused. "For myself, I will not be mentioning the matter to His Majesty."

"You would not keep your position long if you did."

He acknowledged this with a gentle nod. "May the gods judge us wisely."

"They might, but it's His Majesty's judgement that matters now. And mine if you don't answer me. Where has the boy been all these years?"

The old man eyed me speculatively. "Living with a priest named Jian."

"A priest who was known to you?"

"I think you specified one question, Excellency."

"In fact I did not specify at all," I said, mimicking his calm. "You will answer the question. I won't ask again."

Across the table, our eyes met—his harder than I had expected, but I would not back down. Not on this or anything.

"You are very like your father," he said, looking into his empty cup.

"I do not consider that a compliment. Answer my question."

"Yes, I know the priest. Once I called him brother."

"They tortured him."

"I know." He brushed a hand down the front of his pale robe. "It is in the hands of the gods now."

Having learnt what I wanted, I made to rise, but before I could get past my knees, Father Kokoro said, "We have not yet discussed why you came, Your Excellency. Or why an Eye of Vice would have your family crest on it and have been in your father's possession."

They were all the questions I didn't want to answer, didn't even want to think about, but he smiled his serene smile, and I settled back on the cushion with as bored and long-suffering a look as I could summon. "I didn't like my father at all, Father Kokoro, but even I would acquit him of having anything to do with crimes that happened well after his death. The eye is an old symbol repurposed by monsters. He lacked all sense of foresight, but again, even I cannot fault him for that." I sighed. "Now, if you would excuse me, Father, I have to get back to Mei'lian. As should you before His Majesty notes the ongoing absence of his priest."

This time Kokoro rose with me, the pair of us getting to our feet with a shifting of silk. "You are right, of course," he said with the groan of an old man with bad joints. "Your father always wore that necklace. One might almost conclude that whichever monster started the Vices was trying to deliberately blacken his name." That smile again, as much a weapon as the words. "But surely there's no one who disliked him *that* much."

"Your intimation is heavy-handed," I said, holding the door so he could not escape on what he had no doubt hoped to be a parting shot. "As his son, I would have to have been a fool to blacken the Laroth name. And were your accusations true, His Majesty would have been a fool to take me into his service at all, let alone make me minister of the left."

I let go of the door, and with one last beatific smile, the priest slid it open. "I have been saying that these many years, Your Excellency. Perhaps he will soon see the error in his judgement. Good day, Minister."

He walked out on the words, nodding to a serving girl in the passage and blessing her with good fortune.

The twin gatehouses of Mei'lian greeted me in the fading light, their stern boltholes like narrowed eyes. Despite the slide toward dusk, the gates were still open, a mass of people gathered and waiting to enter. I looked from the large group to the blackened clouds upon the horizon. This was going to take hours I did not have.

A stand of tallow bushes ran down the centre of the road, blocking one gatehouse from view of the other. It was the Leaving Gate, but at this hour, and with a storm threatening, it would be deserted.

I wheeled my horse around, pushing back through the still-gathering crowd of merchants and commoners with bundles thrown over their shoulders. Tallow leaves flapped against my shoulders as my horse pushed between their trunks.

"Excuse me, my lord." A guard rushed up as I approached. "This is the Leaving Gate."

"And I am Lord Laroth," I said, hearing unintended irritation creep into my voice. "I am well aware this is the Leaving Gate, but no one is leaving and I have somewhere to be."

"Your Excellency." He swallowed and glanced through the bushes to the mass of people getting impatient before the other gate. "A bit of a crush."

"An understatement. Now let me through, man. I'm in a hurry."

He swallowed again. An annoying habit. "Strictly speaking, I'm not allowed to let anyone—"

"I am not just anyone. I am the minister of the left and can change your orders since I outrank whoever issued them."

A third swallow bobbed his throat. "Yes, Your Excellency. Of course, Your Excellency. You have your papers?"

"My papers?" For a moment, I wasn't even sure I was carrying them—I had left the palace in such a hurry—but they were folded tightly into my sash pouch and I pulled them free. "Here, take them. You must be the first man to ask for them in years. You ought to be congratulated."

He took the papers and opened them, but as he read the words, he kept looking up at me as though afraid this was a test. When he overemphasised his check of the paper quality and looked up for approval, I was sure of it.

Eventually, the guard handed them back. "Thank you, Your Excellency. Long live Emperor Kin."

"Long live Emperor Kin," I said, taking them from his hand.

Like a good citizen, I usually carried my papers wherever I went, but no one ever asked for a minister's papers. Not even to be sure I really was a minister. I glanced down at the neat lines written in four different hands.

These papers are to attest that their owner is a true
citizen of the Imperial Expanse of Kisia 1346

Darius Kirei Laroth
Born the fifty-third day of spring 1346

Father
Lord Nyraek Laroth, Fifth Count of Esvar
Born the eighty-third day of summer 1312

Mother
Lady Melia Laroth, Countess of Esvar
Born Melia Chinya, second daughter of Lord Eri Chinya
Second day of summer 1323

Ascended to the title on the thirty-first day of winter, 1359
Lord Darius Laroth, Sixth Count of Esvar

Elected Councillor to the court of Emperor Kin Ts'ai,
first of his name, spring 1367
Councillor Laroth, Sixth Count of Esvar

Minister of the Left to the court of Emperor Kin Ts'ai,
first of his name, summer 1369
Lord Darius Laroth, Sixth Count of Esvar and Minister of the Left

No children

Allowing myself a wry smile, I folded the papers and slid them back into my sash. The guard watched me warily. The words were so dry, so official. There was no mention of the time when I had not used my papers at all, had not even owned the name written therein. No mention either of just how my father had passed, leaving me the title so sonorously declared in its black ink. It was just a list, a construction, the shroud I had created for myself to escape it all, to escape *him*. But he refused to leave me alone.

I rode into the city. The sun was setting, piercing the storm clouds with its last rays, and in the fast-fading light, the Tiankashi Square was crammed with people. Thunder would have gone unheard beneath the noise of criers and hawkers and guards trying to direct the tide of new arrivals.

I had no liking for crowds and soon slipped into side streets where I found the city on its cusp. When I had been that young man without papers, I had lived for the cusp, for the time when the city began to change. Dusk would creep through the streets, and in the declining light, merchants hurriedly packed their wares, shops closed their shutters, and processions of well-attended night ladies made their way to evening engagements. Passing through the streets, I felt like that boy again, looking everywhere for the signs that it was time to play. During the day, Mei'lian moved like a lazy beetle, full of its own importance, but the night was furtive and quick. Away from the link-boys' bright torches, a different city existed in the shadows, a city where I had learnt to hunt.

I rode now into those dark corners of the city, cramped buildings blocking the last of the sun from view. Thunder rumbled, and the first heavy drop landed on the road. Another hit my sleeve.

I left my horse at the entrance to the Pleasure Quarter, slipping a silver coin into a rein-boy's hand. Others hollered, declaring they would take better care of my horse, but I waved them away. In a few hours, it would be a busy prospect, even in the rain, with scores of link-boys chattering beneath their torches and a constant stream of palanquins halting at the mounting stone.

The rain grew heavier, its fat drops failing to dampen the buzz of activity. Passing beneath the string of red lanterns was like walking into a different world. Here, all men were customers, our carnal desires making us as much like meat as the women in the whore-houses. Hawkers dogged my steps.

"Want to see the most beautiful girls in the empire, my lord?"

"Exotic beauties, plump breasts bigger than your head."

"Follow me for fair Chiltaen girls. Hairless bodies."

They followed, even though I moved on without acknowledging them.

"How about boys, my lord?"

I strode on, and one by one they fell back to cluster around a newcomer.

The Pleasure Quarter was a welcoming place, all brightly lit doorways and winking lanterns, but past the long fountain, the colours and noise began to die away, leaving nothing but the rain. There the shadowed forms of old houses rose neglected from the street. Someone else might get lost in the tangle of alleyways, but

I had come this way too many times. Even in the drenching rain, it called to me, a faded house stripped of all glory I had long called home.

The Gilded Cherry.

It had been years, but the memories returned in an instant. Nothing had changed. No attempt had been made to salvage the building, the world happy to leave the rotting timbers to their ghosts.

Ducking beneath the jutting portico roof, I found respite from the rain. All the windows were dark, but a welcome lantern hung over the door.

He was waiting.

I set my hand to the door and it swung in, light from the welcome lantern slashing through the darkness, drawing old furnishings from the gloom. And his smell. My heart betrayed me.

It had been five years.

"You are late, yes?"

The voice pierced my flesh. In a different life, I had known it better than my own.

"As you say," I said, surprised by my even tone. I could only hope years of practise had made the act true.

A figure shifted into the shaft of light. There an arm clad in fine silk and the tip of a sleek black ponytail.

"Darius," he said.

"Malice."

I could not see his face, but I knew he smiled. He had always liked the sound of his adopted name.

"You've changed."

"And you haven't," I said.

The ghost of a laugh sounded in his next breath. "Perhaps it only looks like you have, yes? Come closer so I can see you."

I was tempted to obey but dared not. "Why are you here?"

"Is it wrong to want to see you?" he asked, that same laugh in his voice. "You got my message, yes?"

Kun. He had knelt in my place, Malice's blood staining his skin along with the Traitor's Mark. And now Takehiko Otako would have it, too. *No, don't think about Takehiko.*

"Yes," I said. "As you see."

"Angry with me? Because of the boy? Your heart has grown quite soft, yes? He was...different, too, wasn't he? Did you think helping him would change anything?"

"What do you want, Malice?"

He stepped farther into the light. "What do you think I want?" he said, another step bringing him close. I took a deep breath and caught the vague trace of opium lingering on his skin. How great had the habit become, I wondered, standing my ground as he came closer still.

"How should I know?" I said. "A position at court, perhaps. I'm afraid I will have to disappoint you there. Kin takes commoners into his service, but he only keeps men who work hard."

Malice smiled. "I see your sense of humour is as strange as ever, yes? I would not work a moment in service to your *Emperor* Kin."

"Then to whom? Katashi Otako perhaps. I hear he is calling himself Monarch these days."

"You leap ahead, Darius." Malice rested his fingers upon his brow and shook his head. "There is no dealing with you at all, yes? Do not leap. Let us reach important points by steps, baby steps. Whatever happened to the pleasantries? I remember you used to talk for hours at a time, then be silent as long, your energy as erratic as your humour."

"Nostalgic?"

"You left me." He gripped my chin in his long fingers, and as though he breathed his soul out through his fingertips, I felt the touch of his Empathy. Five years. It took all my self-control not to lower my shield. Takehiko's skill had been nothing to it.

"Where are you hiding, Darius?" he said, his eyes roaming my face. "What have you done to yourself?"

I didn't answer, didn't move. Malice had not withdrawn his touch, and though I expected another attack, I was not prepared for the blow that came. It crashed into my shield like a mace, sending my mind reeling. The tips of his fingers dug into my cheek. "I am sick of waiting, yes? Drop your pathetic charade."

I pulled away, and his hand remained lifted as though frozen in place. "What do you want?" he said when I did not answer. "An apology?"

"No. I want you to leave me alone."

A flash of anger darkened his face. "I have left you alone for years to get over your sulks."

"My sulks?"

"What else can I call it?"

"Conscience."

"You don't have one."

"And I thought you knew me so well," I said.

Finally, he lowered his hand. "I do. No one knows you better than I do, yes? I know you don't want to remain this pathetic shell you've created for yourself. I've missed you, Darius. Even Hana has missed you, yes?"

Hana. The name set my pulse thrumming. I knew him too well to doubt why he mentioned her. *I met her brother today.* In another lifetime, I would have told him everything, but not now.

"How is she?" I managed calm disinterest.

"She's grown up since you left us. She's a young woman now, yes? Five years makes great change. Not that she's calling herself Hana at the moment or even being a woman." Laughter lit his face.

"She heard about Katashi and his Pikes and wanted oh so much to be able to meet him. Maybe even to fight against the tyrant usurper herself."

I closed my eyes, allowing myself that moment of weakness. I had thought her safe, had thought Malice would take care of her as I had once done.

As though reading my thoughts, he said, "I took no oath, yes? She is spirited. She wants glory and revenge and her great cousin to take her maidenhead. What sort of guardian would deny her such excitement? You would, of course."

"I did take an oath."

I had only been a boy. "*Protect Lady Hana,*" my father had said. "*You are all she has.*" And so, I had given my word and spoken my first oath to the baby in my arms.

> *I swear on the bones of my forebears*
> *On my name and my honour*
> *That I will do all in my power to protect you from harm*
> *I will mind not pain*
> *I will mind not suffering*
> *I will give every last ounce of my strength*
> *I will give every last ounce of my intellect*
> *I will die in service to you if the gods so will it*
> *I will renounce every honour*
> *I will give every coin*
> *I will be as nothing and no one in service to you*

Malice's voice cut across the memory. "Oh, Darius, you are such a spoilsport. I haven't even told you the best part yet. She wanted to fight with Katashi, yes? Wanted to be noticed. So I gave her command of my Vices and let her go play Captains with him, and—" He broke off, laughter bringing tears to his eyes. "And though I am very sure he's realised she's not a man under those clothes, he has no idea who she really is. No idea she'd have a better claim to the throne than him if only she had a cock." He ended on a rising note, barely getting the words out before amusement consumed him.

I could almost imagine him impressing upon her how important it was that Katashi not know, perhaps even drawing out the old stories of how much their fathers had hated each other and now were both dead. She probably believed Katashi would kill her if he knew the truth, when in fact, marrying her would give him an unassailable claim to the throne that would make him twice as dangerous as he already was.

Malice wiped his eyes, still chuckling. It was a cruel trick to play on them both and so very like him, but if he had no interest in seeing her married to Katashi, then he must have had another purpose in mind for her.

"You should have left Hana out of this," I said.

His laughter faded to a brittle smile. "And you should not have abandoned us."

"She could die."

"Yes, she could. Or Kin might. I can't say I really care. You can look after her again soon, though, my dear."

His face gave nothing away. "What do you mean?"

"Only that you might see her when she comes looking for her birth documents. They're in the inner palace, are they not? In the imperial archive, not the one beneath the spire but the one near the throne room?"

"There is no archive near the throne room."

Malice put his hand to his lips. "Oops," he mocked. "At least she will be happy to see you when the guards catch her then, yes?"

The room spun. For five years, I had made a life away from him, having to wake up each and every day and choose to keep being a good man. Foolish to think Malice would let me stay away forever.

Foolish to think he might care enough about Hana not to use her against me. Lady Hana Otako. I had told Kin so many truths but never about her. I couldn't risk her safety.

I let go a slow breath. "Why?"

"Why?" He did not pretend to misunderstand my question but gripped my face between both his hands. "Because I know you. I know you won't let her die. 'The gods judge us on our choices, not our fame,' yes?"

And they would judge me on mine. I could still see the silk band knotted around Takehiko's left wrist. He had tried to read me, the gentle prod of his immature Empathy like the nagging tug of a small child.

Without warning, Malice forced his own Empathy through my skin. It ripped through me, and for a brief moment, I had nothing: no thoughts, no emotions, no memories, everything sucked out through the palms of his hands.

He let go and I stepped back, shaking. He had taken all he could and left behind the memory of a boy in a singed robe, his face covered in dirt and ash. Me. Me as he first remembered me. Me with a fierce hatred of all life burning in my eyes.

"There's another Empath?" Shock froze Malice in place. "Is that why you were late? Oh . . . oho!" He started to laugh again. "And you let him go? Do you truly hate the blood that much?"

"Leave him alone," I managed to say, standing straight though my legs shook. "You'll regret it if you touch him."

"Why? Who is he?"

Prince Takehiko Otako. The name shot into my head and I pushed it away just in time. Malice gripped my face again, and before I could pull away, his Empathy dug into me.

"Where is he?"

I couldn't block him. It had been too long, and unbidden, an image of the guardhouse at Shimai flashed into my mind, its tall stone tower half swallowed by ivy.

Malice let his Empathy ebb, eyes hungry. "Shimai? You are out of practice, Darius. It's pitiful."

"He won't be there anymore."

"Other people might believe your lies, but I am used to them, yes?" Eyeing me critically, he brushed a stray lock of hair off my brow. "Am I playing too rough for you? We can't have Minister Laroth with a hair out of place. Answer one more question and perhaps I'll keep Hana safely at home tonight. Who is he?"

He was giving me the opportunity to exchange one Otako for another, but whatever my duty to Hana, I could not do it. The boy was far more dangerous—Otako and Empath in one deadly package. I had seen too much of what Empaths could do.

"No? Then we'll try this one more time, yes? Who is he?"

His Empathy was like a blade slipped into my gut, paralysing my body. *The boy, the boy, don't think about the boy. He has no name.*

"Who is he?"

"His name is Endymion and his mother was a whore. Just like yours."

Malice slapped me. My breath caught in my throat as I touched my stinging skin. "And you are more whore than any woman," he snarled, pressing me against the wall. The moulding dug into my spine. "You've sold your soul to the highest power. Do you enjoy him so much that you won't even answer me one simple question?" He stroked my smarting cheek. "Tell me who the boy is."

"No."

His fingernails cut into my skin. "Could I tear your flesh away, I wonder? I'd hate to mar your prettiness, but I'm curious now."

Stale opium was on his breath. It clung about him like a shroud, caught to every strand of the silken hair that tickled my arm. "Get off me."

"I would love to see you make me. In fact, that is why I came. Do it, Darius. Make me let go."

His nails dug deeper, and I clenched my teeth against the pain. "Well?"

His Empathy snuck under my guard, digging through my soul. "Fight me, Darius," he hissed. "Fight back!"

"No. Give me up as dead."

He growled, his nails gouging my cheek as his Sight cleaved through me. He wanted me to fight, but I knew all too well where that led.

Thoughts and memories filled my mind and I could not control them. Shimai, the guardhouse, the worried crease between the boy's brows and the sweat on his hands. Beside the glinting tea, a silver eye saw everything. Kokoro had tapped his cup, punctuating his serenity with fear as the name echoed around the room—Takehiko. Takehiko. Takehiko.

Malice let go. In the silence, his every breath sounded harsh. When he laughed, it was a high-pitched sound that echoed strangely. "Another Otako. Well, doesn't this game get more and more delicious."

He smeared blood down my cheek. "Should I apologise? I think not. You will thank me when you come to your senses, yes? Now it seems I have somewhere else I need to be."

Malice turned and was at the door in an instant, the rain outside like golden needles in the lantern light. "Give my love to Hana, yes?" he said and strode out into the rain, the tip of his ponytail the last thing I saw before it flicked out of sight.

———————◆———————

I climbed the stairs to the outer palace, striding past Lord Pirin, the master of the court. It was cold for a summer night, the rising wind making the paper screens snap taut in their frames as I passed, while candle flames danced even within the protection of their lantern husks.

"Your Excellency!" The master of the court called after me as I passed through a small courtyard, its flower bed pelted with rain. Lantern light glinted off every slick surface, but there was no time to admire its beauty, no time to even care that I was sopping wet.

"Minister? Is everything all right?" Lord Pirin called as he followed the trail of water dripping from my robe.

"Perfectly fine, Lord Pirin," I said, not stopping. "I have been for a pleasant stroll."

The brightly lit palace was strange after the darkness of the city. The shadowed haunts had better suited my mood.

"Minister? Are you aware you're bleeding?"

I lifted my hand to show I had heard but continued into a long passage without answering. A court secretary stopped to stare at me, his arms filled with parchment scrolls.

"You!" I said, and the man gave a start of horror.

"Me, Your Excellency?"

"Who else? There is a conspicuous lack of others present. Drop the scrolls."

"E-excuse me, Your Excellency?"

"It isn't a difficult instruction to understand. Drop them. Now."

The man let the scrolls go, and they bounced around the floor before settling at his feet.

"Good," I said. "Leave them, they aren't going anywhere. I need you to do something for me, and I need you to do it now."

"Yes, Your Excellency, whatever you wish."

I parted my lips, but words did not immediately come. I had two problems that needed solving now and only one of me. Either I could go to Shimai and protect the boy or stay here and protect Hana and, by extension, myself. If Kin found out about her... If he found out that I had known all along...

"What I wish is that you run as fast as you can to the messenger's yard. Tell them I want their fastest rider on their fastest horse to take a message to the Shimai guardhouse, leaving immediately. Say nothing about this to anyone else and you will be well rewarded."

"Yes, Your Excellency. And what is the message?"

"They have a prisoner there by the name of Endymion. Order them to keep him safe by any means necessary. Tell them ... Tell them the Vices are coming for him."

7. ENDYMION

I opened my eyes to white-hot sunlight and jolted back, slamming my head against a metal bar. A mute cry parted my lips.

"Looks like the boy is finally awake."

I tried to open my eyes again, blinking fast. Wheels rumbled beneath me. Sweat stuck my robe to my skin, and the air stank of unwashed bodies and piss. A little way off, a horse snorted.

When I adjusted to the brightness, I found myself in a caged cart, and I wasn't alone. Half a dozen men and a boy shared my fate, each one unkempt and red from the sun. My hands were tied to one of the bars, the metal warm and slippery with my sweat. Everything ached. My cheek and the back of my head stung so much my eyes watered, and shifting my legs made me wince.

"You can go ahead and ask him now," said an older man with sparse grey hair.

"He might eat me if I ask," the boy returned.

"Be better for him if he did. Looks like walking bones, he does."

"But he's probably dangerous. Why else is he the only one tied up?"

I looked around. The others' hands were all free. One man slept in the corner, another had his legs dangling through the bars, and the rest looked to be playing dice with an irregularly shaped rock.

One of the players shot me a sidelong glance. "I heard he was tied up because he attacked guards in Shimai. The men were talking about it when we stopped there, said they heard screaming, like he was burning them. Maybe he's one of them witches."

"They wouldn't put him in here with us if he was," one of the others said. "Would they?"

I was broken. Shattered. Emotions seeped in through the cracks, stronger than ever before. These men were angry. They might laugh and jab at one another, but they were angry in their hearts, the feeling so strong it stained the air, drowning out my every attempt to think about what had happened. To me. To the guards. To Jian.

"Well, go on then, boy," the old man said, nudging him. "Ask him."

"All right." He looked at me, defiance edging its own tinge into the air. He had a cut above his lip that gave him a strange, lilting smile. "Why did they brand you three times?"

My mind felt fuzzy. Everything was wrong. The boy had a Traitor's Mark on his cheek, as did every other man in the cage, three horizontal lines crossed by a diagonal. I found myself blinking again, expecting the mark to change, to meld into something else, but it remained a red welt upon his skin.

"Perhaps he doesn't talk," one of the others suggested, picking up the rock.

"Well?" the boy said. "Can you talk?"

The brand on his cheek was strange, distorted, as though the hand that administered it hadn't been entirely steady.

"Just leave him alone."

Frustration, resignation, anger. It smelt like the eel stew that was famous in the Chiltaen port cities—a strange concoction of ingredients that somehow made a tasty meal. The saltiness always left my tongue dry. It was dry now, an awful taste left behind. The men had a water skin, but although I knew how to ask, knew how to be polite, I could not form a single word. My lips were stuck shut.

"Will there be work for us in Chiltae, do you think?" the boy asked, watching the stone roll across the rocking boards.

From up front, the driver barked a laugh. "You wish, boy," he said. "Chiltaens ain't any different from us. They hate traitors same as we do. You ask them for work, and they'll spit on you straight."

"Traitor to who?" the old man said. "The Usurper or the True Emperor?"

"You watch what you say."

"Why? Are you going to brand me again like the poor dumb shit over here? Kin's blood is no more royal than yours or mine or dumb shit's. What do you think about that?"

The driver didn't say anything, but one of the other men shrugged and spat onto the stained cart boards. "I couldn't care less who sits on the throne, it's all the same to me. The Otakos weren't gods. They sucked at their mothers' tits the same as all of us."

"Until they were slaughtered in their beds," the old man said. "From the emperor in his grand apartments to his baby daughter in the nursery. All dead. And there sits Kin on the throne when it was *his* job to protect them. General Kin, *commander of the Imperial Guard.*"

Only the rumble of the cart broke the silence. It was another hot summer day. Birds chirped, fluttering from branch to branch as we passed beneath a broad canopy, dappled sunlight touching every haggard face.

"Didn't his brother kill him?" the boy said at last. "Grace Tianto?"

"Emperor Tianto," the old man corrected, touching his branding with pride. "That's just lies. What man would kill his own brother?"

Again, a pause, then the boy said, "I don't know about you, but I have a brother. I've gone for him more than once."

"Of course, boys fight, that's just what they do. You wouldn't harm him though."

"I broke his arm. I think he got off light. I was trying to slam his head into the stones."

The old man looked horrified and turned his shoulder a little, until he realised that meant he was looking at me. I stared at him and he turned away again.

"It doesn't matter," he said with a sniff. "What matters is it was all Ts'ai propaganda."

One of the other men rolled the stone. "Big word."

"It means—"

"I know what it means. I was a scholar at Aysi."

"Then you should know better than to claim any but an Otako as emperor of Kisia. Emperor Tianto—"

"Is dead. Leave it be or I'll piss on you."

The old man scowled, but when others murmured agreement, he fell silent.

The cart drove on, leaving the brief shade behind. For the rest of the afternoon, we travelled through a world that was bright and harsh, full of distractions, of waving trees and fields of red poppies, of scudding clouds and tiptoeing herons. It was a vivid patchwork. Every colour was brighter, every smell stronger, and every breath so thick with emotion that I felt none of my own.

There was no time, no thought, nothing but pain and thirst and a landscape that flickered through the bars like a variegated painting. The sun grew hotter, my tongue drier. My eyes began to droop.

I tried to sleep, but there was no more a comfortable position here than there had been in that cell. With my hands bound, I could only lean back against the bars, and all it took was a rut to bang my head against the metal and shock me awake, eyes watering.

Afternoon sank into night. I was only vaguely aware of stopping in a town, and of another prisoner being added to our cage. Complaints washed over me. There was not enough space. The boards of the cart needed cleaning. Where was the food. Our new driver spat in the boy's face when he grumbled that it was crowded. "Shut it, scum. Go ahead and sit on someone's lap. They might like that. You're probably the prettiest piece of meat to come their way in a long time, eh?"

I heard laughter, but it was pain that twisted inside me.

The town dragged on. Tangled threads of emotion clogged the air. It was hard to concentrate, hard to breathe. The wheels bumped over cobbles. The cart swayed. Whispering voices hissed around me.

Slowly, as the air cleared of souls, I was drawn toward wakefulness. We were leaving the town behind, the warm night containing nothing but the men trapped with me. My arms ached. The smell of rain tickled my nose, tantalising, my mouth drier than ever.

Darkness closed its hand upon us, the empty road stretching ahead into nothing. I could have walked faster. The cartwheels turned but we seemed barely to move, the steady clip-clop of the horse's hooves melding into a soporific pattern.

The boy turned his head, staring into the night. The horse walked on. Another head turned. I felt the change, like a gentle tug drawing my gaze. Then the hoofbeats fell out of rhythm. Faster. Faster. More heads turned to stare into the darkness.

A bell clanged. The driver was humming to himself and did not hear, though the prisoners all scrambled to the back of the cart, pushing and shoving to see. A shout rang out and the bell clanged again, much louder now. Four riders appeared in our lantern light, slowing as they came alongside. Their crimson sashes proclaimed imperial allegiance, and each man was clad in armour, a helmet upon his head.

"Halt!" one ordered, slowing alongside the driver.

He dragged on the reins and the cart began to slow, the horse throwing its head back at such handling. "What's going on?"

"We have orders from Mei'lian," the rider said. "We're looking for a prisoner named Endymion, a recently branded exile. Do you have him?"

The cart slowed to a halt, its wheels juddering on the rough edge of the road. Around us, the other riders reined in their mounts, each horse backing uneasily into the long grass.

"How am I supposed to know the names of these stinking rats?" the driver complained.

The rider turned his horse, the medallions hanging from its bridle glinting in the lantern light. He held out his hand. Impatience snapped in the air. "Give me your manifest."

Shifting the lantern, the driver began hunting under his seat and produced the papers with a grumble. They were snatched from his hand.

"There, Endymion," the rider said, jabbing at the page in triumph. "Which one of you is Endymion?"

No one spoke. The others kept their eyes averted, only the boy daring to look, wide-eyed, upon the soldier.

"Come on! Speak up." The man slid from his horse and stalked to the cage. He glared up at the boy. "What's your name?"

"Virrik, my lord."

"And which one of these men is Endymion?"

The boy shook his head. "I don't know, my lord, but there's one that doesn't talk."

He pointed at me, all eyes following his accusing finger. The soldier came around the cart, his boots crunching on loose stones. "He's tied up. Why is this man tied up?"

The driver grunted and mumbled something indistinct.

"We heard he killed men, back in Shimai," one of the others offered.

"Then he's the one we want." The soldier nodded to his companions. "Get him untied and out of there and be quick about it. Driver, get the key."

Someone tugged at the knot that bound my hands, mutters issuing from the shadowed faces of the other prisoners. All except the boy who had given me away. He was looking back along the road.

Another head turned.

From out beyond our lantern-lit sphere came the rumble of approaching riders.

Fingers stopped working at the knot holding my wrists. "Captain," the man said, his warm breath dancing across my hands. The captain looked up, and for an instant, everyone stood frozen in place.

The thundering hooves grew louder.

"They're here!"

"Vices!"

The captain dashed to his horse, tearing his sword from its scabbard. "Quick, to your horses! Form up!"

A black stallion burst from the night. The imperial soldier upon its back had dispensed with the traditional helmet, instead allowing a ponytail to fly wild like the unknotted mane of his horse. A large sickle sliced into the captain's stomach, its barbs ripping flesh, but the newcomer did not even slow. He rode on, dragging the mangled torso behind him.

The pain shuddered through my body, there and gone as more of the strange soldiers streaked past. Some crowded about the cart, each horse a black stallion, each man's head unadorned, ponytails flying. Short stabs of pain bit me all over like prickling thorns.

Our driver had taken up a bow and was shouting, his words

inaudible beneath the clattering of hooves dancing around us. His fingers trembled as he nocked an arrow, but before he could loose, pain stung like a whip across my throat and the driver's head rolled free. It hit the ground an instant before his body toppled back, blood spurting from his open neck.

With a screech, the horse bolted and the cart lurched forward, jolting over rough ground. Branches whipped at the bars. My companions swore and kicked each other, trying to get free of the writhing pile of limbs. I could only brace a foot against a bar and hope. Every attempt to wriggle my hands free only deepened the grazes around my wrists.

A black horse appeared, keeping pace with the cart, its rider ducking reaching branches. Hooves pounded the dirt. Men shouted. And crashing through a nest of bushes, the panicked cart-horse charged into an open field. The lantern bounced, and its light gleamed off the flanks of dark horses running close.

The cartwheels dropped into a rut, throwing my companions off balance. One of my hands yanked free, the other aching as though my shoulder had been torn from its socket. But it ripped free too as we slammed into a ditch, and no longer restrained, I hit the bars so hard my head spun. Or perhaps it was the cage rolling, for we rolled with it, even the moon turning upside down. My shoulder struck the side bars. Blades of onion grass tickled my face, their smell spiced with sweat from the stinking blanket of elbows and knees piled on my back.

"The cage is open!"

I couldn't tell who spoke, but the men dug their feet into my gut and my back and my side in their desperation to escape. Clawing over one another, they clambered toward the moon and freedom. Outside, the old man dropped onto the ground.

"I'm free!" he crowed, kicking the bars by my head. "I'm—"

Blood sprayed the grass. His head landed with a heavy thud, rolling a little way toward a surviving lantern as his body crumpled.

"We want Endymion."

A man stepped into the light, as like an imperial soldier as it was possible to get but for the sickle in his hand, blood dripping from its barbed points.

No one spoke.

"Are you all deaf? Conceit, light another lantern. Get the rest of those rats out of the cage."

I let the others climb out first, happy to crouch in the shadows and nurse my aching head while the man stalked back and forth, swinging his sickle so it caressed the grass with every step. The others had long ponytails, but this man's was short, protruding from the back of his head like a fistful of needles.

"Your turn." The voice came from above, where the open cage gaped at the night sky. A pair of strong hands reached down and gripped my arms, and with a grunt, I was pulled up, sandalled feet scrabbling at the bars. Balancing on top of the cart, I found my saviour wasn't one of the other prisoners but one of the ponytailed soldiers.

"Here," he said, his voice unexpectedly gentle. "I'll help you down. Give me your hand."

He didn't wait, just gripped my hand, and skin to skin, the connection was instant. I didn't force it, didn't seek it, it was just there, bright and blinding, like his soul was on fire. Whispers filled my head.

Stinking prison carts. We're good at this kindness to all men thing, huh? What is he doing? Is he going to climb down or just stand there staring at me?

I yanked my hand away, but not fast enough. The shock of recognition leached up my arm.

"Wait!"

I leapt, but instead of hitting the ground, I slammed back against the bars, feet dangling. He had hold of my arm where they had branded me for the third time, and though my charred skin cracked, I could not scream. Through holes in the scorched linen, connection flared again. The man let go with a gasp, and I hit the ground, knees buckling. "He's here! This is the one. He's like the Master."

I scrambled up and ran, my arm a throbbing, oozing mess clutched tight against me. Shouts followed. Tall grass whipped at my legs as I rounded the front of the cart seeking help, somewhere to run, a weapon—anything but more imprisonment.

"There's no point running," a voice called behind me as I caught sight of the driver's bow hooked on the lantern post. "We will follow you wherever you go."

The quiver was tucked beneath the smashed seat. There were only two arrows. I grabbed both, biting one between my teeth and nocking the other to the string.

On foot, the riders gathered in the light, and I spun to face them, aiming the tip of my arrow at their leader's eye. "Are you Endymion?" he said.

I kept the bow drawn, the effort making my arms shake.

"That's him." The young man who had helped me out of the cart stepped forward. "I felt him."

Every breath was difficult, and I swallowed as best I could with the arrow still between my teeth. Almost I gagged but mastered the impulse and dug my teeth in with a crunch of wood.

"Put it away, boy, we aren't going to kill you."

"Just let him loose the damn thing at you, then maybe we can get out of here," another said. "I'm sick of riding."

"We haven't eaten since we left Mei'lian."

"Shut up your moaning," snapped the man I thought of as their leader. I had not turned my arrow away, yet he showed not the smallest fear. He set his lantern down and spread his arms wide.

"Go on, then," he said. "We don't have all night. The Master wants to see you, and we do as the Master commands."

My grip on the string tightened. I could loose this arrow and the next, but there were too many of them. The only solace was in knowing if they'd wanted me dead, I'd already be gone.

I lowered the bow.

Disappointment showered around me. "Really?" one of them said. "That was anticlimactic."

"Drop the bow," their leader ordered.

I let it fall from my shaking fingers. I needed food. I needed sleep. I needed silence. Taking the second arrow out of my mouth, I licked my lips, eyeing my saviours warily.

All danger having passed, their leader jerked up one shoulder. The movement seemed to dislodge something, and a flurry of white flakes fell from him like snow. Each was a piece of white-hot anger, solid for an instant before it faded into the night.

Someone laughed. "Look, he's shedding."

"Shut it, Parsimony," the leader snapped, shaking the last of the flakes off like a dog shedding water. "We ride to Nivi Fen. Hope, bring the boy."

He turned as he spoke, stepping on his lantern. The thin bamboo cage snapped, tearing the waxed paper. The night clawed back a little more darkness. There were other lanterns, but even without them, I could feel the movement of each soul around me. One came forward.

"You're riding with me," said the young man who had helped me from the cage. His hand was all too close to his sickle. "My name is Hope," he went on when I said nothing. "The man you tried to put an arrow through is called Ire."

It was a strange name but somehow suited him.

"You don't talk?"

I shook my head.

"But you understand?"

I nodded.

"Good. Come, we have a long way to ride, and the Master is waiting."

8. HANA

We camped out in the circle of light beneath the well's mouth, waiting for night to come. I had not thought to bring any food and sat getting hungrier and hungrier, while around me the Pikes slowly chewed through their personal supplies, no doubt as much for something to do as because they were hungry. The first time Shin held out a strip of jerky to me, I refused with a shake of my head. The second time, I pretended to be engrossed in an arrhythmic drip. The third time came after my stomach made a loud grumble, and I could not refuse because he threw it at me.

"I will not be discovered because of your stomach," he said, and a few sniggers echoed along the dim passages.

Eventually, the circle of daylight overhead darkened to night, and the Pikes began to get restless. We had been sitting there for hours—all afternoon and well into the evening—when Shin finally gave the order to light the torches. Firelight flared, reflecting back off pools of water and slimy stones.

"It's time to go."

In both directions, the dripping tunnels of the Zavhi Waterway stretched into darkness. The roof was low and covered in moss, and blackened gratings barred dozens of smaller passages. It all looked the same to me, but without hesitation, Shin strode off along one of the tunnels and we all followed.

Between the ringing echo and the roar of water, conversation was impossible. We could only nod and grimace at one another and be grateful Shin knew where he was going, though how he knew was its own mystery. At the first grating, he did not so much as pause, just turned, edging around a sheet of falling water into a narrow tunnel.

The water level rose. Soon, great rivers roared along channels and poured down falls, drawn ever deeper into the earth. To most Kisians, the Zavhi Waterway was more myth than reality. Legend said it was connected to a network of underground rivers and caves and that anyone sucked into its bowels would never return. The Pikes seemed to have this on their minds, gripping tightly to walls, bars, or each other whenever the water rose above knee height.

Yet Shin led us on, saturated and stinking. We waded through high water and skidded along slippery stones, the tunnels a maze to all but him. Over and over I reminded myself why I had come and just kept walking, though the farther we went, the worse the smell became. I held my breath when I could, sucking damp air through my mouth in a vain attempt not to taste it.

Eventually Shin stopped beneath a sluice that rose up into the darkness. Wen went first to light the way, and the rest of us followed, gripping mossy cracks and wedging ourselves between the narrow walls. My limbs burned with fatigue, but I would not give up. If the men could climb it, so could I.

At the top, a bar had been removed from the grating, so we could slide through on our bellies. I was small and made it with ease, but some of the others struggled, black metal bars digging into their backs as they dragged themselves through. On the other side, a ladder climbed into a dark opening. Its rungs were pitted and old, and when I touched it, the smell of metal stuck to my fingers.

We gathered at the bottom, a silent group in the tense air. Flames danced from the torch in Wen's hand, and across its pool of fire-light, Shin stared at me. A long stare full of silent warning, but he must have known as well as I that there was no going back now. I gave an infinitesimal shake of my head.

Shin scowled and, taking the torch from Wen, plunged it into a stagnant pool. It went out with a hiss, the sudden darkness full of flare-light ghosts. Afraid to be left behind, I reached blind for the ladder and began to climb.

The others followed.

A few rungs took me up into a cramped tunnel. I took a deep breath and reminded myself I was not trapped, but it did little to lessen my discomfort. Sounds muffled in the thick air. My clothes stuck to me, puckered and tight like a second skin.

Up another few rungs and my reaching hand brushed something smooth. Drips of condensation fell on my face. I climbed higher and, putting my shoulder to a hatch, pushed it open. The hinges squealed. Someone hissed in warning, but no knives greeted me. No spears. No sounds.

We were in.

The others climbed out of the hole in my wake, each a mere shape in the darkness except for Shin. Something about the way he stood made him recognisable even in shadow.

Once we had tipped half the waterway from our boots and wrung water from our uniforms, Shin went to the door. Outside, more darkness stretched away, the silence oppressive.

As a closely gathered group, we made our way along the passage by touch alone, dragging our fingertips over cold stone walls. For a time there was sign of neither light nor life, until a faint glow heralded a flight of stone steps. These led to a passage with torches in rusted brackets and rooms bearing all the signs of frequent use—storerooms, cellars, a game larder, a silk room, and then, with a scream that pierced the silence, the first sign of life. A high-pitched scream quivered with panic, and we froze, pressing flat to the walls. Words ran together as a woman's pleas caught on sobs.

Ignoring Shin's warning stare, I crept to the open door and peered inside. A guard had his back to the aperture, wrestling with a woman whose wrists he caught as he pushed her against a workbench. Pulling one arm free, she sent a container of pins flying. A bolt of crimson cloth followed, unravelling like a stream of blood.

"What a noise you make, girl," he said, gripping her jaw in one large hand. "Just relax."

She whimpered, but he laughed and untied his belt.

I stepped in, but Shin grabbed my arm. It was dangerous, of course, and he was running out of time to complete his mission, but what if it had been me in there? Perhaps he couldn't understand her plight, too influenced by the prick between his legs to imagine her fear. I snatched my arm away and went in.

The guard was gathering up the front of the woman's serving robe, forcing her legs apart. Intent on his object, he did not hear me, did not see me, did not sense they were no longer alone.

With a few silent steps, I came up behind him and slid the tip of my dagger into his throat. The skin resisted but the soft flesh did not as I dragged the blade across his cords. Blood sprayed onto the woman's clothes. Sobbing, she scrambled off the table, scattering needles and scraps of fabric. The man gurgled. Swayed. Lifeless on his feet, he would have fallen if not for Shin locking his arms around his chest and lowering him to the floor with no sound but the little, intimate grunts of his effort. Blood pooled on the floor, the smell such that it cut through every other scent, its cloying fingers reaching down my throat. I stared at it, determined not to retch and not to be sorry.

The woman huddled in a corner, her sobs catching on the air. She held her arms before her like a shield, the pale fabric of her robe now owning a delicate pattern of blood spray.

"We can't risk her raising the alarm," Shin said, stepping toward her.

Little else might have pulled me from my shock, but I lunged to grab his arm. "No. She is in no state to talk to anyone."

"You trust her not to shout about this?"

The woman had her loose robe clutched across her chest. Her shoulders shook, and she tried to wipe streaming eyes with her bloodied hands.

"I won't kill an innocent woman, nor let you," I said. "Just leave her and keep moving."

Shin grunted his assent and handed me a scrap of fabric, nodding at the thick layer of blood on my hands. I wiped them as best I could, before rejoining the others in the passage.

Tension ran high after that. We moved with more urgency, flitting along the passage like ghosts. At almost every turning, I thought to leave them and go about my own mission, but I could not walk away without them following, without having to explain, without putting their whole mission in jeopardy. Shin seemed to suspect too, his gaze so often upon me, so often containing silent warning that I was as trapped by his awareness as by my own damned integrity.

I would go with them. A bit farther. A bit farther. A bit farther.

Until at last Shin halted outside a door that looked the same as every other and, less invested in their mission though I was, I sucked a sharp breath. At a nod from Shin, Wen oiled the hinges and Kai opened his pouch, disgorging a stack of knives with bent tips. He knelt in front of the lock and set to work, the insistent scratch of his tools loud in the empty passage.

When at last the door swung open, stale air wafted out, heavy with the scent of parchment. The room was full of dim, hazy light, a covered lantern illuminating the office of an excruciatingly tidy man. Neat piles of parchment sat squared upon the desk, books were stored by size, and every slot in the scroll case was labelled. And at the far end of the room sat more than a hundred strongboxes, all different sizes, and a board of glinting keys.

And beside the desk, a spray of greying hair spread across a pillow. I drew my knife, but Shin stayed my hand with a shake of his head. I frowned my question, and he pointed first at the wall of strongboxes and then at the board of keys. No pattern. No labels. This man, snuffling into his pillow, was the only one who could help them find what they'd come for if trial and error failed.

While Shin settled on his haunches beside the sleeping man, Kai took the first key and tried it in the first box. It did not open, so he moved to the next, and on along the rows, until at last a lock clicked, disgorging papers. Wen had already grabbed another key, and Habachi another, and caught to their mission, I took one too and began the silent search for the box it would open. Some had family names or crests upon them, others nothing, but though there was entertainment of a sort in wondering what each new box would have to offer, it soon faded to annoyance as we danced around one another in the narrow space, all damp clothes and reaching arms.

A few boxes contained nothing at all, but others were crammed full of documents, or such luxuries as gold, jewels, and fine robes. One even disgorged the rolled-up portrait of a naked lady, another a stack of old linen. I almost bit through my lip when I saw the name *Laroth* upon one large box, though I should not have been surprised. He lived here. He was a rich man. And yet it seemed so traitorous.

After what felt like hours in that dusty hell, Wen tapped my shoulder, his eyes gleaming. The others had clustered around a box, even Shin abandoning his post beside the sleeping man to catch a glimpse.

Inside the strongbox, demurely perched upon a woven mat, was a crown—an elaborate gold headpiece so finely wrought it looked too fragile to move. Luminous amber symbols embellished its rim and each string of fine gold links ended in a tiny amber charm.

The Hian Crown.

It was old. Legend said the gods themselves had gifted it to the first emperor, but now it was only used once a year when Emperor Kin carried it to Koi for the Ceremony of Avowal. Without it, his vows would mean nothing.

I ran my finger along the spiky ridges. Despite the apparent fragility, there was a strength to it, a strength I could wear, could own, could embody. I lifted it from its hiding place.

"Thieves!"

As though an invisible wire had connected him to the crown, the sleeping man lurched upright. "Guards! Guards! St—" His words ended in a gurgle as blood bubbled on his lips. He fell back, sliding off Shin's knife, but any hope he had not woken the palace died with the sound of running steps. Wen grabbed the crown.

"Take it. Take it!" I shouted, shoving him toward the door. "Go. Get out of here now!"

Each man bolted for the door, pushing and shoving to get through in Wen's wake. Shin grabbed my arm. "Come on."

I shook him off. "No, I'm staying. Besides, you won't make it unless someone creates a distraction. Go, get out of here."

His lidless eye narrowed. "If you get caught here, you're finished."

"So are you."

"I'm not an Otako princess."

Two guards appeared in the doorway and swore at the sight of us, but before they could call for backup, Shin darted in. He dodged a thrust aimed for his gut and jabbed the man in the side. Kidney. Throat. That was what Ire had taught me, his style of fighting far more rough and to the point than anything Darius had imparted.

The first guard hit the floor, and the other doubled over as Shin jammed his knee between the man's legs. He met the point of Shin's knife on the way down, but the rebel slammed him into the wall for good measure. His skull connected with a crunch, and the guard slid to the stones with his neck at a horrific angle.

I could learn even more from Shin if the opportunity ever arose.

"Come on," he said again, striding for the door.

Out in the passage, shouts and footsteps echoed, and I hoped the confusion might work in my favour. If I could get far enough from here to lose their interest, I could do the job I had come to do.

Barely had we gone a dozen steps when a flurry of footsteps neared. Shin gripped my sleeve and pulled me into a storeroom, where he stood between me and the door while the guards ran past.

"You should get back to the others," I whispered once they'd gone. "I have something to do."

"Something that's going to get you killed?"

"I know how to look after myself."

"Bullshit." He turned on me in the darkness, and I was glad I could not make out his expression. "What are you here for?"

I held my ground, though I wanted to step back from his unyielding form. "That's my own business. Go back."

I made for the door, but he stepped in my way. "This isn't just about you. If you get caught, you could give away Monarch's plan, and I can't have that."

"Does he know? Did you tell him who I am?"

It was hardly important in the moment, and yet I needed to know, needed to understand him. And to understand Katashi.

"No."

"Why? Did you think he'd hurt me if he knew?"

"Because I wanted to be sure first. You hide well, but you look too much like your mother. He'll see it soon if you keep letting him get closer."

"How do you know my—?"

He took a step toward the door. "We can talk about this once we're safe. Let's go."

"No. I came to get my birth papers and I am not leaving without them."

"You've got to be fucking kidding me," he said as I walked past him to the door. "Like that is going to make a difference."

"And what would you know about it?" I hissed. "Just go away and let me do what I need to do."

The whole outer palace was alive with noise now, shouts echoing along every passage, but taking confidence from my imperial uniform, I strode out, making for a nearby stairwell. Shin followed, hard on my heels. He pushed ahead as I reached the narrow stairs.

"I don't need your help," I said, but Shin had already disappeared around the sharp bend in the stairway. I ran after him. There was a muffled cry from above and something, or rather someone, hit the wall.

"Watch that one. You'll have to step over him."

I did so, hearing a burbling whimper in the dark. "You know we're dressed as guards. We don't have to kill them all; we can just walk."

"We're dressed like soldiers, not imperial guards. There's a difference. Enough of a difference to make them suspicious so close to the scene of a theft."

"While finding a dead body on the stairs isn't going to make it obvious we've gone this way?"

Shin hesitated at the top of the stairs. "Shit. Well we better fucking hurry now."

"I don't need your help."

"Just shut up. Soldiers look less suspicious in pairs."

It was a pathetic reason, but I didn't really want to be alone, so I let him lead the way out onto the main palace floor. We were in a short passage with an archway at either end and another leading into the gardens. Commotion sounded all around. A trio of guards ran past one of the archways. And for a moment, the sheer enormity of what I was trying to do held me frozen in place. I could just go back.

"The inner palace is through the gardens," Shin said, pointing to the archway covered in twisting vines. The night air was thick with the smell of summer flowers. And rain. "If you're sure about this, we go that way."

"Then we go that way," I said and ripped aside a trailing vine. Rain hit my face like dozens of needles. It poured fast and heavy from the night sky, bending boughs beneath the force of its anger.

"Which way do we go now?" I shouted over the storm.

"To the middle!"

Everything was almost indistinguishable in the rain. A few stone lanterns lit the main paths, but away from their guidance, all was hazy as we trampled through flower beds and rock gardens toward the indistinct shape of the inner palace. Its great spire grew larger as we approached, pitching up out of the gardens like the prow of a ship.

As we neared its base, Shin shouted something I could not hear. When I didn't answer, he turned to see I was still with him and pointed at something ahead. "What is it?" I said, drawing closer to him as we reached the protective bulk of the inner palace's tall walls. In its lee, the storm eased.

"Something's wrong." Shin pointed to where a pair of legs stuck out from the lit colonnade—the single covered walkway that connected the inner palace to the outer. Shin crept closer and I followed, not sure whether fear or hope bubbled more ferociously at the sight of a guard laid prone upon the stones.

"He's alive," Shin said, his fingers pressed to the man's throat. "Knocked out. Look, there's another one."

"Is…is someone trying to help us?" Malice had said nothing about helping, but he was never one to communicate if the surprise could be more amusing.

Shin's eyes darted toward the open doors where a third guard lay as good as dead. The ice-cold vials of Tishwa seemed suddenly to burn against my skin. If *you want the throne, you take the throne, but at least a dead man won't fight you for it.*

"If…if the guards are all unconscious…"

Shin stood up. "What are you thinking now?"

"We could kill Kin."

"What? Don't you think we'd have done that already if we thought it was possible? Even if every single one of his guards has been knocked unconscious, you can't just kill an emperor and sit on his throne and say, hey, it's mine now. It doesn't work like that."

"Kin did."

"He had the loyalty of more than half the Kisian army. Everything is easier when you have the most people with sharp stabby things. We can get your papers, but then we're getting the fuck out of here and sticking to Monarch's plan, all right?"

I made no answer, just walked toward the open doors. Twinkling lanterns invited us in, and on the threshold, I shook the rain from my hair and looked up the stairs to a balcony bounded in exquisite ironwork. From there, more stairs led to another balcony, and another, curving ever higher up the spire, but there was no sign of life, no sound beyond the roar of the rain.

Shin strode toward a pair of guards lying at the base of the stairs. A quick touch to their necks and he straightened. "We shouldn't linger. This is unnatural."

With my goal in sight, I took the stairs two at a time, leaving puddles on the worn wood. At the top, half a dozen guards lay as though they had fallen asleep, light shining through the ironwork to make patterns on their faces. Shin rolled one of their heads with his foot, snapping a string of drool. "They might as well be dead."

The clack of wooden sandals sounded in the lower hall, echoing above the drumming rain. I glanced over the railing. Shadows danced below, but there was no sign of movement.

"It seems your helper didn't get them all," Shin said, drawing a bloodstained knife from his sash. "Wait here, I'll get this one."

Silent steps took him down the stairs, his weapon a mere extension of his arm. I crept into a shadowed corner where thick wooden pillars hid me from the stairs, and there I waited. A breathless minute passed, lacking all sound, then footsteps sounded on the stairs. The loud clacking of wooden sandals.

"Hana?"

The voice was low, hardly more than a whisper, but I could never have mistaken it.

Darius.

My heart leapt, betraying me with a joy I had sworn I would not feel, the very sound of his voice sweeping away so many years of anger.

"Hana?"

"What do you want?" I said, trying to sound chilly and proud.

A slow step came across the floor. "You have to leave."

"You would say that. You want your emperor on the throne instead of me."

"No, you have to go because you'll die if you get caught here, and I swore an oath to keep you—"

"Alive, yes," I snapped. "You mean still breathing, even if I'm dead inside."

He appeared around the pillar, his beautiful face hardly changed, though a nest of fresh cuts marred his cheek. "Dramatic," he said. "Now stop arguing and get out of here. Your friend is waiting downstairs."

Darius gripped my elbow, but I pulled free, backing across the landing. "Don't touch me. I've come too far to leave now."

"Hana—"

He stopped, ears pricked at the sound of distant footsteps.

"Get out of here," he hissed, pushing me toward the stairs. "I'll deal with them."

But instead of taking the stairs down, I sprinted up the next flight, the steps disappearing in pairs beneath me. There were two doors at the top and another flight of stairs. I stared at the doors, unable to recall which floor held the throne room.

"Hana!" Darius stood on the top step, his eyes flashing like he was his old self again. "Getting your birth papers won't change anything."

"How do you know what I'm here for?"

"Malice told me. And then he laughed about having convinced you that the archive was up here. It's downstairs, Hana, and your birth papers aren't there. He's been lying to you."

Knowing Malice as I did, his words were too believable to doubt, and a lead weight of shame and embarrassment sank into my stomach. "He wouldn't," I said. But he would. To other people. I had just thought I was special.

"Leave, Hana. You can still walk away from this."

"And then what?" I turned on him. "You send me back to live with farmers in obscurity for the rest of my days? I don't want that, Darius. That is my father's throne—" I jabbed in the vague direction of the next flight of stairs. "—*my* throne. It doesn't belong to the Usurper."

"The people of Kisia are not goods and chattel. This is not the time. Go."

Blind with hurt and fury, I walked toward the last flight of stairs, sure if nothing else that the emperor's apartments would be up there. Darius gripped my arm. "Where are you going?"

"Perhaps everyone will stop thinking I'm such a stupid little girl if I kill him."

"I can't let you do that."

"Then what are you going to do about it? Call the guards and have me arrested? You gave an oath to protect my life."

I ripped free of his hand and started up the stairs, my heart pounding and angry tears pricking at my eyes. I would do it. I would show them. Malice had probably only given me the Tishwa as a fallback in case the lure of papers hadn't been enough—I bet he'd never thought I could use it.

"Guards!" The sound of Darius's voice froze my feet to the upper landing as it froze my blood in my veins. "Guards!"

I turned, looking down at him halfway up the stairs behind me, his expression a set mask I could not read. "I gave an oath to protect his life too," he said.

If he had further explanations and excuses, there was no time for them, his shout having roused a palace that just moments ago had been sleeping. Doors slid and running steps rose like thunder, all converging upon us. I lunged for the closest door, but even as I tried the handle, steps slowed behind me as guards gathered. Swords scraped in scabbards. Then a terrible silence fell, dozens of eyes pinned to the back of my head.

"Good evening," spoke a mild voice, its cold civility more frightening than any shout would have been. "That, I'm afraid to say, is the wrong door."

I turned slowly. A ring of weapons surrounded me, light glinting off sharp blades. From the group of guards, a tall man in crimson watched, unsmiling. Only one man was allowed to wear a crimson robe.

Emperor Kin stepped forward, leaving the safety of his guards. "A boy," he said, his head tilted to the side as though examining something unpleasant. "Forty-seven failed assassination attempts and the great rebel mastermind sends a boy."

He circled slowly, dark eyes looking me up and down. I stood proud, though I wanted to buckle, wanted to curl into a ball on the floor and scream until it was all undone. The risk had seemed so minimal, the sacrifice so glorious, but face to face with Emperor Kin, I knew it for madness. Fear shuddered through me as though the night was suddenly icy cold.

"The uniform is a good touch," he said when I didn't answer. "The wrong uniform, but it looks real. Killed one of my soldiers, did you?"

Darius had not moved from the stairs, did not move at all, though I silently begged for his help. This man who had just betrayed me was all I had.

"You are silent, I see," Kin went on. "If your friends were at all intelligent, they would have cut out your tongue before you came, because I can assure you we know how to make a man talk. A boy should pose little difficulty."

He took a step closer, seeming to own no fear. There was no fear left for him even had he needed it, because it was all inside me, sickening my stomach as I thought of all the ways they could hurt me until I told them everything. Until I betrayed Katashi.

"Tell me, how were you planning to have me leave this world?" Kin said, privy only to the outward signs of confidence I was desperately trying to maintain. He nodded, and one of his guards came forward, gripping my arms in search of concealed blades. I felt sure he must find the vials, but he just pointed to the weapons hanging from my belt. "It looks like he's just carrying these, Your Majesty."

"Planning to kill me with an imperial army blade. How poetic. The soldier emperor stabbed in the back by one of his loyal men. Not very elegant, but it makes a good story."

The guard took my belt and I did not try to stop him, though at the sight of the sword being carried away, I cursed myself for not having drawn it, for not having given them a reason to kill me. It would have been so much easier to die here.

Kin sighed. "Very well, then. Perhaps you will feel more like talking in the morning. A few hours to consider your situation might loosen your tongue. Take him away."

A rough grip closed around my arm, and I was thrust toward the stairs, the guards barely parting to let me through. They jeered at me. One spat in my face, but though inside I was screaming, I clenched my fists and walked on, lifting my head proudly as the spit ran down my cheek.

9. DARIUS

I told myself there had been no other way to stop Hana, but even as she was led away, I thought of a dozen things I could have said or done to turn her from her path. They might not have worked, but they might have, and I could now be cleaning up her mess rather than watching her life, and mine, hover on the edge of destruction.

Activity flowed around me. People spoke to me, and I must have given answers, for they went away again, satisfied, but the world felt disjointed like a nightmare. From every shadow, Malice laughed.

"Excellency. Excellency?"

A man touched my shoulder, the pressure pulling my attention. I turned, looking straight into the stern lines of General Ryoji's face. "Yes, General," I said, my steady voice belying the headache that crippled my thoughts.

"What happened?"

"We caught an assassin," I said. "Why? Where were you?"

"I was here for that! I want to know what happened before we arrived. I have upward of thirty men lying unconscious. Did you see what happened? If that boy is capable of witchcraft—"

Summoning my most derisive look, I said, "He would not have let himself be led away trembling, General."

"No, Your Excellency, but … what did you see?"

Around us, all was noise. Kin barked orders, servants bowed with placating croons of "Yes, Your Majesty" and "No, Your Majesty," and the imperial chancellor buzzed about like a lost fly. Pairs of Ryoji's guards trooped past, supporting unconscious comrades like a group of actors removing props at the end of a bad play.

"I could not sleep," I said. "And having work to finish, I was on my way to the archives. There is nothing more soporific than a late-night dose of dust, don't you think?"

"I wouldn't know."

"No, I suppose not. Reading is not your forte."

General Ryoji ignored this. "And you just happened across an assassin creeping up the stairs?"

"What else? I saw him. I shouted for the guards. And here you are milling around, making a great noise in the hope His Majesty will not notice your failure, a failure that led to a rebel boy being able to make it unchallenged into the very heart of the palace."

The general was not one to be so cowed. "And the unconscious guards?"

"I saw nothing. A slow poison, perhaps? Or something in the air, though you would be better off posing that question to our new guest," I said, praying to any god who might listen that he wouldn't. Hana had the Otako temper. Given the opportunity, she could see me executed. Her very existence was enough to take me down, although with my head throbbing fit to burst, perhaps beheading would be a pleasant end.

Kin stalked the floor, his crimson skirts caressing the sea of wet footprints. "Wake the council," he ordered, stopping the agitated chancellor in his tracks. "I want them gathered in ten minutes, even if you have to pull them out of each other's beds and drag them here by their night-robes."

He didn't look at me but moved on, his gaze searching the thinning audience. "Where's the chamberlain?"

No one answered.

"Someone find him. The council will need breakfast."

Emperor Kin strode away on the words, leaving the remaining servants flustered. Through the shuttered windows, a pale glow was beginning to light the rain-soaked sky. I had been awake all night waiting, a dozen times on the verge of retiring to bed, but Malice was not one for idle threats.

I turned back to find the general gone. When had he left? I felt like my mind was slipping away, seeping out through holes I could not plug.

Councillor Ahmet slithered up the steps, an embryonic slime just oozed from his mother's womb. "Laroth," he drawled. "You must allow me to send compliments to your man. Never have I seen a servant capable of turning a gentleman out at such an hour looking as though he never went to sleep at all."

"Haven't you heard, Councillor? Monsters require very little in the way of sleep. In fact, we are capable of going without it for weeks at a time."

"But your beauty sleep! Positively, I see a wrinkle forming between your brows. And those cuts, so disfiguring. Trouble with a new woman, Laroth?"

"Hardly, Councillor."

Still fretting around like a startled hare, the chancellor stopped and bowed to us, rather too low, but one could forgive him his nerves. He was a man of routine.

"Your Excellency, Councillor," he said. "His Majesty is awaiting the council."

"Then by all means let us go in."

I let Ahmet go ahead without me, needing just a few moments

of peace to calm my racing thoughts, though from experience, I knew nothing would help the pounding headache. That had to be slept away, though Malice had often eased them with a touch of his hand.

No, don't think about him, don't think about that.

When I reached the chamber, it was almost full. Kin knelt at the head of the long table, his face a picture of scorn. Morning air blew in around the edges of the shuttered windows, each gust chilly after the heavy rain and scented with damp grass.

I knelt at Kin's side, in the place where Kun had knelt, his lifeless body slumped onto the table. The thought made my headache worsen, like hands were pressing in upon my skull, trying to splinter bone.

Talk went on around me until half a dozen serving girls brought the breakfast Kin had ordered. A little army of teapots clinked as a tray slid onto the table. Another long tray slid in beside it, holding a dish of grilled fish, twelve individual bowls of rice, and pickled plums. It was not the breakfast most councillors were used to. Chiltaen bread and sweetmeats had become popular in Mei'lian over the last few years, but Kin would not have them at his table.

While the girls served, I watched. Kin waved away a bowl, taking only tea. It was so like him to order breakfast though he had no intention of eating it himself. A general has to be sensitive to such things, practical and organised.

"You stare," he said, having taken a sip of tea.

"I am marvelling at your composure, Majesty," I said.

"I am not in the least composed," he returned. "A boy. They send a boy to kill me." The others broke off their conversations to listen. "Why?" he went on. "Why would Katashi Otako send a boy? Does he think I will not torture a boy? Not kill a boy? Does he think I would make the same mistake twice?"

"Perhaps the boy has some hidden skill, Majesty," said Councillor Ren placatingly. "You yourself were once called the 'Boy General,' so perhaps it is best not to underestimate this assassin based on his age."

"Thank you for the reminder, Councillor," Kin said coldly.

"There must be something more to it," Governor Ohi agreed, leaning in to give his opinion, his teacup halted halfway to his lips. "The rebels have shown themselves to be very cunning. I feel sure Monarch must have had good reason for his choice."

Councillor Ahmet let out a little snort of air. "You think very highly of a rebel leader, Ohi. This boy might not have anything to do with them at all, have you not thought of that?"

A gentle tap sounded at the door, and the imperial chancellor entered, bowing. His face was white and his hands shook. Beckoned in, he knelt beside the emperor and whispered in his ear. Unable to hear the man's words, we all watched Kin's face. His scowl darkened, but only I was close enough to see his fist clench upon his knee beneath the table, buckling the stiff silk.

"Out," he said, the order delivered in an even tone. "All of you. And someone send for Father Kokoro."

The Imperial Council looked at one another, but Kin did not retract his order. Councillor Ahmet was the first to put down his cup and stand, instigating a chorus of clinking ceramic and a rustling of silk as the others followed his lead. One by one they bowed and left, muttering and whispering before they had even made it to the door. I was glad of the chance to escape and prepared to stand, but Kin touched my sleeve. "Stay a moment, Darius," he said, and despite the gentle touch and the use of my name, or perhaps because of them, I was sure he knew. Hana had already talked, already told her guards everything, and this was the end.

With my head throbbing, I sat down again and prepared for the axe to fall.

Kin waited until all the others had gone, leaving bowls of rice and fish in various states of messy incompleteness. In Councillor Ren's place, half a dozen grains of rice scattered the black lacquered table. It was easier to concentrate on such details than to imagine what was coming.

"They stole the Hian Crown."

I heard the words, but they didn't immediately penetrate my head. Kin kept talking. "They got in through an old cellar that connects to the waterway."

"They, Majesty?" I said, latching on to the detail for something to say.

"The guards say there were at least half a dozen, all in imperial uniforms. They killed one and followed the others, only to lose them in the tunnels."

"Do you mean the assassin was a decoy?"

"So it would seem."

The Hian Crown. Malice must have known, but he had played me too. I closed my eyes. "It was still in the strongbox? Were any of the other strongboxes robbed?"

"Worried for your jewels, Darius? Or is it fine robes you keep in there?"

"Both, Majesty," I said mildly, knowing it was always better to weather his ill humour than attempt to placate it.

"You know it's an unpardonable offence to dress better than the emperor."

I looked down at my robe and then at his. "Planning to have me executed?"

Anger and amusement sought possession of his face before he settled for pursing his lips. "Your impudence is your only redeeming feature, Darius."

"Not my intelligence?"

"To someone who needs it perhaps. You seem to forget I am the one who has kept this empire together."

"I don't forget, Majesty. You are a formidable opponent. Witness our current Errant game. It might yet go to you; the last nearly did."

"There is such a thing as too much impudence."

"Is there, Majesty?"

"I don't think you understand. Without the crown—"

"You aren't the true emperor," I said. "The gods gave the Hian Crown to the First Emperor of Kisia and blessed it for a year of moons, not to be renewed until that emperor once more sat upon the throne at Koi and took the Imperial Oath. A vow you are due to take in three weeks."

Kin looked annoyed, as though he would have preferred stupidity. "Katashi Otako with the Hian Crown," he said. "He has a claim to the throne, and now he has the crown. If we cannot get it back, there will be war. I swear to the gods I will squash this rebellion and I will mount every last one of their heads outside the city walls, starting with his."

"Send word to the city gates. No one leaves without having every sack and bag and pouch checked."

"Yes, and we must search the waterway in case they didn't make it out and it can still be recovered."

"And if a list of likely entrances can be put together, the city guards can go door to door. Anything we can find out could be helpful."

Kin knocked upon an invisible door. "Excuse me, sorry to bother you, but you haven't happened to see the emperor's gold crown around, have you?" He gave me a look. "That will go down well."

"That is not what I would instruct them to say."

He looked down at his tea, cooled enough now that no hint of steam rose from its glassy surface. "We all know the Vices have been working with the rebels this last season. Tell me honestly, Darius, how involved in this do you think they were? They proved the other night they could get inside this palace without being seen. Was it a warning, do you think?"

I ought to have known the question was coming, whatever lies I had already told General Ryoji. "It's hard to say, Majesty."

Kin let silence hang for a moment, perhaps waiting for me to elaborate. But without seeing more of the board, I could not guess what game Malice was playing. And no one knew him better than I did.

"I know it was difficult for you to tell me all you did," he said when I made no answer. "If I could let you put it all behind you, I would, but I need your help. I need to know what I am up against."

"If the Vices wanted to get in here and take something, anything, your guards would struggle to keep them out," I said. "They are capable of things most of your men have never seen let alone have the ability to fight." I stopped, and still staring at the cold tea, I let out a sigh. It seemed to only make my headache worse. "In truth, Majesty, I do not think they were involved in this. There are no signs of abnormal activity."

He sagged, relief clear as he let out his own sigh.

"However." I looked up at him, feeling wholly exposed like I had that night five years ago when I had spilled so many secrets, so much hurt. "Their leader is back, and he is up to something."

"Malice?"

The name sounded odd on his lips, and my heart raced as much from fear of it as from the fact that, after all these years, he remembered it.

"Yes."

"Do you know what he wants?"

"No."

"Do you think he has returned to support Katashi Otako?"

"Oh no." I laughed, though it sounded bitter and stretched.

"Malice doesn't give a damn about Katashi. Or the throne. Or anything very much. He just likes . . . manipulating people. He finds it amusing."

Kin's gaze searched every line of my face, but it was the hint of kindness in his expression that cut deepest. I could tell him. I could tell him everything right now, all about my father and Hana and the oath I had taken as a boy, but he had only taken me into his service on the understanding I had confessed everything. And as oversights went, failing to inform him that Lady Hana Otako was alive and living with farmers in the Valley was massive. Because it wasn't only a lie, it was a threat to his throne, and I had failed to warn him it existed—worse, had chosen not to.

"Councillor Ahmet has offered to talk to the assassin," Kin said, and I was grateful to him for asking no more questions. "And to take in that man of his. I've agreed. He has ways and means that get results. I need information and I need it now."

"I'll talk to the boy," I said.

"What?"

"By all means, let Ahmet have his fun, but let me talk to the boy first. My . . . methods of extraction don't kill weaklings before they can utter a single word."

For a long time, he stared at me, barely blinking. There were dark rings beneath his eyes and new lines upon his brow.

"Very well," he said at last. "Bring me back everything you can."

Taking that as my cue to leave, I stood, smoothing the front of my robe. "Yes, Majesty. No guards though, however much General Ryoji insists."

"Why?"

"Because an audience only makes it harder to persuade a man to talk. If you were being questioned with a dozen men watching, wouldn't you be thinking more about your honour than your skin?"

A nod. "Captain Hallan has had him moved to the Pit. You might want to change out of that robe before you go down there."

"And into what?"

"Something uglier and less expensive."

"Apologies, Majesty, but I own no such thing."

His lips twitched. "Impudent! Go on. You have until Ahmet's man arrives."

I bowed and made my escape, slipping out into the gallery. Father Kokoro was there, examining the painting of the great battle while he waited. "Ah, Minister," he said, making no sign he remembered our previous meeting. "You are always the first summoned in troubling times, are you not? I wish our beloved emperor would be as reliant upon the gods. He who neglects not his faith shall never grow old."

I opened my mouth to retort, but the old man went on. "Yes, your witty tongue would remark that I am old. It is, as you well know, a figure of speech."

"Isn't all religion?" I said, having a score to settle. "Metaphor and moral, dictated by man through the lips of gods?"

The look he gave me was full of amused understanding. "Your father was a cynic too," he said. "But he understood before the end."

"I doubt that fate awaits me, Father."

"Perhaps not, but you cannot keep this up indefinitely."

"Keep up what?"

Father Kokoro laid his hand upon my arm, leaning in close. "The lie you live and breathe," he whispered. "It will kill you more surely than the truth."

I stepped away. "You know nothing about it, old man."

"That is what your father said the first time. Remember, the gods are here for you. You will need them one day."

"If so, that will be a sorry day indeed," I said and strode away without another word, sure he was laughing at my back.

I'd never had reason to visit the Pit. In fact, it was high on my mental list of places I'd hoped never to visit, and certainly never as an occupant. The smell had a pungent, organic quality, the sort that made the hairs on the back of my neck stand up in protest. It grew more foul with each step I took down the dim stairwell. My guide seemed not to notice, though the fasteners on his armour were surely about to tarnish.

"What is that smell?" I asked.

"Just filth, Your Excellency," the guard said, not turning around lest he lose his footing on the steep stairs. "There's not much in the way of fresh air down here."

"Yes, but what else is that smell? The whole city stinks of filth in the summer."

His laugh reverberated around us. "Yes, but that isn't the filth of the condemned, destined to see no light until the day that brings the executioner."

"Don't you think it would be more cruel to execute happy people, Captain?"

"Pardon, Your Excellency?"

"It is just a thought. The people kept here are not happy, yes?"

"Would you be happy with no light, no food, and no one but your jailor to talk to, and he spits in your eye when you try?"

"How imaginative a place," I muttered. "No, I would not, and yet we then release them into the soft, warm embrace of death. It must be a relief, no?"

The captain froze on the step, and as he turned, I realised too late where those thoughts had come from. "I see what you mean, Minister. You're saying that if they were happier, death would be something to fear, not welcome. That hope should not be extinguished until the very last moment."

It was exactly what I had meant, but that the idea had come to me as naturally as breathing, with no thought of compassion or empathy, turned my stomach.

"I see you will make a very bad jailor one day, Captain," I said, laughing to make light of it, to disown the very idea. "Opening all the windows."

He gave me an odd look, and we did not speak again until the floor flattened out, dim light welcoming us into a damp stone room so cold it might have been the depths of winter. The guards all huddled under thick furs, their expressions sour, but the two jailors seemed to have developed thick leather skins that made them impervious to the temperature.

"Fur?"

The captain held out a fur cape, shrugging himself into another. Even at this distance, I could smell it, every fibre sucking in the dreadful stink of the place. If I put it on, I would never get the smell off my skin. I took it anyway, holding it away from my robe and trying not to breathe.

"Ah, welcome, Your Excellency," one of the jailors said, his leathery neck rumpled. "To what do we owe the pleasure, Minister?"

"He's here to see the rebel boy," the captain said. "Alone."

The man actually cackled, his eyes glowing in a manic way. "Nowhere can you get more alone than this. We're thirty feet underground here, in natural caverns. The river makes it cold and damp, but we do the rest." He sounded proud, as though bragging over the aptitude of a favourite child. "The boy's in there."

He indicated a rusty grate in the floor, the hole it covered no bigger than the opening of a well. The space below was black, like the end of the world dropping away beneath me. "Down there?"

"That's right." The jailor laughed. "I'll light the torches."

The man unlocked the grating, metal scraping across stone in a way that sent shivers through my skin. His companion handed him a torch. Lowered into the hole, it met the dry fuel of another torch, which burst into life, followed by another. The chain reaction ran all the way down, the line of fire lighting a ladder's thick rungs and a distant stone floor.

"He's all yours."

I looked into the hole. My oath to Hana had made no mention of climbing into a pit smeared with human excrement, yet here I was. I dropped the fur cloak into the hole and it fluttered out of sight like a ragged bird falling from its nest.

"Thank you, gentlemen," I said, setting my foot to the first slippery rung. "Don't let me keep you from your important work."

And down into the pit I descended, trying not to breathe in the awful smell. Overhead, the grating slid back into place, and I had to suppress a bolt of panic and assure myself that when Kin wanted to get rid of me, he would say so to my face.

Once I neared the ground, I dropped the last few feet to the bottom, my sandals sinking into the muck.

Hana sat huddled against the far wall, and snatching up the fur cloak, I made my way over.

"Good morning," I said.

"Are you really here?" she said, her words muffled by her sleeve. "Because if you are, I mean to claw your eyes out." She looked up then. Her face was stained with tears, but her jaw jutted proudly. "Malice said you were Kin's man. I should have believed him."

"Like you believed him about your birth papers?"

"You're both foul."

I dropped the cloak onto her legs. "Here."

She pushed it away. "I don't want it."

"This isn't the time to be stubborn."

"But it's a good time to be an ass?"

They had removed every vestige of her imperial armour, leaving just the thin linen tunic and hose they wore beneath, neither of which was good at holding warmth. "Just put it on, I know you're cold." I crouched down. "Hana, His Majesty is sending a councillor down here with a man well known for... making people talk. If you talk to me now instead, I might be able to stop them."

"And you'll take everything I tell you to Emperor Kin. No, Darius." She tightened her arms over her chest. "Whatever happens to me, I will not betray my cousin."

"Kin doesn't need to know everything, just enough to think he does. He thinks you were a decoy, not that you know anything about Katashi's plans, but if you can tell me where the crown is..."

She had set her jaw. "You really expect me to trust you?"

"No, but do you have another choice?"

"You've chosen the Usurper over me."

"I am as honour-bound to him as I am to you. Perhaps that is something you cannot understand."

She nodded sagely. "Oh yes, little Hana is very stupid. She never understands anything. I would ask you to explain, but I don't want a lecture." She threw the fur cloak back to me. "Don't worry. I won't tell this councillor of yours anything."

"You had better not. It's a short step from discovering you're a woman to finding out who you really are."

"And Kin wouldn't like that, would he? Does he know I'm alive? Did you tell him?"

I had no answer, just threw the cloak back at her. "Put it on."

"You didn't!" she crowed. "You didn't. You lied to him." Hana laughed. "I thought you were meant to be so very good at lying, but I see through you, Darius. You don't want me to talk to anyone else because you're trying to save yourself." She held out her arms. "Why don't you just kill me? That'll make it all nice and neat, tie up the loose ends."

"I took an oath to protect you."

"And how that must *burn* now. I'm not the biddable girl I used to be, I—"

"Not the biddable... Oh how I wish that were true." I leant close, teeth bared in anger. "You let Malice talk you into risking your life for nothing. Nothing! He knew you wouldn't make it. He knew he was sending you to your death, just to see what I would do about it. Anyone but a fool would have known he meant no good by you, but you drank it all in like a naive little girl desperate for attention, and now we're both fucked unless I can find a way out of this."

Hana's cheeks reddened, but she shoved me back so hard I landed on the slimy floor. "How dare you blame me for all this. You left me, Darius. You were my guardian and you left me."

I took a deep breath of foetid air and tried to remember the sweet girl who had once followed me everywhere, hanging on my every word. But she was right. I had left her. In running from my past, I had run from her too, leaving only Malice to take my place.

"I had to get away," I said. "I'd be dead if I hadn't."

She scoffed, and the disdainful sound hardened my anger.

"I don't care what you think of me, Hana. Your great cousin has brought the empire to the verge of civil war, and Kin's plan for your head and Katashi's has nothing to do with them remaining attached to your bodies. He will make sure Katashi Otako goes the same way as his father, who, in case you have forgotten, was executed for contriving the assassination of your father, your mother, and all your brothers. But if you help me, I can help you."

For a moment she was silent, her fingers writhing restlessly amid the fur covering her knees. "Katashi's father was innocent. There was never any proof."

"No, but he lost the war to Kin and his head to the executioner. That is proof enough for most people."

She threw the fur cloak back at me, its matted curls oily to the touch. "You should go."

"Councillor Ahmet's way of asking questions is a lot more physical than mine."

"I'm not afraid of dying, Darius."

"You're shaking."

Once more, she settled her arms over her chest. "It's cold."

There seemed little else I could say to change her mind, so I got to my feet, the hem of my robe damp against my ankles. "Don't die for an ideal, Hana," I said. "The real world is not a storybook. There is no justice, there is no truth, and the gods don't ensure people get what they deserve. The world is just a dirty mess of men willing to spill blood for power. Whatever Malice told you, no man will fight to put you on the throne because your father once sat on it. No one gives their life for nothing."

She said nothing, just lifted her chin, mulish and proud.

I sighed. "I'll do what I can for you, little lamb."

"It's cruel to give a prisoner hope."

I had said something very similar myself not so long since.

"Then I am a cruel man. Be strong, Hana."

10. ENDYMION

I woke to a sound like rain—a forceful splattering on canvas that slowed to a few lingering drops. The smell of piss invaded the close space, and I rolled over, wincing as my injuries made themselves known, followed by memories. The guardhouse. The cart. The men on their black horses. They had not talked much during the journey, but one by one, I had learnt most of their names. Ire, Conceit, Apostasy, Spite, Parsimony, Rancour, Enmity, Pride. I ought to have been more afraid to find myself with these Vices the whole empire seemed to fear, but Hope had smiled and told me everything would be all right, and while in his orbit, I had believed him.

I tested my limbs. They felt bruised and battered, my joints stiff, and the brands as hot as they had been when fresh. I wanted nothing more than to curl up, but the gathering consciousness of the waking camp was like a continual tapping on my attention. I needed to move.

It had been so late when we had arrived the previous night that I had seen nothing but dying fires and the shadowy forms of tents, which made crawling out into the sunlight like entering another world. A light mist clung to the morning, giving the fens a ghostly look. It dulled colours and dampened the air, and the men up and about moved listlessly as though it dulled spirits as well. The tent I had occupied was one of two dozen black tents in a semicircle around an empty space, while the rest of the tents were a disorganised collection. A sea of them spread away through the fens, occupying every piece of high ground, some big, some small, some fine, some frayed beyond uselessness.

Despite the wakefulness of the camp, the only sound came from a group gathered at a central fire. The smell of food made my mouth water.

"I wouldn't go over there if I were you."

Ire was leaning against a large cottonwood tree, eating a collection of berries he cradled to his chest like a child.

I didn't answer, couldn't, but between mouthfuls, he went on. "This little bit of the camp is our camp, the rest of it is their camp. The only thing Pikes hate more than imperial soldiers is us." He put another berry into his mouth and squashed it. "They're rebels from the north, if you don't know. I hope you're not keen on Emperor Kin. He's not well liked around here."

He ate a few more berries, their juice staining his fingers. "You really don't talk, huh? I thought maybe you were just scared of us."

They had a frightening reputation, but there was nothing sinister about the man leaning there eating his berries. He was dressed all in black this morning, yet his face might have belonged to a kind farmer, a little weatherworn from hard work but with a broad, easy smile.

"We're really not that bad. Most of us. Steer clear of Conceit, perhaps, and maybe Rancour, but for the most part, we only give trouble when we get trouble."

A shout echoed through the swamp. The chatter around the cooking fire died. Spoons froze halfway to lips as out in the mist, enormous trees shivered in the morning breeze. Ire went on eating his berries.

He still didn't move when another unintelligible shout sent Pikes lunging for their weapons. Swords were drawn, arrows nocked—the whole camp seeming to pound to the beat of a single frenzied heart—but he stayed leaning against the tree.

Splashing steps heralded a man emerging from the mist, a Pike, wet to his waist. He nearly tripped as his feet found solid ground.

"What's going on?" someone called as the man bent over, trying to catch his breath. His chest was heaving, but his face split in a grin as he straightened.

"Captain Monarch is coming!"

The sense of relief was so profound, I found myself grinning. The Pikes cheered.

"Oh good," Ire drawled. "The Great Fish is back. His Pikes are much better behaved when he's around."

More men appeared through the trees, black-clad and filthy, scabbed cuts and bandaged wounds apparent on every one. They strode through the mire like men who no longer cared how wet they got, kicking up mud and stinking water with every step. Though they were greeted with enthusiasm, they let off a morose air. Some disappeared toward nests of tents, while others made straight for the fire and the pot of porridge sitting in the coals.

Another shout came through the mist. "Wen is injured!"

"Wen is injured!"

"Wake the old bones!"

A young Pike scurried away, carrying the message through the camp while two men struggled out of the swamp with a third held awkwardly between them. Dry blood stained their ashen faces, and their burden's head lolled onto his chest. Pikes ran to help. They gathered around and more men went running, calling for linen and wine.

Another man came through the mist, his long stride bringing him easily out of the mire. He stood taller than them all, the long-bow upon his back making him more imposing still.

"That's Captain Monarch," Ire said, wiping his stained hands on his black tunic while a few more Vices, perhaps attracted by the commotion, poked their heads out of their tents. "He's the reason they're all here."

"You mean he's the reason they aren't still six different bands of rebels who fight each other as much as the emperor," one of the newly woken Vices said—Pride, if memory served. He certainly felt proud, despite the messy shag of hair and the tunic that sat askew. "Without him, the northern lords would have just fought over who should sit on the throne if they ever managed to get rid of Kin."

I must have looked enough like a confused puppy, because Ire said, "He's Katashi Otako. Only son of Tianto Otako, Emperor Lan's younger brother. He thinks the Crimson Throne should be his."

Katashi Otako. I had heard the name during lessons in Kisian history but had never imagined he was a living, breathing man. Son of the traitor who had assassinated his brother and all his family.

"It probably should be his," Pride said. "Otako name and all that."

"You really care?" Spite this time, appearing from his own tent, his fair hair sticking up on one side. "Like it makes a difference to us."

Pride shrugged.

Pikes had gathered around their returning captain, but the relief in the air was corrupting into anger. Katashi Otako looked our way. Heads turned toward us. Someone pointed.

"He's looking for the Master," Spite said with a heavy sigh. "Well he's just going to have to wait, cos he ain't here."

"Do you think they got the crown?" Pride said while the Pike captain shouted a stream of short, sharp orders.

"Don't fucking care. The sooner we finish with this job the better."

Ire had his head on the side, watching the Pikes. "He seems pretty pissed off. Maybe they didn't."

I could have described the worry eating away at the Pikes, could have told them Katashi was angry because he was afraid of something, because something had gone wrong, but without words, I could not. All I could do was watch as Pikes ran in every direction, rushing to fulfil the man's wishes. A bundle of clothes was thrust into his hands, followed by food. Then he strode away into the fen alone without a backward look.

"Ha!" Pride said. "That settles it. He only ever sulks off with his bow when he's annoyed."

I wanted to ask who the Master was and what crown they meant, but the three Vices spent a few minutes reluctantly admitting Katashi Otako was good with his bow before wandering away. Despite the fact that a perfectly good cooking fire had been established over in the Pike side of the camp, the Vices built their own and set about cooking their own food. Most of them ignored me or just stared at me without speaking, only Ire occasionally stopping by to see how I was. On one of these occasions, he examined my brands and called for Hope to look at them.

The youngest of the Vices had been sitting on his own reading, but when Ire called, he set the book face down on a log and came over. "These wounds aren't looking too great," the big man said. "The Master won't be happy if his prize gets sick, eh?"

"I'll look at them," Hope returned in his soft voice. "Just let me get my bag."

He was gone with nothing but a constrained smile and a lingering scent of melancholy, the same smell he brought back with him as though it were a perfume. "Sit here," he said, pointing at a patch of mostly dry ground beside a log. "Then I can sit behind you and see better."

I settled myself on the ground, and with a knee either side of my shoulders, Hope sat on the log behind me as though he were going to trim my hair. "Still not talking, I see," he said, unwittingly repeating Ire's earlier sentiments. "I'm afraid I'm not much of a healer, but I did study with a master for a time before...before coming here."

He touched the brand on my head and I hissed. Or tried to. No sound came out.

"This one is looking red around the edges. It happens a lot with wounds, but you're lucky it's not a deep one. I'll make you up something to put on it, but more than anything, you need to rest. Let me see the one on your cheek now."

I turned my head so he could examine my cheek, followed by my arm. Neither was as bad as the one on my scalp, he said, but all needed tending. "I'll put some of Parsimony's nettle wine on them first, then make a dressing for them. Then you should rest. The Master could be a while, and until he arrives, we just wait."

The wine stung, the dressing stank, and no matter how tired I was, I could get no rest while a camp full of worried souls spilled their doubts upon me. Short dozes were all I could manage curled up in the black tent while the Vices went about their desultory tasks around me.

From one such doze, the sound of cart wheels roused me. They ground upon the dirt, mingling with the creaking of wood and the stamping of hooves—the whole a symphony that was so reminiscent of Jian's wagon, I thought for a moment I would be back there when I opened my eyes. But I was still in the tent, and where Jian was, or if he was even still alive, I did not know.

I curled into a tighter ball beneath the blanket.

"Endymion?" Hope's melancholy intruded before his head appeared between the tent flaps. "The Master wants to see you."

Stepping back, he held the tent open for me, and still aching all over, I once more crawled into the sunlight. The clearing of churned earth around which all the black tents stood now owned a wagon. Not a shabby, chipped thing like Jian's but a brightly coloured wagon hung with at least half a dozen unlit lanterns. Its painted panels were the most colourful things in the whole camp, at odds with the black upon black that seemed to be the Vices' uniform.

A pair of steps at the back were let down, and while the rest of the Vices stopped what they were doing to watch, Hope gestured for me to enter before him.

The inside of the wagon was lantern-lit and cluttered. Thick carpets of crimson and dark blue covered the wooden floor, while curtains of the same colour hung over every window. A pair of rolled sleeping mats leant drunkenly against one another in the corner, half a dozen travelling chests lined one side, and on one wall hung a knot of coloured sashes, one in priest's white, one in yellow, black, green, and purple. It wasn't easy to have sashes made outside your station, especially the very expensive purple of the nobleman, but this man had one. He also had a low table with an Errant board on it, the pieces dotted across its field. I had never taken much interest in the game, but Jian had always called it the game of great men.

The man they called Master sat cross-legged at the table. He tilted his head a little to the side, fine, noble features faintly smiling.

Hope bowed in the doorway. "Master," he said. "We have brought the boy, but he does not speak."

The man curled the tip of a long black ponytail around his finger, the hair tied back with what looked to be a string of finger bones. "Does not speak?" he said. "That is very interesting, yes? Not a word?"

"Not since we found him, Master."

"I see. Do come in, Endymion. Have a seat. You too, Hope. There is wine. It is not the best, but one must make do when one is travelling, yes?"

"Master, if I may," Hope began. "The horses—"

"Avarice will see to the horses. Sit down."

Hope bent at the knees so fast I was sure I heard them snap. There was fear there, fear of this placid man, but also gratitude, loyalty, and anger, the mixture so complicated I could feel nothing at all from the man he called Master.

Shifting an Errant piece on the board, the man said, "Like you, I have another name, but you may call me Malice." He looked me over as he spoke, examining every one of my features in turn. Whether what he saw satisfied him I could not tell, but when I made no answer, he reached across the table. "Give me your hand, Endymion."

Unsure if he knew what I was, I lifted my right hand. Malice shook his head. "That is not the hand I meant. Your left hand, yes?"

I pushed my Empathy out toward him but felt nothing. The man smiled, waiting. I looked at his hand. Every time I had touched skin since the guardhouse, connection had come unbidden. I couldn't control it and did not want to feel it again.

"Your hand."

I held it out, flinching as Malice took it in a tight grip.

Nothing happened. There was no connection, no whispers in my head, nothing at all. I let him turn my hand over and push back the sleeve, revealing my stained silk wristband.

"That is a sad sight to see," he said. "Are you so ashamed of what is under there? Hope, there is a pair of scissors in the box. Bring them, yes?"

"Yes, Master."

I couldn't meet Malice's gaze and stared instead at our joined hands, the colour of our skin so alike we might have been the continuation of one another.

When Hope returned, he proffered the scissors, but Malice shook his head. "Cut it."

The Vice did so, sliding cold metal under the silk. With a snip, the band fell away, curling up on the table.

"Little did I think to see that mark again," Malice said. "Did you show this to Minister Laroth?"

My other hand tightened to a fist in my lap.

"Angry? Let me assure you that you are not the only one angry with him, yes? I wish you could tell me what he said to you." He sighed. "The silence is normal. It won't last forever, though it passes sooner for some than for others. I should know." He drew back his own sleeve, placing his left hand palm up on the table. The man who called himself Malice wore no band. He bore his birthmark with pride. Three horizontal lines crossed by a diagonal.

I had travelled all my life. I had met hundreds, even thousands of people, from beggars to lords, but never had I thought to find another just like me. Another Empath.

"They designed the Traitor's Mark for us a long time ago, but they have since forgotten why." Malice pulled his hand away, letting his sleeve fall. "They have forgotten that—"

Footsteps stomped up the wooden stairs, and amid a flurry of angry shouts, the door burst open. Katashi Otako filled the doorway, exuding a fury that expanded out from him like a poisonous cloud. It choked my veins, and I closed both hands into tight, angry fists.

"Vice," the rebel captain snarled. "You've been playing games with me."

Malice's fine brows went up. "Games? Oh no. I don't play games, I win games."

"My men tell me Captain Regent joined them infiltrating the palace, and after the alarm went up, neither *she* nor Shin walked out."

"Then they are probably dead."

Katashi's fear bit at my skin as though owning teeth, but it was anger he displayed, slamming his hands upon the low table and snarling in Malice's face. "I don't give a damn what happened to the girl you were trying to mock me with, but if Shin is dead because of some stupid game of yours, then I will rip your fingers off and feed them to you."

The Vice Master held up his hands, fingers splayed as he laughed. "Oh, that's a new one, yes? What do you want me to say? I have no idea what happened to your man, but the fate of my girl I am quite curious about."

Katashi straightened up, his contempt oozing. "What did you send her in there to do? All my Pikes nearly died on that mission. That we lost only one in the waterway is a miracle."

"I sent her to get her birth papers because I thought she might like them. And because she would almost certainly get caught, forcing my dear Darius to make a choice between the Usurper and Usurped, yes?"

"What?"

Malice sighed. "Dear Katashi, this would be far more entertaining if you had a little imagination. Although I suppose a wiser man wouldn't have been so blind for so long and would have discovered my ruse weeks ago."

Again, Katashi leant down onto the table, causing the wood to creak. "What are you talking about, freak? What ruse?"

"Regent. My girl, as you call her. I did not make her my captain to mock you with her lack of cock, but because she has a better claim to the throne than you do."

The rebel captain stiffened. "Better claim to the throne? Everyone with a better claim to the throne than me is dead."

"Oh dear, wherever did you get such a foolish idea?"

Katashi gripped the front of Malice's robe and yanked him forward, spilling Errant pieces onto the floor. "Are you saying," he hissed right into the Vice's face, "that Lady Hana Otako is alive? And that you kept this information from me?"

"You never asked, yes?"

His grip on Malice's robe tightened, whitening his knuckles. "You knew who she was, and you let her parade around as a man leading your freaks, you put her in danger every day, you... *sent* her into the palace to get caught by Kin's guards? *Lady Hana Otako*, Uncle Lan's only daughter... you... you..."

He drew back his fist aimed for Malice's face, but as calmly as if he had been swatting a fly, the Vice Master lifted his hand. It ought to have made no difference given the strength behind the punch, but the moment Katashi's fist met Malice's skin, the rebel yanked his arm back with a yowl of pain. He gripped it in his other hand and staggered a few steps, hissing.

"I don't like being punched, yes?" Malice said, calmly adjusting his position on the cushion as though nothing had happened.

Still holding his closed fist, Katashi spat on the floor. "That's all I care for what you like. Why didn't you tell me who she was? Why didn't she tell me? She must have known I was her cousin!"

"She didn't tell you because I warned her not to. Don't forget, Katashi dear, your father had hers assassinated. How could she be sure you would not do the same to her to get the throne you so dearly want?"

"He didn't! Those were just the lies Kin used to bring him down! Father and Uncle Lan argued all the time, but he would never have killed him, let alone his whole family."

"Almost his whole family."

Katashi ran his hands over his face. "Of course I had heard the rumours she survived, but...people just like their stories. She was only a baby, I never thought it could be true."

"Lord Nyraek Laroth saved her, had her raised by good farming folk in the Valley where Kin would never think of looking for her."

"Until you threw her at him." Katashi dropped his hands, his rage renewed. "Do you realise what you've done?" His hands clenched and unclenched as though he very much wished to close them around the Vice Master's throat. "When he realises who she is, she's dead. You think *I* would have killed her? Kin will rip her to tiny pieces rather than let such a threat survive."

Malice shrugged. "Only if Darius lets him. Either way, I will get what I want."

"You should have told me!" Katashi exploded again. "Just think about what we could have achieved together...you...you..." He paced back and forth the short distance from wall to wall. "By the gods, I should kill you and all your men for such a betrayal, I should—"

"No, no," Malice interrupted, wagging a long finger as though the man had been a recalcitrant child. "Don't forget, there is still Koi. If you want to get inside the castle, you need me, yes? And with Hana in Kin's hands, surely the need to get inside is...all the greater."

For the first time, Katashi looked down, his gaze sweeping over Hope to land on me. "Is that what this new freak is for?"

"Oh no, Endymion is my guest."

"Is he a secret Otako too, then?" Katashi jeered and, daring to lean forward, said, "Don't fuck with me again, Vice. Your meddling could already have ruined everything. You get me into Koi and then you're gone. If I see your face again after I take my oath, I'll fill it full of arrows."

A lingering sneer for Hope and he was gone, stomping down the stairs, carrying his rage with him like a cloak.

"Hope," Malice said, smiling after the retreating figure of the rebel captain. "Be sure to look after Endymion well, yes?"

11. HANA

I had been born in this palace. Now I was going to die here, in a cold, wretched hole far from my father's throne. Darius had taken with him both the fur cloak and my last hope of getting out of here. It had been easy to be courageous with him fuelling my anger, but the moment he left me, fear had returned with the darkness.

My stomach rumbled. Despite the foul stench all around me, I could almost imagine the smell of the millet porridge the Pikes made every morning, imagine squashing the grains between my teeth and searching for a single black bean to save for the last spoonful. Katashi had hated the stuff. Perhaps because there had been a time when any food had been his for the asking, when his name had meant something.

I closed my eyes and he was there in my mind, standing close to me, the touch of his breath on my skin and his hand on my cheek. But no matter how hard I tried to imagine the kiss that had never come, the invasive cold always shattered my fantasy. The reality of my situation was too grim, too terrible, to allow escape.

There was always the Tishwa. The guards had been too cock-sure, too disdainful of this *boy* to do more than strip off my armour and throw me in a pit. It had been the work of a moment afterward to check the seals were tight and push first one vial and then the next into the space between my legs, just in case they ever decided on a more thorough search.

When Darius had left upon his tide of dire warnings, I had considered drinking one to free myself from the coming hell, but I was not ready to die.

The grate ground open overhead and new torches flared. In the light, a figure descended the tall ladder, followed by another—more visitors to my little slice of hell. The first halted at the bottom, peering into the darkness as Darius had done. With him lit from behind, I could see no face, but the swish of a skirt made his noble robe apparent. The councillor Darius had warned would come to break me.

I fingered the needle still caught in my sleeve as the councillor came across the floor. His companion joined him, a plainly dressed man with thick armour covering his chest but nowhere else. What I had taken at first for close-cropped hair became a leather cap as he drew near.

"Hello, hello," the councillor said, his singsong voice echoing. "What a way to end so young a life. Stuck in the Pit, the last home of so many would-be rebels and assassins."

I said nothing, just watched his face emerge from the darkness. He was much older than Darius, and where Darius was obscenely beautiful, this man's features had a slightly crumpled look as though he was beginning to dry out.

"Not feeling very chatty?" he said. "Perhaps if I introduce myself. My name is Councillor Ahmet, and this fine young man"—the other man leered—"is Praetor. As I understand it, the closest thing he has to a virtue is his skill with a knife."

When I said nothing, the councillor sighed theatrically. "Very well," he said. "Praetor?"

"Yes, Councillor?" The man grinned through patchy whiskers.

"Check he still has his tongue."

Praetor stepped forward. Every instinct screamed at me to run, but I couldn't let them get to me, couldn't let them win. I clamped my teeth shut and proudly lifted my chin. The man crouched in front of me, his grin showing even teeth ground flat. He gripped my chin, and pain burst through my skull as he smacked my head into the wall. While lightning flashed before my eyes, Praetor's callused fingers prised apart my lips and pinched my tongue. His fingers tasted tinny, covered in dirt from gods knew where.

"It seems you are capable of talking," the councillor said as Praetor let go. "So let me explain how this is going to work. I want information and you are going to give it to me, or Praetor here will slowly slice the flesh from your bones. We will keep you alive for however long this takes, but because I am a kind man, I will give you the chance to avoid excruciating agony and tell me what I want to know now.

"Where is the Hian Crown?"

"I don't know," I said, deciding that giving a bad answer would keep me in one piece longer than giving none. "How should I? I'm stuck down here."

"Oh, a clever one. Very well, where is Monarch?"

"I don't know that either. He moves around, you know, on legs."

The councillor nodded. Praetor gripped the neck of my tunic, ripping it along the shoulder seam. The loose fabric dangled like a flap of skin. I felt sick. This thin layer of cloth was all that stood between me and debilitating womanhood.

"Let's try again," the councillor said. "We wouldn't want to spoil that pretty face for nothing. Who is Monarch? He has another name?"

"I don't know," I said. "How about Emperor?"

He nodded, and Praetor yanked on the torn fabric. My tunic ripped all the way down. Freezing air caressed my stomach.

"I'll ask you one more question," the councillor said. "Before we start them over again. What is Monarch planning?"

"I don't know."

The councillor smiled and nodded. This time as Praetor's fingers took hold of cloth, they slid beneath my bind. The fabric was strong and did not tear when he ripped, but the laces loosened. The bind slipped. My breasts ached at the sudden release of pressure, and I covered them with my hands. Shame and embarrassment washed over me, followed hard by anger. How weak it made me to have these lumps of flesh on my chest, how vulnerable. So many things I couldn't do, couldn't be, all because I had the body of a woman instead of a man. I couldn't even be safe.

Praetor stared, first at my chest and then at his fingers, as though they had performed a feat of magic. The councillor's smile widened. "A girl," he crowed. "Our decoy assassin is nothing but a girl. That is a joke our beloved emperor is unlikely to appreciate." He nodded, a sharp little movement I was fast coming to hate. Praetor's fingers closed around my wrists, prising them from my chest.

"Perhaps we could try this again," the councillor said. "Where is the Hian Crown?"

"I don't know!"

Stale breath blew into my face. The man was still grinning.

"Where is the Hian Crown?"

I stopped fighting. Praetor lifted my hands away from my body, and in the instant he stood appreciating the sight, I slammed my foot into his shin. Ripping from his slackened hold, I scrambled across the damp floor, palms slipping.

A hand gripped my hair, yanking me back.

"Where is Monarch?" The councillor enunciated every word slowly and clearly right by my face while I struggled to be free.

My sight blurred; Praetor's grip tightened until I thought my scalp would tear away, leaving nothing but a cap of bone. I screamed, clawing at his hands.

"Where is Monarch?"

I could barely hear the words, but backlit by the distant torches, the councillor nodded. Terror fuelled, I wrenched free. Hair ripped from my scalp, and I hit the floor stunned, that second of confusion all Praetor needed to dig his knee into my back and pin me down. Wet, foul refuse mushed against my cheek. I gagged at the stench.

"What is Monarch planning?"

A pause, then would come the little nod that creased the wrinkles in the councillor's neck. A hand grasped my waistband, hot despite the frigid air. Panicking, I tried to buck Praetor off, but he slammed me back so hard my hipbone ground against the stones.

"Who is Monarch?" The councillor's voice was strained and breathless.

Monarch. *If he were here now, he would gut you both*, I thought, the bloody imagining renewing my strength. I bucked again, but Praetor was so heavy I barely shifted him.

His hard prick touched my leg and all sense abandoned me. I screamed, bucking and twisting, trying in vain to wrench out of his grip. This was really going to happen. Would the vials break when he rammed his flesh into mine? I hoped they would, hoped the poison would work from inside and set me free. I had no other weapon left.

Except Mama Orde's needle. *"A woman should always be prepared,"* she had said, though at the time, I had not understood why.

I began to work it free of my sleeve.

No more questions came, just the sound of the councillor's fevered breath huffing in the air. I wanted to hurt him. I wanted to hurt them both, but I would only get one chance.

Praetor shifted his weight. He tugged at my breeches and I waited, lying limp, hating my vulnerability as he pressed me into the floor.

His hot skin touched my leg. He parted my thighs. I let out a feigned sob, whitening fingers pinched upon the needle. Praetor gripped my hips. He dragged me back, hot hands pressing my legs farther apart. *Breathe. Wait. You'll only get one chance.* His prick slid up my thigh. I could not wait, could not turn, just thrust the needle into flesh.

Praetor howled. He leapt up, the moment of freedom all I had hoped for. I scrambled to my feet, tugging up my breeches. I had no thought but to get away, no thought but to run, and I slammed full force into the councillor. He gripped my hair and wrenched my head back hard. "I love a spirited woman," he said, running a tongue over his dry lips. "All the more fun to break. Do you really think you can get away? Do you think someone is going to save you? Your rebel dogs have abandoned you."

He didn't care for questions anymore. He was breathing fast, the air hissing out of his nose as he clamped his lips shut. "Kneel," he said.

When I didn't, he tightened his grip.

"I said kneel."

Again I saw that terrible little nod, and Praetor kicked the back of my knees. I hit the stones, blinking back tears.

"It's time you begged for mercy," the councillor said, untying his sash, its end trailing onto the soiled floor.

"If you dare, I'll bite off your cock and spit it in your face."

He let go my hair and struck me. I fell back, touching my stinging cheek with soiled fingers. My whole body ached. I wanted to fight back. I wanted to rip his skin from his flesh and his eyes from their sockets, but I couldn't move. All I could do was hate my womanhood all the more. They could beat me and have their way, and I was powerless to stop them. No revenge would satisfy. There was no equivalent suffering I could ever force them to endure.

The councillor crouched and gripped my chin between his fingers, squeezing so tight I thought my jaw would snap. My mouth was too dry to even spit at him. "You are going to die. Don't you want me to make a woman of you first?"

"Don't I need a man for that?"

His grip tightened. "Before I'm done with you, you're going to wish you hadn't said that."

"Councillor!"

The councillor's head snapped around. "What?"

Scraping steps sounded on the ladder, and another dark figure entered my pit, the firelight burning around him like an aura.

"I bring a message from His Majesty," the man said, coming across the floor. "He demands you bring the prisoner to him immediately. *Unharmed.*"

The emphasis upon the last word made me want to laugh, whatever terrible reason there might be for the emperor's change of heart. I pulled away from the councillor's suddenly slackened grip. "You had better do as Kin tells you," I said, holding up my breeches and hugging the remains of my tunic to my chest.

"Don't you dare utter the emperor's name." The councillor pulled back his hand to hit me again, but the newcomer caught his wrist.

"Let go or I'll have you whipped," Councillor Ahmet hissed.

"I am merely acting on the emperor's orders, Councillor. He said unharmed. He also said now."

"I am ready," I said, stepping forward.

A frown flickered across the newcomer's face—a handsome face by what I could see, though he examined my dishevelled appearance for longer than was required to ascertain the facts. Then with a little bow of his head, the man gestured for me to go before him, and I strode across the slippery floor with as much pride as I could muster. I hoped they might lock the councillor and his man in the Pit behind us, but whatever happened to Praetor, the councillor at least followed us up the ladder.

A contingent of guards met us at the top. They stared at me, and lifting my chin, I tried to appear unconscious of their searching gazes. Had I been a naked man, they would have respectfully looked away, but the mere ownership of femininity was permission to stare.

"What has occurred to cause so sudden a summons, General?" the councillor asked, quickening his pace to walk beside my saviour as the rest of the guards fell in behind.

"You will have to ask him that yourself, Councillor," the general returned, his disapproval patent. "I am not in His Majesty's confidence."

General? He had looked too young for such a rank, but the air of authority that hung about him made it hard to tell.

Staring and whispering had accompanied my journey to the Pit, but now the palace was empty. Silent. I hugged my torn clothes closer. I had been too relieved at first to question the motive for my release, but now every step was touched with trepidation. Had I Darius to thank? Or did Kin just wish to see me suffer in person?

Shin and I had cut through the rain-washed gardens the night before, but now I was marched along the colonnade from the outer palace to the inner, its stone floor flayed with sunlight. Everything looked different in the daylight, the garden bright and all the lanterns unlit. No rain either, but the inner palace was as dead as it had been before, nothing but the echo of our steps cutting the silence. Flight after flight of stairs with apprehension churning my stomach, until at last a pair of enormous black doors blocked our way. Engraved with a thousand lines of Old Kisian, the pattern was so fine it seemed to shift before my eyes.

The Crimson Throne.

I had long dreamed of the moment I would set eyes upon my birthright, but in no dream had I been a prisoner, a captive rebel in my own empire.

A man stood waiting. He exchanged nods with the general before pushing open the doors. Discoloured light spilled onto my filth-smeared feet. Windows of red glass lent the room a crimson hue, stained the hangings, the guards, the pair of carved dragons, and even the air itself. Only the black wooden floor survived its taint—a road to follow now to whatever end.

I stepped forward. The throne stood upon a dais at the far end of the hall, a grand construction of lacquered wood rising in half-moon curls toward the roof. It had once belonged to my father, but I had no memory of him sitting upon it, no memory of him at all. Kin sat upon it now, his long red and gold robes melding into the lacquer as though they had long since become one.

Halfway to the throne, the general and the councillor knelt to bow. I hung back, the group of guards stopping behind me. Still more stood around the walls, their expressions impassive.

"Rise," the emperor said, and as both the general and the councillor got to their feet, Darius came slowly across the floor.

"Your surcoat, General," he said, holding out his hand.

"Excellency?"

"Your surcoat," Darius repeated. "Give it to me."

After a slight hesitation, the general slid the crimson surcoat from his shoulders and hung it over Darius's hand.

Darius uttered no thanks, but holding it as though it smelt bad, he draped it over my shoulders. The silk was warm and soft, smelling of leather; its large panels overlapped across my narrow chest.

Darius stepped back, and glancing at the councillor through half-lidded eyes, he said, "I think the only daughter of Emperor Lan Otako deserves not to be so humiliated, don't you, Councillor?"

The air thinned to a wisp and I could barely breathe. All my life, Darius had warned me not to tell, that to utter my name would be a death sentence. Even in the Pit, he had warned me not to tell the councillor whatever the provocation, had snarled at me for the position I had put him in, and yet here he stood before the Usurper, announcing my identity to the world.

Emperor Kin sat forward, his eyes devouring me. I gripped the surcoat tighter and stared back, more aware than ever of the filth crusting my cheek.

"What?" the councillor barked, finding his voice at last. "What did you say, Laroth?"

"I take it you've now also met Lady Hana Otako, Councillor," Darius said, indicating me. "I hope you treated her with the respect her birth deserves."

Councillor Ahmet stepped forward. "Are you mad, Laroth?" he demanded. "This is a rebel assassin. A girl, as we have discovered, yes, but no lady of imperial blood."

Knowing how I looked, I could almost believe him.

"But I assure you she is, Councillor. She told me so when I questioned her earlier, so while you were busy with your own enquiries, I did some research."

"Told you? A condemned prisoner would say anything to be set free."

"True, but without the trappings of the imperial soldier, there is something... remarkably familiar about her," Darius said, not at all perturbed. "Surely you saw it too. Bring in the portrait."

Movement against the wall soon coalesced into a pair of men carrying a large portrait, its wooden scrolls wired open. The paper had begun to crack a little around the edges, but the paint had been kept away from the sun, leaving the woman staring down at me looking almost as she must have done the day she was painted. A head of glorious golden curls framing a face I had seen every time I looked into the mirror. Only her eyes were different, brighter, as though she could see through time and into my soul.

"Mama," I whispered, my heart aching for this woman I had never known, who had been taken from me before I could even walk.

The councillor stalked toward me and peered into my face. I leant back, blinking away tears. "Her hair is the right colour, I grant you, but that is all. Besides, Princess Hana is buried in the imperial graveyard with her mother."

"Ah, you have not allowed me to finish, Councillor," Darius said. "No doubt you have heard the rumour that not all the Otako graves contain bodies. Rumours often own some degree of truth, as the grave keeper informed me this very day after sifting through the old records. I assume he would forward you the same information should you ask him."

Kin sat silent, no more a part of the proceedings than if he had been watching a play. His gaze leapt from me to the portrait and back without so much as a frown.

"Portraits and empty graves?" Councillor Ahmet spread his hands. "On the basis of this, any Chiltaen brat could claim the name."

"Enough."

The word shocked through the hall, and all eyes turned to Emperor Kin. "Perhaps," he said, his words very calm, "the best course of action would be to ask her." His sharp eyes turned to me. "Tell us, are you Lady Hana Otako?"

I shrank beneath the collective gaze, the general's surcoat my only protection. A long time ago, my name would have been all the protection I needed, but it was a poison chalice now. Still, if I was going to die, I would do so owning the truth.

A breath of hesitation was all I allowed myself before I drew myself up and stepped forward. "Yes," I said. "My name is Hana Aura Otako, princess of Kisia. My father was Emperor Lan Otako, my mother Empress Li. I had four brothers—Prince Yarri, Prince Tanaka, Prince Rikk, and Prince Takehiko Otako. My uncle was executed, my cousins exiled, and here I stand, ready for you to kill me too."

No one spoke. At any moment, the blow would fall. Kin would

order my immediate execution, and no one would dare argue. No one beyond this room would even know.

"Chancellor," Kin said, his low voice breaking the fragile silence. "Have a room prepared for Lady Hana and be sure she has everything she desires. Send for Master Kenji to attend her wounds." He jerked his head toward the divan at his side. "Darius, we need to talk."

Darius. The way he spoke to him was so informal.

A firm hand took my arm, but I could not drag my eyes from the scene. This man had once been my guardian, and now he went to Kin as though they were the best and oldest of friends.

Malice had been right about one thing at least, and now Darius had betrayed me again rather than risk the loss of his position.

"This way, my lady."

Giving in to the insistence of the hand, I allowed myself to be guided from the room. I walked, but I could barely feel my feet moving, could barely see the palace through my numb haze. All I could think of was that portrait. When it was painted, had my mother known someone was coming for her life?

12. DARIUS

I had climbed onto a knife-edge and now could feel the blade slicing deep into the soles of my feet. I had as good as laid my head on the executioner's block for her, and Ahmet would do anything to see it stay there.

It was plain the councillor was struggling. He wanted to argue, but Kin had acknowledged Hana and there was no going back. It had not been difficult. Her resemblance to her mother was remarkable.

"Are you sure this is a good idea, Your Majesty?" Ahmet said when he found his tongue. He would tread no closer to outright criticism, but one glance at Hana had been enough to see what had been happening in the Pit.

"And what would you have me do instead, Councillor?" Kin asked. "Secretly see her grave filled?"

"If she is Hana Otako, then she is a threat to your throne!"

Kin's lips were a thin line. He turned to me. "Darius?" Here this one chance to claw myself back from the precipice, so long as he did not ask me how I had known, how I recognised her when no other had.

"With all due respect, Councillor," I said, taking no small joy in kicking him while he was down. "Katashi Otako is the greatest threat to our emperor's throne. Lady Hana Otako is a woman. She is not a threat. She is an asset."

"An asset?" Ahmet crossed his arms. "In what way, might I ask? Do you seek to bargain with Otako? Exchange his cousin for the Hian Crown?"

"I will do nothing hastily," Kin said. "That Katashi would risk her as decoy is troubling. He may have no interest in bargaining for her safety."

"Then she has no worth! Or may not even be who she says she is if Katashi would risk her life. A complete decoy, in fact."

"No worth, Councillor?" I said, hating the sight of him all the more. It had taken great willpower to keep from hitting him, seeing how Hana had suffered. "I think you are forgetting of what use women are." I turned again to Kin, who was still watching me, waiting, and I had to wonder whether my solution had already occurred to him.

"Marry her, Majesty," I said. "That would give you the stability you crave, and no matter what Katashi does, you will have the greater claim. He won't be able to so much as shake the empire beneath your feet."

"Marry her?" Ahmet looked horrified. "A rebel boy from the Pit?"

One could almost feel sorry for him, so contemptuous was the look Kin shot him, but I had scores to settle.

"Councillor," I said. "You appear to be forgetting that she is not a boy at all and was only in the Pit, only dirty and disgraced, because of us."

"Majesty." He stepped closer to the throne and addressed himself to Kin alone. "If you keep her alive, she may marshal your enemies. If you...marry her, you will legitimise her claim, and she may use that power against you, or worse—kill you. She has already tried to kill you once."

"If she continues to show herself to be utterly an enemy, then of course His Majesty will do whatever is required," I said. "But she is young. Impressionable. May want nothing more than the acknowledgement of her title and a high position. In any other situation,

I would suggest she could be married off to an ally, but to let her marry anyone else would be dangerous."

Councillor Ahmet sniffed. "And maybe she is infiltrating the court so she can stick a blade in our emperor and give her cousin the throne."

"I think General Ryoji's men are well able to keep an eye on her, Councillor."

Kin said nothing, just sat, watching us throw the gauntlet back and forth. Frustratingly, Ahmet had a point, especially given where Hana had been found, but I told myself that even had I no interest in her safety I would argue the same thing. She was exactly what he needed to end the brewing civil war, if he could but charm her.

"As I recall, your father was very close to the Otako family before the...incident," Ahmet said, his flushed cheeks showing his enjoyment of the sport.

"Whatever you might be attempting to insinuate, my father resigned his position as commander of the Imperial Guard three years before the unfortunate death of Emperor Lan. And he was nearly executed himself for refusing to serve Emperor Tianto."

"Dedicated to the true Otako line, then. How heart-warming."

For once, the words that rose instinctively to my lips were the right ones to utter. Leaving in every trace of bitterness, I said, "As you say, Councillor. Dedicated to a family that was not his own. Given a choice, I would not have asked to be born his son."

Ahmet's smile showed all too much enjoyment of my emotional display, a smile only wiped away when Kin said, "Thank you, Councillor. You may return to your duties."

Dismissed, Ahmet bowed and thanked Kin for his time. Then he went to the door, his solemn steps hiding the ill ease surely eating at his soul.

I let go a long breath once he was gone, while Kin just stared at the floor. "You think I should marry her."

"Yes, Majesty," I said, though it was not really a question. "If you announced your marriage to Lady Hana Otako, Katashi's claims would founder, even with the crown. There is, after all, no precedent to remove you from the throne."

"And if I cut off her head?"

I could see no anger, only calculation. He watched me closely.

"Killing her removes an Otako threat, but if you do it publicly, you set her up as a martyr to her cousin's cause, while executing her in secret would see you little better off than you are now. If it is not what you wish for, then there is nothing more to be said, but I cannot, in all devotion to your service, lie and say the marriage would not be ideal. It would unite Kisia as nothing else would. I am sure the council would agree with me."

"And if I do not wish it?"

"Then by all means, remove her head, Majesty."

"You would permit that?"

"It would not be my place to forbid it."

"That is very unlike you, Darius. Your impudence seems to have abandoned you. Have we at last discovered a subject you will take seriously?"

Time for more of my hated honesty. "Perhaps it is the Laroth blood in me," I said. "But as little as I could wish harm upon the daughter of the family my father once swore to protect, I have made my oath to you."

"What were the words of that oath, Darius?"

He spoke quietly. A test? Or a reminder? I couldn't tell how much of Ahmet's speech he had heeded or whether his thoughts had gone back to a time when he himself had given his oath to Hana's father.

"'I swear on the bones of my forebears,'" I began. "'On my name and my honour, that I will be loyal to the one true emperor, the great Emperor Kin, first of his name, that I will never cause him harm nor seek to deceive him and will give every last ounce of my strength, every last ounce of my intellect and die in his service if the gods so will it. I—' "

" 'Would be as nothing and no one in service to you,' " he quoted. "I'm glad you remember." Kin stared at the floor for a long time, leaving me to stew in my own fear, unwilling yet to consider what I would do, what choice I would make, if he ordered Hana executed.

"I knew her grave was empty," he said eventually. "Her body and Prince Takehiko's were never found."

I left a beat for the feigning of surprise. "Takehiko's as well?"

He nodded. "I always knew they could turn up, that with every passing year they grew older and perhaps…angrier that I sit on their father's throne." Kin turned, stiff silk shifting as he looked at me. "I would have liked to know she was still alive. I would like even more to know whether Takehiko is still alive. Unfortunately, the only person I thought might know has now been dead many years."

The look that accompanied these words made it impossible to ignore their meaning. "If my father knew, he never told me," I said, glad it was at least half-true, whatever lies it skirted.

He nodded, not seeming to agree or accept but merely acknowledge, his thoughts elsewhere. For a long time, we sat in silence, and there again I could have spoken, I could have admitted the truth, could have told him about how Takehiko had come my way mere days ago. I could have and I ought to, the truth best for the empire and the protection of the throne, but every time I formed words in my mind, I could not force them out. Kin might spare my life even after such a betrayal, but without this job, without his protection, without everything I had built here in this new life, there would be only Malice. Death would be preferable.

Fear kept my tongue still when I knew I should speak, and all too soon, the opportunity was lost. With a heavy sigh, Kin said, "You may go now. I have a lot to think about."

I could not even be sure he meant to spare Hana—his expression gave nothing away. All I could do was rise and bow and walk out, not daring to utter another word in case it came out as an admission I could not take back.

I would be as nothing and no one in service to you.

I had never wanted to break it. I had taken the oath gladly, having so much I needed to atone for, so much I had wanted to escape. And for five years, it had been true. Then Malice had returned, and with a single touch, my world had begun to crumble.

Leaving the throne room, I found the palace full of whispers. For a full hour, movement had been restricted, and now the courtiers and servants went about their business, gossiping over the cause. At least no one accosted me, a preoccupied scowl all it took to ensure I reached my rooms in peace.

A man was hovering outside my door—the secretary who had carried my message to the messengers' yard. Enough time had passed for a rider to reach Shimai many times over, but I had dared not send another. That was the sort of gossip that spread.

"Your Excellency," the man said, coming quickly forward. "Your message—"

"The first thing you must learn about this court is that important conversations do not take place in corridors." I slid the door. "Do come in."

The young man bowed, twice, before entering my rooms with a tentative step. Perhaps he had heard the rumours that my walls were lined with human skin and hung with the hair of my enemies. The truth was far less interesting. For the most part, my rooms were empty. I owned none of the clutter most men amassed year on year, only my desk showing a tendency to overflow with papers. There was a low table with a single cushion and an Errant board halfway through a game. It had been a gift and was the closest thing I had to a prized possession, that and the sketch of my estate at Esvar that hung on one wall, a constant reminder of things past.

I closed the door behind the unfortunate secretary.

"Now you may speak," I said, forgoing the usual hospitality. I had no patience left for small talk and condescension.

"Your Excellency." He bowed again. "A rider has returned with a message for you."

I bent to move a piece on the Errant board. "So I have surmised. I hope there is an excellent reason why it has taken so long."

"It appears that by the time your message was received, the prisoner had already been signed over to the prison cart." The man faltered as I bent my gaze upon him, but he swallowed hard and continued. "They sent riders after it to bring him back, but the cart was attacked. Most of the prisoners and the riders were found dead, Your Excellency, and were all branded with…with the Eye of Vice."

"And Endymion?"

"No sign of him, Your Excellency. Captain Ash has sent a letter."

He held it out, but I didn't take it. I didn't need to. Takehiko Otako, gone, and with him all hope that his existence might never trouble Emperor Kin. Malice would make sure it did, if only for the satisfaction of having power over the most powerful man in the empire. And of destroying me.

The secretary ducked as I threw the Errant board at the wall, its flat top smacking the wood with a fierce clap. It did nothing to alleviate my feelings. I could only snarl at my own uselessness and watch the pieces fall about my feet, dancing like wooden rain.

13. ENDYMION

Hope was watching. Hope was always watching, his orders not to let me out of his sight. He didn't talk much though, just stared, his only words a daily recommendation to rest more and apply his salve more thickly on my brands.

The wagon hit a bump, and I gripped the edge of the running board. Beneath my dangling feet, the lantern-lit road disappeared, snatches of grass visible between the stones. A team of black horses drew the wagon on, their sweating coats gleaming in the moonlight, while ahead, a covered lantern swung ponderously from the back of Katashi's cart. I couldn't see the rebel leader, but I knew he was there, wisps of him drifting back to me on the night air.

"You seen a message yet?" Avarice called from the box seat, the reins in his competent hands. I had spent the first night up beside him, but unlike Jian, the man barely spoke at all—grunts and monosyllables his standard fare.

"Not yet." Hope sat wedged in front of the closed door. He was never far away. Whether I was stretching my legs or ducking into the trees to piss, he was always there, barely out of earshot and never out of sight.

I leant back, lulled by the movement of the wagon. Both the Vices and the Pikes preferred to travel at night, but I had so far failed to adjust to their nocturnal habits and spent the days lying awake and the nights fighting drooping eyes.

The wagon slowed as we caught up to the cart ahead. Katashi was sitting on its backboard now, his bow watching over him like an ever-present sentinel. There was something...intoxicating about him. I had watched him shout and rage at Malice, had watched him try to punch the Vice, but I had not been afraid. Angry, yes, hurt even, worried—feeling every one of his emotions as clearly as I had ever felt my own.

"He's signing." Hope stretched his neck to see better. Katashi had lifted his hands and was moving them slowly from one shape to the next.

"No doubt he's saying the same thing he says every night," Avarice said. "Turn off ahead."

Hope got to his feet. Katashi and his Pikes used a version of the old merchant sign language that had been adopted by the priesthood. Jian had liked it for the ability to converse with other priests on the road without having to shout, and learning it had whiled away dull hours on the road. Katashi seemed to have taught the Vices a few necessary words, but no more.

"Five...miles..." Hope said. "River? I think he says there's a river."

"Five miles?" Avarice growled. "It will be getting light by then."

By the time we reached the river and the cart ahead slowed, a pale predawn glow was touching the horizon. Avarice tightened his grip on the reins, and his horses slackened their pace as Katashi's cart began to turn. It banked steeply, one wheel leaving the road, followed by the rest, and I caught a glimpse of men beneath the canvas cover, huddled like animals in the dark.

Our wagon lurched off the road in its wake. I gripped the rail. Onion grass brushed my dangling feet, its sharp reek upon the air.

Ahead of us, Katashi's cart pushed through the thick grass, squeezing between a stand of cedars and a thread of water more mountain brook than river. Avarice had to focus on navigating the narrow pass, and though low branches scraped the wagon's roof, I had watched Jian drive long enough to know it had been that or tip into the brook.

At the lowest point, the wheels of Katashi's cart sank into churning mud, and throwing aside the canvas cover, a handful of Pikes leapt from the backboard and began to push. Katashi didn't move, just sat watching me, his head tilted as though asking a silent question.

After a mile of heavy ground, we turned away from the brook, following a rocky track that rose steeply into the forest. The Pike cart pulled ahead, jolting violently over loose stones. Avarice slowed our wagon to a crawl, muttering under his breath as the vehicle began to vibrate, shaking up my stomach.

The weight of souls grew steadily heavier. It began as a whisper, mounting until hundreds of hearts called out in the morning sunlight, clogging my Empathy.

At the crest of the hill, we found the camp already growing, tents rising amid the trees. There were carts and animal pens, and the sound of hammering echoed over the hillside. Whatever their crudity, the Pikes were well practised and, in the presence of their captain, disciplined.

The great rebel leader slid from the cart as it stopped and was immediately surrounded. Avarice drove on, taking the wagon as far as he could before the trees grew too dense. It was every morning's habit to put as much space as possible between us and the noisy Pikes. The rest of the Vices followed in a desultory line, their black stallions sweating.

When he could go no farther, Avarice halted his team, holding them steady. "Chock the wheels."

Spite did so while the others rode past. My muscles tingled from a night juddering over uneven roads, and I got down from the cart gingerly, smothering a yawn. To stretch my legs, I walked a lap around the wagon, returning to the front in time to see Katashi stride past alone. Avarice was unharnessing the horses and paid him no heed, but though the other Vices watched him as one might watch a stalking animal to be sure it won't strike, it was my gaze he met. Just like back on the road, his eyes narrowed in an unspoken question.

It lasted only a moment before he vanished into the trees, but as though he had me hooked, I felt the urge to follow. The Vices returned to their tasks, setting up their tents and preparing food, Hope nowhere to be seen for a single, blessed instant, no doubt getting orders from Malice. Determined to be gone before he emerged, I hurried away along the ridge. Attention prickled my back, but no one called out to me.

There was no sign of Katashi beyond the edge of the camp, but I could feel him, could feel the lingering trace of his soul drawing me on. It was an odd addition to my abilities, one I couldn't even explain. I'd never been able to sense people so completely before, never been able to see their souls as though they were made of coloured light.

The thud of an arrow hitting its target caused a moment of silence in the natural symphony. Frogs hiccupped mid-croak, and birds ceased their squawking.

Katashi appeared ahead of me, a dark figure between mossy trunks. His bow was drawn, the string at full stretch. Rounding the bend behind him, I cared nothing for a puddle of water invading the path, seeking the soles of my already muddy sandals. There was just him, just the bulge of his muscles and the flick of his fingers as he let the arrow fly. With a satisfying thud, it buried its tip deep into the woven target.

My foot snapped a stick and he wheeled around, another arrow already in his hand. From beneath heavy brows, his piercing blue eyes were as sharp as the arrowhead aimed at my face.

"Ah, the Vices' new friend," he said, those sharp eyes looking me up and down. "I hear you don't talk."

I shook my head.

"Are you really a friend of Malice's?"

I hesitated a moment, then shook my head again. Katashi kept the bow drawn, aiming at my left eye. If he let go, the arrow would come out the back of my skull. I ought to have been afraid, but I knew he would not hurt me. I could feel it. He projected everything, entirely lacking the boundaries others grew like protective shells. No wonder men followed him.

With a nod at the bow, I lifted my hands and signed the number *one hundred* in the old travelling language.

Katashi stared at my hands, then laughed. "One hundred and twenty. She's a deceiving thing." The change in his mood was so sudden I flinched. He lowered the bow, his smile as warm as the sun's caress, except it was artlessly lopsided.

"So you know a thing or two about archery?"

I nodded.

"You can't be all bad, then, even if you are one of Malice's... guests. Endymion was your name, wasn't it? I knew a few Endymions in the years I lived exiled in Chiltae." He spoke easily, but he watched me with every word. "Are you Chiltaen, Endymion?"

I shook my head.

"Kisian?"

A pause, but again I shook my head.

"Then where?"

I don't know where I belong, I signed.

"Well, we have that in common too, then. I was born here, but I was young when I was exiled, and even living across the border it was never safe to stay anywhere long. We travelled a lot in the hope that if Kin sent someone to finish us off, they wouldn't be able to find us."

Again I had the feeling that although he was telling me personal information, it was me that was being interrogated, my every reaction and expression under scrutiny.

Whatever he saw couldn't have displeased him, for he nodded toward the target he'd hung on an arrow protruding from the trunk. "Why don't you retrieve for me?"

I nodded, and once again, he nocked the arrow he had intended for my head. Aiming this time for the target, he leant into his bow. His technique was faultless, his draw that of a man who had dedicated a lifetime to honing his skill. With an easy flick, he let the arrow fly, hitting the target so hard it bounced against the tree.

Katashi had a dozen more arrows stuck point first in the ground at his feet, and he pulled another free with a quick jerk.

"That Traitor's Mark looks fresh," he said. "I bet the one on the back of your head was painful."

I nodded.

He loosed another arrow. "You should be proud of it."

It was a strange idea, being proud of something that disfigured my face, of having been brutally used by men I had given little reason to hate me. When I didn't answer, he glanced at me and seemed to register my confusion.

"A man who is a traitor to one man may well be the loyal servant of his enemy," he said. "I have good reason to like men who have no love for the Usurper."

Another arrow flew to the target.

"Every arrow I loose is aimed at his face."

Not Malice's? I would have asked had he glanced my way again, but he kept taking arrows and loosing them with agonising ease and beauty until the last set the target bouncing.

I went to fetch them. All eighteen of Katashi's arrows were grouped around the centre of the target, wedged into tight coils of cloth capable of withstanding the punishment. Careful not to crush the eagle-feather fletching, I gripped the shaft of each and yanked. They were not barbed like war arrows and pulled out cleanly, but that would be little consolation to the man who found one of these stuck in his flesh.

Gathering them all, I turned back to see Katashi run a hand through his hair and roll his shoulders. Trouble stained the air around him. It made my stomach squirm. I felt more connected to this man than I ever had to anyone, and though I knew it was just the effect of my Empathy, that I did not really know him, could never really be his friend, I let the curiosity carry me back to him with the bundle of arrows deliberately held so he would have to touch me to take them.

When our fingers met, the connection was blinding, his whole body a complex weave of glowing threads and knots.

No, she's on her own. To go after her now would risk everything.

I expected him to growl and pull away, sensing my intrusion, but nothing happened. Katashi had the arrows in his grip, his fingers touching mine, and desperate to hear more, I could not let them go.

He'll find out she's an Otako. The damn Vice thinks the only fear is that he might kill her. Never occurred to the Spider that he might force her to marry him, and what then of my claim to the throne? What then of her?

Katashi gave me a strange look and stared down at the arrows. "Are you going to let them go?"

I let go like they had become hot irons. The last echo of his voice died away, the knit of his every thought fading from his skin.

Seemingly ignorant of the intimate connection we'd just had, Katashi drove the arrows, one after the other, into the churned earth at his feet. "I lost my quiver," he said, as though I had asked him why. "Had it since I was a boy."

He pushed his hair back and, without another word, nocked an arrow. I had touched him and we had connected, but he remained oblivious. Was he stupid? Even without a brief glimpse into his soul, I knew he was not, the serious cleft between his brows a sure sign his mind never ceased turning. No, not stupid. Open. He hadn't felt it because there had been no intrusion. He kept nothing closed away. All he was he gifted the world, and people loved him for it.

"Katashi?" a voice called through the woods, seeming to come from everywhere and nowhere.

Katashi lowered his bow and turned, seeking it. "Kimiko? I'm here!"

"Where is here?" the woman returned, and it was definitely a woman. She appeared around a clump of featherbarks and mountain saplings a few moments later looking nothing like her rich voice sounded. Short enough that she might still have been growing, she was made smaller still by the possession of such a profusion of dark, unruly curls that they could have accounted for half her body weight. She walked straight into Katashi's arms without either slowing or registering my existence, and he crushed her to him, her head barely reaching his shoulder.

"Aw, did you miss me, Brother?" she mocked as she stepped back. "I was only gone a few weeks. Everyone seems to have gotten surlier while I was away, and what is this I hear about Shin? What happened?"

He glanced at me, and the young woman saw me for the first time. "Oh, who is this?"

"A guest of the Vice," Katashi said. "He doesn't talk, but he likes archery."

I lifted my hands and signed a simple greeting, complete with a little bow.

"Oh, but he knows sign," she said even as she returned the gesture. "That makes it a bit easier." She spoke with the same ease as

204 • *Devin Madson*

her brother and had the same watchfulness, throwing him a questioning look as though wondering what he was up to. "My name's Kimiko," she said. "You probably already know I have the misfortune of being this lump's twin sister. It is quite dreadful."

Both watched for my reaction, and I wondered whether their use of the truth as a test was a conscious choice or a protective mechanism they had learnt out of need.

Whichever it was, I must have passed, for Katashi took up an arrow and nocked it to his string. It flew to the target with the same breathtaking ease. "I got the crown," he said as he took another arrow from the ground at his feet.

Kimiko glanced my way, still assessing, but did not answer.

"And do you remember that boy I told you about who captained the Vices?"

"You mean the girl you were desperately keen on?"

"Not just a girl. A lady. Our cousin."

For an instant shock held Kimiko in place. "What?" she exclaimed. "Hana?"

Katashi loosed another arrow, so apparently at his ease that his twin strode up to him and gripped his bow arm. "Are you sure?" she hissed, glancing at me again.

"Very sure. Malice told me. The fucker knew all along and how very funny he thought it." He shook off her hand and nocked another arrow. "He sent her on some fool's mission into the palace and she didn't come back out. Shin too, though I don't know what happened or if they're still alive."

"Well," she huffed after letting all the information settle in. "That's a bump in the plan. A fucking massive one."

"How eloquent you are, my love," he drawled. "We did get the crown though. And the Vice still says he can get us into Koi."

Kimiko jerked her head my way. "Is that what he's for?"

"I don't know what he's for."

It looked like there was a lot she would have liked to say, but she held the words back behind pursed lips and once more examined my face. Her scrutiny made me want to look away, but I forced myself to stand still and stare right back. Though I hadn't known Katashi Otako had a twin sister, the resemblance was marked, as much in their mannerisms and their actions as in their faces. Only in height were they utterly dissimilar.

"Where are you from?" she asked while Katashi loosed his fourth last arrow.

Born here. Lived in Chiltae, I signed.

"Just like us." Her smile was brittle yet bright. "We've always said home is a state of mind, never a place."

Katashi took up his third last arrow. I watched him loose it as much for the joy of watching his technique as to know when it was time to fetch them for him again. He grabbed the second last.

"Katashi," Kimiko said. "Give the boy a go."

He turned an instant after loosing it. "What?"

"Look," she said, gesturing at me. "He's clearly mooning over Hacho."

I backed away a step, shaking my head, but though I tried to deny it with a series of quick, disjointed signs, Katashi held out his bow to me. It was beautiful, its smooth wood seeming to glow from within, yet I did not take it. Could not. A true archer never took another man's bow without expressed permission.

He grinned, once more warming the day with unexpected joy. "I knew I wasn't wrong about you. Take her. Her name is Hacho. I want to see you try. I pride myself on being able to judge a man by the way he handles a bow."

I looked up into his face, unsure, but I could neither see nor sense any malice in the offer and let my fingers curl around the bow's upper limb. Her power was invigorating. Hacho. It was a good name, a name that had been engraved into the glossy wood.

A one-hundred-twenty-pound draw was heavier than the bow I had left behind in Jian's wagon, but I understood the difference in technique, in tapered arrows and a silk string.

Taking his place at the mark, I turned my shoulder to the target. "You can move a little closer if you like."

He was laughing at me. I didn't move, just adjusted my grip and pulled the last arrow from the ground. The motions were instinctive: to hold, to nock, to draw, leaning in, the extra draw-weight enough to make my muscles strain. It was the same action every time, a little altered for a different bow and a different arrow, but enough like my own that my heart soared. I was alive again.

Just as Katashi's had done, my arrow hit the target with enough force to make it bounce. Excitement tingled over my skin.

"Oh, she's good," I said, and it was a moment before I realised I had said it, that the words I had thought had found their way past my lips. After days of involuntary silence, it was a joy, and I laughed.

"He speaks!" the Otako twins cried together, Kimiko adding, "Really I just have the very best ideas, don't I, Brother."

"You do indeed, but now we have a new conundrum." Katashi tilted his head as he looked at me. "Who are you?"

"My name is Endymion."

"But Endymion who? That's not the way a commoner uses a bow. You grip like a nobleman, yet you pause before release, which means a soldier didn't train you. You are a man who draws for the joy, not the kill."

He held out his hand for Hacho, and I gave her gently back to her master. "A priest taught me."

It was half-true. Jian had taught me the basics until I outstripped him in skill and needed another teacher.

"A priest? What was this priest's name?"

I sensed an approaching soul before I heard their footsteps, but as soon as the new sound broke upon us, Katashi drew his bow again, a second arrow held curled in his little finger.

Hope stepped into the clearing out of breath and froze at the sight of an arrow, but there was a flash of relief all the same. "I am well aware you dislike us, Lord Otako," he said in his quiet voice. "But I am not aware of having done anything to earn such a threat."

Katashi didn't release the string but spun and loosed the arrow at the target. I heard the thud behind me as it found its mark. "What do you want, Vice?"

"I am here for Endymion. I was afraid he might have gotten lost and been unable to call for help."

"He has been quite safe here with me," Katashi said. "We've been having a very interesting conversation."

"Conversation?"

"Don't take it too personally. To Hacho goes the credit. He's a natural archer and, as it happens, a natural talker too. Who is he?"

"I already told you my name," I said.

"One of your names."

"I'm afraid it's the only one I have."

Hope stepped forward. "Come, Endymion. The Master wants to see you."

"That's good, because I'd like to see him too."

———————◆———————

I went in without announcing myself, halting a moment on the threshold while my eyes adjusted to the darkness. After the smells of the camp, sandalwood smoke was a vast improvement.

I blinked. Malice was sitting at the same low table as last time, his chin propped on his hand, long fingers pinching the top of an Errant piece. In this attitude he had frozen, one eyebrow raised, his long hair pouring loose over his shoulder.

"Endymion," he said, his lips smiling though he did not look pleased.

"Malice," I said.

His other brow went up and he let go of the Errant piece. "I see you have found your voice, yes? How miraculous. I had not expected it to happen so soon."

I sat. Jian had long ago taught me it was rude to sit without being invited, but I needed to be bold for what I wanted to say.

"Well?" Malice said after I let a long silence stretch. "I sent Hope to make sure you hadn't run into trouble, and now here you are looking quite cross. Like you might even scold me. It's very cute, yes?"

"You were worried I'd run away." Even with an arrow in his face, Hope had been so relieved. Out of breath from hunting for me. "Why?"

"These woods can be dangerous."

It was as much admission as I needed. I couldn't feel him like I could feel the others, and his face was only expressive when he wanted it to be, but I had grown up listening for small confessions left unsaid. Jian had always said that everyone who strikes up conversation with a priest wants to be forgiven for something, and it was his job to find out what.

Feeling more sure of myself, I settled my hands on the table. "Why did you send your men after me?"

"Would you have preferred to remain a prisoner? To find yourself working as a slave, exiled far beyond the borders of your homeland?"

That was an attempted distraction, so easy to see when you were looking for them. "Did I say that?"

We stared at one another. Malice was the first to smile. "You're not afraid of me, yes? That is refreshing."

"No, I'm not," I said, though it was not entirely true. "You haven't given me any reason to be."

"Have I not? How remiss of me."

"You still haven't answered my question."

Malice leant forward, resting both elbows upon the table, his face close enough that I could see every imperfection in his skin and knew him for a man as real as any other. "There are not many of us," he said at last. "Empaths are rare creatures. It would have been madness to let anything happen to you, yes?"

"And how did you know I was an Empath?"

"You would be surprised how much I know, *Endymion*."

A boastful mistake. I had worried him, but it was exactly the opening I needed. "You know who I am."

"I know who you are, yes. I also know who your parents were and I know the name you were born with."

"Tell me."

Malice leant back, tapping a fingernail upon the edge of the Errant board. "Is that all you want? The past?"

"What else? Until I know my past I cannot decide on my future."

"I had thought perhaps you harboured a lot of anger toward the man who did this to you," he said, touching his cheek to make it clear what he meant. "Because Darius also knew who you were and still let that happen. Still let it happen even though his family swore to protect yours." He shook his head, clicking his tongue. "The future you could make of your past frightened him, yes?"

My pulse quickened and I could not draw my gaze away from him. "Who am I, Malice?"

He sat back, and, untying the bone-ribbon from his wrist, began to gather his long hair. "You'll stay with us until the task at Koi is done, yes? I may need a second Empath for what is ahead."

It seemed a small price to pay for the truth. "All right. Now tell me who I am. Why did Lord Laroth have me branded a traitor?"

"Because, little lamb, you are meant to be dead. There is a gravestone in Mei'lian with your name on it."

Trying to keep my hand from shaking, I balled it into a fist. "And what name is that?"

Malice's smile broadened into the same gleeful grin he had worn telling Katashi about his cousin. "Takehiko," he said, with a laugh. "You were born Prince Takehiko Otako, and you are the only surviving son of Emperor Lan, the last true emperor of Kisia. Oh, Katashi is going to *hate* me. But he is going to hate *you* even more."

14. HANA

The Usurper had yet to show his face.

It had been two days. Purple and black bruises blossomed on my knees, my arms, and across my back. Even my skull felt bruised, and I pressed the tender flesh every day to ensure no kindness Kin offered could take away my anger.

The room that was my prison already overflowed with what the maids called *the emperor's generosity*. There were fine silk robes, hairpins, face powder, scent bottles, and a pair of the wooden sandals procured from the imperial artisan, not to mention books, inks and brushes, a bowl of fresh fruit, and another of sugared chestnuts. I had left it all, for the most part, untouched. I needed clothes, but I had taken one look at the feminine robes sent to me and felt the chains of womanhood click tighter.

I had sent instructions to the seamstress, not expecting them to be carried out, until she came to the door with a parcel wrapped in thin rice paper. "Your robe, my lady," she said, prostrating herself on the floor.

It rustled as I unwrapped it, silk tumbling out. Pale blue with a myriad of white flowers, and while it was still most of a robe, it could no longer be called feminine. A tunic and breeches. The front of the tunic was exactly what I had specified—black, its cut making no attempt to accentuate a womanly figure. The back and the sleeves were made from the blue silk and were almost all that remained of the original robe, with wide sleeves dipping to deep points and a pale silk lining that was cool to the touch. The result was perfect, and as I held up the breeches to inspect the fine needle-work, I couldn't help but glance at the pile of trinkets Kin had sent and smile. If he dared to show himself, he would find his opponent no weak woman to be bought with pretty things.

"This is perfect," I said to the still bowing seamstress. "Sit up. Please, help me to dress."

The woman did as instructed. "Thank you, my lady. Anything you wish, my lady."

This servility made me pause in the act of untying my sash. "I fear your master will be angry with you for making this. I will try to ensure he keeps his anger directed at me."

"It is of no matter, my lady. I would do anything for you."

She had turned her head, and I spotted a fading bruise crawling up the side of her neck. "Wait...are you...?"

Gaze averted, she said, "You saved me, my lady."

Her hands were balled into fists upon the matting, and below her neat bun, the soft curls of hair at her nape trembled with her. She ran a fist across her eyes. "I knew it was you as soon as I saw your face. I'm sorry, my lady." She took a deep breath and let it out, the air shuddering over suppressed sobs. "I didn't mean to...I—"

A knock sounded on the door. The seamstress let out a little cry and dabbed her eyes with her sleeve.

"Quick," I said. "Help me dress." Raising my voice, I added, "A moment, if you please."

She shook out the new clothes and handed me each piece. "What do you wish me to do with this one, my lady?" she said, folding the discarded robe over her arm.

"Can you make me another? I will not go to the executioner dressed in a woman's robe."

"My lady—"

The knock came again, and I tied a quick knot in my old sash, cleaned now of all traces of blood. "Come," I said, straightening proudly.

The door slid in its soundless groove, and in the passage, a serving man bowed low. "His Imperial Majesty, Emperor Kin Ts'ai, requests a moment of your time, my lady."

"Well, you can tell him I would rather jump out the window."

The servant unbent with more speed than grace, his eyes starting from his head. Framed by the dark passage, Emperor Kin appeared in the doorway. Without looking at me, he strode to one of the windows and forced it open, its hinges squealing their reluctance. "Your window, my lady," he said.

"Why don't you be a gentleman and jump first?"

He scowled and looked as though he might have retorted had not the seamstress caught his attention. "You may go," he said.

Rising from her bow, she backed out of the room.

"I hope," he said as the door slid closed behind her, "that you have been made comfortable."

"Oh yes. My father's palace is very nice."

"The fact that it's no longer your father's palace is a complaint you should direct at your cousin Katashi, not me."

He said the name casually yet watched for a reaction I was determined not to give. "I'm not sure how or why I would do that."

"You seem to think I am ill informed. I assure you I am not. Now do sit down so we can—" He glanced down my person for the first time and his brows collided. "What are you wearing?"

"One of the robes you sent me," I said. "Only it didn't fit."

"Women do not wear breeches."

"I do."

"You will not do so in my palace."

Determined pride had been keeping me from buckling beneath the oppressive authority of his presence, but so domineering a statement made me bristle from head to toe. "Oh, will I not? And what do you plan to do about it? Have some of your guards strip me? They'll have to force me into a robe while they are at it, because I won't wear one willingly. I would rather wear nothing at all."

Emperor Kin slammed the window shut. "You are very vulgar for a lady."

"I grew up a commoner and became a soldier," I said. "Just like you."

"You are no soldier. You are a rebel."

"And you weren't?" I smiled sweetly, growing more furious by the moment. "Who were you fighting? The true divine heir to the Crimson Throne, Emperor Tianto Otako."

He turned from me, picking up a trinket off the mantelpiece and weighing it in his hand. "You are very naive."

Darius had said the same, and it stung to hear it repeated, to have them both look down on me as nothing but an idealistic little girl who couldn't possibly understand the way the world worked.

Perhaps he saw my flash of anger, for he said, "I didn't come here to argue with you."

"Then why did you come? Have you decided the day and time of my execution?"

He gestured to a cushion before the central table. "Why don't you sit."

"So you can stand grandly over me? No, thank you, I will stand."

Kin pressed his lips tight and began to pace the floor. His robe swirled around his feet with every turn, light catching on the gold threads of his hem. He did not look how I had imagined. This man was no mere soldier, and yet he was no emperor either, no nobleman of birth. From the stories I had been told, I had always envisioned him with cruel, beady eyes and a thin-lipped sneer, but honesty forced me to admit he had neither.

He stopped pacing as suddenly as he had begun and stood before me. "As Kisia's emperor, I have a responsibility to this empire and to its people. A responsibility to provide stability. And as nothing could more surely unite all in common cause than the marriage of the last Otako princess to their emperor, I ask you to marry me. By so doing, you would ensure that your children will sit upon the throne of your ancestors and rule a whole, united empire, not one that has been torn apart by civil war."

"Marry you." I repeated the words dumbly, sure I could not have heard him right. All my life I had been warned that this man would want me dead if he knew I had survived, and instead he was offering me the chance to sit in the place that had once belonged to my mother. Long had I dreamed of being the Empress of Kisia, but always of sitting on the throne, not beside it.

"I understand this may come as a surprise to you," he went on when I gave no answer. "Perhaps you would have preferred I court you in the usual style, but I feel that would insult your intelligence as well as my honour. I do not know you and you do not know me. I dare say both of us would rather choose a different marriage partner, but I am an emperor. Your father believed that meant he could do as he wished without consequence, that he had no responsibilities, only rights. But he was wrong."

"You suggest I will be wrong if I refuse."

His brows rose. "Not my intention, but your point is valid. If you accept me, you protect the people of Kisia from this war. If you refuse, you will be condemning them to years of fighting, famine, and death. It is, as I have already said, not ideal, but though

I may have been born a commoner, I am now an emperor in every sense of the word. I will do what needs to be done to protect my people."

"Which ones? The northern families whose land you took away, leaving them no way of feeding themselves or supporting their tenants? Or the southern merchants you made sure would have lower port fees and taxes along the Ribbon so they could increase their wealth?"

"The port taxes are for all merchants, not merely those in the south."

"But land was only taken from northern estates."

He clasped his hands behind his back and looked grave. "I will not discuss the terms of treaties or imperial policy with you."

"Then the answer is no. I do not wish to be kept as a pet and allowed no voice."

Kin gave a curt nod. "I see. I should have known that would be your answer. You are an Otako. You have chosen to love your blood more than your empire, and on your head be it."

"Your choice to assume that as my reason says much more about you than it does about me," I said. "I didn't refuse because of my name or yours."

He had swept toward the door, but he stopped at that and turned. "You are right. I will leave you now, Lady Hana. I assure you that you are in no danger from me, no matter what decision you make. The court leaves for Koi tomorrow, and you will travel with us as my guest. Perhaps this is a subject we might discuss again later."

"I will not even consider changing my mind unless you change yours."

"Agree to treat you like a councillor rather than a wife?"

"No, you probably talk down to them too. Talk to me like you talk to Darius, and maybe then I will consider your proposal."

Kin froze, his whole body seeming to stiffen from his lips to the hem of his robe. For an instant, he closed his eyes, his chest rising as he drew in a deep breath. "Darius," he said at last, letting it out slowly. "Lord Laroth has lived at court for five years, and in all that time, I am the only one who has ever called him Darius. Do tell me, Lady Hana, how long have you known him?"

15. DARIUS

While the court prepared for the journey north, I buried myself in work, in payrolls and district orders and reports and all the other little minutiae I loved about possessing a ministerial position. But it was not enough. Emperor Kin had not come to the last council meeting. He had not called for me. Our Errant game had gone unfinished. The longer his silence, the harder it became to focus on all I needed to do.

My spies had little to report. Hana was being treated well, although it seemed no offer of marriage had been made, and certainly none accepted. Had I misjudged him? Had the mere suggestion of such a marriage betrayed my divided interests? I felt like I had cut myself open. A headache had become part of every day's struggle to maintain the mask, the shield. The prison.

The teapot steamed. I sat tapping my nails upon the desk as it steeped. In the corner, a secretary was writing replies to my correspondence, tensing every time I tapped a particularly irritating rhythm. Such was my mood that I kept tapping, watching the curls of steam rise and fade to nothing.

The door slid open. There was a sharp intake of breath and papers scattered as the secretary leapt to his feet. Kin stood in the doorway, his face a collection of severe, unmerciful lines.

The room felt suddenly airless.

"You may leave," Kin said, and the secretary departed at speed, bent double in a sort of hurried bow. He closed the door behind him, shutting me in with my fears.

Kin did not move. "Aren't you going to invite me in, Darius," he said. He spoke gently, his tone of regret more troubling than anger.

I bowed. "Forgive me. This is an unexpected honour, Majesty. Do come in."

He did so, glancing about him as he approached the table. He looked at the bare walls and the sparse furnishings, his gaze lingering on the sketch of Esvar. "It seems I deprive you, Darius."

"Not at all, Majesty. I prefer my surroundings simple."

"Perhaps you miss your home?"

He knelt at the table as he spoke, and I resumed my place, hospitality giving me an excellent excuse for ignoring his question. "Tea, Majesty?" I said, the pot tinkling as I gripped its handle.

"No. We will finish that game of Errant we started. No game should be left unfinished, don't you think?"

"That depends on the skill of the opponent, Majesty," I replied, comforted by the sound of my usual untroubled timbre.

"You are, of course, a very formidable player." He removed the pieces from the board. "But I would be interested to know how you perceive me. Have I such mean intelligence that you cannot respect me?"

This was a game. Something had happened, something had changed. He was disappointed. I could see it in the downturn of his lips. Had he tried to woo Hana only to find her thoroughly intractable? Perhaps it had been foolish to hope they could figure something out between them, that it might all fall into place, leaving Malice's new weapon castrated. Katashi Otako would be nothing to the threat of Takehiko.

"I have a very high respect for you, Majesty," I said after a pause. "I would go so far as to say you are the only person in this city I do hold in respect."

"And yet you betray me."

The words shot out like a slap, catching me off guard. It wasn't a question. My hand shook as I took up my pieces. He probably wouldn't notice, but it was worse that I did.

"One must surmise that you have been talking to Lady Hana," I said as I set my pieces in place.

"And why is that?"

"Because I will not insult your intelligence by feigning ignorance of the crimes you are charging me with. I was not lying when I said you were the only person in the city I hold in respect."

A smile twitched the corners of his lips, but he repressed it so severely I knew there was no going back, no matter what I said.

With the board ready, our eyes met. In the third and deciding round of any Errant game, the pieces were placed at random. The king could be anywhere. It added an element of chance, the winner the one who created the best lines and used their opponent to their advantage.

"Do you know how to tell the truth, Laroth?" Kin asked, his fingers pinching a piece in readiness.

"Yes, Majesty."

"Then I will make a deal with you. My trust of you was built on openness, on the honesty and vulnerability you showed me five years ago. While I have not until now had reason to doubt you or be sorry in my choice, the foundation has been shattered and my trust cannot be regained. But if you grant me a sliver of that same truth for every piece I turn, I will be lenient with your life. Do we have a deal?"

Had he but known it, it would have been so much kinder to order my execution. Dead, Malice couldn't reach me. I could have said so, could have tried to make him understand, but I could not have borne his pity, and so I nodded. "Yes, Majesty."

"Swear on your name. I would ask you to swear on your oath, but you've broken that. But Laroths, Laroths care about their name. I sometimes wonder if it is the only thing you do care about."

Once again, I chose not to argue, not to explain how much I hated it. It seemed a fitting thing to swear my downfall on, at least.

"As you wish." I touched a finger to my left cheek. "I, Darius Laroth," I began. "In the presence of my emperor, do swear on my honour and my name to speak the truth for the duration of this game. But not a second longer."

Again I thought I saw a smile, but perhaps it was just hope.

Kin nodded and, making no further acknowledgement, began to play. He moved a piece and I mirrored, considering my strategy. I could play into his hands and let him ask his questions, but he would want to fight for them, to know the answers were true. I would have to protect my pieces and make a play for his. I would have to act as though inside I were not breaking.

We played in silence, the dull, muted sounds of the palace all that dared disturb our game. Heavy footsteps passed in the passage; doors slid closed and distant voices droned. The teapot chilled at my elbow, its sweet smell fading.

The first question came too soon. Kin took two of my pieces. I watched him turn them over, black for white, neither the king that would have released me from hell.

"How long have you known Lady Hana Otako?"

"Since I was ten years old" was my reply, lips dry, each word easy to speak, though the whole was hard. I had sworn to protect her and keep her hidden away, not spill all I knew at the feet of a rival emperor. "She was just a baby."

"How did she escape alive?"

"My father saved her. I don't know how. He never told me. One day he just came home with her in his arms and that was that."

Kin gave a curt little nod and we played on. Despite the rapid thump of my heart and the squares of hot sunlight pooling on the floor, I felt cold to the core of my bones.

"Why didn't you tell me she was alive?" he asked, turning another piece.

" 'I swear on the bones of my forebears,' " I said, " 'on my name and my honour, that I will do all in my power to protect you from harm. I will mind not pain. I will mind not suffering. I will give every last ounce of my strength. I will give every last ounce of my intellect. I will die in service to you if the gods so will it. I will renounce every honour. I will give every coin. I will be as nothing and no one in service to you.' "

"The Imperial Pledge with a few additions."

It wasn't a question, but I nodded. "My father wanted to be sure. He wrote it out for me and I spoke it to a sleeping child. I couldn't...I couldn't afford to ever take the risk with her life, no matter what I feared the omission would one day cost me."

Was that pity that crossed his face? Its flicker was the lash of a whip on raw wounds, but like a starved animal, I wanted more of it, wanted to know he cared however much it hurt and however little difference it would make.

Kin returned to the game, his brow creased into its harsh lines. I could try to finish this, make a push for his Gate, but the deeper I pressed into his territory the more pieces I sacrificed to his hunger for knowledge.

Another piece was turned. "What do you know of Katashi's plans? Why send her as a decoy?"

"I know nothing of his plans. I have never met him. But..." Kin lifted his brows as I paused and I found I could not meet his gaze. "That wasn't his doing," I went on at last, staring at a patch of sunlight on the floor and thinking back to that night at the Gilded

Cherry with Malice. "When I left, Malice stepped in as her guardian and has been whispering in her ear, manipulating her to his own ends. He sent her after her birth papers because he wanted her to get caught. Katashi had no idea who she was and possibly didn't even know she came here, though I don't doubt Malice will have told him by now. He likes it when people are... enraged."

"You told me the Vices had no involvement in what happened the other night."

I couldn't hold back my sad little smile. "I did and it was true. Malice didn't steal your crown and he didn't help Hana. He just... made her think this was her birthright and that she needed the papers."

He didn't immediately move another piece, but when he did, the attacks came fast.

"Did *you* know Lady Hana was masquerading as a rebel?" he said.

"Not until it was too late. I thought she was in the country."

"Why didn't you tell me as soon as she was caught?"

"I needed time to think. I had to be sure she would be safe."

Kin nodded. Then: "What did you do to my guards?"

I hesitated. I hadn't expected that question. The words sat on my tongue, their poison insidious after so many years of pretence. I had sworn honesty, but the moment I framed the truth, I knew I could not speak it, could not explain without destroying everything I had worked for. Without risking his respect.

"A compound produced from seaweed, Majesty," I said, appalled at the ease with which the lie came, destroying my honour in a single sentence. "They will be well again soon, I assure you."

"I'm glad to hear it."

Wanting nothing more than for the game to be over, I clustered my remaining pieces. Kin's were spread out, no strategy in their pattern. A few turns could get me to the corner, but I would have to take his pieces, risking more questions.

Again, the underside of the next piece I turned was plain black. I was beginning to doubt the white crown existed at all.

Kin grasped a piece and looked up at me through thin lashes. His options were clear. He could make a play for the Gate or convert a whole string of my men. I held my breath, my heart hammering as I waited for the axe to fall. He lifted the piece and held it hovering over the board. Then, with a muted click, he lowered it.

Toward the Gate.

I let out a long breath, hating his mercy as much as his questions. It meant he knew how hard this was for me, and I wanted to hate him for it, wanted to feel as sure about the world as Hana did.

I made my next move. The end was in sight. He could not convert my lone attacker nor break the string that led all the way to his gate. His only choices were to make a throwaway move or turn one last piece.

He took the question. Turning my piece, black for white, Kin folded his arms on the edge of the table. "Why did you enter my service?"

Was this the question I had dreaded most? There were so many answers, so many explanations, but they clogged my mind and I could not speak. I could remember the fire, Malice laughing, and the way my father had looked at me with such hatred. And then the storm had come. I had told him so much that night five years ago, but there had been such deep pools of hurt I could not open for anyone. Not even for him, now, after years of friendship given despite everything I had once been.

I met Kin's gaze. I wouldn't lie again, but neither would I give details where none were requested. "To escape," I said.

He hadn't expected that, and he gave himself away. His lips parted as though he would speak, but sure I would break beneath any offered kindness, I quickly took my final piece and leapt it along his string to the Gate, ending the game.

Kin sat back and the room came into focus. The pot of tea still sat upon its tray, steam no longer issuing from its spout. At the desk in the corner, the secretary's unfinished work lay scattered, his brush discarded with ink drying upon its bristles. I could smell the oil Kin used in his hair and the faint traces of wood smoke seeping up from the kitchens. It all seemed more real, louder, brighter than it had before.

Kin let out a sigh. "You are an unusual man, Darius," he said.

"I wouldn't want to be the same as everyone else, Majesty."

"I don't know whether to like you, hate you, or pity you."

"I don't want your pity."

"That doesn't leave me with many options."

"Nor me, Majesty."

The muscles around his jaw tightened, as they always did when he was thinking. Then he sighed again and splayed his fingers upon the table. "I will not relieve you of your oath. You may do no harm to me, and I will do no harm to you. Perhaps I am a fool, but I cannot and will not see you executed."

I could not thank him.

"Given the dangerous situation in the north, you will come with the court to Koi," he said. "I will take my oath, with or without the Hian Crown, and you will remain in my service until it is done. After that, you may go back home and live out your life in whatever way you wish. I will no longer require your services."

The day I had found the strength to live as I wished, I had travelled to Mei'lian and sworn an oath to Emperor Kin. And now he needed me more than ever. If Katashi had the crown, then Kin was walking into a trap and he knew it. War was coming. General Kin had dealt with many wars, but Emperor Kin was too close to his empire now, loved it too much, and that would be his greatest failing. Only marriage to Hana could shield him against the coming storm.

"What will happen to Hana?" I asked.

"She will travel with me to Koi, either as my wife or my guest, whichever suits her best."

There was hope there then. No doubt they had spoken, and things had not gone so very ill, but it was impossible to forget how she had glowed in speaking her cousin's name.

"And Katashi Otako? Do you seek a meeting with him before this comes to war?"

Kin looked a little surprised. "You know me so well."

"He will not retreat."

"You don't think so?"

"No, Majesty. He doesn't just want money or land or even the throne. He wants vengeance. For the death of his father and the insult to his family. What I see are not the actions of a man determined to take back the Crimson Throne but a man so consumed by his need for revenge that he will do anything, *anything*, to see you suffer."

"A pleasant thought. You've always had a skill for reading people, Darius." His smile twisted bitterly. "You will fast make me wish we'd never had this conversation."

Kin rose from his place at the table, assuming his full height. There seemed little else to say, yet he was in no hurry to leave. "Your ward," he said after a pause, "Lady Hana, has refused to marry me. She says unless I speak to her with the same respect and deference to her judgement as I show you, she will not even consider it."

I laughed and he laughed, and almost it was as though nothing had changed. We were not quite friends yet more than just an emperor and his minister. Neither of us had ever been good at friends, but he was the closest I'd ever had. "I beg you will not ask me to persuade her otherwise, Majesty," I said. "I assure you, she dislikes me quite as much as she dislikes you."

He seemed to feel the same awkwardness in our situation, the same bitterness as I, and pressed his own smile flat between his lips. "And yet you are caught in her service, held fast by your own words." Kin walked to the door, but lingering with his hand upon the frame, he said, "My poor Darius," and then was gone.

16. ENDYMION

Prince Takehiko Otako. The shock had held me motionless for a full minute, staring into Malice's laughing eyes. It had been on my lips to refute such a ridiculous suggestion, but Malice told me the story of how Lord Nyraek Laroth had been the commander of the Imperial Guard, how he had taken an oath to protect my family—*my family*, I could not get enough of those words—and how he had saved me and my sister from the assassin, though she had been but a baby at the time.

Father Kokoro had known. And from the moment Lord Laroth entered my prison, he too had known. He had known and he had condemned me anyway, seen me branded a traitor.

It had been even harder to sleep than usual that day, though I had wanted to more than ever, wanted to fall into a dream where I might see my mother and know her for who she was, understand her sad smile as I cuddled into her furs. Empress Li had been Chiltaen, Malice had said when I told him about my memories, so our Kisian winters had been hard on her.

Li. My mother had a name.

"No," Malice had said just before he banished me to my tent. "That was just her adopted name to appear more Kisian, yes? Your mother's name was Liviana."

Liviana Otako. Empress Li. I sat on the wagon's running board the next day, as silent as if I had been mute again, thoughts and words for no one else. Avarice drove the team, Hope sat in the doorway, Vices on horseback came and went around us, but the only person I sought was Katashi. Glimpses of him at rest stops, the feel of his presence on the cart ahead, the sound of his voice shouting an order to one of his men—I couldn't get enough. I was obsessed with this man who would hate me for who I was.

The morning was a long time coming, but eventually we were once more leaving the road, and then the Vices were making camp away from the Pikes, and though I had seen it all before, I had never seen it through the eyes of Takehiko Otako. The knowledge coloured everything with new interest and new fear.

As he had the day before, Katashi strode off into the trees while the camp took shape. Avarice was tending the horses, Spite and Ire were building a cooking fire, Conceit was pulling the rolled-up tents from the storage net beneath the wagon while Apostasy and Rancour laid them out. It was a well-oiled machine, but like the day before, Hope was nowhere to be seen.

"Where's Hope?" I asked of no one in particular.

Beside me, Apostasy dropped a tent roll on the grass. "With the Master," he said. "The Master never lets him wander far."

Pride sniggered, jabbing at the first sparks of the fire. "Lucky boy."

I slipped away.

Katashi was easy to find. He had taken the same target with him into the woods, but he hadn't started his session when I arrived. He was sitting on the ground with Hacho across his lap. He looked up as I approached, pausing in the act of waxing her string.

"I thought it might be you," he said. "Did you get the answers you wanted yesterday?"

The leading question shocked an honest answer from my lips that I couldn't recall. "Yes."

"And?"

He wasn't looking at me, rather focusing on his bowstring, but Jian had often done just that when seeking an answer—appear disinterested and people will try to fill the space with the most interesting or shocking answer they have just to attract your attention. The thought steadied me, and with Jian on my mind, I said, "He thinks my friend was branded a traitor too and exiled across the border."

"Your friend?"

"The priest I've travelled with since I was...orphaned." I had always known my parents were dead, yet now they had faces and names, it was so much harder to say, so much harder to admit. Foreseeing his next question, I added, "I never knew my parents. Brother Jian picked me up somewhere near Risian, and I've been with him ever since." Honesty enough without the truth, and his interest seemed to wane.

"You want to have another go with Hacho?" he said. "I should have brought another bow out with me. I'll find you one tomorrow if you like."

Katashi had no reason to be nice to me, didn't even know we were related, yet the offer was so genuine in its kindness, I wished I could tell him the truth. Had my sister stood just so before and wondered the same? Had she been as desperate to be accepted as family as me?

"He's your cousin," Malice had said. *"His father was executed for ordering the assassination of yours, though Katashi will deny it."*

"I'd like that," I managed to say. "I lost my bow when I was thrown in prison."

"Why were you arrested?"

"Witchcraft."

Wariness crept into his bearing and into the mix of emotions he didn't keep confined to his skin. "The Vice said you weren't one of them."

He emphasised the word *them*, had slowed his strokes with the glob of wax. My heart hammered. "I'm not one of them. I'm not even sure what they are."

Katashi looked up, threat in his gaze. "Then what are you?"

Once again, the sudden shift in his mood threw me off balance, the whole forest seeming to darken with his temper. "I'm like him. Malice. I mean…" I stammered. "I'm an Empath." Katashi had nocked an arrow to his bowstring, and I lifted my hands in supplication. "No, please! I just feel things, emotions, presences, fears. I can't… I can't hurt you."

But I had hurt those guards. I had killed them all, and they had deserved it.

"Malice can hurt people." He hadn't drawn the string back nor risen from the ground, but he was still frightening when enraged. "Touching him is like putting your hand in a fire made of needles and thunder. And even when the pain fades, the lingering feeling that you want to die sticks around. Do you do that?"

"No." But I had seen Katashi try to punch Malice, had seen him jerk back in shock and marvelled at how completely it seemed to break him. "Perhaps… perhaps not all Empaths are the same."

"You don't know?"

"No. I'd never met another one before."

His stormy mood seemed to be passing, and he let the arrow fall back with its fellows. "All right," he said. "I'll find you a bow for tomorrow. Maybe we can have a little competition."

He grinned, his mercurial temper more disorienting than a high wind. "We could even find something to stake on the outcome, though don't get any ideas, it won't be Hacho."

"I wouldn't dream of taking your bow!"

Katashi's smile became a laugh, and he thumped the ground with his hand in an invitation to join him. "Come, sit. I knew I liked you."

Had I been able to see my emotions as I could see other people's, my whole soul would have glowed as I sat down beside him. So long dreaming of my family, so long seeking my home, and here was Katashi Otako, accepting me like a brother. There could be no more exquisite joy.

"I have a bow that Shin—"

"Wait." I turned at touch of someone else in my Sight. "Someone is coming."

A few moments later, footsteps joined the weight of the approaching soul, and Katashi set Hacho down. "Well, that's a useful skill. Even more useful to know the Vice has it too."

"I'm not sure he does."

Leaves shifted under a light step, and a man approached through the trees. He was dressed for riding and carried a leather saddlebag over his shoulder.

"Ah, Raven," Katashi said. "You found us."

"Don't I always?" The man gestured at me. "Who's this?"

"A new friend. Don't trouble yourself over him. Did you bring the supplies?"

Raven dropped the saddlebag on the ground. "Here's what you asked for special. I've left the rest with your men."

"Good."

Katashi dug a leather pouch from his sash and threw it to the newcomer. The man untied it with more speed than politeness, drawing out a gold disc pinched between thumb and forefinger. He held it to the sunlight, and an engraved pike swam across the coin's surface.

"Another bag of trinkets?"

"I don't think my father's coronation coins can be called trinkets," Katashi said coldly. "Take them or leave them."

"Oh, I'll take them. Gold is gold. They might have no greater worth, but they can always be melted down. Until next week?"

"Perhaps."

"Perhaps?"

"You might hear some interesting news before then."

"I will wait with bated breath," Raven said dryly. "And follow you with open hands. Until next time, Great Fish." He bowed, and letting his gaze linger on me a moment longer than was polite, the stranger turned back into the trees. His footsteps retreated, fading into the distant sounds of the camp.

"You're selling your father's belongings?"

Katashi threw a stick into the undergrowth. "What choice do I have? Without their estates, the northern lords only had so much to give. And men without food and wine do not fight, not even for me."

"A steep price."

"You think so? What do a few coins compare to getting back what we lost? Come. Look at this." He beckoned me closer, and I crouched in a patch of spiky grass beside him. From beneath his tunic, Katashi disgorged another pouch and untied the strings with quick fingers. Inside, a gold crown gleamed.

"What is that?" I said.

"The Hian Crown, you simpleton. Your new friend helped me get into the palace and take it—half of the deal I made with him. You see, without this, Emperor Kin cannot take his oath. But I can."

Katashi closed the pouch and slipped it back beneath his tunic. My eyes followed it all the way. If my father had not been killed, would that crown have belonged to me? There had been mention of brothers, but my knowledge of my own family history was poor compared to the day-to-day politics of Chiltae. Kisia had never really been my home.

With a tired groan, Katashi got to his feet. "I look forward to sleeping in a proper bed again one day soon," he said reminding me that Kisia had never really been his home either. "I got so used to Chiltaen beds that sleeping on the ground on a mat is uncomfortable." He stretched, lifting his bow high over his head as he did so, before handing her to me. "Here, you can go first today. Show me that unusual drawing action of yours again."

———————•

He was good to his word and brought a bow with him the next day. It was no Hacho, but it was good and sturdy and closer to my weight, and more importantly, it was mine. Though I had to ask him three times if he was sure first.

We had a competition to see who could put the most arrows around the edge of the target. He won, but I didn't care. He was also only spending time with me to find out more about Malice, but I didn't care about that either. The great Katashi Otako was talking to me, laughing with me, and calling me friend, as he might had he known we were cousins.

Every night on the road, I looked forward to arriving, looked forward to the hour I could spend basking in his presence. The world always felt colder after we parted, the souls in the camp heavier, louder, crushing me with their troubles.

He never failed to join me until on the morning we reached Koi. I waited for him in vain. When he didn't come, I went in search of him, braving the noise of the Pike camp. They were all busy setting up tents and working around the cooking pots and paid no heed to me—at least no heed beyond jeering or giving me a wide berth depending on their opinions of Vices. I didn't wear their clothes and wasn't bound to their tasks, but they treated me like one all the same.

Katashi's tent was larger than the others, though as I wound my way through the Pike camp, I caught sight of a fine construction in brightly coloured silk going up at the far end and wondered if there were new arrivals.

I didn't need to wonder if Katashi was inside his tent, however; his presence bled through everything.

"Captain?"

A Pike stood at the entrance, a bowl in each hand. Katashi's voice sounded over the hum of the camp, and the man went in, returning a moment later, empty-handed and frowning. He strode away, trailing the smell of leather and oil and the unmistakable scent of uneasiness.

I stepped closer to the tent, catching the clink of bowls and the rustle of paper. "But I have gone through every record, Katashi," came the sound of Kimiko's voice. "My eyes are near parched with reading. There is no way in."

"There has to be. The empire is riddled with passages and escape routes. You cannot tell me they built miles of passages in and out of Mei'lian but never built an escape route out of Koi."

"That is exactly what I am telling you. You know how hard that stone is."

Katashi's low growl sounded through the canvas. "There must be something," he said. "We must have missed something. I have to get inside the castle, and I don't want to have to deal with Malice again if I can help it."

"You know Mama took everything when we lost Koi. She burned all the accounts and crammed every scroll from the archives into sacks. She wouldn't have missed anything. She knew it was the end."

There was a long pause, then with a sigh, she added, "I think you're going to have to deal with him or give this up for another plan. Perhaps it's worth meeting with Kin to see what he'll offer for the crown. We might even be able to get Hana back."

"If it wasn't for that fucking Vice, we wouldn't even have to consider that. And I won't give it back to Kin no matter what he offers. If we don't take the castle now, if we don't see this through now, how long do you think I'll keep Lord Kirita and Vitako on my side? A victory here would get me generals. Manshin and Roi are already itching to fight for me if I can but prove I'm not the poor bet they fear I am."

Inside the tent, it sounded as though they were throwing papers into a pile. "Then go see the Vice. If so much hinges on this, then find out what he wants and do it."

A chest slammed. Footsteps strode back and forth. "And we still don't know what happened to Shin," Katashi said as though reading from a mental list of grievances. "If he is dead because of Malice. If Hana is dead—"

"There is no point worrying about that until we know. Shin is very well capable of looking after himself. There is every chance if Hana confided in him that he has hung around to be sure she is safe. It is the sort of thing he would do, because whatever his past actions, if he believed something to be in our interest, he would do it, whatever the danger."

"I know you don't like him, but—"

"You know I like him very well. I just cannot... forgive where his actions have left us. Having to make deals with vipers. Go on, Katashi, go see the Vice and be done. The sooner this is over and we are rid of him the better."

"You are wiser by far than I," Katashi said, the last words muffled. "I go. I go."

I darted away as he pushed through the canvas flap, emerging, blinking, into the bright light of day. He didn't see me, and with my heart thudding hard, I followed him through the camp, protected in the lee of his presence. It was no happy, glowing Katashi I followed, but even in a troubled state, it was better to feel only him than the hundreds of others that crowded close.

In our separate little camp, Avarice was still tending the horses, taking his time to croon to each in a language I didn't understand.

He looked up as Katashi approached the wagon and sidestepped into his path. "The master is resting."

"Get out of the way." Katashi pushed past him, striding to the wagon's steps. "I want to see Malice."

"Well he might not want to see you," Spite said, appearing around the front of the wagon. "You want to see the Master? You wait until you're called."

Ignoring him, Katashi mounted the steps. "You can't just walk in." Hope blocked the doorway.

"And you're going to stop me?" The Pike glared down from his great height. "What's your freak ability, Hope? Are you going to lull me into lethargy? Or make me giggle like a little girl?"

"You don't want to know."

Katashi was thoroughly unimpressed and reached over the young man's head to pound on the door. "Malice, call off your dogs!"

No reply came. Katashi went to push Hope out of the way, but the Vice had wedged himself in the doorway and wouldn't budge. "Woof," he said when the rebel snarled at him. "Want to scrap?"

"You'd lose, Chow Chow."

The door opened behind Hope, and he stumbled back against Malice. "Must you piss all over my wagon, Otako?" Malice asked, steadying the young Vice.

"I want to talk to you."

"How sweet. Did you bring me a gift?"

"Shut up."

Katashi shouldered the recovering Hope out of the way and strode in. I followed, leaping up the steps and ducking under Hope's arm before he could close the door.

Retreating to his divan amid curls of opium smoke, Malice groaned at the sight of me. "Do go away, Endymion, yes? I find nothing so tiring as being forced to talk to you."

"Then he can stay," Katashi said, swatting at the fumes as though he thought it might help. "Hope, leave that door open."

"Close it," Malice said, reclining on a pile of silk cushions.

It slammed closed, and Malice smiled up at Katashi. "And now? What can I do for the great Monarch?"

"You promised me a way into Koi, and I need it," Katashi said, standing beneath the golden star painted on the wagon's ceiling. "I don't want to be left waiting on your humour."

"But since you need me, you're in no position to make demands, yes?"

Katashi crushed his hands into fists, irritation radiating from him like he was leaking darkness. "Then why don't we just have a little chat about it. That castle is as much a stronghold as it ever was. There are no old tunnels to weaken its defence. The entrance is so well defended that no intruder has ever reached the second gatehouse still standing—"

"Perhaps you should try to crawl in then, yes?"

"The outer defences," Katashi went on, ignoring him, "are a maze—"

"Surely not a maze to you," Malice interrupted again. "Koi was your father's stronghold, yes? In fact, surely it was outside Koi that his head was removed." Malice seemed to be enjoying himself and dragged a long fingernail across his own throat.

Katashi's lips whitened. "Short of throwing thousands of men at the walls and climbing to the top of the keep over a pile of corpses," he said, "how did you plan to get me inside?"

"I do not give when nothing is offered in return, yes?"

"Then perhaps I'll just ask Endymion to help me. He's an Empath." Katashi gestured in my direction, and I felt it for the half joke it was, but Malice sat up fast, his eyes bright.

"No," he said, the word like a snap of his fingers. "If you want to get into Koi, you make a deal with me."

Katashi turned to me in earnest. "Could you do it?"

"I...I can't," I said, though I hated to admit it. "I don't know how. I told you I'm not like him."

"Oh? Did you now?" Malice said, his voice deceptively cool. "Let us see, shall we? Start small. Endymion, how many people are standing outside this door?"

I could feel Katashi's mounting interest, and desperate to please him, I closed my eyes. "One," I said. "It's Hope. He always feels a little forlorn." At short distances, it was a trick I had always been able to play, but the longer I kept my eyes closed, the more souls came to me through the darkness, each like a voice calling out in the night. I began to count them and they came to me in dozens, the total leaping to my tongue. "But in this camp, there are currently nine hundred and twenty-three men, Pikes and Vices, and eighteen watchmen in the surrounding trees."

When I opened my eyes, even Malice was staring, his jaw a little slack. "Very good, Endymion. I'm sure even Katashi could not corroborate the truth of that." His gaze flicked to the Pike leader, then back to me, bright and hungry. "I see you are not convinced. A further test, yes? Yes, I insist, it will be fun. Hope!"

The door opened to admit the young Vice, his dark hair tousled. "Yes, Master?"

"Bring me a Pike."

Katashi's brows snapped together. "What?"

"A Pike," Malice repeated. "One of your men. We will do a little experiment."

"Why not do it on your own men? On Hope here. I'm sure he can scream and snivel better than any Pike."

Malice nodded to Hope and he left. "I'm afraid Hope is rather resistant to such things, yes? All Vices are, by definition of being Vices. But don't fear, Great Fish, none of your stinking rebels will die."

Hope returned a few moments later with an unfortunate rebel skulking in his wake.

"Captain," the Pike said, nodding to Katashi. "You need something?"

"Sit down, Tori." Katashi pointed to the step, those bright blue eyes more than a little curious.

Fear dripped off the luckless man, but he did as he was bid, lowering himself onto the step before Malice's divan. Although the opium pipe lay discarded, the air was full of smoke. It made my head buzz.

"Now, Endymion," Malice said, patting the edge of his divan. "Let's start simply, yes?"

I sat beside him, the cushion-covered divan like a scented trap from which one might never rise. Malice gripped my face between his hands and made me look up at Katashi. "Look at your audience, Endymion. This is a performance, yes? Now, can you feel him?"

I glanced at the Pike sitting in front of me, his head little more than a bowl of short hair crisscrossed with a dozen little scars. "Yes," I said.

"What do you feel?"

"Fear."

"Is that so? He is afraid of me, yes?"

"I don't know."

"No, of course, that is merely supposition," Malice said. "But one can make deductions with enough intelligence. It is clear. He does not look at me. He shifts his weight. He twitches and sweats. And now I suspect he is beginning to look at his captain in a way that confesses just how afraid he is of what we can do to his head. Touch him."

I touched the damp skin at his neck, and the man's soul burst into flames before my eyes. Every part of him seemed to move and shift and connect, thoughts running like streams though his body, the pulse of his fear like the concerted tick of a hundred tiny golden cogs.

Then came the whisper. *His hands are cold. Weird freaks with their cold blood, worse than snakes. At least snakes don't walk around and pretend to be normal.*

"Endymion?"

From somewhere beyond the shining complexities of the man's soul, someone had said my name. I heard it, yet the whispering would not stop.

Oh gods, I wish he would let go. Freak. No, he's not going to hurt me. The captain wouldn't let them hurt me. I haven't done anything wrong. Does he know about the jugs of wine I sold in Sina? No one ever saw me. That was weeks ago.

"—does he know about the jugs of wine I sold in Sina? No one ever saw me. That was weeks ago," I said, my lips moving in time to the whisper now. "Oh fuck, he's reading my mind. No, I'm not saying that. I'm not thinking that. Shut up, shut up, shut up!"

The man wrenched away from me and the connection broke. He pressed his back against the wall, chest heaving, his eyes darting from me to Katashi.

"You stole the wine?" Katashi said.

"I didn't mean any harm, Captain, honest. I just—" His explanations died beneath Katashi's stare.

"Don't blame him," I said. "He lost his mother at a young age. He was brought up by a dishonest landlord who sent him out to beg from the mule trains and would beat him if he came back empty-handed."

I could feel the weight of Malice's eyes on me, hot and hungry. I could not remember ever having such clarity before the incident in Shimai.

"Sit, Pike," Malice ordered.

Katashi pushed Tori back down onto the step.

"Now let's see just how strong you are, Endymion, yes? Touch him."

This time I hesitated, but I wanted to do it. I wanted to know how much I could see, and once more I touched his neck. The connection reignited, the desperate whisper unending.

Don't think about anything. Nothing. There is a floor and there are walls. What is that freak staring at? He looks like his eyes are going to pop out of his head.

Malice gripped my other hand. The connection was not immediate, but he pushed it through, and for the first time, I could see beneath his skin. A flood of emotion burned into me, anger, jealousy, hurt. It rent thought from instinct like splintering bone.

Tori's dry lips parted. His cry was silent, parched, desperate. The skin at his neck flamed red, raw and hot beneath my hand. The rebel jerked. His heel slammed into the floor. A rattling groan crept up his throat, rising to a scream, a shriek, and I was back in the guardhouse at Shimai. My grip tightened. The stones were cold. Men pinned my arms and my legs, pressing my cheek to the floor. I wanted the screaming to stop.

I could make it stop.

Do it. Make them suffer.

The power was there. It was so easy. I could stop them hurting me. I could bring back the silence.

They deserve it. Look how they treated you. You're an Otako. You're an Empath. You're a god.

Anger ran through my fingers like molten metal, and my ears rang with their screams.

You deserve no mercy from me.

The silence was sudden. Complete. All connection severed. Tori leant against the wall, his eyes bulging. He did not move. He did not breathe. The pulse at his throat was still, his whispering thoughts silent. And I could remember a dozen men laid lifeless on a stone floor.

Malice cradled his hand, crushing his silk sleeve, but it was Katashi who broke the silence. "I thought you said you wouldn't kill him."

Malice didn't immediately answer, and sick to the pit of my stomach, I knew why. He hadn't killed the man. He had only given me the means to do so.

One of Malice's false smiles spread his lips. "Accidents happen. You are a commander of men, you know this, yes? It was not my intention. Let us say I am unused to this particular tool. Hope, throw the body out. Its presence is irritating."

"Yes, Master."

"Wait." Katashi blocked Hope's way. "We haven't finished yet. You owe me for this little stunt. Get me into Koi Castle and we'll call it even."

Malice laughed. "Passage into Kisia's greatest stronghold for the life of that thief weasel? No. He was nothing and you know it. You would not otherwise have let me play, yes?"

"You know I cannot pay gold, we—"

"I have enough gold."

Katashi inclined his head. "Then what do you want?"

"A soul."

"Another? You just killed one of my men."

"Then he is dead and useless. Hope, I told you to get it out of here, yes? Already it starts to stink."

Hope stepped forward, but Katashi held out his arm to block the young man's way. "No, let it stink. Tell me what you want. I need to get inside those walls."

"You know what I want," Malice said. "You know how this works. You give me a Vice and I give you what you need. I don't take peasants and I don't take scum. They come from proud names. They have honour. They are lords and artisans and scholars, and each is important to the man who sold them. Look at our dear Hope, yes? He is Arata Toi, son of Lord Toi, the duke of Syan, or he was until his dear father needed my help."

Hope did not meet my gaze. His lips pressed into a hard line while the two great men stared at one another. Then Katashi's voice came out quieter than I had ever heard it before. "Who do you want?"

"The only one you won't part with."

Katashi did not answer, and Malice's lips widened into a broad smile. "Think about it, yes? Take as long as you like, but there is only one way inside those walls."

17. HANA

Kin rode ahead, proudly erect in the saddle of his brindle stallion. I had to lie on my stomach to see him, lifting the corner of the curtain just enough so as not to draw anyone's attention.

Since setting out from Mei'lian, Kin had dispensed with his imperial robes. Instead, he wore traditional armour, layers of leather and linen and mail cinched by his sash. A line of gold fasteners ran down each arm, while the Ts'ai dragon wound around his cuffs. His crimson surcoat showed the same allegiance, its broad back bearing the feathered tail of the southern dragon.

Beneath it, his horse swished its black tail lazily. Never had I seen an animal like it. It was a bay stallion, strong but otherwise unremarkable until one saw the brindle pattern on its right hindquarter. It was a fan of white tears, as though the bay skin had been stretched so tight it split, revealing the true horse beneath.

Today one of Kin's generals rode with him at the head of the procession. The man was leaning a little out of his saddle to hear his emperor's words, and I caught his smile, heard Kin laugh, and propped my head on my hands to watch, curious to see how he acted around the men he respected rather than the woman he didn't. Emperor Kin had always been part of my life. His name had often been spoken and his character wondered over, but always from a distance, his face never seen and his voice never heard, his

236 • *Devin Madson*

likeness trapped motionless inside statues and portraits and coins. Now he talked and moved and even laughed, leading his court through a bright summer day, its sultry air punctuated with the sound of hooves and endless footsteps.

Kin turned in his saddle, a gleam of laughter still shining in his eyes as his gaze fell upon me. I dropped the curtain and retreated into the scented palanquin, heart pounding. My cheeks burned. Had I really been staring that hard?

Someone cleared their throat. "My lady, His Imperial Majesty requests a word."

"Tell him—"

The curtain was yanked aside, bright light spilling in. Kin's horse was level with my palanquin, its muscles shifting beneath the brindle. From its back, the emperor looked down at me, something all too like an amused smile playing about his lips. "Surely we would do better if you aren't given the opportunity to be rude," he said. "There being no windows here to jump out of."

I deigned no reply, just watched him. He sat tall in the saddle, moving so easily it might have been his throne. By comparison, my palanquin was a silken cage, created by men to convince women they were useless creatures. Its sway was sickening.

"There is something you wish to say?" I said, refusing to be drawn into such banter.

"Not especially. It rather looked like you had something you wished to say to me."

"I was watching you because I am curious to see how you conduct yourself around the men you deem worthy of your respect."

If my forthright reply threw him, he showed no sign of it. "Ah, Raijin will be disappointed that you were not staring at him. He has become very vain these last few years."

"Raijin?"

"My horse."

Closer up, the animal was even more impressive, but though Kin was clearly trying to be charming, I would not be charmed. "The brindle pattern is certainly startling," I said with as much disinterest as I could cram into the words. He would not make me change my mind with talk of horses or the weather or any other inconsequential topic.

Emperor Kin took a breath and began, "It is very—"

"Warm, yes," I interrupted. "I have noticed, but it's quite usual for this time of year. Also, yes, I am still wearing breeches, I find them more comfortable. And before you ask, palanquins are an awful way to travel. They make me feel sleepy and sick."

"But not too sleepy to condemn your emperor's topics of conversation."

"Oh, I'm never too sleepy for that."

"Then what," he said, glancing down at me, "would you deem a good topic to discuss? My lady."

I had been about to suggest something easy like the policy on free rice allowances, but I would make him pay for that belated reminder of my gender and my station. "How about you tell me what happened the night my father died? A lot of people misremember and think Lord Nyraek Laroth was the commander of the Imperial Guard at the time, but I've seen his family records, and he wasn't. It was you."

"It was," he said, with admirable speed. "And not a day goes by that I do not question every order and every decision I made that day and think if I had just done one thing different, perhaps it wouldn't have happened. Although that one thing might have led to you dying with them, so perhaps it is best to leave the past where it is."

Emboldened by his honest answer, I said, "Were you there when it happened?"

"In the palace? No. Your father had sent me into the city." He hesitated on saying more, looking at the road, the horizon, anywhere but at me, before settling on silence.

"You had some special task?" I prodded. I had never had answers before, only questions. Darius knew only the little he had been told, but here was a man who had been there, whose job it had been to protect my family.

"I suggest the answer to that is not...worthy of your ears, my lady," he said stiffly.

Again, that little *my lady* to remind me that some things were not fit for a woman. As though my ears were any different to his. "You were perhaps escorting my father's whore?"

"No, I was not," he said, disapproval lowering his brows into a single severe line. "I was..."

"You were...?" I prompted when he didn't answer.

"She was not a...a whore. She was a lady, the daughter of a well-respected nobleman."

"I feel one can be born a lady and still be a whore," I said, shocked at how much anger I suddenly had for this woman I'd never known and the father long gone.

"I still feel to call her so is unfair. She...your father..." Kin heaved a sigh and looked around him again as though hoping someone or something might come to his rescue. "This history is so long gone its secrets no longer matter, but little did I think to be having this conversation, to be...admitting these things at such a time."

I waited, afraid that to speak would only remind him to whom he was telling this story, and after another long minute of silence, he said, "Your father was going to set your mother aside and take a new wife to be his empress." Kin spoke the words quickly, as though they had been dammed behind his lips for so long they were desperate to spill free. "I was escorting his new wife."

It was not the answer I had expected, and though I stared at him, it was the portrait of my mother I saw, this woman who had given me life. It hurt so much that I could not throw my arms around her, could not cry with her, mourning the sorrows of a world built by men.

Neither of us spoke for a long time. Kin's horse kept easy pace with my palanquin, but his attention was elsewhere while I blinked away tears. It left an uncomfortable silence, and I wished he would go away.

"It was a complicated time," he said at last. "And difficult for everyone involved. The common people suffered greatly through the civil war that year. All wars are bad for food production and prosperity and population growth, but with civil wars, that damage is concentrated into one society rather than spread over two. It took years to recover, with Chiltae pecking at our border, and the mountain tribes almost took Giana twice, and—" He stopped, a grim statue beneath the summer sunshine. "I have worked hard to ensure it would never happen again, to ensure Kisia had the stability it needed to grow and thrive, but your cousin cares nothing for the people and thinks only of his own desires."

"An easy stone to throw when you are the one sitting in a palace." I spoke the words quietly, hadn't meant to say them at all, so full was I of doubts and questions, but it had been my ambition, not only Katashi's he mocked. It was not Kin who had lost his family.

I had not thought it possible for the dark line of Kin's brow to get any lower, but it dropped into a heavy scowl. He parted his lips as though to defend himself, only to snap his teeth together, so quickly did he change his mind.

"We stop tonight at the estate of Lord Kato, the count of Suway," he said after we had gone on a little way, the palanquin still swaying worse than a fishing raft on the upper Tzitzi. "I would be honoured if you would join me for dinner."

"Should you not be dining with Lord Kato in thanks for his hospitality?"

"Not when he is confined to his mat with an illness, my lady."

There was a slight smile as he batted back the insinuated accusation of incivility, and I liked him the better for choosing not to mock me.

"All right then," I said. "I will dine with you as long as you promise not to bore me with talk about the weather or the state of the roads."

"Requesting promises from your emperor?"

"Why not? I requested answers and you gave them."

Those black brows dropped again. "Only because I chose to."

"Oh no, don't ruin it," I said. "You were doing so well there for a while."

He bowed his head, though whether in acceptance of the criticism or not, it was hard to tell. "My lady," he said, stiffly proud, and letting out his rein, he urged his horse to a trot.

Without his brindle stallion riding alongside, the view from my palanquin was of Darius and his small entourage—what looked to be a pair of secretaries, an imperial guard, and three military messengers in their light armour and bright surcoats. One of them stared after Kin's horse and, when he had moved ahead out of sight, turned to glance at me. No smile, no nod, but with one eye bisected by a long scar, it was impossible not to recognise Shin. He made no attempt at communication beyond allowing his gaze to rest on me a moment too long. Then, looking for all the world like one of Kin's soldiers, he straightened his red sash and marched on.

Tili had been a seamstress in Mei'lian, but when Kin had suggested I travel with a lady's maid, she was the only one I would take. I trusted her. I liked her. And she altered my robes without complaint or censure.

She had two laid out on the matting and was discussing their rival merits while pulling a comb through my short hair.

"I think the blue looks very fine, my lady," she said. "It suits the colour of your eyes and your hair. Although this is perhaps too light a colour to look good against His Majesty's crimson."

"Then I will wear it," I said, wincing as the comb caught on a knotted curl. "I do not want him to think that one pleasant conversation has changed my mind."

"You don't want to be an empress, my lady?"

"Oh, I've wanted to be an empress all my life. I just don't want to take it as a gift from a man who should never have had the position in the first place. I would have grown up a princess in the palace with my family if he had done his job." I thought of the conversation on the road. Kin had not been there. And even if my father hadn't died that night, I would still have grown up without my mother. "Or if not my family, at least my uncle's," I went on. "But for Kin, Emperor Tianto would be on the throne, and he would have taken care of me."

Kin had said he would do anything to stop civil war happening again, but the dangers had not troubled him back when he had incited it, when he had executed my uncle for treason after the Battle of Shami Fields.

Tili said nothing for a time, leaving me to stew in my thoughts. At last when she was done with my hair, she set aside the comb and shook out the tunic sewn from a once-striking robe.

"At least His Majesty is more respectful than most of his court," she said, holding the robe up for a final inspection. "He doesn't have wandering hands or wandering eyes, and he's never down in the servants' quarters pestering one or another of the girls like some."

"Why don't they just tell them to go away?" The words were out before I could think better of them. Tili looked away, no doubt thinking, as I was, of the guard who had not listened to her refusal, who had only been stopped by the edge of my blade. "I'm sorry," I said. "I did not think."

"Oh no, please don't apologise, my lady, it is my silly fault for still being upset about it and for letting—"

I stood and put my arms around her, her words ending in a little shudder of emotion. "No, it's not your fault. He was entirely at fault. You have every reason to still be upset, and I should not have supposed that just because I have some power in my voice, it's a power shared by all women. They did not listen to me when I was in the pit. They did not listen to me at all until they knew my name."

And I had been treated with respect growing up because Mama and Papa Orde had known I was the daughter of a god.

Tili relaxed into my embrace the longer I held her, until her head drooped onto my shoulder and the last of her shuddering breaths eased away. I could have let her go then, should have perhaps, but it had been so long since I had held someone close or been held that I would not move as long as she would stay.

A knock at the door shattered the moment before either of us was ready to part, and with a flustered apology for having been so presumptive, Tili hurried to the door. A low-voiced conversation passed in the passage before she returned, looking at the floor rather than at me.

"A reply from Minister Laroth?" I said.

"No, my lady. Just one of His Majesty's men come to say he is awaiting you on the balcony."

"Well he will have to keep waiting, as I'm not yet dressed and I have half a mind to send Lord Laroth another note."

Tili looked up then. "Oh no, my lady, he must surely have already gotten the other three, and—" She looked down again. "I'm sorry, it is not at all my place to be advising you. Please forgive me. I am...I am not used to being a lady's maid yet, but I am doing my best to learn the proper ways of doing things."

"If the proper way of doing things includes letting me do

something foolish without making a push to change my mind, then please stop learning at once," I said. "You are quite right. Of course he has had my other notes and one more will not make him reply. Come, help me into these clothes. I would much rather stay here and dine with you, but while you won't cut off my head for being absent, Emperor Kin might!"

I said it in jest, but Tili looked shocked. "Do you think he would?"

"No, silly." I gripped her hand and squeezed it as she held out the newly adjusted tunic. "But I would still far rather stay here with you."

"But he is the emperor!"

"And you are my friend."

She blinked back threatening tears and fussed over my clothes long enough that I was able to dry mine too.

Twenty minutes later, I followed a servant through the quiet halls of Lord Kato's house. Quarters had been set aside for the emperor's use and those of his senior councillors, but it was to a balcony overlooking the gardens I was led. There, with a pile of correspondence on the table in front of him, Kin sat cross-legged, his crimson robe pooling about him like blood.

The servant prostrated himself on the threshold, but I did not bow.

"Ah," Kin said, setting a stack of parchment aside and getting to his feet. "Lady Hana."

"My apologies for keeping you waiting, Your Majesty," I said, deciding that I may as well start with the sort of manners that wouldn't make Mama Orde blush in mortification. Whatever Kin might think of me, I would not have him consider my education deficient.

"Oh, you didn't keep me waiting. I had the foresight to send my servant to you half an hour before dinner was to be served."

"Thereby robbing me of the satisfaction of knowing I kept you waiting. Very neat." I pointed at the cushion opposite his. "May I sit?"

"By all means." He looked to the servant. "You may go."

"Very good, Your Majesty."

The man backed out, leaving me alone with Emperor Kin in a setting that might have been romantic with any man I wasn't so set on disliking. Beyond the lattice walls of the balcony, frogs croaked in the garden. Lanterns hung above a series of ornamental ponds and fountains, lighting pretty ripples, the movement of the water more musical than any instrument.

We sat in silence while the meal was served, Kin's gaze not shifting from my face. His unsmiling scrutiny was uncomfortable, but I was determined not to show it and looked at the meal instead. Salted fish, pickled plums, black rice, and clear turtle soup made up the majority of our dinner—not the fancy repast I would have expected a lord to set before his emperor. Kin, however, looked satisfied.

"Do you always eat so simply?"

"Yes," he said. "I'd have ordered something more extravagant for you, but I felt my usual diet was good enough for a rebel outlaw."

"But why?" I asked, refusing to rise to the bait. "You must have asked for these dishes specifically, since no self-respecting cook would set anything so basic before their emperor. I know Darius only eats pear and raw fish and things that will maintain his precious beauty, but you—"

"Have no beauty to keep." Mocking laughter danced in his eyes. "Your honesty is dampening. In truth, old habits are hard to break. I eat like this because I was a soldier and this is standard fare in military camps. Though the soup is usually far less exciting." He set his elbows on the table. "What was it like growing up with Darius for a guardian?"

"Oh, he told you so, did he?" I ought not to have been surprised he had betrayed me so completely. "Well, I didn't, not really. I lived on a farm with a lovely couple. Darius was always away. Always busy."

"A farm? Where?"

I narrowed my eyes at him.

Kin paused in the act of serving himself some fish. "Do you suppose I would have them executed for harbouring you?"

"I don't know, would you?"

"No."

Preferring to let the subject drop, I began to serve myself from the simple repast, but no sooner had I taken some rice than Kin said, "You appear to be better educated than would be expected from common farmers. Was that Darius's doing?"

"If you mean did he teach me himself, no. But he did pay for tutors. I'm sure everyone in the district thought I must be some bastard relation of his." I met his frowning gaze. "The only thing Darius taught me himself was how to use a blade, and then only because he couldn't find someone willing to teach a girl."

Kin gave a surprised little grunt. "I wasn't aware he knew how. Amusing to imagine him doing anything that would lead to a hair being out of place."

"I have only ever seen him properly dishevelled once, and I can assure you it looks as strange as you imagine."

His laugh was short-lived, hastily crushed beneath his heavy brow as it sank once more into a scowl.

"He didn't have to call the guards, you know," I said, watching him stab a plum with more force than was required.

"Pardon?"

"Darius, the night I was caught in your palace. He could have just let me go, but he chose to risk my life rather than yours. Given our history, I feel I have a greater right to be angry about that than you do."

"What a delightful companion you are. Is there anything I do right? Or are you quite set on finding fault with my every decision, right down to how I feel about the betrayal of my most trusted minister?"

His vehemence took me aback, and before I could answer, he added, "You requested respect and serious conversation, and I am complying with both, while you seem only prepared to bestow one."

"If you want my respect, you have to earn it!"

"I could have said the same thing to you, my lady."

A terrible silence followed. I scowled down at my bowl as ferociously as he did, my anger not at all lessened by the nagging feeling that he had a point. I had demanded respect as a basic right, a right I hadn't always accorded him in return. That he was a man—an emperor!—and therefore able to weather it, was a poor excuse.

Caught halfway between making an apology and stubbornly holding my ground, I said nothing and would happily have left the silence untouched for the rest of the meal, but Kin would not. After a few minutes passed, filled with nothing but the croak of frogs and the splash of fountains, he said, "You have criticised my every decision because you do not trust my judgement, but perhaps you would do well to remember that I have been emperor of Kisia almost as long as you have been alive, and whatever your birth, your intentions, or your education, nothing can replace experience. Not only *my* experience but that of all my advisors."

"All of whom are rich men and were chosen by you for—" I stopped. He looked ready to murder me had the table not been between us, but I lifted my chin and gave no ground. "How often do you listen to the advice of farmers? Fishermen? Cart drivers?" I said. "How often do you speak to the people who are actually out doing the relevant tasks before you make decisions? How many of your advisors set foot outside the capital for anything other than this yearly trek to Koi? You may be making what appear to be the best decisions for the empire, but while you rely only upon your own life experience and that of your sheltered ministers, how can you even hope to get it right?"

"As if the god Otakos ever cared whether they did the right thing," he snapped.

"And what is that to do with anything? My father is dead. My brothers are dead. My uncle is dead. If you are making a judgement on how I, or my cousin, would choose to rule Kisia that is based entirely on our family name, then I will bid you goodnight."

I rose, though my meal was as unfinished as my speech. I wanted nothing more than to return to my room and sit in silence, and even had he apologised or explained or entreated, it would have made no difference. But he did none of those things, only got to his feet in an unexpected show of respect and thrust a small lacquered box into my hands. "I had this made for you," he said, his tone as cold as his expression. "Goodnight, Lady Otako."

"Goodnight, Your Majesty."

I followed a servant back through the empty passages, the box pressed between my hands. I considered leaving it somewhere, on a side table or a step, but I would give him no reason to call me childish or petty.

Tili was waiting for me when I returned, her figure made hazy by steam. It rose in languid curls from a wooden tub, leaving the surface of the bathwater barely visible.

"Back already, my lady?" she said. "I was hoping this would have time to cool. I'm afraid I made it too hot. Would you believe I've never had to draw a bath for anyone before?"

"I think a hot bath will be good," I said, setting the box down. "I feel strange. And tired."

"Perhaps the food did not agree with you, my lady."

"Perhaps."

While she helped me out of my clothes, I stared at myself in the mirror. Was that me looking back? I tried to imagine it was my mother, her eyes older, more knowing, able to see what I could not. What had the Kin she knew looked like? Younger, of course, and less careworn. Had he smiled more?

My skin tingled as I sank gratefully into the hot water, the feeling so close to pain I hoped it would burn every thought from my mind.

"My lady, it's—" Tili was holding the box. "I'm sorry, my lady, I did not realise it was a gift, I—"

"Never mind, Tili, what is it?"

She brought the box over, its lid discarded upon the sleeping mat. "It's a sash, my lady."

Rolled inside sat a dusty pink sash—a noblewoman's sash with a family crest picked out in silver thread. Two pikes circled in the water of the fabric.

"It's beautiful," Tili said, unrolling it. "Look, it even has the family motto. That is a nice touch."

I leant closer, reading the line of arresting characters that shimmered along the tail.

We conquer. You bleed.

18. ENDYMION

Koi Castle rose above the trees, the curved roofs of the great keep outlined against the setting sun. Despite its beauty, it had an ominous presence, more like an eagle awaiting prey than the flock of banded crescents it had been designed to emulate. This the old Otako stronghold, the impenetrable keep that had assured Kisian dominance would hold so far north.

And now from its highest point, a crimson flag snapped in the wind.

Emperor Kin had arrived.

We had been waiting a few days, days in which I hadn't dared leave the confines of the Vice camp. Having killed one of his rebels with nothing but a touch of my hand, I was too ashamed to face Katashi, though my Empathy followed him wherever he went. He embodied the family I had yearned for all my life, and he had even begun to accept me, until my abilities had ruined everything. Again. Perhaps Father Kokoro had been right and I had killed my mother and my father and my brothers, leaving only myself and my baby sister to be discovered and rescued in the aftermath.

I twanged the string of the bow Katashi had given me and sank deeper into my misery. If not for me, Jian would not have suffered either.

I leant my head back against the wheel of Malice's wagon and closed my eyes. One thousand four hundred and two. Katashi had been gaining rebels by the hour, and their excitement and fervour was like the prick of a thousand needles in my skin, drowning all fear.

My Sight followed Katashi, from invisible group to invisible group, talking, planning, preparing, captivating all he passed. Was it an Otako trait, this magnificence? Might I have been like that had I not been cursed with Empathy? It was a glorious imagining that died upon my thoughts at the sound of his voice close by.

"Is that where you've been hiding?" His irritability seeped into my flesh like cold fingers. "I was beginning to wonder if you had run off."

I had thought about it, but the possibility that he might forgive me, might accept me again after what I had done, had kept me there—a sentiment so pathetic I couldn't bring myself to utter it.

"Though I imagine Malice has opinions about his toys running off."

Toy.

I shrank farther back against the wheel.

"Is the monster in?"

Shame. Anger. Grief. It all swirled like a storm, and I hardly knew what was his and what was mine, but so much emotion choked my voice that I could not answer.

"If you're upset about Tori, don't be," Katashi said when I made no answer. "He's no great loss. As long as you don't ever plan to use that deadly hand of yours against me."

He laughed but fear rattled in it.

The wagon door creaked open behind me. "Ah, Great Fish," Malice said. "I thought I heard your lovely voice, yes? Do come in."

"Endymion too," Katashi said. "I need him."

"Then by all means, Endymion, do join us," Malice crooned and disappeared back into the wagon.

"Come on." Katashi gripped my collar and dragged me roughly up. A blinding flash burst through the night as his hand touched my neck, leaving his whispers on my tongue and his memories before my eyes. A man lowered his head to the executioner's block. Dark hair fell around him, and I too could hear the people cheering.

The connection broke as he let me go. He was striding to the wagon steps, but I could not immediately follow, so thickly did grief and anger fill my body like an overstuffed scarecrow.

"Kin has requested a meeting," he was saying when I stepped through the door into the sweetly scented interior of Malice's wagon. "Tonight. Outside the walls. I am going to take Endymion."

Malice didn't even lift a brow in surprise. "Are we dogs now to order around?"

"No, but let's cut the posturing and admit you want eyes in that tent as much as I want someone who can feel people. It saves time."

"You could have asked for me."

"Yes, but while Endymion might be fucking creepy, he isn't also an arrogant shit that oozes everywhere. I'll pick my freaks wisely."

I wanted to sink through the floor. For those few, glorious days, I'd had a family; I had belonged. Now I was just the freak again, and I couldn't even blame him after what I had done, could only wish for the thousandth time in my life that I had not been born an accursed Empath.

Malice's smile was faint but amused. "Very well, you may take him. But do allow me to dress him rather more appropriately for an audience with our great emperor, yes?"

"You have one hour."

A slight bow, and on that, Katashi could have left, could have strode off about his preparations, but he stood rooted to the worn boards like a tree grown out of place.

"There is something else you want, Great Fish?"

"That deal you offered," Katashi said, the words drawn from him as though by force. "I accept it. We'll meet you in the trees beyond the north wall, after the meeting."

Out there, a whole camp was sure he could get into that castle, that he could kill Kin and do the impossible, but to make it happen, Katashi was here accepting a deal he hated, and only I could feel his heart breaking.

Malice gave a solemn bow. "As you wish."

Katashi's lips parted as though he might snap that *wish* was hardly the right word, but whatever pain he might have admitted he shut away with a little shake of his head and strode toward the door. Without another word, he was gone, stalking away into the fading daylight.

"Hope," Malice called to the Vice who was never far away. "Close the door, yes?"

"Yes, Master," the young man said, appearing briefly in the open aperture before he closed the door, shutting off the ingress of fresh air. Without it, sandalwood and opium smoke choked every breath. The haze made the air dry, dulling every bright colour.

Malice folded his arms. "Your idea, Endymion?"

"What was?"

"Going to the meeting. It is understandable that you are curious about the man sitting on your throne, and as it seems Emperor Kin has not yet discovered Darius's treachery, he is likely to be there too. Almost I am envious of you, yes? A meeting of giants. I would give much to see Kin and Katashi attempting civility, almost as much as I would give to see Darius's face when he sees you with your cousin, whose claim to the throne is so vastly inferior to your own."

"I don't want the throne, I just want…"

"Just want…?" he prompted after a short silence. "A friend? The family that you lost? Oh, don't look surprised I can read you,

Endymion, I'm an Empath too, yes? And you are terrible at masking. Now take off your clothes."

"What? With you watching?"

"You think I want you? Let me assure you that you awaken not one iota of desire in me. On those grounds, if no other, you have no need to fear me. Now take off your clothes. You cannot meet the emperor dressed like that. You're dirty." He took up the long opium pipe that was never far from his hand and pointed it at my clothing. "Mud and grass there. Specks of blood on your sleeve, oil on your collar, and that sash can no longer be called white. You are a filthy specimen."

He began to sift through a chest of clothes scented with cinnamon. "If it is family you want, then don't forget you have a sister, yes?" he said as he pulled out robes. "Trapped in Koi at this very moment, a prisoner of Emperor Kin."

There seemed to be no purpose behind his words, no continuation of the thought as he went on through robes, but my Empathy skittered away across the moors in search of the sister I had never known. I had been so enamoured of Katashi I had not even thought of her, had not considered her plight. If Katashi could get inside the castle and take the throne, perhaps we could be reunited. Perhaps I could be more than just a freak again.

Malice pulled a robe free with a triumphant swish, and I buried my new thoughts as deep as I could, hoping he would not see them.

"This is the one. It will look glorious, yes? Clothes off."

Under his eagle eye, I removed my offending robe. Hope brought hot water, and I washed and even let Malice drag a comb through my hair and fix my nails, wondering all the while if such things would seem normal had I remained the prince I had been born.

The robe Malice chose was pale blue silk over white linen, its sleeves covered in a myriad of thread-thin branches. I watched it shimmer in the mirror while Malice tied my sash, his hands moving with practised speed. Upon my cheek, the Traitor's Mark glared. The skin had scabbed, forming an unsightly mess that even the thickest layer of paint would not hide.

"Stay still for this part, yes?" Malice pinched my ear. A soundless cry lodged in my throat as something hot slid through my lobe, only to be removed as quickly. He waved a thin needle in front of my face. "There, that was easy," he said, putting the intimidating instrument down. "Now again, don't move."

"Why did you do that?" I said, tentatively touching the newly pierced hole.

"Because you are not properly dressed without it. I said don't move, yes?" With a linen cloth, Malice washed the injury he had just inflicted, the gesture oddly tender in one so seemingly selfish. When he had finished, he slid an earring through it, the weight of it causing the skin to stretch painfully.

"You are now correctly dressed," he said, returning to his divan. "Give my love to Darius, yes?"

He lay down and took up his book, shutting himself off so completely that I might no longer have existed. Feeling like the lost sheep for which Jian had named me, I let myself out of the hazy wagon. Hope was sitting on the steps.

"They are waiting for you at the northern boundary," he said. "Might I walk with you?"

"You haven't needed permission before."

He did not reply, just fell in beside me, his lantern lighting our path. It turned the grass golden beneath our feet and made my silk skirt shimmer. I had never worn a nobleman's robe before. It felt strange, heavy and yet soft, the hem catching on the grass with every step.

"Avarice says you'll be staying for a while," Hope said as we made our way through a tight knot of cedars, their needles prickly.

Not sure what to say, I did not answer. A hare dashed away from our steps, sending wineberries swinging on their boughs. At the edge of the copse, a group of shadowy figures was lighting lanterns.

Hope stopped, his hand on my arm. "Whatever it is you think you want from Malice, whatever he is offering you, don't take it. Nothing is so important. Trust me."

His youthful face looked worn and aged in the golden light. Son of the duke of Syan, Malice had said. He had been someone once.

"He isn't offering me anything."

"If he hasn't offered you anything yet, then run while you still can, before he has reason to call in your debts."

His gaze was so full of open hurt that I flinched. I gestured at the waiting escort, Katashi's presence brighter than any lantern. "I . . . have to go."

"You don't, but I'm sure my father would have said the same thing until it was too late to walk away. Run, Endymion. Don't stop running and never look back." With a little bow and a waft of melancholy, Hope left me to go the rest of the way on my own.

"I was sure he would send you not dressed at all," Katashi said in greeting, his restless fingers curling the mane of a chestnut stallion. "But instead you look more lord than I. Do you ride?"

I shook my head, reluctant to explain the difficulty I had with animals. It would only make him dislike me all the more.

"Looks like you're walking, then."

Katashi threw his leg over his horse with the same effortless grace he brought to everything, but as he settled himself in the saddle, I realised he was not carrying Hacho. A meeting of peace, then. Nothing else could induce him to part with her.

With lanterns held high, Katashi's entourage moved off through the dense trees, shadows running ahead. Not wanting to be parted from him, I kept pace beside his horse, watching my step as best I could in the shifting light.

Breaking from the cover of trees, we found ourselves on a wide field before the walls of Koi, the castle a lighted beacon in the night. Katashi did not hesitate, and I marvelled at his daring, so easily did he advance upon his enemy's stronghold.

A large pavilion had been erected in the middle of the field, glowing from within like a silk lantern dropped from the city walls.

"You'll stand behind me," Katashi said, his horse tossing its head as it caught my scent on the breeze. "I want to know everything you can tell me about Kin and his men, anything you can get."

"I can only do so much without touch," I replied.

"Then do what you can. I need everything you can give me."

We were the first to arrive, only a servant present to greet us with fragile anxiety. Perhaps he knew not what to say to a man who was both lord and rebel, heir and exile, and settled for saying nothing at all, just bowing, a lantern trembling in his hand. Katashi dismounted and, leaving his horse with a group of Pikes outside, strode into the tent.

Inside the pavilion, a dozen lanterns winked at us, shining their light upon a low table in the middle of the floor. It was set with wine jugs and a stack of earthenware bowls, but no other attempt at hospitality or decoration had been made. A practical man then, our emperor, above the ostentation of the nobility. I had to admit I was curious about this man who was so hated by all other Otakos, curious too how Lord Laroth would react at the sight of me standing behind Katashi, bearing the branding he had all but given me with his own hand.

Awaiting no invitation, Katashi knelt at the table. A slight tang of nervousness spiced the air.

A few minutes passed in silence before the thud of horses' hooves grew from the night. I closed my eyes. Ten new souls approached, bringing tension and anger and a murmur of voices. I strained my ears but caught only the fevered thrum of my own heart.

The tent opened. Crimson sashes and surcoats entered—imperial guards, stiff and solemn. I had hardly a moment to catch my breath before Kin was there, pausing on the threshold, his crimson robe flowing to the floor like water. He stood tall, firm-featured and determined, an Emperor in every sense of the word. He wore a soldier's topknot and his skin was weathered, but his assurance was like a rock.

Emperor Kin stepped forward and the gold threads of his sash gleamed in the lantern light. There, the Ts'ai dragon undulated down the crimson silk, gripping the grand characters of their motto in its curling claws: *Honour is Wealth*.

"Seated before you," a servant intoned as the emperor knelt across from Katashi, "is His Imperial Majesty, the great Emperor Kin, first of his name, Lord Protector of the Kisian Empire. And His Excellency Lord Darius Laroth, sixth count of Esvar and minister of the left."

My eyes shot up. In the opening, Lord Laroth stood framed by the night. A gasp caught in my throat. I could not breathe, but when those violet eyes travelled slowly over the company, they passed me with barely a flicker.

One of Katashi's Pikes stepped forward. "All bow before His Grace the duke of Koi, Lord Katashi Otako, prince of Kisia and true heir to the Crimson Throne."

A shock of anger tarnished the air. Lord Laroth paused in the act of kneeling, but still he did not look at me. Did he not recognise me in these clothes? Had he forgotten me?

Emperor Kin stared across the table. Words were already snapping from Katashi's lips. "—I'm an Otako and proud of it," he was saying. "I am my father's heir, and he was the last true Divine Emperor to sit upon the throne."

"I make no such claim to divinity," Emperor Kin returned. "But I am Emperor of Kisia in more than just name. Your family lost the crown when your father lost his head, and there the Otako reign came to an end."

"And what of the claims of my cousin, Lady Hana? I do hope you are treating her well."

"Of course. I have offered her a place at my side."

My chest tightened. Disbelief. Fury. Katashi's hands balled into fists. "And she accepts you?" he demanded, a hard note in his voice.

"We are still discussing terms, but an announcement will come. It is, after all, best for Kisia. And that way her children, legitimate heirs of the Otako blood, will sit upon the throne when I am gone."

"You have forced yourself upon her! I should have expected no less from a man of common blood."

Kin reacted for the first time, his heavy brows drawing together. I was reminded of all the stories I had heard, of the battles General Kin had won and the men he had killed, turning the rivers of Kisia red with blood. The man had a temper.

"I would have no unwilling wife," he said.

"Then you will not have my cousin. She is an Otako, and we know what is due to our name and our blood."

When Emperor Kin did not answer, Katashi leant forward, his elbows on the table. "I want to see her," he said. "To be sure you are treating her well."

"That is not possible."

"Then what assurance can you offer that she is even alive and this is not all a fiction to anger me?"

With a cold little smile, Minister Laroth spoke for the first time. "You do not accept His Majesty's word as a matter of honour because you have none yourself," he said. "This fault is yours, not ours."

"Ah, Lord Laroth," Katashi said. "How charming it is to meet you at last. I have heard much about you."

"If you are seeking to discompose me, you will have to do better than that," he said.

Divorced from these pleasantries, Emperor Kin gestured to a servant. The man knelt and served the wine, offering a bowl to the emperor and the minister and then to Katashi. "No," the Pike said, waving the bowl away. "I will pour one myself."

The air chilled. With trembling hands, the servant withdrew the bowl. He looked to his emperor, who nodded. The wine jug was handed over. It was an insult to question a lord's hospitality, but Kin, it seemed, was not fool enough to let Katashi rile him so pettily.

While Katashi poured himself a bowl, Emperor Kin's eyes strayed to my face, fixing upon my branded cheek. From there, his gaze fell to my robe and sash before snapping back. Malice had said I resembled neither my mother nor my father very closely, yet Emperor Kin went on staring. He knew my sister had survived our parents' assassination; did he know I had too?

"You are staring at my companion," Katashi said. "His Traitor's Mark offends you, perhaps. But you see, men who are deemed traitors to the Usurper are heroes to the true emperor of Kisia."

"Beyond your warmongering, it does not seem to me that the name of Kisia's emperor is in doubt."

Katashi lowered his wine bowl. "You think not? But you see, I learnt my history, the same as every noble son of Kisia, and, do correct me if I am wrong, but it was to the *Otako* family the gods gave this empire. There was no stipulation that anyone who conquered them might take the throne, as there is no law in this land that allows a commoner the right to behead a true and sworn emperor of Kisia."

"No stipulation because no stipulation is required," Kin returned, his words clipped. "If you give a gift to a man and that man's estate is taken, then the gift belongs to the conqueror. That is the law."

"The Crimson Throne is not a gift."

"No. Neither is it a right or a privilege. It is a duty. The oath states as much, but your ancestors stopped treating it so when they chose to suck more and more gold and resources from their own people to build ever grander palaces, when they chose to put themselves and their godhood above everything, chose to execute any and all who did not pay proper obeisance. They took the trust placed in them by their own people and drove this empire to the edge of ruin."

Their glares locked across the table, and though neither knew it, I felt the sting of the words as much as Katashi. This was my family the emperor was talking about, the family I had yearned for all my life, only to find it eking an existence in broken pieces. Had our fathers really deserved what had happened to them? Had they really ruled so poorly?

"I give you my terms," Kin went on, seeming to regain control over his temper. "Return the Hian Crown and disband your rebels. If you do, you may still leave Kisia with your life."

"You think having the crown will make you Kisia's true emperor?" Katashi said. "Even with it, you have been nothing but a Usurper for sixteen years."

"And you are nothing but a rebel. Hear me when I say the Crimson Throne will never again belong to an Otako of your blood. Lady Hana will marry me, and through her, you must be satisfied. If you return the crown and renounce your claim to the throne, you will live. If you fight, you will die. Those are my demands."

"I am the true heir to the Crimson Throne, as you will discover before long. There is no mercy for my father's murderer, but if you release Hana and abdicate the throne, you will save the lives of thousands of the people you claim to serve above yourself."

"I will never give the Crimson Throne to you or anyone."

The heavy silence seemed to suck sound away. No one spoke. No one moved. There would be no compromise, not for these men so steeped in their enmity. Old wounds had never healed, and now here they sat, two scabs on the page of history. And me. I had told Malice I didn't want the throne and it had been true, but as these men glared at each other, a thrill of fear rippled through me that I knew for my own. If either of them knew my true name, everything would change.

Katashi let out a snort of mirthless laughter. "If you have nothing else to say, I think it is time to abandon this pointless attempt at mediation," he said, throwing back the last of his wine. "I should have known better than to expect sense from you. You detest all Otakos as much as we detest you."

"I do not detest all Otakos."

"No, you were in love with Empress Li, weren't you? Have you fallen in love with Hana too?"

"I will not deign to discuss Lady Hana with you, but you may be assured that *you* are the only Otako I hate. You are very like your father and seem bent on the same course—removing the true emperor from the throne by whatever means it takes. I stopped him and I will stop you."

Katashi slammed his wine bowl on the table. The thin lip shattered, shards of earthenware skittering across the wood. "And you will suffer for what you did to him," he snarled. "I will watch them slice your flesh into a thousand pieces and feed you every one."

Kin did not flinch, but the tension grew tenfold. "There is a saying," he said with controlled calm. "'Before you embark on a journey of revenge, dig two graves.' If you succeed in killing me, you will not live to enjoy it, I promise."

"That we will see."

Kin looked down at the broken wine bowl. "You have until the morning to think better of your rash decision. If you bring the Hian Crown to the castle, you have my word you will not be harmed, and we can continue this discussion like sensible men. If not, you have until morning to remove your rebels from my woods, or not a single man will wake from his mat when the sun rises."

"Your kindness is without equal, Usurper."

Emperor Kin grunted and rose from the table, the tendons in his hands sticking out like whipcord.

Lord Laroth joined him, rising with stately grace. Still he did not look at me, had not since he entered, and I wanted to shout at him, to lunge across the table and slap him so he could not ignore me. *Look at me*, I shouted in the silence of my head, standing my ground. *Look at what you did to me!*

Emperor Kin strode out into the night, but Lord Laroth paused. For an instant, he lingered on the threshold, and at last he turned those violet eyes my way. His lips tightened into a smile, and he touched the single earring that hung from his ear, sending the bright amethyst swinging. I touched the one in my ear before I could stop myself, but he had already vanished into the night. The imperial guards followed, the tent silk shifting as they passed.

"It's time to go." Katashi had gotten to his feet and set his hand on my shoulder, his thumb grazing the bare skin of my neck. And once again, not seeming to notice the intrusion, connection flared. His anger prickled my skin.

I will have my revenge. Stinking shit, how dare he sit on my throne? How dare he speak so of my father! How dare he marry Hana. I will see him rot.

Screams sounded from the darkness. With fine robes torn, men ran through hallways littered with the dead, blood running in rivulets across old floors. It was Katashi's dream, the deepest desire of his soul. And there, staring at the point of a drawn arrow, was Emperor Kin, his face crusted with blood.

They will die. They will all die tonight.

19. DARIUS

The city of Koi buzzed with excitement as we made our way back through the lantern-lit streets. People waved flags and paper lanterns on strings, while children ran alongside the guards, waving and calling out to their emperor. With the oath ceremony to take place in the morning, the city was full to bursting—a lot of innocent people unprepared for the destruction I feared was coming.

He had dressed the boy to taunt me. Malice himself had worn that robe the night we first met. *Look at him*, it seemed to say. *Just remember you belong to me.*

"I should not have gone with you," I said, breaking the silence that had crushed us since leaving the tent on the moor. "When Malice hears I am still in your good graces, he will strike again to try to dislodge me."

Kin looked over, the frown he had worn for the last half an hour unshifting. "Dislodge you?"

"You once asked what it is that he wants. I wasn't sure then, but I am now. It's me he wants, Majesty. The old me. He wants to erase the last five years and punish me for ever leaving him." The honesty and the vulnerability tore at the shield I had built myself, but I had to make him understand and ploughed on. "He doesn't give a damn about Katashi, but he will make use of whatever tools are available to get what he wants. If Katashi intends to strike tonight, then the Vices will be with him. Unless I go to Malice now."

The speech was out, it was done, but Kin did not immediately answer, did not even look at me, rather stared ahead at the flickering threads of General Ryoji's surcoat.

"You once told me you never wanted to return. Never wanted to be... *that* again."

"I don't."

The chatter of the excited city folk followed us up the hill toward the towering castle.

"It seems I have required many sacrifices of you, Darius."

"Sacrifices I have been glad to make, Majesty."

"Until now."

No lie would convince either of us. "Until now," I agreed.

"You are sworn to my service until I take my oath in the morning."

"I am, but I beg you will let me go now so I may protect you from what is coming."

Again he stared at the back of General Ryoji's surcoat as the man led the way through the city streets, the cheering of the crowd at odds with the constriction in my throat.

"Koi Castle is impenetrable—"

"Excuse me, Majesty, but it is not. Not to men who can do things men ought not be able to do."

He held up his hand in acknowledgement of the crowd, waving as he said, "And if the Vices still attack with Katashi as you surmise, regardless of your sacrifice, who will be able to advise on the defence of the castle? Hoping for the best is not a viable strategy."

"More lookouts. More guards. Total lockdown. Don't let anyone in or out. Every soldier who knows how to use a bow must be given one. Most Vices require short range to—"

"You can give these orders to the council yourself. If, after we have done all we can to protect the keep, you still wish to leave, I will not stop you. But neither will I ask you to go. No, Darius," he went on when I would have spoken. "Don't argue with me. I don't doubt you believe in your assessment of the situation, but you are an asset against the Vices, not merely a magnet to possible attack. Who else knows as much as you do of how they function?"

I hated to admit he was right almost as much as I hated the loyalty he was showing me—loyalty I had done nothing to deserve. Takehiko Otako had stood behind Katashi at that meeting, and if Kin was right, if Malice was in this for greater ends, then Katashi was only the start of Kin's troubles.

"Tell me, Darius," he said, shifting the topic into calmer waters. "What did you think of Katashi Otako? What sort of man did you see?"

"I saw a man who speaks a fraction slower than is usual because he likes the sound of his own voice," I said, far preferring to talk of anyone but myself. "He also holds his hands so he is always touching some part of himself with the tips of his fingers. You will never be able to persuade such a man that he is wrong. It is his divine right to sit upon the Crimson Throne." I turned enough in my saddle to meet Kin's gaze directly. "I told you he would not be satisfied with just taking the throne from you. He wants you to suffer. He wants revenge even more than he wants the throne."

"What a cheery thought."

"Isn't it though?" I agreed. "If only you could go back and execute him with his father before he could become such a thorn."

Kin snorted. "If I could go back, that would not be the first thing I would change."

"You surprise me."

"Do I? Good. I had started to fear I was entirely predictable."

The crowd thinned as the castle's outer wall loomed. It would take another ten minutes to make our slow way through the maze of its defences, perhaps the last ten minutes I would ever have as a trusted advisor.

"You need to marry Hana," I said as the gates opened and we left the crowds behind for an endless stream of desultory "Your Majesty"s from the men on duty. "And if you don't, you have to let her go, otherwise Katashi will tell the world she is alive and imprisoned, and once he spins a good story, you will not be able to undo the damage. Once he paints you as a monster, you will not even be able to marry her without it being said you forced her into it. You saw tonight how quick he was to leap to that assumption."

"By the gods, Darius, I am trying," he said, lowering his voice to keep the pained growl from reaching the ears of his guards. "But I swear I can do nothing right with her. I can say the most seemingly innocuous thing, and all of a sudden it is monstrous to have even thought it. What sort of tutors did you give her?"

"No one out of the ordinary. I could not trust any of the great masters, nor would they have travelled so far from the capital nor taught a girl."

"That is not at all reassuring."

It was not a conversation I had ever thought to have with anyone, let alone the Emperor of Kisia, but knowing the end would soon come, I revelled in its bittersweet joy. "How so, Majesty?"

"Consider that if she does not think this way because she was taught to by philosophical masters, then she does so because it is in her nature. That, Darius, is frightening. No, don't laugh. She told me I could not call Katashi selfish for desiring to take the throne however grave the consequences of war, because it was easy for me to throw stones while living in a palace."

"There is some wisdom in that observation. I'm impressed."

Kin glowered at me. "In truth, you would prefer I abdicate rather than fight to protect the stability Kisia already has?"

"Hardly, Majesty. Katashi is an unknown. He could be a terrible leader and that uncertainty alone is worth fighting against. But there is an admirable sort of honesty in admitting that you fight as much for your own pride and honour—because you *want* to be Kisia's emperor."

He was silent as we passed through the next gatehouse to another chorus of bows and "long live Emperor Kin"s from the guards on duty. As our horses took the turn and started up the next slope beside the sheer rock wall, he said, "You make it sound sordid to say it like that."

"Hana won't think so. She has wanted the position she feels she is owed ever since she was little."

"I still feel it would have been much better had you told me at the beginning that she was still alive, Darius."

They were chilling words and, in their wake, the brief moment of friendship could not be recovered. He seemed to realise this as I did and added, "Still, I am not without hope. I will speak to her again before I call the council meeting to organise our defences. If she accepts me, she may yet be a useful tool against Katashi."

"Yes indeed, Your Majesty."

His sidelong look was full of calculation and bitterness. "I wish I could be sure I could trust you, Darius, but for all the openness in our conversations of late, I become only more assured that I cannot. You have been a good minister and a good friend, and I will miss you. More I cannot say and you ought not assume."

"To have been of service to you has been an honour, Majesty," I said, and I meant it. That it had been the only five years of my life I could be proud of I could not say, nor that I dreaded every day that would come hereafter.

20. HANA

The castle was quiet, this castle that had once been Katashi's home. I could not but imagine him walking its every hall, playing in every garden as a child and practicing his archery in the courtyards. I had no memory of the place at all, but I could not be inside an Otako stronghold without feeling the very walls themselves beat with a heart as proud as my own.

Though the whole compound was a sprawling maze, I had not been allowed out of the keep, barely out of my room—a space made gloomy by a profusion of square pillars, blackened with age. The roof had the same dark skeleton, with a central spine and dozens of branching ribs. In contrast, the paper screens that delineated the rooms were so fragile, painted with delicate birds, blossoms, and branches that seemed to tremble in even the gentlest draft.

As though giving voice to this susurrus, the guards outside my room continued their desultory conversation. They were ostensibly there for my safety, but locked away in this great keep, I felt more like a prisoner than ever. Kin had barely spoken to me since our ill-fated dinner, but I often felt his eyes on me, those dark orbs having a weight all their own. And while he watched me, I watched him, trying to make sense of a man as ferocious as he was kind, as blind as he was wise, and whose force of purpose led him to bury all sense of self beneath a thick layer of duty. Katashi had vengeance in his heart rather than duty, but I was slowly starting to think the two men had more in common than either would have appreciated.

A cluster of lights appeared through the main gatehouse, shifting like fireflies. That meant Kin had returned from his meeting with Katashi, and like the castle itself, the feelings that produced in me were both complex and ever-changing.

I finished my meal while watching the constellation of lanterns meander up the path and over the bridge. They came through the second gatehouse and then the third, twisting through the maze of walls and dark gardens, a group of shadowy figures on horseback. As they passed beneath my window, I pushed my tray aside and stood, peering down in time to catch a glimpse of crimson silk before it disappeared.

Had Kin really believed diplomacy could save Kisia? Katashi wouldn't.

With Kin's procession having vanished from sight, there was nothing to do and nothing to see, and I slumped onto the cushions with a sigh. Was it worth sending another message to Darius? He had ignored them all so far, and I had caught nothing more than the occasional glimpse of Shin, continuing to impersonate a military messenger in Lord Laroth's train. That Darius kept him nearby was interesting. Did he think Kin more of a threat to my safety than he would have me believe?

"Lady Hana Otako languishing in despair? I never thought to see it."

I hadn't heard the door slide, but there was Kin, framed by the heavy timbers. Dressed in his imperial robes, he was once again the Kin of Mei'lian, not the armour-clad warrior I had known of late.

"I do not languish," I said, sitting up. "I am just bored."

"Finally, you appear ladylike," he said, sliding the thin screen closed. "I hope you have everything you desire."

"No, there is nothing to do and I have only my maid for

company. Why can't I walk around the keep and the gardens? The castle is well enough guarded, is it not?"

"It is," he agreed. "But for now, you will stay here. Once the area is safe, I have no objection to you walking wherever you choose."

"You mean once you are free of Katashi."

He did not immediately agree, just looked at me as though trying to read my thoughts. "I have just been to meet him," he said after a time. "He is calling himself the *one true heir*, and had the audacity to describe in detail the death he has planned for me." He stopped speaking, a scowl darkening his already fierce features.

"I could have told you meeting him would be pointless," I said.

"No doubt, but I wanted to meet the man who would take my throne from me."

"As you took it from his father."

"And his father took it from yours."

I looked back out the window, preferring the nothingness of the night to his brooding frown. Behind me, footsteps marked his journey from one side of the room to the other and back.

"What is Katashi planning?"

The silence had been preferable. I did not turn from the window. "Do you really expect me to tell you?"

"I don't know what I expect. But I'm asking."

I hesitated. As a captain of Malice's Vices, I had not been privy to Katashi's plans, but there had been talk enough to make some guesses. That Katashi had asked Malice for a way inside the impenetrable keep, I knew, but in no part of the plan had I been captured, and Malice might yet betray Katashi as he had betrayed me.

"You make no answer. Will you tell me what you know?"

I shook my head slowly. "No, I will not."

"I see. Again, it is a choice I should have expected. I have allowed myself to hope too much."

"A willingness to betray confidences is a strange trait to hope for in a wife."

"It is only betraying confidences if you speak your secrets to an enemy. That answers my next question before I even need ask. I shall leave you now, my lady, and—"

"Stop calling me that whenever you're angry with me!"

Kin had turned to go, but he spun back on the heel of one sandal. "Calling you what?"

"*My lady* with such a mocking emphasis. I don't know anything, all right? Katashi never told me anything. He didn't even know who I was."

It was his turn to stare out the window while I fought the urge to gather my knees to my chest and hold them close. His presence unbalanced me, made my stomach knot, and I wished he would leave me to my boredom.

Again, he paced from one side of the room to the other and back, seemingly struck by the same agitation. Then, as though the words were drawn from him, he said, "Well he knows now. Perhaps it will please you to know he asked after you. He wanted to be sure you were well and being looked after." For a moment, he seemed sure to say more, but he pursed his lips and kept all further thoughts on the subject to himself.

I was not sure what to say or how to feel. That Katashi would not want me here, would not want me to marry Kin, would not want me to do anything that might get in his way, troubled me as much as it satisfied me. Again, I was struck by the likeness between the two men, though their age and birth and experience of life were so dissimilar.

Kin paced another lap of the room, not seeming to want to stay still. I wished he would speak as much as I wished he would leave.

"Hana." His skirts rustled as he neared, the smell of horsehair and leather clinging to the silk. "I have … come to ask again that you do me the honour of becoming my wife. My empress. I hope I have shown myself prepared to discuss important subjects and... and to treat you with the respect you both requested and deserve."

I ought to have seen it coming, maybe I had, but my heart raced with panic because I had no answer. It had been so easy back in Mei'lian to throw refusal in his face, to be definite and sure even in the shock of the moment, but there could be no such confidence here. Out there beyond the walls, Katashi was awaiting his moment to strike, and here and now I was being asked to make a final, definite decision between my family and Kisia. And something in Kin's look, in the earnestness of his expression, told me it was a final choice, that he would not ask me again.

"Would you grant me equal rights under the law?" I said, hoping he didn't catch the tremor in my voice. "As your empress?"

"Not equal, but..." He had answered before thinking and trailed off, the room suddenly hot and stuffy. "Equal rights would be... complicated, and... unprecedented. This would not be a good time to make such changes to—"

"If not to save your empire from the threat of civil war, then when would be a good time? If not to unite Kisia, then when? Marriage may be the goal given to every young woman of rank, but I would live unwed before I would agree to be nothing but a man's adjunct, even when that man is the Emperor of Kisia."

"Even if he was Katashi Otako?"

"Yes! Even him."

Silence wallowed around us. Was it our curse that every encounter ended like this, so prone were we to speak our minds?

Hasty words make for a meal of regret! It had been one of Mama Orde's favourite scolds, and I could see her now, bustling around the farmhouse while the scent of spices seared in the pan. Papa wouldn't be in from the fields until the sun drew low, but she would be keeping herself company with tunes hummed between dry lips. I would still be there had Malice not come, not whispered of adventures and plans and all that might be. All that should have been. Or if I had not listened. But too much had I wanted to be someone.

I turned away, blinking at tears. Kin did not move, just stood with his heavy gaze fixed to the side of my face.

"If you have nothing else to say, I would ask you to leave," I said.

"You're crying."

"I am not crying."

"You're a bad liar."

Bitter tears trickled down my cheeks. "Oh, just go away!"

The soft divan sank beneath his weight, tipping me toward him. I had to put out a hand to right myself.

"Lady Hana Otako should not cry," Kin said. "Look at me."

Pride stinging, I kept my face averted and rubbed away the tears with the back of my hand.

His fingers closed around my wrist. "Hana." I had expected a strong grip that crushed my bones, but his touch was gentle though his skin was rough. "Hana, look at me. I...I am asking you to marry me out of duty to the empire, but I am...not sorry that such a duty falls to me, that..." He faltered and stopped. A sigh blew past his lips. "By the gods, you would think that after sixteen years on the throne, I would be better at making speeches."

I turned, surely red-eyed but no longer caring. "Will you give me what I want?"

"There is plenty of time to discuss the details when—"

"When I have agreed and have no more leverage. And you can go back to being imperial and overbearing."

"And risk being scolded? I wouldn't dare. But is it really so terrible to want a wife, a companion, a mother to my children, rather than an equal under the law?"

I closed my eyes, disappointment weighing down my shoulders.

"Must one preclude the other?" I pulled my hand from his. "Marriage was not any part of my future plans when I left my home not so long ago, and you must excuse me if I am in no hurry to change that. Whatever my…feelings and opinions on the subject, what you are asking of me is no small thing. Exile or not, Katashi is my cousin and the head of my family, and my responsibility to him and to my name cannot lightly be thrown away."

He looked down at the hand that had held mine, closed to a fist now upon his knee. "It is a difficult position you find yourself in, indeed," he said, brisk and cold. "As caught between loyalties and desires as poor Darius was. May the night bring you good counsel, my lady."

The divan sprang back, a cold space opening beside me. He strode to the door, fists clenched tight, and for one mad instant, I thought to call him back. But I held my tongue, and he was gone, leaving the air considerably chilled behind him.

The urge to cry was almost overwhelming, but I would not. Not for any man who looked at me and saw only a woman.

I sent for Tili, and by the time she arrived, I had composed myself and no longer wanted to scream into the cushions.

"My lady? You sent for me?" She slid the door closed behind her. "I am sorry if you should be in a hurry for warm washing water, but this castle—"

"No, Tili, nothing like that. I want you to take a message to Minister Laroth. I don't care where he is or what he's doing, tell him I want to see him and insist he comes. Now."

"If…if that is what you need, my lady, of course, but…is everything all right?"

"No, Tili, it isn't. I need to get out of here. Tonight."

21. ENDYMION

Malice waited at the edge of the forest, watching distant figures walk the castle walls. Moonlight scattered around his feet and speckled his robe, shifting with every movement of the clouds. Hope and Avarice stood at a distance, neither ever far away.

"You're late, yes?" Malice said as we approached through the thinning trees. Just the two of us, as Katashi had sent his guards back to the camp with his horse.

"In a hurry, Vice?" he retorted. "Do you have somewhere more important to be?"

"As a matter of fact, I do."

Koi's lantern-lit walls were visible as flashes of gold through the trees. The keep loomed above them, a silent beast in the night. More than anything, it had been built as a symbol of power, and the proud northerners were quick to remind anyone who might mistake that the throne room in Mei'lian was only a replica of the one originally built at Koi.

"And your payment?" Malice said, shadows dancing upon his face.

"Coming," Katashi snapped. The meeting with Kin had left him furious, and for the first time, I could feel him trying to bury it. He was trying to hide the trouble that knitted his brows, but the world went on sucking in its breath when he did, its very threads responding to his strength.

We waited beneath the last of the trees like a small group at vigil, listening to the sounds of the night—the bark of night herons and the unceasing chitter of insects in the heat. Hope was watching me. *Run*, he had said. *Don't stop running and never look back.* But Katashi was my family. Hana was my family. And after a lifetime of wondering, of dreaming, of yearning, the word held such power, such allure, that no warning Hope uttered could make me abandon them now.

I felt a soul approach but did not look up until Katashi did, his ears having caught the dull thud of hooves. He had crouched in the grass but rose as Kimiko reined in her mount. "Katashi, what's going on?" She slid from the saddle, sending her curls bouncing. "Tan said you needed me."

She looked up into his face and touched his arm, but he did not speak, just patted her horse's neck. "Katashi?"

He took a step away. "Just do it."

"Do what?" Kimiko scanned the shadows and found Malice standing beneath the trees. "Why is he here?" Her panic flared bright. "You made the deal."

"He did, yes," Malice said. "And you are the payment, my dear. But don't be afraid. I am not going to hurt you, yes?"

"Me? No!" Kimiko grasped Katashi's arm. "I know how important this is, but there has to be another way."

"You said yourself that there is no other way! Our father deserves vengeance. Kisia deserves vengeance. And I will do whatever it takes to see it happen."

She stepped back. His heart may have broken back in Malice's wagon, but it was as hard as stone now, hot with fury. It was hers that ached. "It was never supposed to be about revenge," she said, the words no less fierce for being quietly spoken. "It was supposed to be about family. About regaining what had been lost and for the right reasons. Kin took away everything we had, everything we were, but if Hana is alive, then maybe Takehiko is too, and then the Crimson Throne does not even belong to you."

My heart hammered uncomfortably at the sound of my name. And I flinched when Katashi hissed a gout of fury back at his twin. "Takehiko is gone. If he was still alive, he would already have come to claim it. No son of Emperor Lan would hide in the shadows."

All I had wanted was a family. The desire sounded so pathetic as Katashi tore the dream apart around me. Here stood the brave and great Katashi Otako, willing to sacrifice anything, even his own twin sister, for the good of a name I could not even admit I possessed. Too afraid. Too unsure. Too desperate for his love and acceptance to risk drawing his ire. I wanted a family, but he wanted a throne.

"He might," she said. "Those who have been through troubles are not as they were born but as life made us, and if he knows who he was born, then Takehiko has more reason than most to be afraid. Tell me, you would give everything, even me, to fight Kin for the throne, but would you give it to the rightful Otako heir if he returned?"

I could not breathe. The intensity of Malice's gaze on me ought to have drawn their attention, but neither seemed to recall we were there. Katashi looked away. I wanted him to answer, needed to hear his reply though I feared it to the core of my being.

"I have no choice, Kimiko," he said at last, his avoidance of the question all the answer I needed. "I've come too far. I sit on that throne at dawn or the Otakos die here, bettered by a commoner."

"If that is all that drives you, then let us die!"

"Our name is all we are, all we have left. We are the divine Otakos, and by the gods, we will have vengeance for what was done to us."

Tears stood in her eyes. "And you will sacrifice every honour to achieve it. I thought I knew you better, but now I weep for you, Katashi."

He turned his back on her, scowling upon each of us watching in silence. "What are you waiting for, Vice?" he demanded. "I have brought your payment."

"And a charming payment she is, yes?" Malice beckoned to Kimiko, but she held her ground, glaring at everyone present in turn with unflinching pride. But her fear fluttered my heart. I wanted to be sick.

Malice strode toward her, but still she did not flinch, just eyed Avarice warily as he approached in his master's wake. "What will happen to me?"

"I am going to mark you," Malice said. "It will bind you to me as well as giving you a new...aspect of yourself. A special skill, triggered by emotion, often whichever is most heightened at the time, though in your case, your brother requires a particular skill generated with a particular emotion—one no other Vice of mine currently possesses."

"Why not?"

"Why not? Because it killed the last one who did, yes? And as useful as it is, I did not deem the recreation of it worth the risk." He smiled so sweetly as he said it, first at her and then at Katashi, that the air chilled. "Shall we?"

Across the odd gathering in the shadows, I stared at Katashi. I could tell him the truth, I could beg him to change his mind, but no words came out no matter how fiercely I thought them. He would do this, and while I stood by in silence, I could not even condemn him for it. Silent, it became my crime too.

Run, Hope had said. *Don't stop running and never look back.*

"I hope this is worth it, Brother," Kimiko said as Avarice took up a position behind her. "I hope you get what you need."

He didn't answer, didn't look.

Malice lifted his hand. Again, I begged in silence for Katashi to speak, to challenge, to change his mind, but he set his jaw hard and stared at the trees. Kimiko flinched as Malice's fingers touched her cheek, then her eyes widened. Her lips parted in a silent scream, and when she would have fallen back, Avarice locked his hands at her stomach and did not let her go.

The trees shivered. An eerie moan parted Kimiko's lips, a terrible keening, and though I wanted to look away, I wanted as much to see all there was to see, to feel the shift of power, the change Malice was capable of creating with seemingly little effort. For so long, I had thought of my Empathy as nothing, a burden owning no use but in the helping of others, but Malice could do things I had never thought to dream of—he could change people, use people, hurt people, kill. He could move through the world, shaping it to his own ends, with no reason to ever be afraid again, no need to ever suffer.

In our quiet little clearing, Kimiko's silent wail rose to a scream, and Avarice clamped his hand over her mouth, but the muffled cry was no less chilling. It ended abruptly when Malice withdrew his hand, and like a formless doll, Kimiko slid out of Avarice's grip and onto the grass.

Hope moved first, holding out a hand to her heaving shoulders. Kimiko yelped and backed away, animal-like, her feet scattering leaves across the forest floor.

"Lady Kimiko?" Hope held out his hand, each step a light tread upon the grass as he crept closer.

Katashi hurried forward only to walk into Avarice's outstretched arm. "What's wrong with her?"

"Hush, Otako," Malice said. "Your dear sister is in shock, yes? Recovery was once a long process, but fortunately for you, we now have our dear Hope."

"Then make him—"

"Oh no." The Vice Master wagged a finger. "Hope cannot be hurried."

The young Vice ignored this interchange and continued his cautious approach, his hands raised before Kimiko to show he meant no harm. "Let me help you," he said. "Take my hand."

She hesitated, eyes flicking from Hope to me to Malice, her whole body poised, ready to flee. But she let him come, let him crouch before her and take her face gingerly between his hands. And there they froze, only the breeze stirring their hair and the loose material of their clothes.

"Endymion." Though it was Katashi speaking my name, it was an effort to withdraw my gaze from Hope's narrow shoulders. "Endymion." He gripped my arm. "Tell me what you felt from Kin? Is he worried? Afraid?"

He had turned his back on Kimiko and Hope, but over his shoulder I could still see them. "No," I said, trying to focus on his question. "Well, worried, yes, a little, I think, though it's hard to tell different people apart in a close space. Not afraid though. Determined. Angry. He meant everything he said; there was no bravado. He is as sure about the world as you are."

Katashi's snort of wry amusement sounded close to my ear, an intimate sound for me alone. "Then I will just have to make him see he's wrong."

And if he failed, our family would fracture still more. Right now, he was all I had. "What's your plan once you're through the walls?"

He narrowed his eyes at me in the gloom. "I won't risk that answer to anyone."

"I heard what you said about the defences. Even if Malice gets you through the walls, the keep will be full of soldiers and guards."

"Why do you care what I do once I get in? Worried for me?"

Because I'm an Otako too. The words were there on my tongue, but his earlier admission kept them trapped behind my lips.

"I can help you," I said instead of answering. "I know you don't like what I can do, but having an Empath with you in there would make it much easier. I can sense people before you can see them or hear them or even smell them."

He eyed me with disfavour. "Why would you help me?"

Because maybe if you win, we can be a real family. Because maybe if I help you, you won't look at me like I'm a monster.

Instead I tapped the Traitor's Brand on my cheek. "I have my own reasons to dislike Kin. One man's traitor can be his enemy's friend, remember?"

Again he made that little snort of amusement. "All right then." He walked over to where Kimiko had left her horse and began going through the saddlebags. She and Hope still hadn't moved from their places, seemingly frozen on the grass, but when I glanced his way, I found Malice's eyes on me. No emotion in his face, nothing in his soul I could read. Would he try to stop me going?

Within a minute, Katashi was back, Hacho's upper limb once more standing proud above his head. He held out a bow, different again to the other he had given me.

"In the absence of Shin, you'll have to do," he said and thrust a holster and a ball of black clothing into my arms. "Wear these. They should fit close enough."

Stepping away into the trees, I changed as quickly as Malice's complicated sash-knot would allow before returning to the small group. I found Kimiko sitting up, hugging her knees while Katashi paced. Hope had moved away to lean against a tree a little way off, a hand pressed to his head.

"At last you return, Endymion," Malice said as Avarice took the fine robe from me. "I get quite sick of standing around watching the Great Fish wriggle."

He held down his hand to Kimiko, but she pushed it away. "I don't need your help. I can stand on my own."

"As you wish, my dear. Shall we go?"

"No."

Avarice froze, thick fingers clasping silk.

"No?" Moonlight dusted Malice's face. "Perhaps you don't understand. You have been marked by me. That means whatever I command, you must obey, yes?"

"You can do whatever you like, but I will not obey you."

Hope covered his eyes with shaking hands. Malice didn't speak, didn't move, but pain leaked its elusive tang into the air. Starting as a dull ache, it grew, an ever-increasing agony tearing through the night. Kimiko winced, then she doubled over, pale, her arms clasped across her stomach as the disobedience stirred within her like knives.

Malice crouched beside her, his whispered words barely catching on the breeze. "It is not me you should hate, yes?" he said. "I am your master now, and you will do as I say. Do you understand? This is where you say, 'Yes, Master,' like a good Vice."

She said nothing.

"I can make this much, much worse, and I will enjoy it. 'Yes, Master.'"

"Yes ... Master," she gasped.

"Good."

The pain eased, flowing back into the night.

Malice straightened. "We go to the wall. Avarice, Hope, stay here and wait for me."

"Yes, Master."

Holding tight to her pride, Kimiko got slowly to her feet, her legs a little shaky. Her brother's hand was there, but she steadied herself on a tree trunk instead, turning her back on us all. Malice was already disappearing through the trees, and she followed him without another word.

Trembling, Hope slumped to the ground. He looked barely conscious, little more than a black heap on the grass.

"Quit staring and get on," Avarice said, jerking his head at us. "He isn't dead yet."

"Come on." Katashi brushed past me to follow in Kimiko's wake. "We're running out of time."

Koi Castle sat at the western edge of the city atop a steep hill, down which the growing populace had spilled. Its outer wall met that of the city's part way around, the rest left to jut out and protect itself. Not that it had any trouble with this, the outer wall being only the beginning of the castle's defences.

Space had been cleared between the wall and the surrounding forest, and we found Malice and Kimiko waiting at the edge of a copse, crouched low in the shifting shadows. The moonlit moor stood between them and the long shadow of the castle wall—a wall lined with guards. The moment anyone stepped out, they would immediately be seen.

"I think we're expected," Katashi whispered. "There's no other reason Kin would have so many guards on a part of the wall with no gates."

"Yes, it's very sweet." Malice did not look at all troubled. "Shall we test your new skill, my dear?" He pointed to a short stone wall nearby, jutting from the ground like a manmade cliff. There were lots of them around the edge of the forest, as though the line of trees marked more than an arbitrary boundary.

"What are those?" I said, though the weight of souls upon the wall kept drawing my gaze.

Katashi reached the short wall in half a dozen long strides. "It's the crypt. They couldn't build it beneath the keep because the hill is made of iron-hard rock, so they built it beside the castle instead. These walls are at least four blocks thick though and made of iron-stone. They're not entrances."

"How do you get in then?"

"There's an entrance in the gardens," Kimiko said. "No tunnel could go right into the keep because of the hardness of the rock. So even if you could get through here," she added, glancing at Malice, "it still doesn't get you inside the keep itself."

The keep that rose behind her, its narrow windows like slitted eyes. I could sense life. There were a dozen men on this portion of the outer wall, another dozen on the other side. Eight in the gate-house, twenty-one on the front wall, twenty-four in the grounds, and another twelve upon the second wall—one of them fast asleep. Stretching myself thin, I could just reach the keep, there another two hundred and fourteen souls, each a small flame in a sea of light.

"Getting inside the walls was the job asked of me, yes?" Malice said.

"I am going to help with the rest."

Kimiko's eyes turned to me in the darkness, but it was Malice who laughed. "Oh, Endymion, you are a sweet brother, no?" My heart leapt into my throat so close did his words come to exposing me, but he went on speaking as though it had not happened. "Here, my dear." He gestured to Kimiko. "Rest your hand on the stone."

Kimiko hesitated but only for a moment. Against the rough stonework, her hand looked small and pale.

"Now the emotion you need is sadness, and not just ordinary sadness, yes? The sort of sadness that edges into despair, the feeling that you wished you no longer existed and never had existed before."

"I don't know how to do that."

"Yes, you do. It is a feeling everyone knows intimately whether they admit it to themselves or not. It is a feeling for dark corners and lonely moors, for the nights when you wake and worry and wish it all over, and the days that break your heart with their slow erosion of all comfort and pride and honour, all sense of self-worth. Here." He touched his open palm to the back of her hand, and a sadness bloomed in the air until every breath stank of it, of such great despair that I wanted to retch. Then, as though her flesh were as insubstantial as smoke, her fingers slid into the wall.

Kimiko pulled them back out and stared at them, touched them with the other hand to be sure they really did exist. "How did I do that?"

"It is the gift I gave you by infusing your whole body with an emotion only meant to be felt by the soul. The process creates... great variation, but I have had reason to perfect this particular skill before, yes?"

She set her hand back on the stones. "You said the last one died."

"He did. Don't ever let the emotion go while you are... mid transition." Holding out his hand, Malice added, "Here, let me get you started again and you try to hold it."

I had never seen Malice so gentle, speaking calmly and teaching with patience, as for the next twenty minutes or more, Kimiko worked on maintaining and then creating the emotion she needed. There was a hunger in her while she worked at it, over and over, all objection to being made a Vice temporarily forgotten in the joy of so miraculous an ability.

Katashi watched, and though he was usually easy to read, it was impossible beneath the sheer depth of despair Kimiko had to produce. When at last she had managed to create and maintain it on her own, she held out her hand to Katashi. "Ready when you are, Brother."

Bitterness laced every word, but he did not answer, just put his hand in hers, their fingers entwining so naturally they might have been one. The sadness returned. Her other hand slipped into the stone first, her fingers vanishing, then one step closer, two. It was hesitant, unsure, but the wall did not repulse her, and she stepped more confidently forward, drawing Katashi into the stone.

Malice scowled at the place where the two ill-fated Otakos had disappeared, and he waited, his breath held. The sadness did not fade.

"She learns quickly," he said after a time. "Perhaps I will have more than one reason to celebrate this night after all."

"You never said you were going to use Kimiko."

His brows rose in their characteristic expression of mock surprise. "You did not ask. Who else would it have harmed him to part with, yes? No one should be given what they want most without paying more dearly for it than they really want to. That is part of the fun, part of the game, the test, the hunt. People really are quite fascinating."

"She was my cousin."

"Still is, she's just now also a Vice and bound to me, not her family." He pressed his hand to his lips. "Oh no, you were trying to fix your family, weren't you, to bring them all together. Don't worry, you still have Katashi, and if you're in time, you might even save Hana. That's why you're going in there, yes?"

"Yes, but... how can I? I don't know where she is, and even if I find her, she has no reason to trust me."

A breeze caught his long hair and he smiled. "No, but Darius will know where she is, and—" He held up his hand, silencing my complaint that I could hardly trust Minister Laroth a second time. "And... since Emperor Kin would be very unhappy to find out Darius knew all about you, it is even more in his interests than yours to ensure you are not found, yes? Regardless, the whole keep will soon be swarming with Pikes, which should keep you quite safe."

He drew a small canister from his sash, the sort Jian used for ink. "Here. She may not trust you, but she will trust me. Give this to her, yes?"

I took it from his outstretched hand. The whole container seemed to whisper, to thrum with its own heartbeat. "What's in it?"

"Blood." He held up his hands as I thrust it back at him. "Ah, still so much to learn, yes? Don't fear, little one. Hana has been with me long enough to understand what to do with it. One day, I will teach you this little trick."

The sadness was growing again, drawing close, and I tucked the flat canister into the pouch beneath my sash, trying to dismiss the feeling I had just hidden a living creature against my stomach. A moment later, Kimiko reappeared, stepping soundlessly through the stones. She looked pale but triumphant. "I did it. We had to walk all the way along because the stone doors at the other end are kept blocked off when no one is in residence, but I got him through." She looked to me. "Are you ready to go? He's waiting for you inside."

The stone edifice looked solid. And when I touched it, it felt solid. If something could smell solid, this would, this construction of stone and mortar, centuries old.

Kimiko took my hand. I was growing used to connecting on contact, used to the insight and the whispers, but... *Oh, I forgot, he's like Malice*, her whispers said. *Only somehow worse. Right under my skin.* She ripped her hand away.

"I'm... I'm sorry," I stammered. "I'll try not to, I'm just not... not very good at this."

Horror lit her eyes, and she glanced at Malice, but of course there would be no sympathy there. Katashi was waiting and she had to obey, yet even as she had to draw upon soul-crushing sadness, having to touch my skin was worse.

Her very soul seemed to shiver as she once more took my hand. No immediate whisper this time, but memories were there, the memories she used to draw the emotion, and I closed my eyes, trying not to see them. Short snippets. Sharp. Fast like her heartbeat. The smell of parchment and the clink of coins—a merchant's counting room. Laughter. The kind smile of a golden-haired man. Then the memories turned sour, fuelling her sadness. Rain. Cold streets. The claw of hunger. And Kimiko pulled me into the stone.

The wall did not part, but I did. The tingle started in my skin only to dig down, cutting me open as every piece of my body separated to pass through the stone, my pores like a sieve. The pain of it touched every inch of me, inside and out. It stung. It burned. And when I parted my lips to breathe, it stabbed into my lungs.

This is so strange. No, Kimiko, don't think about it or the wall might become solid again. Why does his hand feel so cold? Malice's didn't.

Kimiko's thoughts continued to churn and I wanted to let go, hating the intrusion that laid her soul bare before me, her life one that many would cringe to behold. Unable to free her, I tried to turn it off, to stop the connection, but her voice continued its whispered monologue in my head.

Look what you have done to me, Katashi, she said. *You fool, you stupid, selfish fool. You're in here, aren't you, Endymion? Get out of my head!*

Emerging the other side, my constricted lungs sucked musty air and my knees buckled. Kimiko tore her hand free.

"Will we have to do that again?" I asked, the words little more than an indrawn breath.

"There is another wall at the other end that leads into one of the gardens."

A torch had been thrust into a mound of dirt against the wall, its flickering light filling the crypt with shadows. Kimiko snatched it up and began to walk without waiting. I hurried after her along the shadowy row between two lines of stone caskets, each covered in carved script and a thick layer of dust and dirt.

I'm sorry. I tried to force the words out as we sped through the vaulted hall, each pillar appearing like a stationary figure from the darkness. *I'm sorry I didn't stop him. I'm sorry I didn't speak.* The words sounded weak even in my head, the words of someone who wants their guilt absolved merely to lighten their own burden. Thanks to us, she would be a Vice for the rest of her life.

"Here," she said, slowing at last as we reached another wall. "Let's get this over with." Kimiko slid the torch into an empty bracket and held out her hand. "I'll try to make it quick."

And it was, this wall more like a thick door and far easier to pass through. We reached the other side to breathe mouthfuls of scented night air, and I let go a sigh as she dropped my hand. There was no sign of Katashi, but two souls were approaching.

"Stop," I hissed as Kimiko made to step out from the lee of the wall. "Someone is coming." I pulled her back as two guards rounded the corner, talking in low voices. I tried to keep my Empathy close, tried not to listen, tried not to exist at all in the hope they wouldn't see us in the shadows.

Footsteps approached. "You think so?" One of them laughed. "I heard he's leaving."

"What do you suppose he did?" the other asked. "They've always been so happily married."

His companion sniggered and his footsteps brought him closer. They were going to walk right past us. I prayed the shadows were deep enough. "You think it goes that far? I've always thought Minister Laroth a bloodless man."

Minister Laroth. The mention of his name piqued my curiosity. What were they saying of him? Was he leaving?

"Did you feel that?"

Their footsteps halted.

"Feel what?"

"Like a . . . weight."

"A weight?"

"You know, like the air was touching me."

His companion started to laugh, but I balled my hands to fists and tucked them into my armpits. Had that been me? No one had ever felt the touch of my Empathy like a physical thing before.

"It's not funny. You know there are ghosts here. They say the ghost of Emperor Tianto walks these grounds. I wouldn't want him creeping up behind me."

We cut off his head and stole his castle. Then his empire. Oh gods, I don't want him creeping up behind me.

The whisper came to me though I hadn't been touching him. Heart fluttering in panic, I tried to pull my Empathy back, but it was too late. He turned toward me, drawn by my intrusion.

"Who's there?" the man demanded.

"Shit," Kimiko hissed. I felt the sadness an instant before the pain crawled up my back, stinging like I had fallen into icy water.

Idiot can't keep to himself. Yes, I'm talking about you, Endymion, I know you can hear me. That guard felt you and you weren't even touching him. After this, I hope I never have to touch you again.

"What are you talking about? There's no one there."

The muffled voice sounded far away.

"I tell you they were here!"

"And just disappeared into the wall? More of your ghosts?"

"Would it be any wonder? Do you know how many men have died protecting this keep?"

"Stop getting morose. The general doesn't care about ghosts, only rebels. Let's go."

There were no more words, just the strange stifled roar of the stone in my ears. Every inch of my skin was beginning to itch, but I could not move my arm without more pain scything through me. What would happen if Kimiko let go? Would the stone close around me? Would it slide down my throat and fill my body? It was unbearable to even think about.

Back out in the thin air, I shivered. Kimiko let go. The guards had gone. "Any more?" she whispered.

I barely needed to let my Empathy wander. There were men on the walls, but down here we were alone. "No."

She didn't wait but set off around the edge of the garden. A mixture of smells from the nearby workshops danced in the air— paint, wood shavings, and dye—but there was no light and no sign of life. Until, like the flames of a great fire, Katashi's soul began to fill every crevice of my awareness. Soon we found him crouched in the shadows, his face lit by scratches of moonlight. Rising above us, the curved roofs of the keep were tipped in silver, its crimson flags barely rippling.

Without so much as a nod or a smile, Kimiko left us to our task and returned the way we had come. Katashi scowled after her, but he could not, or would not, call her back.

Guards? he mouthed to me.

My Empathy never lied. There were four on the wall behind us and three in the garden. I held up the right number of fingers, and he nodded before breaking cover from the trees.

I followed, trying to float across the ground as he did, dis- turbing neither stick nor stone, but I lacked his skill. He crept, half-crouched in the shadows, managing to look like he was himself made of flickering darkness. More important still, he knew where he was going. The looming keep watched our progress with glowing eyes as, one after the other, we crept over moss-covered stones and through garden beds, crushing clumps of fragile anemones beneath our feet.

We met our first guard at a small pavilion. He did not see us. Did not hear us. He stood perfectly still, one hand resting on a stone lion while he stared out at the garden, the babble of water and the call of night birds lulling him to something like a standing doze.

Katashi pressed a finger to his lips. A breeze caught loose strands of his dark hair, and I could see him marking a path with his eyes, every stick and every blade of moonlight shaping his way. In his hand a long dagger, on his brow a heavy crease. Leaving me crouched in the shadows, he stalked across the soft ground, animal in his grace.

Katashi clamped the man's mouth, wrenching him back. With a flick of his wrist, he drove his dagger into the guard's kidney and yanked it out. Distance alone saved me from agony. The pain was quick, blinding, as Katashi cut deep into the man's throat. Blood sprayed, peppering the ground and the face of the stone lion that watched, impassive.

The guard jerked, blood spurting sluggishly from his mangled neck. Katashi held him as he thrashed, held him until his legs no longer kicked and he fell quiet. Then he prised his hand from the dead man's lips and lowered him to the ground.

I could not move, could only watch as Katashi cleaned his dagger on the guard's red sash before returning across the shadowy ground. "Any more?"

"No." I touched my neck to be sure it was still intact. "Not here."

Katashi strode on, excitement pouring off him as he climbed the rising ground to where a line of willows edged a moat. There he crouched beneath the trees, joining the reeds and shadows gathered beside the still water. Across the moat, a short wharf jutted from the keep's lowest level, lapping at the water like a tongue.

Upon the jetty, two guards stood bathed in the light of a single flambeau, its fire casting gold ribbons across the water. We could go no farther without being seen. Katashi slid Hacho from her holster. "Only two?" he asked, his breath warm against my cheek.

Again, I let my Empathy wander at his bidding, bringing back nothing but a quiet boredom. I nodded.

"Could you hit one from here?"

I considered the distance, the angle, the wind, but however much I might pride myself on my skill, I had never used a bow to harm someone. These men had done nothing to earn my ire.

Katashi regarded me with raised brows, the shadows of willow fronds shifting upon his face.

"If you can think of a better way, I'm listening," he said.

"I've never—" But I had killed people. I had killed Tori and all the guards back in Shimai. I had just never done it on purpose.

"I was idealistic once," Katashi whispered. "There was a time I knew, as solid and sure as you stand here, that they could not kill my father. He was the sworn emperor of Kisia and had done nothing to earn such hatred. Right up until the moment the headsman lifted the axe, I knew they could not do it." He moved away, leaving the side of my face cold where his breath had touched. Taking an arrow from his quiver he handed it to me. "I was wrong."

I took the arrow. Father Kokoro had said something similar the night he ordered my arrest. *Sometimes we do things because they are right*, he had said as the guards led me out. *But sometimes we do things because we must.*

I took out my bow.

"The one on the left is a clearer shot," Katashi said. "He's yours.

But we have to do this at the same time and you can't miss. If only one of them dies, the other will have time to raise the alarm."

My well-practised hands nocked the single arrow and I nodded. There was hardly a breath of wind. Close to my ear came the sound of Hacho's tightening string.

"On three then," Katashi said. "One..."

The bow quivered in my hand. I had to tell myself it wasn't a man at all but a target, its flesh-coloured coils bound in a red sash.

"Two. Three."

I let go, revelling in the joy of the familiar motion. My arrow struck, my target was thrown back and almost I crowed with such visceral delight. Even the pain in my throat was satisfying while it lasted, the strings of my heart humming like my bow.

Katashi had nocked a second arrow but lowered Hacho with a wry smile. "I had to be ready," he said with a boyish shrug. "You might have missed. Are we alone?"

I reeled out my Empathy but sucked it back quickly. "Almost," I said. "Your man's not dead. But he will be soon."

The cold sweat of pain shattered the thrill, turning me sick. No man should have to suffer such agony.

His foot jerked, banging on the boards.

Katashi snorted and began to undress. Leather tunic, linen shirt, breeches, underclothes, and soft leather shoes, all removed until he stood naked beneath the swaying willow fronds. Not at all embarrassed, he bundled up his clothes and tied them together with his black sash. Then he threw them to the wharf, where they landed with a gentle thud, rolling into the shadows.

"Joining me or staying here?" he asked, sliding soundlessly into the water, as smooth and graceful as an otter.

I undressed as quickly as I could while Katashi swam out into the moonlight, Hacho held above his head. No shouts came, nor cries of "intruder." But for the gentle lap of the water, there might have been no sound at all.

Having balled my clothes around Malice's canister and thrown them to the wharf, I lowered myself into the moat. The water was cold despite the sultry summer warmth, and I moved quickly, trying to make no splash, no sound. Keeping my bow out of the water was tiring, but I swam on, pushing from my mind all thought of what creatures might live in the black water.

Already at the far side, Katashi laid Hacho on the boards and pulled himself out, water streaming off him. My arm burned. The water seemed to be getting thicker as I tired, but I dragged myself the rest of the way and threw my bow up onto the wharf. Katashi held down his hand and I gripped it without thinking.

So close, came the whisper of his thoughts. *I will avenge them all.*

A woman lay on a tattered sleeping mat in a robe that might once have been beautiful. Its brilliance had faded like her face, its beauty worn thin, her hair little but wisps curling from her head. She smiled wanly up at me, hardly breathing, hardly seeming to live at all.

And I stood dripping on the planks.

"I felt that," Katashi said, his eyes narrowed. "I thought it was nothing the first time, but it's not, is it? It's you. Every time I touch you, I see something I've never seen before. Malice has never done that."

"Who was the woman you were just thinking about?"

"My mother," he said, beginning to dress. "She died a pauper, heartbroken, exiled from her homeland with no way of feeding herself or her children, no family, no shelter, nothing. She was a noblewoman. She had never worked a day in her life, but of course there is always a way for a woman to earn a living."

His anger was palpable. He did not look at me as he spoke but stretched his black sash between his hands.

"That's why you wear a black sash."

"Yes. I'm not a gentleman, whatever my birth. Kin saw to that."

Katashi buckled on his holster then slid Hacho into it. While I dressed, he dragged first one corpse and then the other to the end of the wharf. There was only the gentlest of splashes as he lowered each into the water's welcoming embrace, the weight of their armour sinking them beneath the surface.

"All right, I know where we're going," he said when he was done. "So just tell me when you feel someone and I'll do the rest."

"Where *are* we going?"

"To open the Willow Gate. It enters off a secondary courtyard near where we came through the crypt. Kimiko will bring my men through the walls while we open the gate."

I imagined a whole army of Pikes waiting in the crypt, ready to attack. Katashi might really get what he wanted this night, but it would never get him back his sister. Or mine, if the battle went ill. The canister tucked into my sash hummed with its own life.

"I'll go with you as far as I can."

His eyes narrowed. "You're here for Laroth?" He grinned at my surprise, his ever-mercurial temper unsettling. "You think about him a lot. It's always him I see when you touch me. If he's the reason you have that branding, then I hope you get the revenge you want. You get me near the gate and I can do the rest. Is anyone around?"

"No, not here."

"Good, let's go." He went ahead, his long dagger already free of its sheath.

The keep's lower level was a maze of tunnels built into the foundations. Cold emanated from the stones, and already chilled by the swim, my skin pimpled.

Despite the dim light, Katashi strode the passages unerring, looking to me only to be sure we were alone. Occasionally a presence would pass overhead, but down here there was nothing but an empty chill.

When we climbed the narrow stairway to the next level, I slowed and touched Katashi's shoulder. He turned, the castle so quiet I could hear his clothing shift. I pointed ahead and lifted a single finger. With a nod, he hurried along the torchlit passage to where a narrow hallway branched. There he leant against the cold stones and waited.

Footsteps grew louder. The echo made it hard to judge distance, and every moment I expected a man to appear. Katashi stood poised, watching the mouth of the passage, his dagger ready.

A guard appeared. A lantern lit youthful features, but Katashi did not hesitate. Two long strides and he had his hand over the man's mouth. I tried to pull my Empathy away, but the knife slid in; the knife slid out. Shock hammered my heart. The light was too bright and my head spun, then the blade ripped my throat and I was on my hands and knees, retching. The pain vanished as quickly as it had come, but I could not forget. My arms trembled as I lowered my forehead to the cold stone floor.

Katashi went past, dragging the body. Out of the corner of my eye, his feet passed, then a limp arm and the smell of blood. I took a deep breath, air shuddering out of my lungs.

When Katashi returned I sat up, steadying myself on the wall. "Felt that, huh?" he said. "It's the quickest and quietest way I know to kill a man. We can't chance anyone going down to find the wharf unguarded."

"I know."

"Do you feel everything?"

"Yes."

"Anger?"

"Yes."

"Lust?"

I paused. "Yes."

"What an interesting life you must lead."

"You'd be surprised."

"Perhaps," he said, crushing the guard's discarded paper lantern beneath his foot and kicking it into the shadows. "Not much surprises me. Let's keep moving."

I pushed to my feet. My legs shook, but there was no time to rest and I followed him back into the maze.

Up another set of stairs, the stone tunnels became passages of blackened wood. Most of the servants were asleep, but enough roamed the halls to make our progress slow. Katashi tried to avoid as many as he could, but when there was no choice, he killed, and I gritted my teeth as the pain slid across my throat again and again.

From passage to passage, we moved through the keep, climbing until we reached what Katashi called the court floor. The castle rose farther above us, but the last stairwell spat us out into a narrow hallway lined with bamboo screens. The air was heavy, filled with the smell of dust, incense, and reed matting—the smells of age, of a building that had lasted centuries and would go on existing long after my body rotted in the ground.

"Lots of guards?" Katashi asked, his voice a whisper.

"Hard to tell," I said. "Lots of people."

The weight was oppressive. Even though many slept, I could tell something was wrong, some disturbance yet beyond the reach of my Empathy.

"There's a wall that runs from the armoury to the Willow Gate," Katashi said. "Once there, we'll be able to open the first gate."

"Is it close?"

"Close enough, why? Is this where you leave me?"

There was accusation in his tone, but I nodded. He had sold his sister to Malice; I was determined to save mine.

"Then I hope you kill your man," he said. "It certainly won't harm my cause." Katashi nodded, tapping Hacho as though she were a good luck charm. "I'll see you at dawn."

"Or in the hells."

"Whichever comes first."

He winked, and with a flash of his boyish grin, he was gone.

22. DARIUS

Malice was close. I could smell him, could feel him behind me at every step, the sound of his footsteps falling with mine. It was all I could do to keep from turning to see if it was real. And from my memories, he laughed.

Outside the council chamber, I stopped to smooth the furrow from my brow. The rest of Kin's council were already gathered, Kin himself kneeling at the head of the table. Composing my features into something like my usual mask, I entered, hoping no one would see the cracks in my facade, hoping Kin had been kind enough to keep my departure secret. Many eyes watched as I knelt and bowed upon the matting. The threads of my robe caught on the rough, well-worn reeds, and I tried not to breathe in their dust.

"Rise, Darius," Kin said. "Join us and we may start."

"Yes, Majesty."

Receiving few nods and even fewer smiles, I took my place at Kin's right hand. With Minister Bahain and half the council left behind in Mei'lian, it was Councillor Ahmet who sat across the table from me, engaged in making the most of this place of favour.

"It is certainly to be expected," he was saying to Kin. "You are right to be on your guard, Your Majesty. Think of the timing too. Tomorrow will mark the anniversary, not only of your oath but of his father's execution."

"I assure you, Councillor," General Ryoji said, leaning forward, "that we are fully prepared for such an event. Steps have been taken to ensure His Majesty's safety tonight."

"Such as?"

General Ryoji gave the councillor a long stare. "In the circumstances, Councillor, you must forgive my silence. It is, as you say, an inauspicious time."

"You do not trust His Majesty's own council?"

"My job is to keep His Majesty safe, and to that end, I will keep my own counsel."

There were some mutters at this, but when Kin showed no disapproval, Councillor Ahmet merely smiled an unfriendly smile. Making friends like that, I would put my money on General Ryoji taking my place before long.

The door slid open, and the entrance of half a dozen serving girls kept the conversation minimal. Kneeling, they served refreshments, and I clenched my hands into fists in frustration at the need for every slow ritual. Seconds could make the difference tonight, but Kin seemed intent on maintaining the appearance at least of normality and control.

Roasted tea, sweet rice, and red bean cake all made it onto the table, but wine was conspicuously lacking. Those councillors who weren't watching the maids turned reproachful eyes toward the head of the table. Kin's expression was more than ordinarily grim. He seemed only to be present in body, his dark eyes fixed upon nothing. The others would assume the meeting with Katashi had gone poorly, and it had, but having counselled him to speak again to Hana, I was sure his frown could be attributed to more than just Katashi's inflammatory behaviour.

The serving girls finished their duties and bowed themselves out, and while the councillors cupped their bowls of tea, expectant eyes turned back to Kin. He gripped the edge of the table. "Katashi

Otako will not back down," he said. "He saw fit to ignore my every demand. He will not trade the crown and he will not renounce his claim upon my throne. Worse, we have reason to suspect the Vices are still working closely with him and may attack tonight, before I can take my oath."

The combined outcry kept any one man's words from being heard, but the shock at least was clear. Only General Ryoji remained silent, watching and waiting as I did, and I added another mark to his promotion card. Kin disliked effusiveness as much as he disliked sycophants.

Having weathered a minute of blustering noise, Kin cleared his throat and held up a hand. "Minister Laroth has already begun implementing a plan for the further protection of this castle against unknown forces, to which I suggest you all listen. Darius."

All eyes turned to me, every expression part fear part accusation. "Thank you, Your Majesty," I said. "I will keep this brief. The Vices are dangerous. They proved this the first time they terrorised Kisia, and this time is different only in that they appear to have allied themselves with Katashi Otako."

"How do you know this?" Councillor Rhim asked, the skin around his eyes wrinkling as he peered over his tea bowl. "There has been no intelligence that either rebel group has been active since the theft of the Hian crown."

"Until tonight. A known Vice stood behind Katashi at the meeting." It was not entirely true, but there was no time for nuance, though my words made Kin's gaze snap my way. I ought to explain, but more than he needed to know about Endymion, I needed to finish this, needed to leave, and I went on, trying to appear unconscious of his scrutiny. "A man who entertains no deals is a man who needs no deals. That means Katashi Otako has a plan. Now, all our information suggests that Vices are only capable of performing their witchcraft at close range, so every capable archer in Koi's standing battalion is on duty tonight. If they can be killed before they have a chance to use their . . . magic, then so much the better."

Would you really want to see me dead, Darius?

It was a voice from my memory, and yet it seemed to live in the room with me, so real I expected the others to have heard it. But they were all watching me with intent horror.

I pressed on. "We are also aware from past intelligence that they can be capable of deceptions powerful enough to get them inside even heavily protected buildings, unseen. We are not sure exactly how they manage this"—I had seen too many different skills to guess which Malice might use—"but as a precaution, I have ordered the castle into total lockdown. No one comes in, no one goes out, and we have standing guards on all walls and gatehouses, as well as men patrolling, leaving no inch of the castle unwatched."

"And if there is no attack?" Councillor Rhim again, sipping his tea now the steam had begun to dissipate.

"Then we shall all be a little tired tomorrow, Councillor. I am sure His Majesty will forgive the odd stifled yawn through the ceremony."

Compressed smiles. Humourless titters. These were worried men, and I could be satisfied my words had been effective. As one man, the council lifted tea bowls and crunched on bean cake, eyes on Kin. At last, he settled clasped hands on the table, his gold signet ring glinting. "It is a small risk but one worth being prepared for. In the morning, we will open the gates to those who have come for the ceremony, and I will take the oath as usual, though of course security will be doubled for that as well, and we will set forth for Mei'lian the day after rather than stay a few weeks as originally planned."

Kin turned to the young man at the far end of the table. "Hallan, you have reports?"

The imperial secretary laid his hands upon a pile of papers. "Yes,

Your Majesty, though this first one I believe was wrongly directed to my hands instead of Minister Laroth's, as it is from General Jikuko."

"And what has the general to say?"

Master Hallan's eyes darted my way as though expecting me to interrupt, but that the message hadn't come to my hands was just the first step toward Kin's ultimate replacement of me. "He says he lost another thirty-four men in raids last night and twenty-two the night before. They are having difficulty tracking the rebels during the day. A similar message came from General Yi. I think it is safe to say that not all the Pikes are here with their leader and that they have not ceased activity. A . . . temporary lull is all it was."

"Perhaps Otako is trying to divert our attention with this," Ahmet said. "Or the threat on the castle might be a diversion. Koi has always been impenetrable."

Councillor Rhim nodded. "Yes, and if there are bands of rebels hitting our northern military camps, then whatever Otako's plans, he hasn't got his full force with him here. Why sit and wait for them to come to us when we could hit him now? There is still a standing battalion in the city, is there not, Laroth?"

"There is," I said. "Though many have been deployed in the protection of the castle, allowing General Ryoji's men to focus on the emperor's personal safety. I feel this discussion ought to wait until Master Hallan has finished speaking, however, or he might burst."

The young man had been opening and closing his mouth with every interjection and kept looking down at the scroll in his hand. He did so again now, reddening as my words sent all eyes back his way. "It is just . . ." He wriggled on his cushion. "The other report is from one of our spies. A list of lords known to be in contact with Otako. I know we expected many of his father's old allies and the deposed nobility and exiles, but the list is . . . extensive. Some are noted as having housed him, while others are known to have financed his campaigns. I have yet to go through it in detail, but—"

"Names," Kin ordered.

"Your Majesty, I am not sure that, without proper verification—"

"Give it here, boy." Ahmet held out his hand and, bowing his head, Master Hallan gave him the scroll. Unrolling it, Councillor Ahmet began to read. "Lord Sulaya, count of Ya, known to be in contact. Lord Kirita, count of Veil, known to be in contact and believed to have housed Otako exiles. Lady Muya, duchess of Lin'ya, believed to have given substantial financial support." That name sent whispers about pirates hissing along the table while Ahmet continued unrolling the scroll, his eyes darting back and forth. "Tishan Mei, deposed and exiled count of Risian, and his son, Tan Mei. And—" The councillor stopped abruptly and looked up. "—Lord Manshin, general of the sixth district, known to be in contact."

"Send a rider immediately to Kogahaera and have General Manshin removed from his position," Kin said. "Quietly."

I cleared my throat. "And General Roi."

"General Roi, Minister?" Ahmet said. "His name is not on this list."

"If Manshin is in this, then so is Roi."

Kin turned to me as though he might speak but thought better of it. As minister of the left, it was my job to deal with such problems, but after tonight, it wasn't going to be my job anymore. He would have to deal with it himself.

As though I were already absent, the council went on without my input. Ahmet continued with his list of names. The possibility that General Tikita might also be tempted to take the Otako side was raised, Master Hallan reminding the assembled councillors that Tikita was the youngest son of a border lord, brought up to support the Otakos. I let them talk, let them discuss such petty enemies. Generals or peasants, they were nothing compared to Malice. And every moment I waited, he stalked ever closer.

"And you are sure about the oath, Majesty?" Councillor Rhim said, at last drawing my attention back to the table.

Beside me, Kin took a deep breath, compressing his thin lips. "The divinity of the Hian Crown is nothing but a myth. I have ruled this empire for sixteen years, not because I wore the crown and spoke some words but because I have done the job. Anyone who denies my right to sit upon the Crimson Throne because of superstition deserves the war that will come to them. I will not let Katashi Otako win."

No one dared argue with the scowl he used to cow us. But we were not the danger. It was Katashi who would take any excuse offered to weaken Kin's claim and strengthen his own.

A knock sounded on the door. Many held breaths eased, the council grateful for the interruption. Upon being summoned, an imperial guard stepped in. "Your Majesty," he said, bowing low. "My apologies for the interruption, but Lady Otako's maid is here. She brings a message for Minister Laroth."

Eyebrows rose. The councillors exchanged amused glances, and Kin's jaw muscles tightened. At any other time, I might have been angry at the attention so ill-timed and ill-advised a message had brought, but what did it matter what anyone said as long as I could use it as an excuse to escape?

I was about to rise, about to speak, but Kin tapped the table with nervous fingers and said, "Did Lady Hana's maid give a reason?"

"No, Your Majesty."

"Then inform her she will have to wait. Lord Laroth is not currently available."

"As you say, Your Majesty."

The man slipped back out of the room, closing the door behind him.

For a few long minutes that felt like hours, discussion of the crown continued, until at last Kin heaved a sigh. "This council is adjourned," he said, pushing up from the table. Every member of the council hurried to do the same, bowing as he made for the door. "You are all dismissed about your duties, and we will meet back here in an hour. Hallan, make copies of that list of conspirators, we have a lot of decisions to make."

"Yes, Your Majesty."

"Your Majesty," Councillor Ahmet said, sliding obsequiously into the emperor's path. "I feel that if Lady Otako has something she wishes to say to a member of the council, it would be in the best interests of all to hear it, especially as it may be about her cousin's plans. As Lord Laroth has much more important tasks to attend to, I would be perfectly happy to visit her in his place."

It was on the tip of my tongue to refuse his offer, sure the last person Hana wanted to see was the man who had attacked her in the Pit, but Kin's thoughts appeared to be elsewhere, for with nothing but a distracted wave of his hand, he said, "Very well, Councillor. Darius. Walk with me."

"As you wish, Majesty," I said, following him out into the passage. At least I could be sure Ahmet wouldn't dare do anything stupid this time, and Hana was well able to look after herself. Shin too would be loitering nearby, something the man had proved very good at.

Despite a large number of lanterns, the hallway we walked was gloomy. Koi Castle was always dark, its thick, iron-hard timbers blackened by fire and the passing of so many years.

There was a new notch between Kin's brows as we walked through shadows. "Are you still determined to leave tonight?" he said, when we had put enough distance between us and the council chamber.

"Almost at once. I have a few things to collect from my room, but I will not linger. I already fear I have left it too late."

"What makes you say so?"

"Just... a feeling, Majesty, that Malice is close by."

Kin stopped walking, shadows upon his face. "Inside?"

"I don't know, but I fear your life is in danger every moment you remain here. Would it not be better to return to Mei'lian at once and take the oath there?"

"And have people say I am a coward? That I surrendered Koi to Katashi without a fight? Every emperor in Kisian history has sat upon the throne at Koi and spoken their vows, year on year, and I intend to do the same."

"They also did so while wearing the Hian Crown. It seems contradictory to insist upon half the tradition while letting the other half go."

"You are as severe upon me as Lady Hana."

He had not spoken of her at the meeting, as sure a sign as his current scowl that his mission had not fared well. "She still refuses?"

"She is demanding I give her equal rights as my empress without having proved herself capable of ruling so much as an ant nest. Her interest in rearing children is not high either. By the gods, Darius, I wish you had never suggested I marry her."

"You would rather have executed her?"

"No! Not that, but..." He sighed. "I am near to pulling my hair out trying to understand her."

"What is there to understand? She wants to share your position, not be subjugated, wants to be important and seen and loved. She's an Otako to the core."

"Not entirely. She has a lot of her mother in her."

Kin stared at the floor as though looking through time. I had never known Empress Li, only heard of her by report, but that he had kept her portrait near his rooms in Mei'lian long after her death gave some credibility to the rumour he had loved her. That he had refused all attempts by his council to encourage him to marry until now lent more still.

"What will you do if she decides against you, Majesty? I do not think it would be wise to keep her locked away."

"No, but…the more time I spend with her the more I…don't dislike the idea of marrying her, as…frustrating and determined and—you're grinning."

"I would not dare, Your Majesty. Ministers do not do such things. Especially heartless ones who are rumoured to be the awakened dead."

A rueful smile made him appear years younger, and as we both stood smiling in the passage, I could believe, just for a moment, that everything might work out all right. "Damn you, Darius," he said. "You make me feel like I'm ten years old, and she makes me feel as though I'm eighty." He sighed. "Yet I have only to wish I had not been so hasty in dismissing you, for you to once more make me question my trust in you. Not that it matters now, but you never told me the boy with Katashi was a Vice."

"Because I was not be entirely sure, Majesty. It was only a feeling I got, not that I recognised him."

"I thought he looked familiar. Something about his eyes. Though perhaps it was only that Katashi had dressed him like you—an interesting touch, I thought, to mock my advisor as well as me."

"Indeed, Majesty."

He said nothing, seeming to expect me to fill the silence with more as yet unuttered truths, but there was no time. I had to go.

Kin held out his hand. It was a final act of dismissal, of acceptance, and I knelt before him to kiss his fingers.

"Thank you, Your Majesty," I said. "For the great honour of allowing me to serve you."

"Goodbye, Darius."

In an instant, he had pulled his hand away and was gone, the skirt of his robe brushing the smooth wood with every step. Around me, the palace hummed gently with a myriad of soft sounds—footsteps, whispers, and the crackle of burning torches. Dawn was a long way off yet, but the castle felt none of man's anxiety. The paintings and ancient screens had watched dozens of emperors walk these halls, coming and going, living and dying, and after them, Kisia lived on, for better or worse. The empire never died.

It was time to go, with nothing left to do but hope I had done enough, hope he would make it through the night, because without him, nothing stood between me and the power of my blood.

I turned and walked toward my room, sure that even Kin could not understand how desperately I needed him to win, to go on proving a man could rule this empire.

I had to believe Kisia needed no gods.

23. ENDYMION

I tapped on the minister's door and got no answer. I couldn't feel anyone inside, but I hadn't been able to feel him at the meeting either, and I tapped again. I could go in and wait, but if Katashi struck soon, he might not be back in time.

Not comfortable standing longer in the passage, I slipped inside. It was empty, no sign of habitation beyond a few travelling chests along one wall, exactly like the ones Malice had in his wagon, right down to the spider carved upon their lids.

Just like the spider etched into the pendant Nyraek Laroth had given me and his son had taken away. The eye had been a sign of love and protection, Jian had said.

I lifted the lid of the first chest, and the smell of kiri wood assailed me. Pale shavings covered a neatly folded robe, but I brushed them out of the way and peeled back the sheet of thin paper separating it from the next. Sky-blue silk. Then a heavy winter robe in dark green. Sliding my hand down the side, I felt nothing but soft fabric and closed the lid again.

Sitting back on my haunches, I wondered where I would find his jewellery. Did the servants keep it in a special place? Or would it be buried in one of these chests?

Footsteps sounded outside. Crouched, I froze, listening to the steady paces. They drew close only to fade with their attendant soul back into the silence.

I moved to the next chest. It was full of personal belongings, of parchment scrolls and sticks of ink. There was a roll of silk containing brushes of all sizes, a few mixing stones, two spare pairs of wooden sandals with the Laroth crest branded into the heel, a trio of shaving blades, a collection of leather-bound books, and an Errant board. Throwing each of these items onto the floor, I dug deeper, unearthing a box containing a pair of small scissors and some pincers.

"A thief now as well as a traitor?"

I sucked in a breath. Lord Laroth stood in the doorway, the same picture of precision I had first seen back in Shimai. He looked around at the scattered belongings and blinked slowly, taking it all in with no change to his expression.

"Was it necessary to make such a mess?" he asked at last. "You were perhaps looking for something specific?"

"My necklace."

"Your necklace."

"The one your father gave me."

"I am well aware which necklace you mean," he said, stepping into the room and closing the door. "But I was not aware I was under any obligation to return it to you."

With a theatrical wince at the strewn belongings, Lord Laroth indicated the table. "Won't you please join me? I am afraid I have no refreshments, however, as I was expecting someone quite different."

"Your friend Malice perhaps."

"I would rather have called him your friend. You wore his robe at the meeting after all."

"You must know him well to know the robe was his."

"I never said that I did not."

We stared at one another. My heart was hammering so fast it turned my stomach sick. I had not come to argue with him, had come only for Hana, but this man had known my name and still condemned me, leaving me to break beneath the branding iron.

"You are very alike, you and Malice," I said, holding in my wrath with tightly curled fists. "You are both monsters clad in expensive silk."

Without a word, Lord Laroth came forward, slow steps bringing him across the matting. His expression did not alter. He did not hurry and he did not speak, just knelt at the table and clasped his hands in his lap.

"Tell me, Endymion," he said as I joined him. "Are you trying to make me angry? Or afraid?"

"My name is Takehiko Otako and you know it."

His eyes bored into mine. "I see Malice has been sharing secrets."

"You knew."

"Yes."

"But you condemned me anyway."

With great deliberation, he blinked, so calmly I wanted to hit him. I controlled the urge with an effort.

"What else did Malice tell you, Endymion?" he asked.

"He told me my name and that your father was honour-bound to protect me, an honour you should have upheld."

Ignoring the second part of this, he said, "But names mean so little. Take Malice, for example. You cannot be fool enough to think that is his true name. Even if it was he must have a family name, too."

"I don't see your point," I said, beginning to wish he would direct those sharp violet eyes somewhere else. "My father was an Otako, so I am an Otako."

And there came the first change in his expression. The impassive face came to life, perfect lips turning into a sneering smile. "Not your friend then, Malice."

"What do you mean?"

"What do you think I mean?" Lord Laroth leant forward. "He's lying to you, Endymion."

"And you're not?"

He sat back. "I never said that. But I have not lied to you yet."

"You lied about my father."

"No. I did not lie to you then and I have not lied to you now."

It was hypnotic, staring into those expressionless eyes. He spoke with such assurance that I wanted to believe him, wanted to trust him. But there was no warmth in him, no life, his blood as cold as a cunning snake.

"My father was Emperor Lan Otako," I said. "He was not some honourless traitor like you said. Your father swore an oath to protect my family, and you betrayed that honour when you condemned me to this fate."

Something like anger lashed at my senses, gone in an instant. The minister's expression remained impassive. "How grievously at fault I am, to be sure," he said in a mild tone.

"Grievously at fault?" I repeated. "You—"

"Why did you come here, Endymion?" Lord Laroth interrupted, clasping his hands tightly upon the table.

"To save my sister."

In perfect imitation of Malice's surprised expression, the minister's brow rose to thin arcs. "A sister you have never met? How perfectly sweet." He sounded like Malice too, the mocking jeer owning all the same tones. "But if you could find my room, you could find hers, yet here you are. You're angry with me."

"You think I would not be?" I said, hating how much truth was in his words. "Look what you did to me! I was branded not once.

Not twice. But three times." I pulled up my sleeve so he could see the last and deepest of the brands upon my arm, still red and scabbing. "They broke me. You broke me."

"I did what I had to do. Do you think Kin would have been glad to hear of your existence? I saved you. I could have ordered your execution. I could have left you to burn."

"Then why didn't you?"

Lord Laroth slammed his palms upon the table. "Because I am not the monster everyone thinks me!"

He was breathing fast, and I flinched at the sudden hit of emotion. Already his barriers were returning, thick like the carefully controlled walls of a fortified city, but I had seen life within. A hot-blooded man was in there somewhere.

A tentative knock sounded on the door. I froze, and for a moment, the minister's eyes scoured my face.

The knock came again.

Lord Laroth got quickly to his feet and pointed one slim finger at the corner. I wanted to ignore his command, to throw it back in his face and stay seated at the table, but discovery would not help Hana. I had no choice but to trust him.

I went to the corner and wedged myself in beside a scroll cabinet. He schooled his features to a frown and slid the door. "Well?" he said, his tone chilly. "What is it?"

"Your Excellency, I have a message from General Ryoji," the invisible man said. "He requests your presence in the main hall immediately. Katashi Otako is on his way, desirous of an audience with the emperor."

But Katashi was already inside the walls. Was this part of his plan, too?

"He comes alone?" Lord Laroth asked.

"No, Your Excellency. He has been allowed to bring two of his men with him. They approached the front gates carrying a white flag."

I shivered, unable to shake the feeling a feather had brushed across my soul. Growing insistent, the pressure increased, its gentle fingers drawing forth fear and confusion.

"Fools!" Lord Laroth snapped, and the pressure was gone. "Tell them not to let anyone in until I get there. Go! Quickly!"

"Yes, Your Excellency!"

Footsteps hurried away and Lord Laroth slid the door closed with a crack of timbers. "How did you get in?" he demanded, turning on me. "Did Malice get you in here?"

"Why should I tell you?"

His anger was there now, free and unfettered and fuelling my own, the fire fizzling back and forth between us.

"Because you owe me your life!"

"Owe you? You should have these brands, not me."

Lord Laroth snarled. "And what would you know? What would you know of what I have done for this empire?" His own words seemed to check his wrath, and he came toward me with quick strides. "I have to go." He gripped my shoulders. "Hana will be safe, you can be sure of that, but I need you to stay here and wait for me."

"Why?"

"Listen to me. You didn't come to save Hana, you came because Malice wanted you to come, just like he wanted her to come. You have been thrown at me to make me choose between protecting myself and protecting you, and by the gods, I will not let him win. You have to trust me."

"And sit here while you go call the guards?"

Shaking me roughly, he snapped, "You fool! You've put your faith in the wrong man." His eyes burned, no longer cold, no longer dead. "Only a Vice could get in here undetected. What did you give him?"

I pushed past him toward the door, but Lord Laroth's fingers clamped around my wrist. "Don't do it, Endymion. Don't listen to Malice. Don't let him have you."

Skin on skin there was no connection. Since the incident at Shimai, there had only been one other person I had failed to connect with at first touch—Malice.

"Who are you?" I asked the question, though I did not have to. He had let go his barriers, had laid himself open, and all it took was a little push, driving my Empathy into his veins, into his heart, his very soul. The connection flared, and under my touch, he burned hotter than fire. Here was a man more alive even than Katashi, more complex, more closed. He owned places no one else was allowed to go.

Where did this strength come from? came the whisper of Lord Laroth's thoughts. *A Whisperer? Get out! Get out of my head!*

He tried to push me away, but with my skin touching his, a memory hit me with all the force of a hurled stone...

"And if I don't want to do this anymore?"

"Do what?" Malice stood threateningly close, an arm on either side of my head, blocking my escape.

"I am not your tool."

"No, Darius, we do this together. You're my brother, yes?"

"Half."

Malice took my left hand and pulled it awkwardly up before my eyes. There he drew back both his sleeve and mine, holding them so I couldn't but see the two identical birthmarks. "Half?" he said. "You are more my brother than if we shared the same mother."

His Empathy whipped out, striking the shield I held between us. "I am not your tool," I repeated.

"You are my brother!"

"Yes, that I cannot change. But this I can." I pulled my hand away and pressed it to my heart.

318 • *Devin Madson*

Malice began to laugh. "A heart? You? Don't be such a fool. Why seek to change what makes you better? You know we can do this together, achieve the impossible, rule as gods. It is our duty, yes?"

"I don't believe that," I said.

"I can see through your lies, Darius."

"Then I will make the lie true!"

Malice shoved me into the wall, knocking breath out of me. "You will not leave me," he snarled. "You cannot, yes?"

"You can't stop me."

"Oh no?"

He struck again with all the force of his rage, but I kept the shield raised. "You think I don't know you?" I said. "I can keep you out." A laugh came from my dry lips, but it sounded far away. "You might as well let me go. I'm going to leave you whether you like it or not."

The laugh caught in my throat, choked to a cry. Pain filled my chest like cold pressure, and there was Malice, so close I could feel his breath. A little smile turned his lips, dampened by a circuit of his tongue. Then he drew the blade back out, the tip sliding free of my ribs. I gasped, sucking in air laced with pain. My blood was hot. It clogged my robe and ran onto my hands as I pressed them to my chest.

And in my ear, Malice whispered, the words a gentle caress. "No, Brother," he said. "You're not going anywhere."

Lord Laroth pulled away, the shock knocking me back into the present. Viewing the memory had been the work of an instant, but his jaw had dropped, and all I could do was stare back, my thoughts in a whirl.

Without warning, he pinched my earlobe between his thumb and forefinger, squeezing fresh pain from the piercing Malice had inflicted.

"Do you even know what this is?" he demanded, dragging me down by my ear. Obedient to the pain, I followed, knees collapsing onto the matting. "This"—he pinched harder, causing the earring's hook to dig into my skin—"is your name. This is your place. You let him brand you without asking why."

All at once, he let go. I went to touch my ear, but a loop of silk caught my wrist.

"What are you doing?" I tried to pull free of the tightening knots, but they were yanked tighter, and my wrists banged into the leg of a divan.

"That question is a waste of breath," Lord Laroth said behind me. "As is this answer."

His hands touched mine without the ingress of connection.

"Why don't I connect to you unless I try?" I said. "Who are you?"

He gave the silk one last tug, locking my wrists. Then, looking more dishevelled than I had ever seen him, Lord Laroth straightened. He adjusted his sash and smoothed his hair, his expression slowly settling into its naturally impassive lines.

"Tell me who you are," I said again. "Tell me!"

Lord Laroth went to the door. "Wrong question, Endymion," he said, laying his hand upon the wood. "I am Lord Darius Laroth. What you should be asking is who you are."

He slid the door, but before he stepped out into the passage, he tapped the earring that hung from his left ear. A silver medallion swung, glinting in the light.

24. HANA

Tea sat cooling upon the tray. It was the second tray I had sent for, but still Darius had not come. Again and again I had gone over my arguments, had considered my options, had wondered which threats might force him to act out of self-preservation, but nothing I could tell Kin about Darius's past would matter if Darius never came.

I tried to relax, to be patient, but at every sound beyond my door, I tensed, only for the footsteps and voices to pass on, leaving my heart hammering for nothing. I blew a gust of air out through my lips and slumped back against the worn cushions of the divan. Of course, there was an easier path. I could send Emperor Kin a message instead, tell him I would marry him, that I would do my duty to the empire and help protect its people, whatever the damage and hurt it would do to Katashi. I could even hope to get the power I wanted if I argued long enough, but I had not snuck away from home to join Malice and his much-maligned Vices just to become a wife.

An even easier course would be to kill Kin. Since the Pit, I had carried the Tishwa Malice had given me tucked into my sash, the presence of the vials comforting in the absence of any blades. I tapped them as the tea chilled on the table undrunk. It wouldn't be hard. If I sent for Kin, I could put the poison on the rim of the tea bowl and suggest we drink to our future. If I did it right, no one would be able to prove I had done anything at all.

There was some joy in so dispassionate a consideration of my position, but I could not kill him. If Kin had been right about only one thing, it was that Kisia was better with stability. If Kin died, there would be war, because no one, not even Katashi, had enough support to take the throne without repercussions, even from a dead man.

Voices floated along the passage and I sat up straight, moving my fingers away from the vials of poison. It didn't sound like Darius's voice, if only because Darius rarely raised his and the man coming closer was snapping in frustration.

"—a maid, how dare you—"

"Lady Hana Otako's maid"—that was Tili's voice—"and I would be remiss in my duty to my lady if I did not speak. The query she had for Lord Laroth was of a personal nature, and you cannot—"

The door slid open and Councillor Ahmet stepped in, Tili fuming behind him. "Ah, Lady Otako," he said, a laugh in his eyes as he bowed. "We meet again and under more...appropriate circumstances."

I tried not to think of the Pit and of his little nod, of the weight of Praetor's body pressing me into the dank stones.

"Councillor," I said, fury that Darius would even consider sending such a man in his place curling my fingers into claws. "It is Lord Laroth with whom I wish to speak. If he is currently unavailable, then I will await his leisure."

"I fear that Lord Laroth is likely to be busy for some time, my lady, but I assure you I will take an accurate message to him should you deign to speak your mind to me."

"I would not speak my mind to you if you were the last man in Kisia!"

His smile widened, or rather he showed more of his teeth. "Fortunately, that is not the case. Fetch us some wine," he said to Tili and slid the door closed in her face.

I swallowed the urge to call her back and sat statue still, trying to channel as much of Darius's disdain as I could muster.

Councillor Ahmet lowered himself onto the other end of the divan, his keen eyes travelling over me, from my ankles to my curls, a sneer of distaste twisting his lips.

"You are determined to draw attention to yourself in those foolish outfits," he said. "You may not have much in the way of womanly curve, but in such mannish things you attract no one."

"As I have no interest in...attracting anyone, that works very well for me. Now as I have already informed you that I have nothing to say to you, I must again ask you to leave."

"Lord Laroth *is* very pretty, isn't he? Is that what you like in a man? That he look like a fine doll?"

"Your insinuation is distasteful."

The councillor laughed and clapped his hands in derisive appreciation. "Very good," he said, settling his hands back upon his spread legs. "You really are very good at the virtuous lady act, but it was a mistake to send Lord Laroth a message in the middle of a council meeting. It makes you appear...desperate. Even more desperate than sending him a dozen messages upon the road here."

He slid along the divan until he was almost beside me—a place Kin had occupied not so long since, his clasp upon my hand very different to the hand Councillor Ahmet rested on my knee. "I am not as pretty as Lord Laroth, but his little affairs are notoriously short-lived. Even if he takes an interest in you, he will tire of you within a week and then where will you be?"

I stared at the hand lying hot and heavy on my leg, stunned to a moment of immobility. Did Kin's council not know he had asked me to marry him? Did his pride extend to being unable to admit to his advisors that I had refused him? There could be no other explanation for Councillor Ahmet's belief that I sought to be Darius's mistress. Perhaps he even considered it possible Darius would try to marry me himself.

Had it not been for the hand on my leg, I would have laughed.

"You are quite mistaken, Councillor," I said. "I am not Lord Laroth's . . . Lord Laroth's lover. It was on quite another subject that I wished to consult with him."

The hand did not move. I tried not to think about it, sure that to push it off would only incite worse. There were guards outside I could call, but they had let him in, would perhaps turn a blind eye if he had slipped them enough gold. At least Tili would be back at any moment with the wine he had ordered.

"Perhaps you wished to discuss how best to go on making Emperor Kin believe you're an Otako," the councillor said. "Oh, don't look so shocked, my dear, I have grown used to Laroth's little games. He likes to make us all dance to his tune, but really it takes no great amount of intelligence to piece it all together. Everyone knows his father was dismissed from court after the scandal over Takehiko. That boy was never Emperor Lan's son, just as you are not his daughter. You're a Laroth bastard, and all of this is nothing but an elaborate plan to make Emperor Kin bend before Kisia's most intolerable family."

I wanted to deny it, to say I was no bastard, no puppet to be played, but the words would not come. It was all too easy to imagine Malice as a puppeteer, why not Darius too? Holding all our strings, every word from my lips penned by his hand.

A tap on the door heralded Tili's return, a tray balanced on one hand. "Your wine, Councillor. My lady."

He didn't remove his hand from my leg, just leered at her. "Finally. Set it on the table and serve, then you may go."

"No." The word was out of my lips before I even knew what

I meant to do. "No, just leave it on the table, Tili. I will serve it myself."

It was a mark of great respect to serve for someone, and Ahmet's smile broadened. "As you wish, my dear."

The look in Tili's eyes as she brought it in was all question, but I forced a grim smile and nodded, though it did nothing to lighten her worried frown.

Once the door had closed behind her, I slid off the divan, setting myself between the councillor and the table. I had seen girls employ all sorts of tactics to get the attention of men before, from drawing up their sleeves and cutting their robes low at the neck, to making suggestive motions with their hands, but as I bent over in front of the councillor, I felt exposed and embarrassed, fear all but knocking my heart from my chest.

He gave a little grunt, and I hoped my arse would keep his eyes off my hands for the few seconds I needed. I withdrew a vial of Tishwa from my sash. One twist broke the wax seal, and with no time for finesse, I poured the entire contents over the rim of one bowl. With shaking hands, I tucked the empty vial back into my sash and snatched up the wine jug, pouring so hastily I spilled wine upon the tray to join the splash of escaped Tishwa.

The poisoned bowl winked at me as I picked it up. "Your wine, Councillor," I said, holding it out with two hands to keep them from trembling.

"Come here. Perhaps we can come to an agreement, and I will keep your secret if you're...suitably grateful." Councillor Ahmet patted one silk-clad knee, and I went to him, no longer as afraid with the bowl in my hands. But as I sat upon his leg, he slid his arm around my waist, and at his touch, I was back in the Pit, struggling beneath Praetor's weight as my hipbone ground into the stone.

I thrust the bowl out for him to take.

"Put it down. Wine can wait." He gripped my thigh. The breeches made it easier for him to touch me, easier to slide his hand up between my legs, and the shock of revulsion was impossible to master. I slammed the poisoned rim into his teeth. The shock threw him back with a cry, wine splashing over his face as I pinned him to the cushions, digging my knee into his gut. Red-faced, he spluttered, but I gripped his short hair and wormed the edge of the bowl between his lips. "The answer is *no*, Councillor," I said. "I would rather watch you die."

He shoved me from him with a snarl, and I hit the floor, my shoulder banging into the edge of the table. Broken shards of ceramic scattered across the matting.

"You little bitch, what have you done? What was—"

His voice faltered. His ruddy colour rose. He lunged at me and gripped my leg, but there was no strength in his hand, and I yanked my foot free, crawling away over crackling reeds.

Kneeling beside the divan, the councillor clawed at his throat, his fingernails ripping into his skin. A cry quavered free, but his eyes bulged. And with his mouth hanging open, he shuffled slowly toward me. I backed into the wall as the councillor dragged himself along the floor, his bloodstained fingers reaching for my ankle. His bloodshot eyes rolled. His neck twisted, kinking to a horrific angle like a dying bird.

I must have screamed. All I could hear was my pounding heart, but the door opened. Guards dashed in. Shin was there too, and Tili, all slowing at the sight of the councillor twitching on the floor.

"What's wrong with him?" one of the guards demanded. "What happened?"

I could not drag my eyes from the dying man.

Shin knelt beside the councillor as he stilled, his lifeless eyes staring up at the dark beams above. "He's dead," he said.

"We'd better send for Master Kenji," one of the guards said. "And His Majesty should be informed. What happened? Did he choke on something?"

"My lady, are you all right?" Tili patted my shoulder. Tears were running down my cheeks, but all I could do was shake my head. He was dead. I hiccupped on the start of a laugh. He was dead.

"I'll run for Master Kenji," one of the guards was saying. "Then you can inform His Majesty."

"He's dead, he doesn't need a physician. We should inform the general."

Tili went on patting my shoulder. I wanted to move, to speak, to show in some way that I did not care a man lay dead, but I could only stare at his bulging eyes and the hand that had reached out to me so desperately.

"I don't think it is safe for Lady Hana to stay here," Shin said, addressing the two guards. "What if someone was trying to poison her and got the councillor by mistake? I was on my way back to Minister Laroth's rooms. Let me take her and her maid with me. That way one of you can run for the physician and the other can inform His Majesty without any loss of time."

I had never heard him speak so many words in one go, but something in his rolling western accent was almost hypnotic and carried more authority than either fearful guard. Both men agreed, and we were soon all out in the passage, the two guards rushing off about their tasks while Shin strode ahead of Tili and me in the opposite direction.

The keep was quiet, the only sounds the crackle of torches and the shuffle of our steps. "Are we really going to see Darius?" I said once they were out of earshot, every sound seeming to come through a distant haze. Had I gotten enough Tishwa on my skin to kill me too? Did it even work like that? My head spun at the panicked thought, and Tili tightened her grip on my arm.

"Are you all right, my lady?"

Shin turned back to look at me. "She's just breathed in too much Tishwa. That shit makes you dizzy. Unless you drink it, then it makes you dead."

Out of the corner of my eye, I caught Tili's horrified glance but said nothing.

"Let's just get her to Lord Laroth before she faints. It's about time he upheld his side of the bargain and got us the hells out of here."

"What bargain?" I said.

"You think I've just been hanging around because it's fun to play messenger boy?" Shin gave me a stern look over his shoulder. "I met your friend the night you got caught. He said if I stayed to help keep an eye on you, he'd get you out as soon as it was safe."

He stopped outside a door and tapped on the frame. "Excellency?" he called while he glanced both ways along the passage. "Excellency?"

No answer came, and with a grunt of annoyance, Shin slid open the door and stepped in. "Laroth," he said, all pretence at respect falling away. "You have to—Who the fuck are you?"

Pulling free of Tili's grip, I stepped in after him. The room was dark, seemingly empty, but as my eyes adjusted, I caught the wriggle of a figure sitting on the floor before the divan. Black clothes melded into the black night, but the answering whimper of annoyance didn't belong to Darius.

"Can you please untie me?" the young man said, attempting to squirm into a more dignified position. "I have to find Lord Laroth, he—"

Past Shin, our eyes met, and the man tied to the divan froze as though turned to stone. With light now eking in through the open door to the passage, I could make out his face as a series of hazy features, and a Traitor's Mark branded upon his cheek. Plenty of the

Pikes owned similar marks, but none of them wore single earrings dangling from their ears. But Darius did. And so did Malice.

"Who are you?" I said, repeating the unanswered question.

I took a step forward only to find Shin's arm blocking my way. "Careful."

"I'm..." the young man began only to stop, looking up at us like a puppy begging for scraps. "Please can you untie me?"

"Not until you tell us why you're tied up in the first place."

Someone shouted in the distance, and whip fast, the young man turned in the direction of the sound, tugging at whatever bound him with agitated haste. "Lord Laroth just wanted me to wait for him. I have...I have a message, for you." He nodded at me, and the intensity of his gaze made my stomach squirm even more than the Tishwa had. His stare had real weight, pressure even, seeming to press into my flesh.

"A message for me?" My heart sped to a sickening pace. Who was this man? "What do you mean a message for me? How do you know who I am?"

"You're Hana. Lady Hana Otako, I mean. The message. It's from Malice, he—"

"I thought you looked like one of his."

Shin knelt closer to the strange man, but not too close, I noticed, the natural wariness of Vices kicking in. "The Vice Master sent you?"

"Yes, I mean no. Sort of. I wanted to come. Wanted to help. But I knew you wouldn't listen to me, so he gave me something for you."

"Gave you what?"

"If you untie me, I can get it."

Shin snorted. "Tell me where it is and I can get it myself."

"It's tucked into my sash."

"We don't have time for this," I said, a wave of dizziness forcing me to set my hand upon the wall for support. "Where's Darius?"

"I don't know, but he said he would be back." The young man wriggled as Shin reached inside his sash. "Please take this even if you won't untie me. Katashi is already inside the castle and Malice is coming. You have to get to safety. I don't know what he's planning to do."

I stared at him, stomach churning. I told myself it was the after-effects of the Tishwa, but it was Kin I thought of, Kin perhaps having laid down upon his mat to sleep, or sitting alone in his room reading his correspondence. Kin having no idea what was coming for him.

"You said you had a message," Shin said. "This is an ink canister."

"Give it to me." I held out my hand. "It won't be ink."

Shin dropped it into my outstretched hand, but I was still staring at the Kin of my imagination as Katashi's Pikes tore him apart. "Come on," Shin said, striding toward the doorway where Tili hovered. "If the Pikes are on their way, then getting out of here will be easy. Better you're not caught up in the bloodshed."

Pinching the canister's tight lid, I managed to prise it open, exhuming a waft of blood. It had always been Malice's favourite way of leaving messages, the sight of it so common as to not even be surprising.

"My lady?" Tili said from the doorway.

Shin returned on impatient steps. "Come on, let's go."

The blood looked black in the dim light, a small puddle in the bottom of the canister. There was nothing Malice could say that would make me trust him again, that would ever make me go back, but anything that could shed light on what was coming, that could allow me to make a difference, was worth knowing.

I touched the blood.

Kisia belongs to you. The Crimson Throne belongs to you. You are Emperor Lan's daughter. How dare the Usurper steal your birthright only to treat you like chattel. Kill him and take what's rightfully yours.

Righteous rage ripped through my veins, setting my mind aflame. My birthright. My throne. I was an Otako. An Otako!

"My lady?"

The voice came from far away, as revelling in the joyous anger, I smeared the blood from my fingers onto the back of my hand. My fingers. My wrist. Letting it inflate me from within, no longer a small, weak woman but a vengeful god who would destroy all in my path. I grabbed the dagger Shin wore on his belt and I drew it from its sheath.

"What are you—?"

I threaded it into the back of my sash and strode to the door.

"No. No! That wasn't meant to happen, grab her! Stop her!"

"My lady? My lady!"

A trail of voices followed like a clinging scent, but they meant nothing beneath the storm of my thundering pulse. I charged through blurring passages. Shin stepped in front of me, but I shouldered past him, chanting the rage that made my soul sing.

Kisia belongs to you. The Crimson Throne belongs to you. Kill him and take what's rightfully yours.

"Lady Hana?" A guard. His face swam as though in a haze. "I'm afraid His Majesty has requested no visitors, he—"

"Kin!"

The door banged open in its track and I strode in. Kin stood by the window, the sight of him flaring my rage so bright he might have been standing in flames. *How dare the Usurper steal your birthright only to treat you like chattel.*

I yanked the blade from my sash.

"Hana?" His gaze slid to the knife in my hand. "Hana! What? Why?"

Hurt throbbed in his voice, fuelling my furious joy. I lunged while shouts roared around us, but though he dodged back, Kin caught my wrist. His fingers smeared Malice's blood as he twisted my arm, forcing me so close that my eyes met a silvery scar tracing its memories across his throat. *Kill him and take what's rightfully yours.*

I tried to wrench free, but his grip bruised my arm. "Let me go," I snarled. "Kisia belongs to me."

"Let you go? Let you go!" He twisted my wrist still further until pain overcome rage and the blade slipped from my hand. "I offered you everything, *everything*, and this is how you repay me? What a fool you make me!"

With a growl, he threw me from him and I hit the screen door, crashing through thin wood and paper, splinters scratching my face. Debris rained down and Kin was there, the hatred in his face a mirror for my own. I leapt, clawing for his throat, but from everywhere, hands closed around my arms, dragging me back though I wriggled and spat, fury all that lived beneath my skin.

Shouts echoed around me, rising like bubbles in my ears.

"Majesty," someone said nearby, seeming to gasp for every breath. "Rebels have taken the Willow Gate."

"Let them come!" Kin snarled. "Get the executioner. I will have this traitor's head before Katashi comes for mine."

25. DARIUS

On the balcony above the main entrance doors, General Ryoji stood like a sentinel. Tonight, he looked older than his years, his expression set in something like Kin's perpetual frown.

"I told you not to let anyone in or out, General," I said, joining him at the railing. A dozen archers stood at intervals along the balcony, each staring down at the closed doors of the hall below.

"Yes, Your Excellency," he said. "But His Majesty's only stipulation was to allow Otako in if he brought the Hian Crown with him. He arrived at the gates some time ago with two of his men. He wants to talk."

"And you believe that, General? You were at the meeting. There is nothing Katashi wants to do less than bargain with Kin. This is a trap!"

He gestured around the room. "As you can see, I am well prepared for that eventuality."

"No," I said, panic beginning to hammer my heart into my ribs. "You're not. Order your men to kill all three of them at once."

"Kill men who approach with a flag of peace? In His Majesty's name?"

"Yes! There is nothing honourable about Katashi Otako and there is nothing honourable about the Vices. Kill them now before you condemn everyone in this castle."

Fear passed fleetingly across his face. "But His Majesty—"

"Would be better off making his oath without the crown than risking his life, and the lives of everyone in this castle, to retrieve it."

I was breathing fast, could not stop myself. Did it even matter what General Ryoji chose to do? Endymion was proof enough that the bastards were already inside the walls.

Three brandings. Fading bruises ghosted across his brow and marred his wrists, and each branding was a scabbing mess. Back in Shimai, his Empathy had been weak and unpractised; now it lacked restraint, ranging over the world with the subtlety of a mallet. Had he made it to adulthood without Maturating only to meet me?

A muffled shout sounded outside. One of Ryoji's men came along the gallery. "They are here, General," he said.

"Archers ready!" General Ryoji called.

"Don't do this, General. If you sent for me because you wanted my advice, then I beg you will not open those doors. Kill them. Now."

Had he been any other general I could have given him a direct order, but the commander of the Imperial Guard was the only one who answered directly to the emperor.

"I'm sorry, Your Excellency. I have my orders. His Majesty wants the crown. Open the doors."

I gritted my teeth but could not call the order back from his lips. Men were already gripping the handles, three to a door required to drag them open over the worn stones. Night spilled in. It licked at the heels of the incoming guards and bathed three men in darkness. They entered with their hoods drawn, their faces only visible to those who could see them at eye level. One of them carried a large bow upon his back while the others appeared not to be armed at all.

A scrap of white silk fluttered in the bowman's hand. Fine hands, long fingers just pinching the corner of the silk. Not the hands of an archer.

The dark hood turned toward me, and I felt the smile I could not see. I took a deep breath and the smell was there, the scent that was always at the very edge of my awareness.

Malice.

"General," I said. "That man is not Katashi Otako."

"You have requested speech with Emperor Kin," General Ryoji said, projecting his voice to the uninvited guests. "Set back your hoods and identify yourselves."

"I have told you who I am," the central figure said. "Your guards have already identified me as Lord Katashi Otako."

Too well did I know that voice.

General Ryoji hesitated, glancing at me, but it was already too late. He had let them inside the walls.

"Few of my guards would know what Katashi Otako looks like," he said, wariness in his tone. He had let his men be fooled by a black sash, a longbow, and noble features. And Kin's foolish desperation to have the crown returned before morning, a desperation he had been unable to voice even to me.

"Draw."

All along the balcony, bowstrings creaked. "Set back your hoods," the general said.

A chuckle sounded softly on the air. "As you wish."

The three imposters put back their hoods. From the centre, Malice looked up at me, his lips twisted into something like a smile. I knew neither of his companions, one a man with slick blond hair, the other a woman with an eruption of wild curls.

"Identify yourselves," General Ryoji said.

Malice made an ironic little bow. "But of course. My name is Malice and these are my Vices, Spite and Adversity." Again, his eyes drifted to me. "Aren't you going to say hello, Darius?"

"Take aim!"

An order to spare Malice leapt to my tongue, but there was

no time to utter it. Arrows flew. A grunt sounded nearby, then a scream gurgled from a blood-clogged throat. Beside me, an archer toppled down the stairs, an arrow buried in his neck. He hit the stones below with a sickening crunch.

Malice hadn't moved. Spite stood in front of him, arrows hovering in the air between his splayed fingers. Sweat beaded his brow and his hands shook, fighting the force that should have seen each sharp tip through his chest. One after another the arrows bounced back, digging deep into legs and necks and eyes.

In less than a minute, every one of General Ryoji's archers lay dead or injured, and like a man gone without water for days, Spite crumpled to the ground.

"Kill them!" General Ryoji cried, and more soldiers spilled into the entrance hall. Leaving Spite where he had fallen, Malice pulled the young woman toward one of the walls. They hit it together and thinned, their flesh sliding through the stone like water.

"Shit! Where did they go?"

Guards dashed forward, patting the stones, but there would be no way through. I had seen that ability before. "Where are you going, Malice?" I said beneath my breath, staring at the patch of stone.

"See if they're in the next passage," Ryoji shouted. "Spread out!"

"You won't find them if they don't want to be found, General," I said. "We need to get Kin out of here."

Shouts came along the upper passage, then a guard tumbled down the stairs to fall in a crumpled heap at my feet, three arrows in his back. "How did they get onto the walls so fast?" General Ryoji demanded.

"That's not them. Malice doesn't know how to use a bow."

"Otako?"

"Who else? What are you waiting for? Go! I'll get Kin."

"His Majesty's life—"

"Trust me this time, General," I said. "Try to keep Katashi from reaching the upper levels. I'll get His Majesty out. Go!"

I didn't wait for a reply, didn't wait to argue, just hurried back the way I had come. Up the stairs to the court floor, the sounds of battle seeming to come from everywhere at once. Out in the courtyard, Kin's dogs were barking. Courtiers and servants ran past me, pushing each other in their haste, while others stuck their heads out of rooms demanding to know what was going on. In the madness, I grabbed a passing guard. "Where is Kin?"

"In the upper audience room, Your Excellency," he replied breathlessly. "He's sent for the headsman. Assassins."

I let the man go and plunged on, taking the stairs and doubling back through the dim passages. Once on the upper floor, I ran to the audience room only to find the doors wide open and soldiers crammed into the aperture.

"Out of the way!"

The imperial guards knew my voice and tried to move, but there was such a press that all I could do was push through the mass of stinking armour and sweat.

Inside the room, hastily lit torches belched black smoke while clustered around Kin, imperial guards stood tense, watching the doors. Kin himself had eyes for no one but Hana, bound and gagged at his feet. He looked wild. Hair had pulled free of his topknot and his jaw was set so hard he might have been grinding unspoken words.

"Majesty, what are you doing?" I said, pushing men out of the way. The sounds of battle were growing every moment, screams echoing through the castle. We were running out of time.

"Removing the head of a traitor, Laroth," he snarled. "You are no longer in my service. Leave now, unless you have a fancy to see your head on a spike beside this one." Kin kicked Hana in the side, sending her rolling. It ought to have looked pathetic, but she struggled fiercely at the chains binding her, fury flashing in her eyes as she chewed at the fabric wadded between her teeth. Though our eyes met, she seemed not to recognise me.

Blood covered both her hands and smeared like paint up one arm. Malice had been here after all.

"Majesty, I—"

Kin gripped the front of my robe, his eyes burning with rage. "Don't push your luck, Laroth," he said. "I will do it. I would see you both burn for the injury you have done me. If I see your face ever again, I will break it."

He shoved me from him, leaving bloody fingerprints on my pale silk. It was all over his palms.

Because Malice was never going to take no for an answer.

"I took an oath," I said. "And I am not relieved of it until the sun rises. Just remember that. Remember I had no choice."

Anger flared in his face, and he was mad enough to have killed me then, but I had already turned, was shoving my way blindly back through the crowd of guards and out through the open doors.

The passages were full of noise. Men shouted, echoes bouncing back as though the walls themselves were screaming. Two imperial soldiers pushed past, sprinting in the direction of the Willow Gate. If Katashi had brought enough men, the castle would soon be overrun, but I could not just leave, could not flee while there might still be a chance to save them, if nothing else.

I turned a corner and almost ran into a Pike. I leapt back as he swung, the sharp spikes of his mace coming so close that air rushed by my face. The weapon smashed into the wall, splintering wood, but as he wrenched it free, I jabbed an elbow into his kidney. Doubled over, he stumbled back...right onto Shin's blade. Blood splattered as he withdrew his knife. A few drops hit the bare skin atop my foot, leaving fleeting pain—something I hadn't felt for years.

"You said you would look after Lady Hana," Shin said as he let the dead Pike fall to the floor. "I agreed to wait while you got her out with your fancy talking, and look where that got us."

"Letting her touch that blood was a very bad idea."

The man snapped his teeth at me. "She wouldn't have been able to if you had gotten her out of here before all this shit. Fix this. Now. I cannot fight them all single-handed."

"Try. Stall them. Do something to keep the executioner busy for a few minutes."

The man didn't even nod, just stalked away like a wolf. I hurried on. At the door of my room, I spoke a silent prayer and slid the screen. Endymion was still there, tied to the divan, but he was not quite as I had left him. Blood dribbled from a split lip, and a Pike stood over him, a sword at his throat.

"Where's the minister, boy?" he said, pressing the tip into Endymion's skin. "Tell me or I'll slice you, eh?"

Endymion saw me, and the rebel spun around. "You!" He grinned, misshaping the faded branding on his cheek.

"Yes?" I said. "Do I know you?"

"No, but I know who you are. I'm going to skin you alive and sell that face to the highest bidder."

He took a step toward me, his sword hovering low.

"I suggest you leave," I said. "Or it might be your skin."

The rebel leered. "Funny."

"Hilarious," I agreed. "Last chance."

Amusement twisted the man's lips. He saw a weak man dressed in expensive clothes whose manicured hands could never get dirty. He saw no weapon, no way I could defend myself, and already mentally narrating this story to his cronies, he waited for my humiliating capitulation.

I looked down at Endymion. The Pike didn't. And Endymion smashed his foot into the man's ankle.

Sucking in a hiss of pain, he turned. "You little—"

I jammed my heel into the back of his knee. His leg buckled, and while he tried to steady himself halfway between standing and falling, I gripped his hair and yanked his head back, exposing his throat to the side of my hand.

The rebel crumpled, gasping. If I had used more force, his throat would have been crushed beyond repair, but he had no breath left to thank me.

Endymion kicked the man's limp foot in petty revenge. "How did you do that?"

"You should have been watching," I said, kneeling beside him. "I did warn him."

With bedraggled hair falling into his eyes, Endymion glared at me. "What's going on out there?"

"We have to save Hana," I said, hating the words that had to come next. "I need your help."

"Why? What's happening?"

"I haven't time to explain, but you're the only one who can help me." I gripped the knot, ready to release him. "Will you come?"

He nodded. One tug upon the sash and it fell loose, allowing Endymion to his feet, but he didn't immediately follow me to the door. "The canister Malice gave me..."

"Oh, it was you, was it?" But of course, that would perfectly suit Malice's sense of humour, sending the boy who wanted to save his sister in with something designed to ensure her death. "I told you not to trust him. Come on."

"What was it?" He had crouched to pick up the discarded container from the floor, nothing but a smear of blood left in the bottom. "It felt...intense."

"It's called a leech implant. Blood filled with extremely potent emotions and thoughts and...whole ideas. Malice has a knack of mixing them all just right so it makes you want more." I took the container from his hand and dropped it into one of my travelling chests. "Don't touch it. Don't ever touch anything Malice gives you."

"Does it only work with blood?"

"It works best with blood." I strode toward the door, and when again he didn't follow, I turned back. "Are you going to help me or not? We're running out of time."

Endymion dragged his gaze from the travelling chest with an effort. "Yes," he said. "What do you need me to do?"

"I need you to take everything you can from me and amplify it, push it out as loud as you can, do you understand?"

"Everything?"

"Everything. Don't pretend you don't know what I mean."

"Yes, but are you—?"

I cut him off, walking out the door. "No more time. Let's go."

Together we made our way back through the keep. Mere minutes had passed since I left Kin and Hana in the audience room, but it felt like an age. An age full of fear, knowing the only way I could save them from Malice was to let Malice win.

We arrived to a scene like a tableau. Hana knelt, her wrists bound. The executioner's burly shoulders were unmistakable in black linen. And in his own well of darkness, Kin stood apart, a deep scowl ravaging his face. The battle beyond this room seemed not to reach him, trapped within the cage of Malice's anger.

I swear on the bones of my forebears.

I took a deep breath and lowered what remained of my shield.

On my name and my honour.

Colour flooded into the world, every soul a chorus of emotion. There was freedom in this world, freedom to breathe, freedom to smell and feel and see and taste.

That I will do all in my power to protect you from harm.

I took Endymion's hand. It was cold and strange, not like the hand I was used to, its fingers shorter, its palm less smooth. Almost my thoughts veered into memory, but the flare of connection seared it all away. Never had I felt anything like his power, his very fingers seeming to reach into my soul.

I will mind not pain.

His mind melded into mine, his memories before my eyes. Through the figures crowding the throne room, rain pounding a dark road. Around me, a pair of strong arms gripped the reins, and with every breath came the stink of the horse between my legs. There were other smells, all so vivid, the blood, the sweat, and the sweet scent of jasmine oil. Then I looked up and saw my father. He was smiling, a smile he had never given me.

I will mind not suffering.

My emotions gathered strength, but with dreadful ease, Endymion ripped them all free, all control gone beyond my hands.

I will give every last ounce of my strength.

For so long, I had tried to eradicate my instincts. I had tried to live without a heart, and now raw emotion ran through me, twinging every nerve and fibre that had so long fought against it.

I will give every last ounce of my intellect.

Like molten metal, it burned along my arm. Anger for my failure, fear for the future, and hatred for what I had been unable to change, for the self I could not escape.

I will die in service to you if the gods so will it.

Endymion's strength tore it all out like poison, long after there was nothing left to give. It boiled inside him. It saturated his soul, held within until he could hold it no longer.

I will renounce every honour.

The blast shook the floor. Guards fell, thrown off their feet. Emotion crackled through the air like sparks, their dense fumes choking every breath.

I will give every coin.

For an instant I saw the scene, the tableau broken. Hana a crumpled heap upon the floor. Kin thrown into the shadows. And darkness came to me as the last shred of soul was sucked out through my fingertips.

I will be as nothing and no one in service to you.

26. ENDYMION

L ord Laroth dropped like a stone. He crumpled, all steel gone, leaving nothing but the fragile bones that held his form. With my heart still thundering, I put my hand to his chest. It rose and fell so slightly I could almost believe I had imagined it.

"Darius?"

I shook him, but he did not stir. His head lolled to the side like a broken doll, and my stomach twisted. I was the only one left standing. Around me, dozens of men lay dead or unconscious, and power hummed through my veins.

"Endymion!"

I spun, shocked to hear a voice in the dead silence. Ire stood in the doorway, his eyes widening at the chaos. "What did you do?"

"I . . . I don't know," I said. "I did what he told me to. I . . . I didn't think it would be so strong."

Kimiko entered silently in his wake, her face pale.

"Well." Ire picked his way carefully across the floor so as not to step on any prone figures. "It looks like you've done the first part of my job for me. He's here, Adversity."

He pointed to a sprawled pile of crimson silk, and Kimiko joined him, still silent, and pressed her hand to Emperor Kin's neck. He did not move, did not so much as twitch beneath her touch. Was he dead? Had I killed the emperor?

Drawing back her hand, Kimiko slapped the immobile man across the cheek.

"What are you doing?" Ire said.

"Hitting the emperor."

The Vice laughed, and feeling giddy, I joined in, sure the whole world had gone mad. Still chuckling, Ire took something from a pouch and waved it beneath the emperor's nose. He jerked violently, sitting up as though attached to strings. Not truly conscious, he began to fall back, but Ire gripped his arms and dragged him up, and between the two of them, they managed to get him on his feet.

"Don't tell Katashi," Kimiko said, looking back to me as they made their slow way toward one wall. "He won't understand I had to obey."

She touched the wood, and pausing only to be sure Ire was ready, she emitted her sadness and stepped forward. A gasp from Kin was all they left behind.

Slowly, some of the unconscious began to stir. Nearby, a guard groaned, lifting his hand to his head, yet at my feet, Lord Laroth did not move. I couldn't get his memory out of my head. The sting of the knife had been so real, as real as the sight of his fair wrist against Malice's.

An Empath.

Lord Laroth was lying on his left arm, but I had to see, I had to know.

I rolled him over. Dark hair had stuck to his forehead, the redness of where his cheek had lain on the wood the only colour in his face.

Running steps sounded along the passage. Pikes appeared, slowing as they entered, the black sashes with which they honoured Katashi's mother drenched in blood.

Katashi strode in after them. He had Hacho in his hand, an arrow loosely held to her string. In a moment, his gaze took in the scene, sweeping across the sea of barely conscious bodies until it came to rest on me.

"What the fuck did you do?" he said, and I winced at the mingled horror and disgust that coloured the question. "Where's Kin?"

I had no energy with which to explain and just shook my head.

Katashi snarled and kicked a fallen scabbard, sending it spinning away across the floor. "Search everywhere," he snapped at his men. "He can't have gone far. Search the keep, search the grounds, search the forests if you have to. I want him found. Go!"

All but a handful departed, their footsteps fading with their souls.

Pain tore across my throat, ghostly in its brevity. It came again, but when I touched my neck, I found nothing but smooth skin. The remaining Pikes were picking their way around the room, turning each semi-conscious man. Most were Kin's guards, and every red belt they found, they thrust into the arms of death.

Blood ran across the floor.

Soon, Malice arrived with Avarice and Conceit in his wake. Brushing past me, the Vice had eyes for no one but the fallen man at my feet, and he dropped at Lord Laroth's side, pressing two fingers to his neck.

Relief.

His broken doll lived, but all too well could I remember Darius's fear of him. Hurried steps brought Katashi back to stand over the pair. "What are *you* doing here? This castle is already home to enough spiders."

Malice didn't look up. "I am merely here for what is mine, yes?"

"For what is yours? This castle is mine now, which means everything in it belongs to me. And every man answers to me, including Lord Laroth."

In the centre of the room, Conceit gripped a Pike's arm. "What do you think you're doing? That's not a red belt, that's Lady Hana."

Hana. I took a step toward the small figure, but Malice gripped my leg in warning, leaving Katashi to dash forward alone. The family I had fought so hard for, reuniting without me.

"Quick, someone find a physician," Katashi said when Hana remained limp in his arms. "Run out into the city and rouse as many as you can find if you must."

"She'll be fine after some rest," Malice said. "Just have someone find her a room unoccupied by a corpse and stay with her until she wakes, yes?"

Katashi turned on him. "You have no right to give orders or make suggestions here, Vice," he said. "This is my castle and she is my cousin."

"My deepest apologies, *Your Majesty*," Malice said, bowing. "I was quite forgetting. By all means, leave her lying on the floor with the dead until you manage to find a physician, it is all the same to me. However, with your permission, we shall return Lord Laroth to his room."

He received a curt nod, and Avarice lifted Lord Laroth without so much as a grunt of effort. He looked thin and fragile in the big man's arms, his grand silk robe like tangled wings clinging to shattered bones.

"Come, Endymion," Malice said as Avarice carried his precious burden away. "Let us leave His Majesty to his preparations. He has an oath to take this morning after all."

"And I would have a Usurper to behead if it wasn't for your interference." Katashi prodded a finger into Malice's chest. "I know it was you, Spider, and if I don't find him, your head will roll instead of his."

Malice's faint smile remained fixed. "I trust you will think better of that threat. But for now, let us part. Endymion?"

"Endymion can stay with me."

"I am sure he is physically capable of such an act, but I think he knows now where he belongs, yes?"

Outside, the sun was rising, light beginning to stretch its fingers over the dead. The Pikes had killed most of them but not all. No one else could know by looking at the sea of bodies, but I knew. I had felt them die, felt their ends like the snapping of strings in my fingers, and it had felt so good.

"Well? Endymion?"

I had wanted nothing but Katashi's acceptance, but whatever his reason for wanting me with him now, there was no friendliness left in his smile. He could see what I had done. Knew what I was. I had thought Lord Laroth a monster, but perhaps the only monster here was me.

I needed to see the underside of Lord Laroth's left wrist. I needed to know for sure.

"I must make sure Lord Laroth is all right," I said, not meeting Katashi's gaze. "I feel responsible for what happened to him."

"Oh, how chivalrous you are, Endymion. His Majesty can't but respect such honour, yes?" Malice took hold of my elbow and, bowing very slightly, turned me toward the door. Silence followed us, and I could not look back.

"Your idea?" Malice said as we gained the comparative peace of the hallway.

"What was?"

His eyebrows went up. "The emotive blast. Any stronger and you would have killed every man in that room, yes?" He walked through the smoke of a guttering torch as he spoke. Its light was no longer needed now morning had come, but there were no servants to douse them. The castle was changing. Even the air felt different. Katashi's aura had spread across the building, taking instant ownership of his birthright.

"I did what he asked me to do."

That made Malice stop. "Darius? But such desperation! And I thought nothing would shift him. Perhaps he missed me after all."

He chuckled and we walked on, the sound of rebels laughing in the distance all that disturbed the peace.

"I remember my first time," he said abruptly, staring straight ahead. "A man had come into my mother's room without permission. He dragged her across the floor by her hair, and when she shouted for her owner, he did not come. She did not fight. She had to be careful of her reputation, you see, but there I was watching, and all she would do was cry. I wanted to hurt her for being weak." He paused, licking his lips. "I still remember the sound of their screaming. I was six years old."

Trying not to think about the horror of those words, I said, "These men didn't scream."

"No, you hit them too hard for that, yes? The human heart can only take so much before it shuts down to protect the body from harm."

We walked on, the truth increasingly hard to ignore.

It had felt good.

So little time had passed since I'd left Lord Laroth's room in his wake, and yet it could have been an age, so different did the world feel. Avarice had already laid Darius upon the divan and now fussed around as though he were a wayward child to be cosseted and lectured.

"How is he?" Malice asked, crossing the floor.

"I've never seen him this bad," the older Vice growled. "You never did this to him, not even in those early days." He turned, blaming me with every ounce of his being.

Malice splayed his long fingers upon the unresponsive chest. It rose and fell gently beneath his touch, but it looked as though the body was just breathing in memory of its function.

"He's in there," Malice said. "Just very weak."

"Who knows how long it will take him to recover." Avarice

glared at me. "You fool. Don't know what you're doing? Nearly sucked the life right out of him."

"He gave it to me."

Avarice lunged, hands reaching for my throat, but Malice stepped between us. "No, Endymion is too strong for his own good," he said, turning the enraged Vice aside. "But Darius wasn't to know that."

"No," I said. "He did know."

"If he dies because of you, I will rip your head off," Avarice snarled.

"No, Avarice. Go now. Check on the others and find Hope. I will sit with Darius, yes?"

For a moment, I thought Avarice would refuse, so protectively did he look at the unconscious man upon the divan, but with nothing more than a grunt, he went to the door. His anger stalked past, disappearing into the passage.

Quick steps took me to the divan. Lord Laroth's hand hung toward the floor, and pinching the fabric between dry fingers, I drew back his sleeve.

A birthmark stared up at me. Three horizontal lines crossed by a diagonal.

Malice had called him brother.

"I'm your brother," I said.

A dry chuckle sounded above my head. "Told you so, did he?"

Had he? He hadn't wanted to.

Bitter tears stung my eyes, but I would not let them fall. Darius had known, from that first moment in Shimai he had known. But he'd had no choice. And the family I had thought I'd gained was not really my family at all.

I looked up at Malice. "You're a Laroth."

"*We* are Laroths, yes?" he said. "Our father was a busy man."

"Are there more of us?"

Malice shook his head. "No. Although until now, we didn't know about you. Your priests hid you well. There was always the rumour Empress Li's last children were his, and here you are to prove it."

"Hana?"

"Painfully normal, I'm afraid. A pity, yes? She is only your half-sister."

"So I'm not an Otako."

"Oh, but you are. Whatever he might have known to the contrary, Emperor Lan formally acknowledged you as his son, yes? You are perfect. Laroth and Otako in one. The key to Kisia's future, here ready to sit upon your father's throne."

"But...I don't want to. I just want...somewhere to belong." And I thought I had found it, but Hana had looked at me as though I didn't exist, and she was right. What good was a bastard freak, neither Otako nor Laroth but caught somewhere in between?

I looked at Darius, still motionless upon the divan. Avarice's anger over my words could not change the truth. He had known I could kill him and he had welcomed it.

There was a sharp knock on the door, and Conceit poked his head inside. "Otako will be taking his oath at noon," he said with something of a wicked grin. "The nobility are already arriving for Kin's and there is...some confusion."

Malice laughed. "Ascension by blood. It will prove an interesting morning, yes?"

"So it would seem, Master."

———————◆———————

Sun shone through the crimson windows, turning everything the colour of blood. It touched every face and turned pale robes red.

Upon the throne, Katashi sat like a returning god, dressed in imperial crimson. From a distance, it might have been Kin himself, but for the black sash and the tall, graceful curve of Hacho rising behind him. Hundreds held their breath. They had come for one emperor only to see another, neither the rightful heir.

The high priest of Koi lowered the Hian Crown onto Katashi's head. The old man was shaking. Only Katashi looked calm, his hands resting easily on the lacquered arms of the throne.

"Here before witnesses, I take the Imperial Oath," he said, his voice carrying with ease. "To Kisia I give my strength. To Kisia I give my heart. In service to the empire, I am nothing. I have no coin. I have no blood. I will protect her from foes, from famine, and from plague. Here and now before the divinity of the gods, I give myself to her. In duty, I am Kisia."

Applause rose to the rafters, but there was a world of whispers in my head. Of doubts and wonders and fears, of questions and assumptions as everyone present made their choices and accepted their own truths. And over it all, a whisper from beside me, repeated and insistent while Malice smiled and twisted the tip of his ponytail around his finger.

That throne is yours, Takehiko Otako. That throne is yours. You were born a god.

Acknowledgements

So, here I find myself in an odd position. The original version of this book was published in 2013 with the following acknowledgements, but while it's important to give thanks to those who helped that original edition exist, there is a lot more to be said now, in 2020. And some things that are...no longer true. So rather than totally rewrite these, I am going to edit them. Ahem. Here we go.

The initial inspiration for *The Blood of Whisperers* came from two sayings. The first was the Confucian saying: *"Before you embark on a journey of revenge, dig two graves."* And the other a Chinese proverb: *"When two tigers fight, one walks away terribly wounded, the other is dead."*
(Still true, but kind of silly to say. Whatever.)
I wanted to write something with this honesty in mind, and so The Vengeance Trilogy was born. It has been a long and very difficult journey (Hahahahahahahaha omg past Devin you have no idea yet), but we made it, no little thanks to the people who have shared the adventure with me. Writing the first draft of a novel is a very solitary experience, but taking that draft through beta reads and edits and producing a finished product involves a lot of amazing people (it really does and they are all still amazing people), all dedicated to the same goal.
So first and foremost, I would like to thank my parents, Louise and Andrew, for their constant love and support, and for not

minding when I call at midnight just for the company because I'm up late working—again. (Still amazing parents, that part sure hasn't changed. And I don't wake them up when I call at midnight, I'm not a jerk; they don't go to bed until 1:00 AM.)

To my husband (rather awkwardly no longer my husband), for all the hours he is left to man the fort without me, and for all the times he thinks he is talking to me, but my mind is somewhere else entirely (possibly why he's no longer my husband?). He never gets tired of hearing about my worlds (hmmm, I think he did...) and my characters and listening to me read aloud, and if he does, he doesn't let me know it (ahem).

To my two little girls, for being the light of my life. I never tire of hearing your views on the world, so simple and yet so true, and you never fail to make me smile even on the darkest of days. (Still true; they are many years older now but still amazing humans.)

Amanda! You are the prince of editors, princess doesn't suit you... (Still doesn't.) Never could I have dreamed of a better partnership than what we have, a friendship I now could not imagine being without. You are equally crazy and amazing, and I hope you will put up with me for many many more books to come.

(Amanda is even more my bestest bud than ever, but she is no longer the editor of these editions of my books, as that role is now taken by the equally amazing but not yet so long-suffering Nivia Evans at Orbit. Hi, Nivia! [She's great and I look forward to working with her on many more books in the future. Yes, these are parentheses within parentheses, is that a problem?] And my very impressive and diligent copy editor, Maya Frank-Levine. Long may she be the final bastion between me and very foolish continuity errors.)

In regards to the book production, I would like to say a humongous thank you to the art/design team behind The Vengeance Trilogy.

To Viktor, for producing the most beautiful depiction of Katashi Otako for the cover that I could ever imagine (FOR THE ORIGINAL cover, which I'm sure can be found somewhere on the internet for the curious; for the new and wonderful version gracing this book, all thanks must go to Gregory Titus for the stunning art and Lisa Marie Pompilio for its design). To Isabelle, for all the hours of design work it took to get it all right. And to Dave, for bringing my vision to life on the inside pages: you are a true gem! (Again, all thanks here has to fantastic art team at Orbit for bringing this beauty to life. A lot more people work behind the scenes to make these things look amazing than you think.)

Thank you to my team of amazing beta readers—Natasha, Carl, Chris, Dave, Kath, and Louise. And an extra special thanks to Chris and Dave for all the times "a minute of your time" became an hour. Your knowledge and patience have been truly inspirational. (I don't have new beta readers to thank on this one, but all of these people were a huge help in the development of my early writing, and I am still much beholden to their generosity and kindness.)

A huge thank you to Lauren Mitchell, and to Dan Allan, book arsonist and vampire bat (honestly no idea why he is listed as a book arsonist or a vampire bat. Dan, if you know, call me). And to Jess and Stef Cola at the View Point Handmade Gallery in Bendigo, for being awesome supporters of all things artsy and all things Bendigo (sadly no longer there, though they were kind enough to hold my first ever book launch and reading... maybe there's a correlation...).
   An extra amazing thank you to Jessica and Julian Avelsgaard, David Hosking, Kim Bartels, and Riyadh Bawa.

And the most important part of all, for helping me raise the funds to see these books produced to a professional standard (I crowdfunded for the production of this original trilogy, so while this has nothing to do with the current edition of the book you are holding in your hand, their donations allowed me to enter the publishing world as a little minnow self-pubber, and I might not be here now without them), I would like to thank all of these amazing people:

Chris Themelco, Jason Maricchiolo, Geoff Brown, Christopher Phillips, Peter Farnaby, Janet Farnaby, Jaana Sauso, David Young, A. C. Flory, Boyce Yates, Matthew Santilli, Col Hoad, Dana Lee, Jessica Cola, Maarja Valdmann, David Stott, Fiona Wright, Dan Allan, Jack Heath, Rebecca Dominguez, Keiko Maber, Stefania Cola, Emma Knights, Lauren O'Brien, David Hosking, Anja Sauso, Jullian Sauso-Bawa, Louise and Andrew Stott, Judy Gersch, Foz Shanahan, Jarryd Fell, Grant Adam, Luke Smith, Tamara Bond, Shari Bird, Marie Berry, Gisela Guillian, Lara Whitehead, Riyadh Bawa, Kim Bartels, Phil Randall, Brendan Hill, Tom and Caryn Avelsgaard, Jessica and Julian Avelsgaard, Kath and Don Macqueen, Jos Roder, Kristin Stefanoff, Cecil and Lynette Stott, Amanda J. Spedding, Carl and Natasha Weibgen, Genevieve Callaghan, Lisa Lawrence, Andrew Bunnell, and Rachael Gunn.

Well, that was fun! I would also like to thank my superhero agent, Julie Crisp, for her tireless work, especially the bit where she has to answer all my alternately rambly and panicky emails. You're a gem!

Thanks to my partner, Chris, as well (who I swear I don't bore as much as I bored my ex-husband with my work, though he has to man the fort about as much) for being an amazing support and best friend through this batshit journey we're on.

Also my Discord fam for putting up with all my screaming and for being generally just the most amazing group of humans I've ever met.

And of course the entire team at Orbit, on both sides of the pond, for all the hard work they have put in to make this happen. Especially Nivia, yes I'm thanking her again, for giving me the wonderful opportunity to go back and revise and rewrite these books and make them part of my world that I can truly be proud of.

extras

www.orbitbooks.net

about the author

Devin Madson is an Aurealis Award–winning fantasy author from Australia. After some sucky teenage years, she gave up reality and is now a dual-wielding rogue who works through every tiny side-quest and always ends up too over-powered for the final boss. Anything but Zen, Devin subsists on tea and chocolate and so much fried zucchini she ought to have turned into one by now. Her fantasy novels come in all shades of grey and are populated with characters of questionable morals and a liking for witty banter.

Find out more about Devin Madson and other Orbit authors by registering for the free monthly newsletter at www.orbitbooks.net.

if you enjoyed
THE BLOOD OF WHISPERERS

look out for

THE GODS OF VICE
The Vengeance Trilogy: Book Two

by

Devin Madson

The war for the Crimson Throne has split Kisia. In the north, Otako supporters rally around their champion, but Katashi Otako wants only vengeance. Caught in the middle, Hana must decide between her family and her heart. Is the true emperor the man the people want? Or the one they need?

As the true heir to the throne, Endymion remains hidden in plain sight, but the Vices know his secret. Malice, scheming to restore the empire to the rule of gods, plans a coup that will tear Kisia apart if Endymion does not find a way to escape. But he is running out of time. His Empathy is consuming him. It grows stronger with every use, spreading him so thin there will soon be nothing left—nothing except the monster he fears to become. When gods fight, empires fall.

1. HANA

I had woken disoriented from many bad dreams before, but never to a stomach intent on spilling my horror onto the matting floor. Tili sang and shushed my cries, patting my back as I purged darkness from my stomach. And it felt like darkness, like a horror and a disgust so deep I might never smile again.

Slowly, the warmth of the sun began to touch my skin, and I didn't just hear her song; I felt it. It was like waking from another layer of dream, trembling and ill.

"It's going to be all right, my lady," Tili said as she rubbed my back. She had draped blankets over me at some point, the weight of them on my shoulders comforting. "Everything is going to be all right."

Outside, birds went on singing. A bee buzzed onto the late-blooming jasmine coiled around the balcony railing. I could not recall my room at Koi having had a balcony, but the smell sent a wistful blade deep into my soul. Tears came next, and Tili held me to her, her weight and her warmth even more comforting than the blankets, and when at last I could cry no more, I finally felt alive. Exhausted, broken, but alive.

"No one seems to know what happened," Tili said, fussing

around while I picked at some thinly sliced fruit. "But everyone who was in the room has suffered like this, and some…"

She stopped. Her fussing got fussier.

"Dead?" I said, my first word, but it felt appropriate. For a while there, death would have been a relief.

"Yes, my lady, but let's not think about that. You are safe and you are well and that is all that matters."

Her words owned a brittle cheeriness, her smile as fragile as glass. "Tili, tell me what happened. Please," I added when she pursed her lips and would not speak. "I need to know."

"Lord Otako—Emperor Katashi, I mean, holds the city now. He's taken the oath and everyone has to kneel before him and swear loyalty to their new emperor and"—Having begun to speak, she seemed unable to stop, words spilling from her like bile had spilled from me—"if they refuse, they are being…being executed, and anyone who had a position with Emperor Kin is being executed, and the imperial guards who didn't escape are all dead, and most of the servants who came from Mei'lian, and…and…" Grief overtook her, tears choking her words. She rubbed her eyes with the sleeve of her robe. "I'm sorry, my lady, I did not mean to tell you until you were feeling better, I—"

"Kin?"

I could remember the fury and the blade and the flash of hurt in his dark eyes but not much else. Had he been in that room with me? Had Katashi caught him?

Tili looked down and shook her head, sending fear thundering through my numb veins. "I'm sorry, my lady, but I don't know. He seems to have just…" She lowered her voice to a whisper. "…disappeared."

"Disappeared?"

"Hush, we should not talk so in case someone is listening, my lady. I do not want to . . . be thought a traitor and . . ." She pressed her sleeve to her eyes and stayed there silently shaking.

Disappeared. Perhaps I had something to thank Malice for after all.

I gripped Tili's arm. "It's going to be all right," I said, repeating her words back to her. "I will not let him hurt you." I let her cry as she had let me cry. Most of the servants who had travelled with us from Mei'lian had been known to her, some of the guards too. She might have exaggerated the number of deaths in her distress, but there were still many lives to fear for.

"What of Minister Laroth?" I said. "What happened to him?"

I had been in his room. Shin had been there. A strange young man too, tied to the divan. All I had wanted to do was get out of the castle, and then he had given me Malice's blood.

"I . . . I hear he hasn't woken, my lady." Tili sniffed. "But there are some men in black robes who are caring for him. Everyone says they are Vices." She whispered the last word with the horror and awe that seemed to follow the Vices everywhere, but to me they were familiar faces.

Almost I told Tili not to worry about them either, but while my ability to protect her from Katashi needed no explanation, I had not the energy to explain Malice.

I nibbled a few individual pomegranate arils and stared at the table while Tili went back to fussing. I appeared to have a lot more robes than before, and she seemed intent on refolding them all.

Kin had disappeared. Katashi had taken the oath. Darius was asleep, while Malice and his Vices were stalking about. And tucked away in this pretty room, I was as inconsequential as the breeze. I crunched a few more arils and tapped the table. I needed to see Katashi.

"I will wash and dress," I said. My body ached at the very thought, but I had to see the new world for myself. I had fallen asleep and everything had changed.

"Are you sure, my lady? You still look very pale and you've hardly eaten anything. Emperor Katashi said I was to look after you and make sure no one troubled you and—"

"I'm fine, Tili, I promise. Just tired, but...not the sort of tired sleep can fix. Will you choose something for me to wear?"

With a nod, she walked away along the line of chests while I finished what I could stomach of my meal. "Blue, my lady?" She held up a lovely light-blue and white robe, edged in dark blue waves. It was pretty but cut low at the back of the neck and not one of mine.

"No, one of the ones you altered for me."

Tili hadn't a smile to lose, but her gaze slid toward the door. "As they were gifts from the Usurper, they have been taken away and replaced with...and unfortunately, my lady, I haven't been able...there just hasn't been time to—"

She sucked a panicked breath, and I leapt up from my mat to take her hands, leaving the pretty robe to fall unheeded on the floor. "Tili, Tili, it's all right; you cannot think I would be mad at you for that. I understand, you're afraid, and if my cousin is making a nuisance of himself, then I can't but—"

"A nuisance? My lady, poor Ilo got executed just for having been born in Ts'ai, he is—"

Again, she looked at the door. Her hands shook.

"Surely there must have been more to it than that," I said.

"No! Ilo would never hurt a fly. I...I was born in Ts'ai, my lady. I lived there all my life until I moved to Mei'lian and took work at the palace. The only reason my head is not out there with theirs is because I am your maid."

Beneath the sound of her shuddering breath, there was

nothing but the patter of footsteps, some chatter, and even a distant laugh—the sounds of a castle in which nothing had changed. And yet Tili trembled all over like an aspen leaf in a storm.

"Tili," I said. "How long have I been asleep?"

"Three days, my lady."

"Three days? I—" I bent and grabbed the robe off the floor. "I have to see Katashi. Here, I don't suppose there is a robe with less of a come-fuck-me neckline, is there?"

Her eyes widened, and cheeks turning pink, she gasped. "My lady!"

I laughed at her look of mingled horror and awe. "I'm sorry, but you shouldn't be surprised anymore that I'm hardly a lady. A less...attention-seeking neckline then, is that better?"

"Yes, but...no. I'm afraid they all have...come-fuck-me necklines." She squeaked at her own daring and covered her mouth with both hands as though she could push the words back in.

For a blissful moment, there was nothing but companionable giggles, but it did not last. All too soon, the knowledge of where we were and what had happened dropped its shroud over us, and she helped me dress in silence. Having grown up on a farm, I was only used to wearing full robes on special occasions. The tunic and breeches style Tili had sewn had been as much for my own comfort as to annoy Emperor Kin. This court robe, however stunning it might look, was both too tight and too loose in all the wrong places, and its neckline that dropped below my fifth vertebra made me squirm.

By the time Tili was finished, I might have walked right out of a court portrait.

I hated the very sight of myself.

"It'll have to do," I said as she tried and failed to make a comb stick in my short hair.

"Shall I come with you, my lady?"

"No, you stay." I walked to the door and slid it open. "I'm sure someone will be able to tell me where—"

"Lady Hana!"

I spun around. A man in an imperial uniform had been standing outside my room, his black sash all that marked him as one of Katashi's men, not one of Kin's. Though I would have known him from one glance at his face. "Wen," I said before I could think better of it and immediately thought better of it as he frowned. Captain Regent of the Vices had known Wen, not Lady Hana Otako.

"I want to see Katashi," I said, drawing myself up to maximum pride in an attempt to cover the mistake.

"Cap—His Majesty is busy with his council, my lady," he said, struggling with his own confusion in a way that might have given us something to laugh over had the situation not been so fraught and unsure. "But I can inform him that you're feeling better and—"

"No. I will see him now." I walked on past Wen, sure that while he might grab my arm if he was very bold, he would not harm me.

He was not very bold, but he did hurry to walk ahead of me as I made my way along the passage. "Lady Hana, His Majesty is meeting with his generals and would not appreciate—"

"You know what else he would not appreciate? His cousin being forced to shout for him in the passage, making a scene. However, if you'd prefer I got his attention that way, by all means stand in my way."

Wen's eyes widened and he fell back. I had shaken him off balance, but he followed as I got my bearings and made for the emperor's apartments.

At the sound of Katashi's voice, my steps faltered. My heart seemed to drop right through the floor as I realised the enormity of what I was about to do. Like Wen, Katashi had only known Captain Regent, never Lady Hana.

I rapped on the door before fear got the better of me.

Inside, the voices halted, and letting out a gust of breath, Wen slid open the door. "Excuse me, Your Majesty," he said, the polished words not coming easily to his tongue. "It's Lady Hana. She is very intent on seeing you."

"Tell her I will see her when I am finished here. We have important business—"

"Then I will join you," I said, stepping in and drawing the gaze of half a dozen men I didn't recognise—and Katashi. He knelt at the end of a long table in the same crimson robes Kin wore, but in all other ways, he was the Captain Monarch I had first met at Nivi Fen, right down to his beautifully lopsided smile. "My dear cousin," he said, emphasising the word as though in reproof for the secret I had kept. "I am so glad to see you are finally up and about. We have all been very concerned for your well-being."

In a flurry of silk and awkward coughs, the other men at the table rose and bowed, murmuring my name.

"My thanks, Your Majesty," I said, acknowledging them with a nod. "I am, as you see, quite well now." I settled myself at an empty place at the table. "Do continue the meeting."

All eyes turned to Katashi, and with a nod to the gathered men, he said, "Family will not wait, it seems. Let us adjourn until General Manshin arrives this afternoon."

With many a nod and bow and murmuring of "Your Majesty," the men once more rose from the table and headed for the door. Annoyed that he would rather send them away than let me take part, I might have protested, but Katashi's smile had vanished beneath a thundercloud. I kept my peace and waited until the last one departed, leaving Wen to slide the door closed behind them.

From the other end of the table, Katashi sighed. "Are you so intent on embarrassing me?" he said. "First you don't tell me who you are so I must suffer the humiliation of having my cousin captured by the Usurper, and now you force your way into an important meeting with generals newly come to my cause. Any who believed you to be in Kin's confidence, or his bed, have only more reason to think so now!"

He could not have shocked me more with a slap. I leant back, fingers gripping the edge of the table. "Excuse me?"

"Why else the desperate need to listen in on our plans?"

Katashi gave a satisfied huff as my jaw dropped. All too well could I see why his allies might make such an assumption. "I am no spy."

"No? Well, Cousin, I feel proper introductions are in order then, since this is the first time we've met. I am Emperor—"

"Oh no, don't do that. I'm sorry, all right? Malice is…very good at…persuasion. He had a hundred reasons why it was important you didn't know who I was, and they all sounded sensible. And some of them were. If you had known who I was, you would never have allowed me to do any of the things I wanted to be a part of, would you?"

"Allow you to parade around as a soldier and risk your life for nothing but the fun of it? No."

"See? I had no interest in exchanging one pair of shackles for another."

He frowned at me across the table, that expression the brooding look I'd often stared at across a crowded camp, wanting him to look my way. "You could have died," he said at last. "And what then?"

"Since you didn't know I was alive, you would never have known let alone cared."

"But I knew *you*. And I would have cared."

The words sent my heart racing, but I shook my head. "Now *that* is nonsense."

His lips curved into an amused smile and my heart beat all the faster. "Is it? You're very sure of yourself. I wondered how different you would be as yourself, how much of Captain Regent had been an act. I'm glad to see not much, since I had begun to like him all too well."

How impossible to respond to such words with my heart in my throat. This was not the conversation I had expected, and I swallowed hard, trying to recall what I'd come to say.

When nothing came out, Katashi nodded at the cushion next to him. "Come, sit closer. I feel like I have to shout with you all the way down there."

Almost I refused, the memory of the kiss that might have been a sudden specter. I had wanted it more than anything in that moment and did not trust myself. Did not trust a body that yearned so fiercely to be near him.

I rose and shifted closer, not to the cushion beside him but to the one a spot farther away. "You think I'm going to bite, sweet Regent?" he mocked.

"No, but you probably shouldn't call me that in case someone hears you."

"There is no one else to hear me. Now why don't you tell me what was so important it couldn't wait until I had finished meeting with my council?"

Could I demand to know how many people he had executed in the last few days? It ought not to have been a question that needed asking. "Did so many people have to die, Katashi?" I said, a softer plea than I had meant to charge him with. "Tili tells me you have not only had Kin's courtiers and councillors executed if they did not swear to you, but servants too."

"I have done no more or less than Kin himself did after he took the throne," he said, brows lifting in surprise. "The number of people who were labelled traitors and executed with my father was in the hundreds, many who had done nothing but be employed by our family. Whatever your maid has told you, I have not gone that far, but neither can I give *anyone* the opportunity to betray me. If I do, this will all have been for nothing. This may look like a big win, Hana, but my power is fragile until I can consolidate my hold on the north. Or find Kin." Eyes that had been looking at the table pinned me then. "It would be good to know where he is."

"You say that like you think I know. I have been asleep for three days."

"And living with him for three weeks."

I attempted haughty disdain. "If you think he told me anything of his plans in that time, then you are very mistaken. He trusted me no more than you seem to."

"You haven't given me any reason to yet."

"How can you say so? I may not have told you who I was, but I fought for you." I reached for his hand only to pull back and rest mine upon the table. "I wanted to fight for the throne and for our family so much that Malice brought his Vices into play. Where would you have been without them? Without us?"

Enter the monthly
Orbit sweepstakes at
www.orbitloot.com

With a different prize every month,
from advance copies of books by
your favourite authors to exclusive
merchandise packs,
**we think you'll find something
you love.**